Critical acclaim for *Billy Gogan, American,* the debut
novel of an exciting series chronicling the life and times
of Billy Gogan during the tumultuous years leading up to
and during the Mexican-American War, when the United
States first learned how to be an imperial power

International Book Awards: 2017 Finalist, Historical Fiction
Hollywood Book Fest: 2018 Honorable Mention
New York Book Festival: 2018 Honorable Mention
Readers' Favorite: 2018 Honorable Mention in Adventure Fiction
Independent Author Network Book of the Year Awards:
2018 Finalist

"Well-written and rich in historical detail, giving a fascinating
glimpse of the period.... Highly recommended."
—Jeff Westerhoff, The Historical Novel Society

"The heartbeat of tenderness, love, and even racial enlightenment
pulses through 'Gotham's' brutal veins...Higgins writes descriptions
so spot-on, you need to close the book and look around your own
room to remind yourself that you really are safe and sound in the
here and now."
—Gary Buslik, author and professor of English

"A sweeping epic saga of one Irish immigrant's passage both across
the Atlantic Ocean to a new land and his coming of age from boy
to man. As an Irish-American...it made me thirst for more...a book
about the melting pot which came to be called America."
—John J. Kelly, *Detroit Free Press* reviewer

"Through Billy we discover what it was like...not only to travel to
and survive in a foreign country, but also to make a new life, and
learn about love, hate, and the myriad emotions in between."
—Susan Keefe, *Midwest Book Review*

"A hypnotizing tale that defines the origin of not only Billy Gogan but of each of us at our point of entry, past historical or recent, into America. A brilliant tour de force."

—Grady Harp, *San Francisco Review of Books*

"Higgins's prose weaves together a world not only of violence, but of love, tenderness, compassion and the incomparable strength of the human spirit."

—Pamela Gossiaux, author of *Russo Romantic Mysteries*

"This riveting historical novel is told in the first person, which lends an immediacy to the story that will resonate with readers. It is the story of what all immigrants are in search of: a better life."

—*Irish American Times*

### Critical acclaim for *Billy Gogan, Gone fer Soldier*

"Fold together the splendid Irish language, the flavors and scents of Ireland and Texas, a dissecting eye of the evils of the crime wherever it appears in the story, and the result is a hypnotizing tale . . . fortunately to be continued!"

—Grady Harp, *San Francisco Review of Books*

# BILLY GOGAN

## GONE FER SOLDIER

# BILLY GOGAN
## GONE FER SOLDIER

A NOVEL BY
ROGER HIGGINS

SOLAS HOUSE FICTION
PALO ALTO

Copyright © 2019 by American Memoir LLC

Travelers' Tales and Solas House are trademarks of Solas House, Inc.
Palo Alto, California 94306
www.travelerstales.com

Cover Design: Creative Communications and Graphics, Inc.
Page Layout: Howie Severson, using the fonts Goudy and California Titling

Library of Congress Cataloging-in-Publication Data is available
upon request.

For more information about the Billy Gogan series, visit BillyGogan.com.

ISBN 978-1-60952-137-0 (paperback)
ISBN 978-1-60952-138-7 (ebook)
ISBN 978-1-60952-175-2 (hardcover)

First Edition
10 9 8 7 6 5 4 3 2 1
Printed in the United States of America

*To Pat, who continues to give Billy his chance to live, and*

*To my grandchildren, may you find and explore many wonderful worlds in the books you will be reading in the years to come*

Historical accuracy is like quicksand. Stay too long in the same place and it will suck you down and there will be no movement, no dynamism to the story. Too much attention to factual detail is undoubtedly an impediment to literary art.

—James Forrester, "The Lying Art of Historical Fiction," *The Guardian* (August 6, 2010)

[Y]ou know that neither numbers nor strength give the victory: but that side which, with the assistance of the gods, attacks with the greatest resolution, is generally irresistible. I have taken notice also that those men who in war seek to preserve their lives at any rate, commonly die with shame and ignominy; while those who look on death as common to all, and unavoidable, and are only solicitous to die with honor, oftener arrive at old age, and while they live, live happier. As therefore we are sensible of these things, it behoves us at this critical juncture, both to act with courage ourselves, and to exhort the rest to do the same.

—Edward Spelman, *Xenophon: The Anabasis* (1839)

The past is never dead. It's not even past.

—William Faulkner, *Requiem for a Nun* (1951)

# Table of Contents

# Foreword

*November 2018*

⌒

THIS SECOND VOLUME OF General Gogan's memoir recounts the General's youthful adventures following the tragic death of his friend and companion, Mary Skiddy, during the Great Fire of New York—the last great fire to afflict old Gotham. I have once again tried to keep a light editing hand on the General's words, which were written in the very same fair, feminine hand as *Billy Gogan, American*. For example, I changed the spelling of the Mexican city to the more modern "Monterrey," from the 19th-century "Monterey," so as not to confuse that city with the *norteamericano* town of Monterey, California. But I left virtually untouched the same type of language in this volume that appeared in the first, language which today is largely unacceptable, but which was of its time. I thus once more ask you to observe who uses such language and why.

In this second volume, the General had originally included what appear to be a number of letters he wrote to his cousin, Evelyn, as well as those written to another young lady to whom the General introduces us. The General does not explain why he had copies of those letters on hand, but it is clear that he intended them to be an integral part of the manuscript. So they remain, as lightly edited as the rest of the manuscript. I selected one of the letters to open this book. It seems to have been written some weeks after Mary's tragic death, from a little frontier village called Corpus Christi, at the confluence of the Nueces River and Aransas Bay. The city today boasts a beautiful waterfront drive, where in the late summer of 1845, a small American army was gathering and training for America's first invasion since 1775 of another country for the express purpose of conquest. (That latter expedition, led by a fellow named Benedict Arnold, had been a disastrous failure.)

When I read my ancestor's account, I was struck by the ambivalence in the months before the Mexican-American War began of (a decided minority, to be clear) West Point-trained, career American military officers about the prospect of invading another country. But this ambivalence did not give rise to guilt among those officers. Quite the opposite, as every one of them was professional in the utmost. Such guilt about the Mexican-American War is an emotion that first arose only in the 1960s for reasons having everything to do with that post-colonial era and not with the 1840s, not the least of which was the confluence of the civil rights movement and mounting opposition to the Vietnam War, particularly in academic and other circles. Since then, I suspect that the Mexican-American War and its politics have once again quietly slipped from view of almost all Americans, even though the United States continues to deal with the consequences of this more than half-forgotten war.

Finally, I have included a list of principal characters. As you might imagine, even in an army of well less than four thousand, Billy encountered scores of officers and enlisted men, not to mention the army's camp followers and civilians living in Corpus Christi, Matamoros, and points south.

I hope you enjoy this next installment of an old man's reminiscence about his youthful exploits on the far southern reaches of *limes americanus*, as the General would have said.

—NIALL GOGAN

# Glossary

| Term | Definition |
|---|---|
| Abigail | A maid. So-called, as Abigail was a common first name for Irish women, and such service was a major source of work for Irish immigrant women. 19ᵗʰ century American slang. |
| Absquatulate | To disappear in the sense of Snagglepuss's famed, "exit stage left." H. L. Mencken called it and words of similar ilk "entirely artificial" in their creation. 19ᵗʰ century American slang. |
|  | By comparison, "skedaddle" was widely used in the U. S. Civil War to mean "rush off," as in fleeing a battlefield, usually dropping one's weapons and shedding one's uniform in the process. The earliest known appearance in print was in 1861. Mencken says that this word likely originated much earlier in the north of England, meaning "to spill." 19ᵗʰ century American military slang. |
| Acknowledge the corn | To admit an error. 19ᵗʰ century American slang. |
| Aguardiente | A generic term for alcoholic beverages that contain between 29 and 60 percent alcohol by volume. Roughly the equivalent of the English "firewater." Sometimes called brandy, although it was rarely distilled from grapes. During much of the 18ᵗʰ century, however, *aguardiente* distilled from grapes was manufactured in Barcelona and shipped to Mexico and other Spanish-American colonies, but such exports largely disappeared after Mexico won her independence from Spain in 1821. Spanish, then Mexican term. |

| Term | Definition |
| --- | --- |
| Alcalde | A town mayor. Spanish, then Mexican term. |
| Arkansas toothpick | A long knife. Also known as a California or Missouri toothpick. Better known today as a bowie knife. 19th century American slang. |
| Battery | An artillery unit roughly equivalent to an infantry company in number of men and the rank of the commanding officer (usually a captain). The number of guns in a battery varied widely, depending upon the type of gun and its availability. |
| Bene cull | A good fellow. "Bene" means "good." English, then American slang. |
| Big Bug | An important person, particularly an aristocrat, or more often a person who considers himself to be important, even when he is not. 19th century American slang. |
| Bog Rat | A derisive term for an Irishman. Alternatively, "bog trotter." Both terms are generally dated to about the mid-19th century, although "bog trotter" may have originated much earlier (the 17th century) and "bog rat" a little later (the late 19th or early 20th centuries). English, then American ethnic slur. |
| Bluebellies | What Northern soldiers affectionately called themselves prior to and early in the Civil War (on account of their uniform blouses). Later in the war, Southerners used the term rather more disparagingly. As the general uses the term, and as used in the Civil War, it applied to all branches of the army, infantry, artillery, and cavalry alike. 19th century American military slang. |
| Bottlehead | A stupid fellow. 19th century American slang. |

| Term | Definition |
|------|------------|
| Bow Legs | Cavalrymen. So-called on the theory that a man must become bow-legged if he is in the saddle all day. Usage dates to well before the Civil War. The term, "yellow-legs," on account of the yellow stripe on a cavalryman's pantaloons, did not come into popular usage until after the Civil War. 19th century American military slang. |
| Buck the Tiger | To go against the odds (the tiger being the God of the odds) and beat a faro dealer at his own game. In other words, to undertake a fool's game. Mid-19th century American slang. |
| Bull Battery | A section of the 3d U. S. Artillery, comprising two 18-pounder wheeled iron siege guns that were ponderously maneuverable, commanded at the Battle of Palo Alto by LT. W. H. Churchill. So-named presumably because the artillery and its accompanying caissons were so heavy that only oxen could haul them. |
| Caballero | A gentleman, perhaps even a nobleman. Usage dates to medieval Spain, when the term meant a "knight." Usage is inextricably tied up in the concept of the *hombre de bien*. Spanish, then Mexican term. |
| Bully Back | A bully who supports another person, according to Grose. Also a bouncer or strong-arm man employed by the madam of a brothel, often her husband or lover. English slang. |
| Cap'n Hackum | One who slashes with a bowie knife. American slang. |
| Casa de sillar | The main house at a *tejano* ranch. Spanish, then Mexican term. |

| Term | Definition |
| --- | --- |
| Carreta | A "curious combination of medieval invention and rudimentary technology," the presence of steel or iron being almost entirely unknown. The carts were hewn from heavy wood, covered with tops of white cotton stretched over hoops of bended wood. They had two enormous wheels constructed from large blocks of wood, usually drawn by a single mule. The *carreteros* (or cart-drivers) were often ranch family members, and the *carreta* routes stretched from "Chihuahua to Missouri, from Nocogdoches to El Paso, and from San Antonio to Mexico City." Their heyday stretched from the 16th century to the middle of the 19th century. Spanish, then Mexican usage. |
| Cavaulting House | A brothel or bordello. Mainly English slang. |
| Chattermag | Gossip. Mid-to-late 19th century American slang. |
|  | Compare to scuttlebutt and the gouge, the latter having the inference of being good information above and beyond mere scuttlebutt. U.S. naval, then later U.S. military, slang. |
| China plate | An old and very close friend. 19th century American slang. |
| Chink | Money, especially coinage. English, then American slang. |
| Coahuila y Tejas | One of the constituent states of the newly established United Mexican States under its 1824 Constitution, which encompassed the present-day Mexican state of Coahuila and the portion of present-day southeastern Texas where land grants had been made in the 18th century to *tejanos* by the Spanish crown. |
| Colossus of the North | One of the more polite ways in which Mexicans of the period began referring to the United States of America. Roughly translates to "*el coloso del norte.*" Mexican term. |

| Term | Definition |
|---|---|
| Confidence Man | As G. W. Matsell defined the term, a "fellow that by means of extraordinary powers of persuasion gains the confidence of his victims to the extent of drawing upon their treasury, almost to an unlimited extent." Later shortened to con man in the 20th century, the con being a fraud or trick. 19th century American slang. |
| Cottonbalers | The United States Army's Seventh Infantry. So-named because the regiment anchored the center of Andrew Jackson's line at the Battle of New Orleans behind cotton bales that caught fire from their musketry. Despite the flames, the Seventh continued to pour fire into the advancing British, thus contributing to a most remarkable defeat of the best the British Army had to offer. The Seventh is one of the oldest regiments in the United States Army. |
| Corrida | Typically a ten-man team of *vaqueros* led by a *caporal*, born of the Spanish ranching tradition dating to the early 16th century. A ranch foreman, or *mayordomo*, would hire them on (if the team was itinerant) or detail a *caporal* to gather them from the ranch's *vaqueros* to round up the ranch's cattle herd to drive it to market (the drive being a *partida*). It is from their skills that modern-day rodeo was born. Spanish, then Mexican terminology. |
| Cove | A man. English, then American slang. |
| Croake | To murder or to die, depending on context. A "croaker" or "croaksman" was mid-19th century slang for a murderer. A "croaker" could also be a doctor, which given the state of medicine in those days is not terribly surprising. 19th century American slang. |
| Criollo | A white man (a woman being a *criolla*) born in Mexico. During colonial times, *criollos* were seen by the Spanish-born *gachupine* as socially inferior. |

| Term | Definition |
| --- | --- |
| Cully | A prostitute's customer. A simpleton. A fool. Comes from the Irish, *cuallaidhe*, meaning companion. Cully originally meant "pal," and then only later evolved in meaning. A "bene cull" is a "good fellow." Irish, then New York slang. |
| Dago | Used throughout the 19th century to refer to both Spaniards and Mexicans, only to be turned on Italians in the early 20th century as Italian immigration to the United States increased. American ethnic slur. |
| (Cutting up the) Didoes | To "cut up the didoes" was to get into mischief. A dido was something fancy or frivolous. 19th American slang. |
| Ding | A worthless person. 19th century American slang. |
| Dog Robber | Man-servant or personal valet. More generally, a subservient person. A term generally used by enlisted men. Officers tended to use the term "striker." 19th century American military slang. |
| Doughboys | The infantry. Although the term was popularized during the First World War, it seems to date to the Mexican-American War. The etymology is unclear. The cavalry derisively used the term for the infantry, based upon the "adobe" dust covering their uniforms as they marched. H. L. Mencken claimed that the pipe clay used to clean soldiers' belts or uniforms would become a doughy mess in the rain. American military slang. |
| Douse (one's) glim | To kill someone. Originally, it meant to douse a light. The colloquialism also had an alternate meaning of giving someone a black eye. 19th century American slang. |

| Term | Definition |
|---|---|
| Dueña | The ubiquitous companion of a *mujer decente*, or an unmarried, proper young lady. Similar to a governess, but so much more central to the protection of an unmarried young lady's virtue and position in society in 19th century Mexico. |
| Dustman | A dead man. 19th century American slang. |
| Dutchy | A German immigrant, particularly one who went to Pennsylvania (e. g., the "Pennsylvania Dutch"). So-called because the Germans called themselves, "*Deutsche*." Usually reserved for immigrants who had yet to shed the ways of their home country. Occasionally derogatory, particularly in the latter sense. 19th century American slang. |
| Eagle | $10 gold coin. A double eagle is $20. 19th century American slang. |
| (To see the) Elephant | As John Russell Bartlett put it in his 1848 *Dictionary of Americanisms*, "to see the elephant" meant "to undergo any disappointment of high-raised expectations." In the Mexican War, to see the elephant was to experience the harsh realities of war—not necessarily battle itself, but also the "stern reality" of disease, moldy hardtack, vicious regular army discipline, and every other form of privation experienced by American armies invading Mexico—experiences which quickly dashed all rosy prewar visions of a romantic war in an exotic land. 19th century American military slang. |

| Term | Definition |
|---|---|
| Enfilade | "Enfilade" is a raking fire in the direction of a trench, line or column of troops. An enfilading battery (of artillery) is one in position to deliver enfilading fire. Justin Smith, in his magisterial (but flawed) 1917 work, THE WAR WITH MEXICO, was harshly critical of Taylor's placement of Fort Texas (later named Fort Brown) on the north shore in the bend of the Rio Grande because it was not placed properly to provide enfilading fire into Mexican defenses. Military term. |
| | Compare to "defilade" fire, which is fire (e. g., from a defilade battery) concealed from its enemy either by natural topography (e. g., hills or ridges) or (less commonly in the era) man-made earthenworks. Military term. |
| Escopeta | Generally, a blunderbuss shotgun or similar type of weapon. Many were coachmen's blunderbusses manufactured in England during the Napoleonic era and exported to Mexico along with the Brown Bess musket (which was in the British Army through the end of the Napoleonic Wars). Other forms of the *escopeta* included cut-down Brown Bess and other muskets, as well as other older, short-barreled weapons manufactured in Spain and elsewhere, dating back well into the 18th century and even earlier. Mexican military terminology. |
| Escudos | A unit of currency of the era (meaning "shield" in both Spanish and Portuguese), worth two bits, affectionately called "scoots" by generations of American military. Spanish. |
| Ewe | A beautiful woman. 19th century American slang. |
| Exfluncticate | To overwhelm or to utterly destroy. 19th century American slang. |
| Faro | Card game with a bank. By the mid-19th century, there was hardly a square faro game to be found. |

## Glossary

| Term | Definition |
| --- | --- |
| Flat | One who is unacquainted with the tricks and schemes of crooked gamblers. Mid-19th century American slang. |
| (Bit of) Fluff | Pubic hair, either male or female. The more modern usage is a pretty, if empty-headed, woman. 19th century American slang. |
| Forlorn Hope | A gambler's last, despairing bet, although it never lost its original military meaning, which was a unit of skirmishers or assault troops sent ahead of the main attacking force, particularly when attacking a fortified or otherwise formidably defended position. English, then American military slang. |
| Flying Artillery | Lightweight horse artillery, using then-new, relatively light-weight bronze six-pounders (the weight of the solid shot), could be towed at a gallop on the battlefield. Unlike other light artillery, every man was mounted. The artillery pieces themselves were also easier to load, and thus had a much higher rate of fire, than other comparably-sized artillery. |
| French Leave | To desert. In the 18th century, taking French leave meant a guest committing the social faux pas of leaving without informing his host. English, then American military slang. |
| French Letters | Prophylactic sheaths for preventing French disease. Also known as condoms or "safes." Typically made from sheep's intestines during this period, they were expensive and relatively difficult to obtain. English, then later American slang. |

| Term | Definition |
|------|------------|
| Gachupine | A Mexican pejorative for Spanish-born white men who held virtually all positions of power in pre-independence Mexico. The *gachupine* were largely expelled from Mexico soon after independence in 1821. It derived from the Aztec "*cac-chopina*," which meant "prickly shoes," apparently referring to the spurs worn by the 16th century Spanish invaders. It thus quickly became the Aztec name for the Spanish. During the course of the war, *norteamericanos* came to call the Mexicans "*gachupine*" as a polite alternative to other, more pejorative names. |
| Gammon and Spinach | Nonsense or humbug. To "gammon" meant to deceive in mid-19th century New York slang. English, then American slang. |
| Get | A bastard child. A general term of abuse in the 19th century. By the late 19th century, the term also meant a swindle, trick, or other means of defrauding a victim. Since then, it has evolved several other meanings, including as a verb, to engage in sexual intercourse. A "whore's get" is a variant with the same meaning. Irish, then American slang. |
| Grapevine | Originally, the "grapevine telegraph," was defined as "a network of unofficial sources, rumours, half-truths, etc., which seems to spread the news faster ... than any sanctioned announcement." American military slang. |
| Greaser | A highly derogatory epithet with a fraught history first used "in connection with the people of Matamoros." It is said that Americans did not especially fancy greasing the wheels of their wagons, and paid the local Mexicans do it for them. Hence they, and presently all Mexicans, came to be termed greasers. There are other, less salubrious derivations. American ethnic slur. |

| Term | Definition |
|------|-----------|
| Gringo | Usage by Mexicans referring to *los norteamericanos* dates to the Mexican-American War. Eric Partridge (and many others) report the story that the word came from a popular song with a refrain, "green grow the rushes, oh." There are other possible derivations. Mexican slang. |
| Guerrillero | A Mexican fighter attached to an informal unit. The Mexican-American War was America's introduction to guerrilla warfare. Mexican *guerrilleros* turned out to be far more successful in the field against the Americans than did Mexico's army. Spanish, then Mexican term. |
| Higglety, Pigglety, and Pop | The first line of a "coarse, vulgar, [and] offensive" nursery rhyme, which clearly stuck in at least one young, impressionable mind. The remaining lines are, "The dog has ate the mop; The pig's in a hurry, The cat's in a flurry—Higglety, pigglety—pop." Old English nursery rhyme. |
| History of the Four Kings | A pack of playing cards. 19th century American slang. |
| Hit | To succeed. 19th century American slang. |
| Hombre de Bien | "An honest man." They were the educated "men about town" in Mexico's urban centers, a white, *criollo*, urban elite who saw the governing of Mexico as their birthright. The concept of *hombres de bien* and their role in Mexican political life in the decades after independence is thoroughly explored in Michael Costeloe's *The Central Republic in Mexico, 1835-1846*, which explores in detail the political state in Mexico in the decade prior to the Mexican American War and the *los Polkos* revolt in February 1847, which was both key to, and emblematic of, Mexico's political and military collapse during the Mexican American War. Mexican socio-political term. |

| Term | Definition |
|---|---|
| (Going) Home | A euphemism for dying. American Civil War military slang. |
| (A skinful of) Honey | A wallet full of money. Mid-19th century American slang. |
| (Tell that to the) Horse Marines | Phrase means "I don't believe it, but somebody else may." A Horse Marine is, of course, an impossibility. Dates to the War of 1812 or earlier. American army slang, likely from the British. |
| Huckleberry above the persimmon | Although it meant no more than "a cut above," the expression was capable of infinite variety in meaning and form. "Huckleberry," by itself, meant a fellow or a boy. Thanks to Mark Twain's *Adventures of Huckleberry Finn*, it eventually came to mean a person of little importance. American slang. |
| (to) Injun | To sneak up on a target without the target knowing. A racial stereotype. 19th century American slang. |
| Jonathan | An American. Originally a Yankee as in someone from New England. Often referred to as "Brother Jonathan." American slang. |
| (to the put the) Kibosh (on someone) | To kill someone. Etymology is uncertain. One school of thought has it coming from the Irish, "*cia baois*," which means "what idle nonsense" in this context. Usage dates to the mid-19th century. American slang. |
| Kinchin Cove | A boy trained to be a thief. Often used to mean "little man" as a term of general abuse. English, then American slang. |
| Kinchin Mort | A girl educated to steal. English, then American slang. |
| Kinker | A circus performer. Star circus performers were seen to be stuck-up by locals. *Geanncach*, became "kinker," an adjective meaning surly or rude. First Irish, then late 19th-early 20th century American slang. |

| Term | Definition |
| --- | --- |
| Knight and barrow pig | A knight and barrow pig is, as Grose says, "more hog than gentleman. A saying of any low pretender to precedency." "Knight of the barrow pigs" is a term of the General's invention. English public school slang. |
| Knocking Shop | A brothel. Mid-19th century American slang.<br><br>Compare, cavaulting house, riding academy, hog ranch, and goosing slum. |
| Knowledge Box | The head. Mid-19th century American slang. |
| Limes Americanus | The American frontier. The term is a play on "*limes Romanus*," or the frontier of the Roman Empire. One such *limes Romanus* with which the General would have been familiar as a young man was "*limes Britannicus*," which was demarcated by Hadrian's Wall. Schoolboy Latin doggerel. |
| Milling Coves | Boxers, who were often used as security at faro games and the like. English, then American slang. |
| Molley | A young woman or an effeminate young man. American slang. |
| Mort | A woman. A "dimber mort" is a pretty, young woman. A "bleak mort" was a beautiful woman, because "bleak" meant pale, and the paler a woman's skin, the more desirable she was by the standards of the day. English, then American slang. |
| Nocky Boy | A simpleton. American slang. |
| (los) Norteños | How *centralistas* viewed Mexicans and *tejanos* living in the borderlands between Mexico proper and the United States. |
| (los) Norteamericanos | A polite name for denizens of the United States of America. Compare, *gringo*, *el otro lado* (the other side). Mexican. |

| Term | Definition |
| --- | --- |
| Other Ranks | "The usual designation for N. C. O.s and privates in orders." English military, then archaic American military terminology. |
| (To Catch an) Oyster | For a woman to have sexual intercourse. American slang. |
| Panocha | Literally means "unrefined brown sugar." Colloquially similar to calling someone a "pussy" in modern-day English. Often used as an insult, and occasionally semi-affectionately. Mexican slang. |
| Parlor House | A better class of bordello or brothel. American slang. |
| Picayune | A "picayune" was worth 6 ½ cents, or a Spanish half-real. Used in Louisiana and Florida. Later became American slang meaning small or insignificant. |
| Pollrumptious | Foolishly confident. 19th century American slang. |
| Presidiales | Militia cavalry attached to presidios, which were fortified towns strung across northern colonial Mexico by the Spanish in the 17th century to defend the northern border against Indian incursions. Mexican military terminology. |
| Pumpkin Rind | A second lieutenant, based on the bare shoulder straps of a second lieutenant (the gold bar was not introduced until World War I). Usage likely dates to the Civil War or earlier, and was still in use as late as World War II. American military slang.<br><br>Compare to "shavetail," which also has the meaning of being a young mule. Query which came first … the untrained, young mule whose hindquarters had been shaved, or the second lieutenant? They have so much in common. |
| Peach | To inform the police or other authorities. Or, to "give the office," "blow the gab," or to "squeal or squeak." 19th century American slang. |

| Term | Definition |
|---|---|
| Plug | A worthless or incompetent person. Mid-19th to mid-20th century American slang. |
| Pulque | An alcoholic beverage made from the fermented sap of the maguey (agave) plant, having the color and texture of a slightly viscous milk, and a sour, yeasty taste. Usage extends back into Meso-American times, when it was considered a sacred drink, the consumption of which was limited to old men and other privileged classes. The drink became secular after the Spanish Conquest, and popularity peaked in the late 19th century, when it was supplanted by beer. Most observers consider it the predecessor to *mescal* and *tequila*. Mexican, from *Nahuatl*. |
| Queer Prancer | A lame or second-rate horse. Could also mean an aging prostitute, although that meaning was archaic by the 19th century. English slang. |
| Quick Time | A quickened pace of marching of 110 28-inch steps per minute. The standard rate was 90 28-inch steps per minute. Double quick time was 165 33-inch steps, but this pace was not introduced until the 1850s. The General must have been mistaken in his reference to its use in the Mexican-American War. American military jargon. |
| Raffle-coffin | A villain or ruffian. American slang. |
| Redlegs | Artillerymen. So-called because of the red stripe on their uniform pantaloons. Usage dates to well before the Civil War. American military slang. |
| Redoubt | An earthen or similar work completely closed by a parapet (a wall or elevation of earth), thus allowing all-around fire. It could also mean a small, rough, usually temporary, enclosed work without a flanking defense, or even a small, detached fieldwork. Originally French, then English and American military terminology. |

| Term | Definition |
|------|-----------|
| Rhino | Money. To be rhino-fat was to be rich. English, then American slang. |
| Riding academy | A brothel. An academician, in this context, is a prostitute. Not surprisingly, an "academy" could also mean a prison. Mainly English slang. |
| (los) Rinches | What *los tejanos* called the Texas Rangers in those days. Needless to say, the Texas Rangers were seen by both *tejanos* and *méxicanos* of the time as little better than bloodthirsty killers. Compare that view to the popular Texan view (even today): "[T]he real Ranger has been a very quiet, deliberate, gentle person who could gaze in the eye of a murderer, divine his thoughts, and anticipate his action, a man who could ride straight up to death." |
| Roll | A bankroll. Mid-19th century American slang. |
| Rumbustious | "Boisterous, noisy, unruly, turbulent." 19th century American slang. |
| Sam Hill | A euphemism for the devil. American slang. |
| Sassenagh | A "*Sassenagh*" (or "*Sassenach*") is an Englishman or Protestant, and use of the term in Ireland is today (and was then) quite derogatory. The term derives from the English, "Saxon," and is usually dated to the early 18th century as a Scottish Gaelic term later coopted by the Irish. Scottish, then Irish slang. |
| Sawbones | A doctor. So-named because the main surgical trick was a swift amputation. American military, then more common slang. |
| Scragged | To be hanged. From the slang word, "scrag," meaning neck. Compare to "jerked to Jesus." English, then American slang. |

| Term | Definition |
| --- | --- |
| Scribblers | Newspaper reporters, many of whom were not professional newspapermen, but who were instead "occasional correspondents" or "special correspondents," a class of newspaperman that might have been best described in the 20th century as newspaper stringers. American slang. |
| Scuttlebutt | What passes through the grapevine telegraph (and over a drink or three). Originally, the scuttlebutt was the place where a ship's crew got fresh drinking water. The scuttle is the hole and the butt is the barrel holding the water. The term first appeared in print in the early 19th century, and it is still in use in today's Navy. American naval, then more generally military slang. |
| Shoulder Strap | An officer, so-called on account of the straps, one on each shoulder of an officer's uniform blouse, which held their rank insignia. Usage dates to at least the Civil War, if not earlier. American military slang. |
| Simkin | A fool. English, then American slang. |
| Skinning | A sure game for the mechanic (a crooked dealer or one who invents ways to cheat at gambling) or a sharper (one who obtains goods by a false representation). Mid-19th century American slang. |
| Slantendicular | Slanting, or at a slant. English, then American slang. |
| Spice | To steal. English, then American slang. |
| Square | Honest. A "square game" is a game that is not fixed, and a square cove is an honest man. Compare, a "square-decker," who is a crooked card-dealer who stacks the deck. 19th century American slang. |
| Squared Away and Before the Wind | The expression has been around since Methuselah was a seaman deuce. "Square-rigged" meant well-dressed. 19th century American nautical slang. |

| Term | Definition |
|---|---|
| Sutler | A civilian merchant licensed to sell his wares at permanent military camps. Lacking any real competition, many sutlers became quite wealthy selling shoddy goods at inflated prices. |
| Take a Powder | To leave in a great hurry. 19th century English slang that later became "thoroughly Americanized." |
| Teas | Heat, passion, excitement or the highest temperature, and it is pronounced, "chazz" or "jazz." Some have attributed the origin of the term, "jazz," to "*teas*." "Jazz" was used during the 19th century "as a common vulgarity among Negroes in the South" as both a verb and a noun to describe sexual intercourse. It was only in the 1920s that "jazz" came to denote the "latest thing in music." Irish. |
| Toploftical | Pompous, haughty, arrogant. English and American slang. |
| (*las*) *Villas del Norte* | *Las villas del norte* comprise six towns strung along the río Bravo (also called the río del Norte)—what in the U. S. is called the Rio Grande. Five of them were on the southern bank: Dolores, Revilla, Mier, Camargo, and Reynosa. Laredo was both the only one on the northern bank, and it was the farthest west of *las villas del norte*. The Spanish established these towns and the accompanying ranchos and haciendas on the south bank of the río Bravo early in the 18th century as the northern *frontera* (a closed border) defending Saltillo and Monterrey from first the depredations of the Comanches and other Indians, and then later from Americans. |
| Wild Geese | Irishmen seeking their fortune abroad as soldiers fighting for other countries from the 17th through the 19th centuries. Irish idiom. |

# Dramatis Personae

## C COMPANY, FOURTH INFANTRY REGIMENT

Finnegan, Rónán, corporal and later, sergeant (*fictional character*)

Gaff, Dennis, private (*fictional character*)

Gogan, Billy, private (*fictional character*)

Grant, Ulysses S. "Sam", lieutenant, platoon and later company commander, C Company, then quartermaster, Fourth Infantry (*historical character*)

Hoggs, C Company First Sergeant (*fictional character*)

LeFort, Josiah, second lieutenant, platoon commander, C Company, Fourth Infantry (*fictional character*)

McCall, George A., captain, company commander, C Company, Fourth Infantry, and a future Union Army brigadier general in the Civil War (*historical character*)

O'Leary, Kenny, private (*fictional character*)

Porter, Theodric, second lieutenant, Grant's best friend and scion of a family of famed naval officers (*historical character*)

Wurster, Hermann, Private (*fictional character*)

## OTHER OFFICERS AND MEN OF THE FOURTH INFANTRY

Crittenden, Aloysius, regimental surgeon, Fourth Infantry (*fictional character*)

BILLY GOGAN: GONE FER SOLDIER

Garland, John, lieutenant colonel, executive officer and later commanding officer, Fourth Infantry, and still later, commanding officer, First Brigade, at the Battle of Monterrey (*historical character*)

Harrison, Francis Marion, captain, brevetted to major after Resaca de la Palma (*fictional character*)

Higgins, Thaddeus, second lieutenant, a casualty of the *Dayton* explosion (*historical character*)

Hoskins, Charles, second lieutenant, regimental adjutant, killed at Monterrey (*historical character*)

Morrison, Pitcairn, captain, bereaved father-in-law of Lieutenant Higgins (*historical character*)

Page, John, captain, mortally wounded at Palo Alto (*historical character*)

Reeves, C. M., corporal, F Company, Fourth Infantry (*historical character*)

Whistler, William, colonel, commanding officer, Fourth Infantry, Army of Observation (*historical character*)

## OTHER NOTEWORTHY MEMBERS OF THE ARMY OF OBSERVATION (WHICH BECAME IN TURN, THE ARMY OF OCCUPATION AND THEN THE ARMY OF INVASION)

Bliss, W. S., captain and later, brevet major, chief of staff, Army of Observation, and son-in-law to General Taylor, known universally as "Perfect" Bliss (*historical character*)

Bragg, Braxton, lieutenant, accomplished artillery officer and noted disciplinarian, and a future Confederate army general in the Civil War (*historical character*)

Churchill, William, captain, Third Artillery, commander of Churchill's Bull Batter of howitzers at the Battle of Palo Alto (*historical character*)

Cross, Truman, colonel, quartermaster of the Army of Observation, who went missing just prior to the commencement of hostilities (*historical character*)

*Dramatis Personae*

Davis, Jefferson, colonel, commanding officer, 1ˢᵗ Mississippi
Volunteer Regiment (aka, the "Mississippi Rifles"), later President
of the Confederate States of America, and General Taylor's former
son-in-law (*historical character*)

Duncan, James, captain, Third Artillery, and commander of Duncan's
Light Battery of flying artillery at the Battle of Palo Alto (*historical character*)

Hitchcock, Ethan Allan, lieutenant colonel, commanding officer,
Third Infantry Regiment, later a Union major general in the Civil
War (*historical character*)

Longstreet, James, second lieutenant, Fourth Artillery, one of Grant's
closest friends, and a future Confederate army general in the Civil
War (*historical character*)

Magruder, "Prince" John, captain, an artillery officer and quondam
thespian and theater impresario, a future Confederate army general in the Civil War, and briefly a general in the Mexican army of
Emperor Maximilian I of Mexico (*historical character*)

May, Charles, captain, Second Dragoons (*historical character*)

McCormac, Danny, private, First Infantry Regiment (*fictional character*)

McManus, John L., captain, commanding officer, Company E (the
"Jackson Fencibles"), 1ˢᵗ Mississippi Volunteer Regiment (aka, the
"Mississippi Rifles") (*historical character*)

O'Brien, Thaddeus, second lieutenant, First Infantry Regiment (*fictional character*)

Pillow, Gideon, brigadier general, commander, Tennessee Brigade
(*historical character*)

Quitman, John A., brigadier general, commander, 2d Volunteer
Brigade (*historical character*)

Rey, Anthony, one of two Catholic priests attached to the Army of
Invasion in 1846 (*historical character*)

Ringgold, Samuel, major, Second Artillery, founder of the famed
"flying artillery," and commander of Ringgold's Light Battery at

the Battle of Palo Alto, where he was mortally wounded (*historical character*)

Russell, Daniel R., lieutenant, 1$^{st}$ Mississippi Volunteer Regiment (aka, the "Mississippi Rifles") (*historical character*)

Taylor, Zachary, brevet brigadier general, Commanding Officer, Army of Observation, and later President of the United States (*historical character*)

Thornton, Seth B., captain, Second Dragoons, captured in the Thornton Affair, just before the commencement of hostilities (*historical character*)

Twiggs, David E., colonel, later brevet brigadier general, commanding officer, Second Dragoons (*historical character*)

Worth, William J., brevet brigadier general, second-in-command of the Army of Observation (*historical character*)

## LOUISIANA VOLUNTEERS IN MATAMOROS

Rocheron, Eddie, corporal, Louisiana Volunteers (*fictional character*)

Rouquette, Antoine "Carambole", captain, then major, a gambler, Louisiana Volunteers (*fictional character*)

The brigadier general of Louisiana volunteers (*fictional character*)

The beastly captain of Louisiana Volunteers (*fictional character*)

## TEXAS RANGERS

Alston, Damien, first lieutenant, Gray's Company, Texas Mounted Volunteers, primarily recruited in Matamoros in August 1846 (*fictional character*)

Chevallie, Michael H., regimental major, First Regiment, Texas Mounted Riflemen (*historical character*)

Gray, Mabry "Mustang", commanding officer, Gray's Company, Texas Mounted Volunteers, primarily recruited in Matamoros in August 1846 (*historical character*)

Hays, Jack, colonel, commanding officer, First Regiment, Texas Mounted Riflemen (*historical character*)

McCulloch, Ben, captain, commanding officer, Company A, First Regiment, Texas Mounted Riflemen (*historical character*)

Moncrief, Sidney "Big Foot", sergeant, First Regiment, Texas Mounted Rifleman (*fictional character*, modeled on Big Foot Wallace, a *historical character*)

Paige, Jedediah, sergeant, Gray's Company, Texas Mounted Volunteers, primarily recruited in Matamoros in August 1846 (*fictional character*)

Pickens, J. T., co-owner and co-founder of *The Picayune*, a New Orleans newspaper, correspondent accompanying the Texas Rangers (*fictional character*)

Walker, Samuel Hamilton, lieutenant colonel, executive officer, First Regiment, Texas Mounted Riflemen (*historical character*)

## CAMP FOLLOWERS OF THE ARMY OF OBSERVATION

Billings, Jenny, protégé of the Great Western, also a laundress to the Seventh Infantry and then subsequently to C Company of the Fourth Infantry (*fictional character*)

Langwell, Sarah, the "Great Western," laundress to the Seventh Infantry and heroine of the Siege of Fort Brown, she was born Sarah Knight, and was married several times, which accounted for her numerous last names, including Borginnis, Bourdette, Davis, and Bowman (*historical character*)

## CIVILIAN SCOUTS TO THE ARMY OF OBSERVATION

Kinney, Henry, founder of Corpus Christi, chief scout to General Taylor, and Texas colonel by courtesy (*historical character*)

Sandoval, Chapita, *tejano* chief scout to Colonel Kinney (*historical character*)

## Denizens of Corpus Christi

Alandra, don Guillermo's wife, and mother to Serafina and Calandria (*fictional character*)

Calandria, don Guillermo's younger daughter (*fictional character*)

Delgado, Juan Pablo, *caporal* of Grant's mule-skinning *corrida* (*fictional character*)

Hart, Mrs., an actress who played Desdemona (*historical character*)

Maria, Pedro's wife (*fictional character*)

Pedro, a retainer of the Rodriguez family (*fictional character*)

Rodriguez, don Guillermo Ñíguez, a *tejano hacendado* and friend of Colonel Kinney (*fictional character*)

Serafina, don Guillermo's elder daughter (*fictional character*)

## Civilians in Matamoros

Adabelita, a prostitute (*fictional character*)

Luis, mayordomo of a hacendado's house in Matamoros (*fictional character*)

## At the Recruiting Station in New York and at Governors Island

Doc (*fictional character*)

Kehoe, Lachlan, recruiting sergeant (*fictional character*)

Mulvaney, Otis, private (*fictional character*)

O'Dea, Dillon, a deserter (*fictional character*)

## Mexican Army Officers & Politicians

Ampudia, Pedro de, general, commander, Army of the North, who was replaced by Arista just prior to the commencement of hostilities, and who subsequently relieved Arista and led the Army of the North at the Battle of Monterrey (*historical character*)

Arista, Mariano, general, commander, Army of the North, at the battles of Palo Alto and Resaca de la Palma, later President of Mexico (*historical character*)

Canales Rosillo, Antonio, a *norteño hacendado* and leader of Mexican irregulars and cavalry during the Mexican American War (*historical character*)

de Herrera, José Joaquin, President of Mexico until deposed on December 30, 1845 (*historical character*)

Falcón, Ramón, a bandit chief or a leader of *guerrilleros*, depending upon your perspective (*historical character*)

Fernandes de la Cruz, Teodoro, Mexico's foreign minister and Isabella's father (*fictional character*)

Paredes y Arrillaga, D. Mariano, President of Mexico from January 4, 1846, through July 28, 1846 (*historical character*)

Santa Anna, General D. Antonio López de, aka "Santa Anna," once and future president of Mexico and generalissimo of Mexican forces during the Mexican American War, returned to Mexico in August 1846 (*historical character*)

Seguin, Juan, once mayor of San Antonio, he was a leader of the Mexican rancheros and *guerrilleros* who fought the American occupation in northern Mexico during the war (*historical character*)

Torrejón, Anastasio, general, Mexican cavalry commander, Army of the North (*historical character*)

## DENIZENS OF SAN FERNANDO DE PRESAS

de la Gerza Flores, Ramón, *hacendado* (*fictional character*)

Fernando de la Cruz, Isabella Maria-Magdalena, don Ramón's niece (*fictional character*)

Maria, Isabella's dueña (fictional character)

Saenz, Bartolome, *alcalde* of San Fernando de Presas (*fictional character*)

## Miscellaneous Characters

Blackie, Magee's right-hand man (*fictional character*)

Cassidy, Magee's nemesis in Gotham (*fictional character*)

Dineen, Cian, one-time protégé of Magee, who went to work for Cassidy (*fictional character*)

Dineen, Lúcás, Cian's brother, a reg'lar Cap'n Hackum (*fictional character*)

Donoho, Con, political boss of the Five Points in the 1840s (*historical character*)

Gogan, Niall P., Billy's father and a noted member of the Loyal National Repeal Association (*fictional character*)

Kendall, George, J. T. Pickens's partner in *The Picayune* (*historical character*)

Levesque, Georges, deacon (*fictional character*)

Levesque, Mary Domithilde, Deacon Levesque's only daughter (*fictional character*)

MacGowan, a mysterious man in black who seems to be Billy's nemesis (*fictional character*)

Magee, saloon-keeper and budding politician in the Big Onion; Billy's erstwhile mentor and now sworn enemy (*fictional character*)

O'Creagh, Evelyn (Eibhlin), Billy's cousin, to whom he writes letters, but who has yet to answer any of them (*fictional character*)

O'Creagh, Seamus, Evelyn's father (*fictional character*)

O'Marran, Brannagh, Billy's friend and erstwhile lover in Gotham before he was gone fer soldier (*fictional character*)

O'Muirhily, Daniel, Catholic priest, Latin master, St. Patrick's School for Boys, Dublin, who was murdered before Billy's eyes (*fictional character*)

Rynders, Isaiah, captain of militia, adventurer, gambler, and New York politician (*historical character*)

*Dramatis Personae*

Skiddy, Fíona, orphaned daughter of Mary Skiddy (*fictional character*)

Skiddy, Mary, Billy's boon companion in *Billy Gogan, American* (*fictional character*)

Shipley, Mrs., who has taken Fíona under her wing (*fictional character*)

*A New Map of Texas, Oregon, and California*, published in 1846

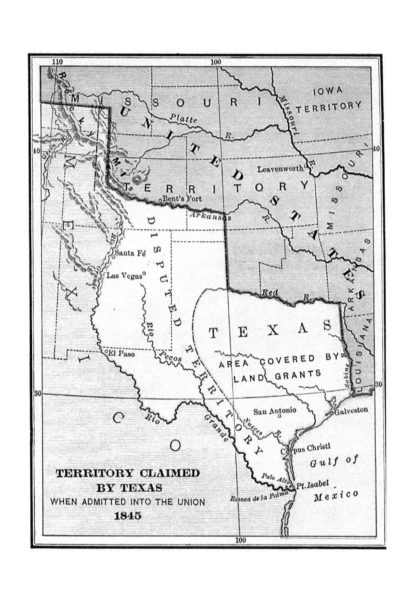

TERRITORY CLAIMED
BY TEXAS
WHEN ADMITTED INTO THE UNION
1845

# Texas

⁓

Sunday, September 29, 1845
Corpus Christi, Texas

My Dearest Evelyn:

I am once again writing to you, care of your headmistress at that fancy *Sassenagh* finishing school you told me about when we last saw each other at your father's house. I have not yet received any letters from you, but if you get this letter, please reply to let me know that you are safe and sound. You can send your letters either to me here, care of Uncle Sam's army, or to the Irish Emigrants Society, which will send the letters along. I look so very much forward to hearing from you.

I do not wish to alarm you, for I am in fine fettle. But I am sorry for not having written sooner. Life has taken a strange turn, and I am no longer in New York.

You see, my dearest Evelyn, I've gone for a soldier. Before I left Gotham, though, I paid my five dollars and became a United States citizen. I'll always be an Irishman in my heart, but now I'm a "reg'lar" Jonathan as well. Only I can't be their president (that's like being the *Sassenagh* Queen) because I'm not native-born. But any native American (what they call white men born in the United States) can become president, and Brother Jonathan takes a lot of stock in that.

A lot of us Irishmen "j'ined up," as the frontiersmen like to say, to fight the *Sassenagh*, because they are fixing to fight old Uncle Sam (that is what the Jonathans call their country) over a place called Oregon. I have enclosed a map for you based on what I remember from the atlas I used to peruse up at Wiley & Putnam's. It got so that you couldn't go a block in Gotham this past summer without a great crowd of patriotic citizens—God fearing Irishmen thick among them—all crying "fifty-four-forty or fight." I guess the *Sassenagh* are fixing to take this virgin land away from the Jonathans and occupy it all the way down to the 42$^{nd}$ parallel like some second coming of Cromwell and his lobster-backs.

Uncle Sam isn't taking too kindly to the prospect of the *Sassenagh* occupying what rightfully belongs to Uncle Sam, and in any case thousands of intrepid Yankee pioneers are trekking two thousand miles by mule-drawn Conestoga wagons from a city called St. Louis to Oregon to settle and start farms. It seems odd that the *Sassenagh* are fixing to fight this war, because there aren't any *Sassenagh* in the Oregon territory at all. Apparently, Oregon is empty except for the Indians, and no one takes any account of them, it seems. Most Jonathans believe that it is their Uncle Sam's *manifest destiny*, straight from God Himself, to expand all the way from the Atlantic Ocean to the Pacific and put farms and churches all across the land. So, unless our President, Mr. Polk, figures out a way to sort things out with the *Sassenagh*, there could be a war there in the next couple of years.

But funny enough, I'm not in Oregon, fighting the *Sassenagh*, like I thought I would be doing. I'm in a place called Texas. I guess that one war isn't enough for the Jonathans, because the Mexicans are mighty upset with Uncle Sam as well. This brings me to explaining why I am here, sitting in the little town of Corpus Christi, on the Nueces River, which is the border between Texas and Mexico. (Although there are many Jonathans who believe that the boundary rightfully is a hundred miles south of here, along the Rio Grande.) I've included another map to show you where I am. Apparently, the Mexicans have never really gotten over losing Texas, which as I mentioned in my last letter to you, is about to become the newest state in the Union.

Back in 1836, Mexico got into a fight with American settlers in Texas whom they'd invited in to settle the country, which up until that time had been occupied only by the Lipán Apache and their mortal enemies, the bloodthirsty Comanche—the Mexicans, *los méxicanos*, they call themselves, refer to the Comanche and every other Indian as *los bárbaros*, or the barbarians. Well, one thing led to another, including the Mexicans under some *caudillo* (which is what the Mexicans call a dictator) named Santa Anna massacring God-fearing Texians at a church mission called the Alamo, which is up in San Antonio de Béxar, about 100 miles northwest of Corpus Christi. Sam Houston, who is a real hero in these parts, and the Texian army later destroyed the Mexican army and captured Santa Anna.

So Texas became an independent republic, and on July 4 (the Jonathans' holiday I mentioned in my last letter), the Texians voted to join the Union. That has riled up the Mexicans something fierce. So President Polk sent General Taylor (we call him "Old Zach" or the "Old Man" on account of his not acting the proverbial huckleberry above the persimmon) with an army down to Corpus Christi. That's why I am down here, a proud member of C Company of the Fourth Infantry Regiment.

A lot of the Irishmen who "j'ined up" are grumbling, though, because they said they signed up to fight the *Sassenagh*, and not the Mexicans, particularly as the Mexicans are very devout Catholics. You may think it funny on account of father being such a free thinker and my not going to church when I was growing up, but I went to services the other day.

I hope and pray that you remain safe and well.

I am Yours Truly

PART ONE

# Poor Old Soldier

~

CORPUS CHRISTI, TEXAS
SEPTEMBER 1845–MAY 7, 1846

CHAPTER 1

# Nothing But a Bluebelly

WHEN THE WIND DIES, mid-September nights in south Texas are hot
and humid to the point of suffocation, even a mere 150 yards from
the cooling ocean. My shirt and the leather stock binding my neck
were sweat-slick and stinking beneath my heavy blue wool serge
uniform blouse as I marched post, musket primed, shouldered, and
bayonet fixed, guarding the bivouac of the Fourth Infantry Regiment
against all enemies, foreign and domestic. Forty paces north and forty
paces south along the 150-foot-high crest of the soft, sandy dune that
formed the backbone of St. Joseph's Island. In daylight, the dune was
a remarkable creation of nature, sloping steeply to the ocean on one
side in brilliant yellow-white sand covered with patches of thorny
vegetation and rather more gently on the other to a pretty and lightly
treed plain that stretched to Aransas Bay. On nights such as this,
black as sin itself under the low-lying clouds that presaged tomorrow's
heat and humidity, the top of the dune seemed as far removed from
the dull glow of the regiment's campfires on the bayside plain as it was
from the bustle of the Five Points two thousand miles away.

Falling asleep on my feet or otherwise tripping in the dark and
dirtying my musket were sins that could earn me a dozen lashes and
a day bucked and gagged and left to broil in the merciless Texas sun.
To pass the time, I concentrated on counting my steps up and down
the soft sand, taking care to plant my brogans in the very same foot-
prints I had been making since I had begun tracing my predecessor's
steps. Inevitably, my mind wandered, turning gloomy in darkness as I

contemplated for the thousandth time in the past few weeks the unal-
terable fact that Mary, poor sweet Mary Skiddy, my boon companion
during the dark days of our passage over the Western Ocean (and
the elder sister I'd never had), was dead and buried in Potter's Field.
Lúcás Dineen and my black-coated Fenian nemesis, MacGowan,
had murdered her, just as the very same MacGowan had murdered
my cousin Seamus O'Creagh in his bed by burning his house down,
leaving cousin Evelyn all alone in the world. Only God knew where
Evelyn was, for I surely did not. I would have made a pact with Old
Nick himself at any price he asked, just to trade places with Mary, if
only to allow her to reunite with her poor, orphaned daughter, Fíona.
And given half the chance I would have made the same pact with
Old Nick to trade places with Seamus, if only to know that Evelyn
were safe and sound. As I marched across the soft and shifting sand, I
thought that the ache in my heart would kill me and the guilt of it all
would bury me in eternal damnation. But such damnation is no more
than mere child's talk, and the long dreamless sleep of death would
not have been punishment enough for me.

By and by, my mind wandered once more to contemplate this
new life of mine as just another bluebelly in C Company of the
Fourth Infantry. I spent my days keeping my skirts clear of Hoggs,
the company First Sergeant, and otherwise doing as little else as possible. The transport ship *Suviah* which had brought us here was gone
now, presumably back to New Orleans for yet another regiment of
doughboys or battalion of redlegs to follow the Fourth on the journey twenty miles south to the little town of Corpus Christi, nestled
at the conjunction of the mouth of the Nueces River and the head
of Aransas Bay, where Old Zach's tiny little Army of Observation
was slowly being assembled. I call Corpus Christi a town, but the
"despatch by grapevine telegraph" stoutly maintained that the
word was too grand by half. Apparently it was a mere frontier trading post hardly able to fend off even the most dilatory Comanche
raid, were those heathen inclined to foray so far east as the Gulf of
Mexico. Proper ships could not reach Corpus Christi on account

of the barrier islands blocking the way and protecting the bay—
St. Joseph's Island, which stretched north, and Mustang and Padre
Islands, which stretched 100 miles south of us to the Rio Grande.
Even if the ships could have found a way in between St. Joseph's and
Padre Islands (a sand bar blocked the way), the bay was so shallow
that boats couldn't transit from the St. Joseph's depot to the main
camp without getting stuck in the mud at least once or twice. The
army was using the southern tip of St. Joseph's Island as a jump-
ing-off spot to debark supply and transport ships for transshipment
to Corpus Christi.

We'd spent two days unloading everything but the fixtures from
*Suviah* onto lighters, which we dragged through the surf onto the
beach where we unloaded them. There were no horses or mules, aside
from the officers' mounts, nor were there carts or wagons to be had.
We had to drag or carry everything by hand up the steep, seaward side
of the dune through the soft, yellow sand and the dense and thorny
vegetation that tore at your clothes and shredded your skin, and down
the other side to where the regiment was now sleeping.

It was backbreaking labor and entirely unnoteworthy. That is,
until I heard a brief cry and a splash as I was loafing on the fo'csle of
the lighter that I had just helped load, and which was tied up alongside
*Suviah*. A man surfaced several feet from the lighter. He seemed to be
laboring a bit in the water, weighed down by his boots and clothes.
Without thinking, I kicked off my brogans, shrugged off my blouse,
and dove into the water. I hadn't been swimming in such a long time
that I wondered briefly whether I was now going to drown along with
the man who had fallen in. I reached him in a couple of strokes, tapped
him on the shoulder as he laboriously trod water, and helped him to
the lighter, where we were unceremoniously dragged on board.

He was a youngish man. A pumpkin rind. Likely still pissing West
Point water, I liverishly thought to myself.

He reached his hand out to shake mine. "Wanted to thank
you, soldier. Mighty charitable, getting yourself wet like that on my
account. What's your name?"

"Gogan—Billy Gogan, sir."

"Nice to meet you, Private. Sam Grant's the name. Maybe I'll see you around sometime."

"Yes sir."

Dripping wet and half-naked, I caught Hoggs giving me the cut eye as I saluted Grant. He made off from the lighter back onboard *Suviah*, presumably to change his clothes and his rather fine looking boots—an opportunity that I would not have, particularly as the wet clothes I wore were the only ones I still had to my name.

⌒

But that had been many hours ago, and I had been immediately turned to some task or another. I had not stopped laboring until I began marching post, guarding against ... what? An attack by Mexican cavalry? Not likely. We'd heard that there were no Mexican soldiers anywhere near us. But it wouldn't have taken much to destroy Old Zach's little army just then. There were hardly a thousand men in camp at Corpus Christi, no artillery to speak of, and only one regiment of cavalry—the Second Dragoons. Here at St. Joseph's Island, twenty miles north, was only the Fourth Infantry Regiment, with little ammunition and food and not a single breastwork with which to defend itself. So, if the Mexican army did arrive, everybody reckoned that we would be in a very poor way, indeed.

But it didn't matter whether I was here, on top of a deserted sand dune on St. Joseph's Island, down at Corpus Christi, or back at Governors Island, standing guard along the pier. I was on sentry duty, pacing forty paces north and forty paces south with a 10-lb. flintlock musket on my shoulder—an exercise that will make your arm and neck muscles scream with pain after even a few minutes, if you are not used to it. But I was used to it now after a month or two of soldiering, and I hardly felt the pain anymore. It was the least of my worries.

Right now, stupefaction was my worst worry, and despite my best efforts, I was in a dreamy state after a couple of hours of pacing, hardly aware of anything. Then a twig broke and a low bush just in front of me rustled oddly.

As I unshipped my musket from my shoulder, I cried in as plangent a tone as I could muster, "Halt, who goes there?"

Silence.

"Halt, who goes there?"

There was more rustling. I checked the charge on the flash pan of my musket.

"Corporal of the guard! Corporal of the guard!"

More rustling.

"Halt or I must shoot." I raised my musket to fire and squinted down the barrel in the direction of the rustling. "Corporal ..."

I saw a shadow just in front of me, and I began to squeeze the trigger. Then I saw what the shadow was—a little boy, not much above seven years old, barefoot and carrying a line from which several fish dangled.

I did not have trouble staying awake after that. The corporal of the guard, Rónán Finnegan, was a good old sort hailing from County Monaghan, and he complimented me on having been alert. He also told me that, notwithstanding the grapevine, St. Joseph's was apparently not entirely uninhabited, as there were a couple of families living in small wooden huts on the bay about a mile north of us, supporting themselves by fishing and providing transport across the bay to whomever needed it. The boy had come from there. He apparently had gotten lost in the dark, and so was to be returned to his family in the morning.

It couldn't have been more than twenty minutes after I had damn near killed the little boy that yet another figure materialized in front of me out of the gloom. It was a most extraordinary coincidence, for a sentry could spend a year marching post and not ever have to challenge a soul, and here I was challenging two different people within an hour of each other.

"Halt," I said. "Or I will shoot."

Like the little boy an hour earlier, the figure did not stop moving, nor did he reply with the countersign.

"Corporal of the guard!" I brought my musket to "charge bayonet"—in other words, I was pointing my bayonet at the figure walking towards me. "Halt. Or I will shoot."

Still the figure did not stop moving. Nor did he reply with the countersign. I could hear Finnegan beginning to rustle down at the base of the dune, a hard running climb of a minute or more. I muttered a foul oath under my breath. Then I saw the face of the figure, hardly more than an inch or two away from my bayonet.

"Lieutenant, the countersign." I could not let him proceed without the countersign—on pain of a dozen lashes or worse.

LeFort ignored me and made to walk past me.

"My apologies, sir." I barred his way with my musket. "But unless you give me the countersign, you are my prisoner until the corporal of the guard arrives."

That seemed to snap LeFort out of his reverie. "You impudent bastard. Stand aside or I'll have your guts for garters."

"Sir ..."

LeFort drew his sword and raised it as if to strike me with the flat of it. I should have parried him and disarmed him, but I did not. In those days, many an officer thought nothing of savagely beating a hapless bluebelly with the flat of his sword merely for having displeased him. So I did not want to think of the consequences of striking an officer, even in the line of duty.

"Lieutenant, Lieutenant ..." It was Corporal Finnegan, panting hard from his uphill run.

LeFort said, maintaining his glare at me, "This man is insubordinate."

"Sir, did you give the countersign?"

LeFort lowered his sword, but he did not reply to Finnegan.

"Sir, Private Gogan was just doing his duty."

LeFort considered Finnegan for a moment, and then acknowledged, "I see."

I breathed a sigh of relief, thinking that I had weathered the storm. Indeed, I was relieved as sentry not long afterwards, and I found my blanket for a couple of hours of sleep before reveille.

⌒

"Wake up, you filthy bog trotter." Deep in my dreams, I heard a scream of agony and only slowly realized that it was me. A hobnailed boot had connected with my ribs, and I was doubled over in pain. I was then jerked to my feet by main force.

"You insubordinate, filthy, little bog rat."

I snapped to attention. "Sergeant!"

"Corporal Finnegan tells me you insulted Lieutenant LeFort on guard duty last night."

"Sergeant?"

"You filthy, insubordinate …" A fist crashed into the side of my head and I tumbled to the ground. I was pulled back up onto my feet. I snapped to attention, my head swimming.

I had been entirely wrong about having weathered the storm. At morning muster, just as the sun peeked over the dune, Hoggs personally paraded me in front of C Company to be bucked and gagged for my insolence to the shavetail. Out of the corner of my eye, I could see Lieutenant LeFort standing at attention in front of the company, with a look of stony indifference on his face … the bastard. I was neither the first man nor the last to be bucked and gagged for seemingly nothing. So I did not feel any shame in the punishment, particularly as Sergeant Hoggs, like so many native Americans, seemed to take pleasure in punishing the Irish and Dutchies who, everyone said, made up half of the army.

That said, I did resent the injustice of it. I had done my duty, and now this. As the drum rolled, I was forced to sit in the sand with my legs bent, my knees crushed against my chest, and my arms clasped around my legs. My hands were tied tight, cinching my legs even tighter to my chest. The drum continued to roll, and I was bucked—a splintery pole was shoved over my left elbow, under the crook of my knees, and over my right elbow, driving a splinter deep into the flesh above my left elbow. The splinter felt like a dagger probing my arm every time the pole moved even infinitesimally, and my shoulders felt as though the downward pressure of the pole would tear them from their sockets. Within a minute or two, my lower back began to spasm with the effort of staying upright and not falling over onto the end of the pole—which would have earned hard kicks from the corporal of the guard. I was in instant agony. But I could not move a muscle.

Grinning sadistically, Sergeant Hoggs looked me in the eye as he bent over and dropped a filthy rag into the sand. With a grunt of satisfaction, he picked the rag up and shoved it in my mouth to gag me. The dust and sand from the rag exploded into my nose, my throat, and my lungs. I began coughing uncontrollably, which caused the gag to slip further into my throat, making matters that much worse.

Gradually, I was able to calm myself and resign myself to sitting until night fell, hatless and shirtless and motionless in the broiling sun, sand tickling my trachea all the while. As I sat there, not a single soldier in the company, nor in the entire army, for that matter, even deigned to notice my existence. Except for the corporal of the guard (Finnegan, as it happened), who periodically walked around me to check that the ropes binding my wrists were still tight and the rag still firmly in place in my mouth. (But not too firmly. Finnegan was a decent sort, and he didn't want to me to asphyxiate. Not on his watch, anyway.) If any other soldier were to have consoled me (let alone to have given me a sip of water to relieve my suffering), he would have simply undergone the same punishment the very next day.

I'm nothing but a fucking bluebelly, I thought. What the newspapers and the cavalry call a doughboy. The newspapers said that we called ourselves doughboys on account of our using pipeclay to whiten our belts. But the newspapers were wrong. The cavalry called us infantry doughboys on account of the "adobe" soil dust that covers us whenever we march. The cavalry rode, and they felt much the superior for it. But they were nothing more than bowlegs, on account of all the riding that they do. But what we called ourselves—or each

14

other—or what the scribblers called us did not signify in the least, and it didn't matter whether we were doughboys, bowlegs, or redlegs, we were all naught but mere chattel of the United States Army by virtue of voluntary servitude. How had I gotten to such a sorry place so far from the heroic dream I had for myself of finding Hawkeye in the far wilderness of the *limes americanus*?

# CHAPTER 2

# Wild Geese

⌒

THE ANSWER WAS PRETTY STRAIGHTFORWARD. MacGowan—a man named "Smith" to you non-Irish speakers—and that reprehensible wretch, Lúcás Dineen, had murdered Mary Skiddy in that awful fire that burned down Magee's boardinghouse and saloon in the heart of Gotham's Five Points, thereby leaving Mary's daughter, Fíona, an orphan. The fire had killed Charlie Backwell, as well, and left three-score poor Irish and German immigrants homeless and bereft of all their worldly possessions. Their arson also, by all accounts, started the last great fire ever to trouble the Big Onion. It was all so unnecessary. Did they really need to burn down Magee's boardinghouse and saloon merely to ease poor, dead Charlie Backwell of whatever riches he may have had behind the flimsy deal door that he refused to properly lock? Or was it more?

In my heart, it was more. Much more. And the presence of MacGowan said it all. Dineen and his boss, Cassidy, may have had the motivation to avenge themselves for their humiliating defeat at the polls and in the betting. Magee and Con Donoho had bamfoozled the two of them beautifully, what with a little voter fraud that Bill Tweed and I cooked up and the coup nicely-engineered by Magee and Donoho to coopt Rynders and his bully backs. Then again, Rynders and his thugs were always ready to rush to the winning side. It was the callous savagery of the fire—and the patent failure to kill Magee—that seemed out of character for Cassidy and Dineen. For as surely as the sun will rise and set each day, Cassidy had reason enough to want to see Magee dead, and Dineen was the sort of dead-eyed son of a bitch to do that. But Magee was still alive. So there had to have to been something else, and MacGowan was it.

But why? That I didn't quite ken. MacGowan had barged into my life on that awful day as I sat in Headmaster's antechamber at St. Patrick's, waiting to learn my fate for beaning a classmate with a well-aimed cricket ball, and instead learned that my father was dead and my childhood was over. I'd next seen the son of a bitch some days later, on Lavitt's quay in Cork, where in front of 300 oblivious souls (and two sentient ones—Fíona and me), he'd casually murdered the one man in the entire world who had any regard for me, whatsoever. Father O'Muirhily, my Latin and Greek master at school. And for what? Had MacGowan quietly and casually stabbed him and thrown him in the filthy waters of the River Lee merely for being the only human on earth with the decency to see me off on my way to the New World?

In the name of the good Lord Jesus Christ himself, how could that be a capital offense?

I'd next seen that bastard MacGowan out of the corner of my eye one day while I was fixing bowling games to chouse feckless tourists from Poughkeepsie out of their hard-earned, and easily gambled, rhino. I put that down as a mere figment of my overheated imagination. Then on the morning of the fire, I received a letter from Headmaster, apologizing profusely to me for doubting me at the time of my father's death. He also adverted me to the chilling news that my cousin, Seamus O'Creagh, and dear, sweet Oonagh, his housekeeper through the ages, were dead in a mysterious arson. The constabulary were, for what it was worth, seeking some chap named MacGowan to pursue further inquiries—seemingly the same MacGowan who had darkened the door to Headmaster's *sanctum sanctorum*. But there'd been no progress beyond that. Worst of all, Seamus's daughter, Eibhlin—Evelyn as she liked to be called so as to sound more English at her swell finishing school—was missing. No one seemed to be looking for her, because there was no one left alive to care. As soon as I read the letter, I ran to gather up Mary and Fíona to take them to safety. On the way, I saw the black-haired and malign man once again. My blood ran cold. It was hardly more than a few minutes later, as I was attempting to disengage myself from Lúcás's younger brother Cian, who begged me not to go back to Magee's boardinghouse, when that plangent and portentous tocsin sounded, slowly at first, and then more insistently. The bell stopped as abruptly as it started. A moment later, it rang three strokes, signifying that the fire was in the 'Points (or at least somewhere in the southern part of the city—the Third Fire District). Within a few minutes, poor Mary was dead and I was kneeling in the mud of the street with her body in my arms.

The crying shame of it was that the three of us would have been in Hoboken in another day or two, well-heeled and safe from those murderous bastards. Mary had wanted to go to a little town called Chicago on the shore of a huge lake in the middle of the continent and open a French restaurant. I had gone woolgathering about another little town called Yerba Buena, near an old Spanish mission called San Francisco in a Mexican province called Alta California, where the summers were reputed to be colder than the winters, which weren't cold at all.

But our dream of leaving wicked Gotham had disappeared on that hot and lazy summer afternoon, as I wept over poor Mary's body. Magee had hissed into my uncomprehending ear that I was to blame, and young Bill Tweed, my erstwhile running mate and boon companion, had muttered to me, "Leave. Leave now. Otherwise, Magee will kill you, or Blackie will, or somebody … so, *slán agat*, my friend." I heard his words. I even comprehended them. But I could do nothing then to act upon them except cradle poor Mary's dead body. Sometime later, how long, I don't know, I felt myself being pulled to my feet. It was a carrion hunter, for Christ's sake, here with his undertaker's cart on account of the fire and the prospect of a customer or two whose families would pay handsomely to avoid interment at Potter's Field. I stood there, foolishly, wordlessly, as I watched her being slung, not unkindly, into the cold meat cart. It was not a sight that I would forget.

I stood there for a while, conscious of the wet stench of the dead fire that Magee's boardinghouse and saloon had become. There was a great hullabaloo half a block away. I saw Blackie and a couple of his stalwarts advancing towards me, staves in hand. I remembered Bill Tweed's parting words to me and was chilled to the core in the sweltering afternoon. They were coming for me. I should have run for my life. But I remained, unmoving, as if the hobnails in my boots had rooted me to the very cobblestones upon which I stood. Closer they came and I looked at them, not feeling the terror that I should. I wasn't feeling much of anything at all, except perhaps a soupçon of relief at the prospect of the oblivion to come.

A monstrous explosion shook the ground, followed by a volley of lesser explosions, and concluded by a final blast that dwarfed all the rest. This, then, was how the Great Fire of New York began. It was only many years later that I learned that a large warehouse over on Broad Street, Crooker & Warren, had blown up as the fire spread. Chock full of saltpeter, it had been. The explosion leveled virtually every building for blocks around, broke a million panes of glass, and shook the city to the bedrock as far north as Canal Street, blocks north of where I stood, in the muck and mire of Mulberry Street, awaiting Blackie and his companions. When I picked myself up from the cobblestones, my palms and knees bloodied from having been flung down as if by a giant's hand, they weren't there anymore. Or, at least, I could no longer see them in the billowing clouds of smoke and dust and ash choking me. To the south of me, even through the fog and fug, I saw flames shooting hundreds of feet in the air, and I felt the blast of the fire and heard its roar.

I scrambled to my feet and ran mindlessly in the opposite direction through the dust and the smoke. I saw no one until I bulled into what felt like a brick wall. I realized with the briefest frisson of terror that I'd just found Blackie. Where his companions were, I hadn't a clue.

⌒

The next morning, I awoke—regained consciousness, more like—in an unfamiliar doorway, with the noonday sun shining bright and hot. I was in my shirtsleeves. My coat and vest were nowhere to be found.

I reflexively felt my pockets, knocking a piece of paper off my chest. With growing trepidation, I realized that I had been stripped of virtually everything I owned … my wallet, my money, my pocket watch (recently repaired and adjusted), the letter from Headmaster telling me of MacGowan's perfidy and murder, and the pouch containing $350 in collections I had made just before the fire started. The pouch had been buttoned securely in the inside pocket of my now-vanished vest. If Tweed's warning to avoid Magee's wrath by fleeing the city had not been enough, the loss of $350 of Magee's money certainly was more than enough. Inexplicably, the lowpads hadn't gotten everything. Secure in an inner pocket of my pantaloons were the safe deposit keys and savings passbooks I had taken from Mary's hand just before the bodysnatcher took her away.

I picked up the piece of paper and looked at it. It was an American army recruiting handbill, just like the hundreds of others I had seen strewn all over the 'Points and the Bowery. I had never deigned to even look at one—until now. It said:

> *A few enterprising young men of good character are wanted for the Service of the United States.*
>
> *All recruits shall be provided with good quarters, an ample sufficiency of good and wholesome diet, an abundance of clothing, and in the case of sickness, the most careful attendance and most skillful medical aid.*
>
> *Sergeants, corporals or privates may save between $400 & $700 during a five-year term of enlistment.*

It was only then that I remembered the date. August 10, 1845, my sixteenth birthday. Mary had hinted yesterday morning, the last time I saw her alive, that she had planned some sort of surprise. Now I would never know what it was.

⌒

I stood up and backed away from the doorway. Standing not three feet from me was a big man in a blue wool uniform blouse with huge white chevrons on the upper sleeves and a smaller dark blue one bordered with red just above each cuff. Behind him was a view from Hell. Black smoke hung over the ruins of the lower reaches of Manhattan. I realized that I was standing near the waterfront in Hoboken, on the other side of the Hudson. It looked as if the fire was out, mostly. Just a few scattered columns of smoke reached lazily into the sky from ruins that lay where there had once been tall buildings. Where the Battery had once been seemed to be alive with scores of ants, which I realized must have been refugees from the explosion and fire.

The big man was talking to me as if the horrors behind him did not exist. "Hello, lad. A bit down on your luck, are yers?" The man was a Paddywhack by the sound of him. "Lookin' for something a bit different to do, mí cully?"

"What?"

He pointed over his head to a hand-lettered sign above the opened door behind him, "United States Army Recruiting Station." In the window next to the door was much larger version of the recruiting bill in my hand.

"Ye be after enlistin', aren't yers? Lost everything after last night, I be after thinkin'."

I couldn't find my voice.

"I been waiting f'yers t'be rousin' yersel' this fine morning. But ye na' be lookin' like ye deserved a cold pig t'be startin' the day with." He looked at me with a slightly amused expression, gesturing to a bucket of water by my side.

I was glad of not having been awoken that way. But I was still quite befuddled, and my voice still did not want to work. "I'm … I'm trying to figure out …"

"How yers got here?" The Irishman completed my sentence for me. "Ye was dumped here, looking a little worse for the wear, just after dawn by some *dead ráibéad*. I saw himsel' walking aways, sayin' somethin' about yer needin' to be away from Gotham for a while."

"Black beard?" My voice hardly sounded like my own.

"Yep."

Blackie. I considered for a moment, savoring the hurt of both my lost dreams of a future with Mary and my pipe dream of Hawkeye and mountainmen in the Rockies, and conscious that I was effectively destitute, save for my account at the Bowery Savings Bank—which might as well have been on the moon as across the river. I decided. "You're right. I do think I want to join the army."

"A mick, are yers, then?"

"Yes sir. Well, I was." I replied, "I'm from Cork. But I'm a naturalized citizen—at Tammany Hall just a few months ago."

"Very good. Most encouraging. This man's army be thick wi' us Paddywhacks." The man replied, his accent thickening just a little, as if to bolster his bona fides. "A right congenial place for those of us needin' to get away." He stuck out a great paw and engulfed my hand in it, "I be Sergeant Kehoe. Call me 'Sergeant.' Don't call me 'sir.' I might be thinkin' yer insultin' me by tellin' me that I'm some idiot pumpkin rind still pissin' water from the 'Point. I'm not a 'sir' ... I am a sergeant."

"Yes, Sergeant."

A figure appeared, silhouetted in the gloom inside the door, and said. "A bit scrawny, he is, Sergeant."

Kehoe smiled." Nay, Private Mulvaney. Himsel' be a roight fine specimen. An' he be lookin' twenty-one." He studied me for second." Every bit o' it, methinks. Four limbs ... an' a citizen of good moral character, to boot." He invited me through the threshold of the recruiting station, adding, "I'm sure of it."

Kehoe sat himself behind a desk with a slight, but satisfied groan of pleasure, and then looked up at me with an air of unctuous concern. "I am right, ain't I, that yer o' 'good moral character' an' all?"

"Yes, Sergeant."

"Very good. An' ye'll be twenty-one, of course?"

"Yes, Sergeant. I turned twenty-one last week."

A snort emanated from the back of the room, but Kehoe affected not to hear it. I knew enough not to react.

Kehoe said, "Well, *mí* son, today be yer lucky day. Ye be after goin' fer soldier. A private in the United States Army. Jes' another one in five generations of wild geese flyin' from Éireann in search of something better."

And so I was, one of the Wild Geese just like my great uncle, fighting another man's fight and not fighting for Ireland's freedom like my father. My great uncle had run off, so Father told me, with a recruiting officer just after the Year of the French and signed up with Napoleon's Irish Legion, the single greatest collection of Wild Geese ever assembled, so Father had said. That is, he added, except the Irishmen who manned His Majesty's Army in those days and fought the Irish Legion wherever they found it. My great uncle wrote home regularly, recounting his adventures in a score of battles and his promotions, first from private to corporal, thence to sergeant until he was awarded an officer's commission for some desperate act of heroism at a place called Walcheren. He continued writing until the winter of 1812, his last letter coming from a little town in Poland, speaking for the first time of a whiff of defeat in the air. It was only much later that his colonel, a fellow named Lawless, wrote a letter speaking of my great uncle's heroism in helping save the Legion's eagle at a place called Löwenburg.

Kehoe continued, "So all that be standin' in yer path is the good lieutenant's signature approving yer enlistment. Then ye'll be havin' a signing bonus of honest chink in your pocket. A full half-eagle, I should think."

"Thank you, Sergeant." I straightened perceptibly. I was going to have to get used to standing at attention.

Kehoe got up from his chair and knocked on the closed door just behind him. A muffled voice answered, and Kehoe entered through the door and closed it behind him. I couldn't understand what the muffled voices were saying until a querulous voice said sharply. "A bit young-looking, ain't he? Awfully scrawny." There was another muffled exchange, and then the querulous voice spoke again, "That could be my commission, Sergeant. Confound it!" The querulous voice paused to consider Kehoe's muffled response. "Oh, all right, Sergeant. We are a bit short this month."

Kehoe came out of the room and sat down again. "Yers ain't peloothered, are ye, lad? Ye be quite sober?"

"Of course, Sergeant." Well, as far as I could recall, I hadn't drunk anything last night, let alone any whiskey. I had kept my pledge to Mary … I gulped a little bit, choking back the rush of tears.

"Come with me, then." Kehoe knocked on a second door, and led me in, saying. "Another one for yers, Doc."

A man in a grubby suit, smoking a cigar, looked up from his newspaper and echoed Private Mulvaney and the unseen lieutenant. "A mite scrawny, ain't he, Sergeant?"

"Himsel' be just fine, Doc. He just ain't been in the grub." Kehoe glanced at me. "That's all."

"Amazing what missing a meal or two will do to a young man." The doctor looked over at me. "Come here. And take that filthy shirt off. Let's have a look at you." He pulled out an old-fashioned wooden stethoscope of dubious cleanliness and looked at me as I held my shirt in my hand. "Holy mackerel, son. Those are some mighty impressive bruises."

Kehoe beamed. "Just shows, Doc. He's a scrapper, this one."

The doctor walked around behind me and sighed. "Well, Sergeant, this is the first candidate this week?"

"Himsel' be the first. Though, maybe we might see some more tomorrow, on account o' the fire an' all."

"Then, he'll do." The doctor sat down in his chair and picked up the cheroot he had been smoking and the newspaper that he'd been reading when we entered his office.

Kehoe said to me as we left the doctor's office. "Congratulations, lad. Ye be ready to enlist. Mulvaney over there'll take yer for some grub, and we be havin' yers over to Governors Island lickety-liner."

I remember to this day the oath of allegiance, which I recited about an hour later to a magistrate over at the local Hoboken court, not the New York magistrate's court where a few weeks earlier a judge had pronounced me an American citizen:

> *I will bear true faith and allegiance to the United*
> *States of America and I will serve them honestly and*
> *faithfully against all their enemies and opposers whom-*
> *soever; and I will obey the orders of the President of*
> *the United States, and the orders of officials appointed*
> *over me, according to the Articles of War.*

"Left foot, right foot" is how you march—the left foot always being the first foot you march with. For those who did not know left from right, the cadence was "straw foot, hay foot." The U. S. Army's infantry marched at 90 steps a minute, and each step was precisely 28 inches long—so Scott's *Infantry Tactics* prescribes. Quick time was 110 steps per minute. Double quick time was a run—165 steps per minute, and each step was (thankfully) a little longer—33 inches. Our squad of twelve recruits mastered these basic skills beautifully within about 20 minutes—notwithstanding the half-dozen or so who truly did not know their left from their right.

It was the command "to the rear, march" that landed Dillon O'Dea and me in the flue. More specifically, it was O'Dea's inability to master the timing of executing that particular command that landed us there.

The corporal drilling us was patient to a fault, although he did observe in as thick an Irish accent as I'd ever heard, "Faith, O'Dea, it'll be a fine Judy you're makin' o' yersel', sure enough, ya conceited *créatur.*" A Judy of "Punch and Judy" fame being a woman of utterly ridiculous appearance.

Despite his frustration at O'Dea's slowness, the corporal kept his starter—which was virtually identical to the one used by Mr. Mounce on *Maryann*—in his belt. After I crashed into O'Dea for the third time because he turned a step too soon, the corporal said, "At ease, lads. Let me show yers how it's done. I be marchin' a few paces in front of yers. And then ye's be takin' a pattern." He showed us. We marched again, and we all turned in unison at the command, "to the rear, march." All of us that is except for Dillon O'Dea, who now that he was marching behind me marched a step too far, causing me this time to stumble over him and drop my musket.

"What's this?"

I straightened up at attention after having picked up my musket.

"You." A sergeant about my height, with baleful breath and a stony countenance that was only slightly belied by a cruel gleam in his eye, poked me in the chest. I instantly hated him for the indignity of it. "And you." The sergeant poked O'Dea in the chest. "Are you both complete Paddywhack half-arses?" The sergeant turned his attention to the corporal.

"Yes, Sergeant Hoggs." The corporal snapped to attention.

"I will teach these two misbegotten bog trotters to march."

"Yes, Sergeant."

O'Dea and I spent the rest of the day in the mud by the water's edge beneath Castle Clinton on Governors Island, within sight of Grace Church's spire on Manhattan Island—which had miraculously escaped the ravages of the Great Fire of New York, marching back and forth in unison, our muskets held over our heads until we could lift them up no longer. I cursed O'Dea and Hoggs in equal measure that afternoon, just so that I could maintain some semblance of concentration. O'Dea dropped his musket first. Hoggs beat O'Dea with his starter until O'Dea fell to his knees. Hoggs continued to beat O'Dea until he staggered to his feet and stumbled back into formation in front of me. Hoggs tormented us for a good two hours more as we sloshed along through the rising tide in a straight line and then, on command, marched to the rear down the same straight line as the water lapped around our ankles, ruining our brogans. Hoggs finally left us to the corporal, who mercifully allowed us to occasionally shoulder our muskets to restore feeling in our arms. At sunset, we were released—which meant that, before we could even think about resting, we had to spend hours cleaning our muskets and restoring our uniforms and brogans for inspection at reveille the next day. As I fell asleep, I couldn't decide who I hated more: O'Dea for his mortal stupidity, or Hoggs for his mindless cruelty.

⌒

About a week later, O'Dea came to me and my tentmate, Hermann Wurster. Hermann was a Dutchy kinker whose circus had folded a month ago, leaving him out of the grub in Hoboken, a month's wages in arrears. With him was Kenny O'Leary. Like me, Kenny was a refugee from the 'Points. The only difference was that no one was looking to kill Kenny. He simply had been starving and unable to find a job, even as a streetsweeper.

"I'm going to desert," O'Dea said to us. "I can't take Hoggs anymore. He'll kill me."

"How are you going to do that?" Hermann asked derisively in his curiously formal manner (stemming from his Dutchy origins, no doubt). "We sit on Governors Island, almost a mile from the city by water."

O'Leary said, "Two guys escaped last month in a washtub. They stole it from the officers' laundry and rowed it to Battery Park."

"You do know what they do to ... what is the word ... *Fahnenflüchtige*."

"Deserters?" I helpfully asked.

"A ... deserter." Hermann considered the word. "*Ja, das ist richtig.* You know, Dillon, my friend, what they do to deserters, even here on Governors Island?"

"They won't catch me." O'Dea was defiant. "My brother's bringing a boat tonight. We've been exchanging notes. We'll row back to Gotham. He says he's got enough blunt for us to head to Pennsylvania. I hear they're hiring to build the railroad."

"*Viel Glück.*" Hermann dismissed O'Leary and O'Dea. "I know where my next meal is coming from, even if it is disgusting. And I thought the Prussian army fed us badly."

"I'm out, too," I said. "I can't go back." Hermann nodded. He had spent many an hour listening patiently as I told him my story. I had listened equally as patiently to his stories about the circus and his career as an acrobat until his circus folded, and before that, his service in the Prussian army—the proceeds of which had paid for his passage to Hoboken two years ago.

Kenny O'Leary looked at us all, each in turn. "I'm out, too. Ain't nothing back in the 'Points for me. Like Hermann said, I know where my next meal is coming from—even if the coffee is a reg'lar suck."

"Well, lads, I be after seein' yers in the next life." With that, O'Dea was gone.

We saw O'Dea the next morning. We recruits, all 300 of us, were paraded into three ranks standing at attention in a three-sided square around a tripod. Sergeant Hoggs led a sorry procession to the tripod. O'Dea was marching behind him, alongside a corporal carrying a baize bag. A drummer beating out a doleful march brought up the rear. O'Dea's head had been shaved (I could see blood glistening where the skin had been scraped away) and his blouse hung from him, the buttons ripped away.

The corporal handed the baize bag to Hoggs and pulled O'Dea's blouse off roughly, leaving him stripped to the waist. The corporal then shoved O'Dea face first toward the tripod, with his back—white and glistening with sweat—facing us, and roughly secured his wrists to the tripod. The drum stopped.

A shoulder strap—that's the polite name we called officers on the rare occasions we actually saw them, and I'd never seen this particular cove before—faced my side of the formation's open square. Hoggs was at his right shoulder, and he was extracting a cat o' nine tails from its baize bag. Designed, it was whispered, to flay a man's back to bare bone in a dozen well-applied lashes. Hoggs looked for all the world like a cat about to play with a cornered mouse.

The shoulder strap brayed in a stentorian tone, and I felt as if he was directly addressing me. "This man is a deserter. He has been court-martialed and sentenced to fifty lashes, branding, and dismissal from the service. If a man deserts in a time of war, which God willing we will have very shortly with Mexico, he will be hanged by the neck until dead. That is all."

With that, the shoulder strap pivoted smartly to the left and beat retreat out of eyeshot. Hoggs pivoted about-face and marched to the tripod. The corporal counted out the lashes. The first one did not break the skin. But the second one did. By the time Hoggs had administered twenty lashes, there was hardly any unblemished skin on O'Dea's back. But O'Dea had emitted not a sound other than a groan of air being forced from his lungs as Hoggs flogged him. O'Dea's silence only encouraged Hoggs, who laid in all the harder as he landed thirty and then forty lashes. I could see Hoggs sweating from the exertion in the early morning August sun. Then he was done. Fifty lashes. The torn flesh and skin hung from O'Dea's back, and I swore that I could see naked bone beneath the bloody waste.

"Cut him down," Hoggs ordered.

The corporal complied. O'Dea staggered, but he did not fall. The drum renewed its doleful march and O'Dea was led away. We remained at attention. Nonetheless, more than one man flinched visibly when we heard an unearthly scream from behind us and the stench of burned flesh assaulted us.

Then the drum began again, this time accompanied by three scratchy flutes bobbling a tune I'd never heard before, but which I would hear many times again in the future: *The Rogue's March*. The sergeants and corporals began singing, and we were commanded to join them:

> *Poor old soldier, poor old soldier*
>
> *Tarred and feathered and sent to Hell, because he*
> *wouldn't soldier well …*

The flutists and drummer preceded O'Dea as he was marched across the parade ground to a boat waiting at the dock. I could see that a giant "D" for deserter had been branded into the flesh of his cheek. So did every other manjack in ranks, each man's face paler than those of his comrades. Somebody said later, echoing the shoulder strap at morning muster, that O'Dea was lucky he hadn't been jerked to Jesus for his sin, as desertion in wartime is a hanging offense and Uncle Sam was fixing to get himself into a couple of them, what with the Mexicans to the south and the *Sassenagh* to the north. I felt more than a little ill at the thought of it all, and I felt quite ashamed of having once hated O'Dea for his stupidity.

At the next day's morning formation, we were told that we would be leaving Governors Island in two days' time to join the Fourth Infantry Regiment in New Orleans, where the regiment awaited a ship to take it to a place called Corpus Christi, which was somewhere in Texas. Before we left, a few men—not an Irishman among them—were given passes for a day to go to the city for one last visit. Hoggs sneered that he didn't trust single bog rat among us not to desert.

Hermann was one of the lucky ones to get a pass. I asked him to take a note to Mrs. Shipley regarding Fíona. I also gave him Mary's and my savings passbooks and the deposit box keys. Hermann had put most of the proceeds, nearly 700 dollars, including a great stack of double eagles that Mary had been hoarding in her deposit box, into an account for Fíona's education and upbringing. Since there was naught I could do to look out for Fíona now that I had joined the army, Hermann had given Mrs. Shipley control of the account and of Fíona's future. I was uncomfortable with my act of vast trust. But Hermann reassured me many times thereafter that I "did the right thing," as it were.

Hermann also took two letters to Evelyn, addressed care of her school's headmistress, along with a note to the Irish Emigrants Society, asking the society to forward Evelyn's letters to me, care of the regimental quartermaster for the Fourth Infantry Regiment.

# CHAPTER 3

# Sam Grant

As I LOOK BACK ON IT, the acts that ended my childhood in Ireland and those that ended my life in Gotham were anything but random. My father had died in debtors' prison, hounded by his creditors, like so many another bankrupt. I didn't know why he was a bankrupt, but such mysterious and grisly ends for bankrupts were all the rage in Mr. Dickens's novels in those days. By those lights, my father's death seemed to be anything but random. Yet there was more, far more, to my father's death. He had been the great O'Connell's trusted advisor during the heady days of the Repeal Year, when it had seemed so certain that Ireland would finally win her independence from the hated *Sassenagh*, who had trampled over the Irish and all they treasured for nigh on 700 years. When Peel, the *Sassenagh* prime minister, put his foot down and made it clear that Ireland would never be independent as long as there was a British empire, my father stood side-by-side with O'Connell as they allowed Dublin Castle to arrest them peacefully. It was the right thing to do, no doubt. Self-sacrificing too, for it obviated any possibility of a senseless repeat of the bloodshed of the uprising of '98, when every Irishman who supported the evanescent chimera of Irish independence was either shot or hanged for his pains. But that brave act ended with my father dying in prison, a disgraced man, just a few weeks before the House of Lords overturned his and O'Connell's convictions on Peel's trumped-up charges and O'Connell walked away from Richmond Prison a free man.

Then there was MacGowan, the mysterious Irishman, who seemed to have been dogging my every step since then. Did MacGowan have anything to do with my father's death? I didn't know. But it seemed almost as certain a likelihood as his assassinating Father O'Muirhily on Lavitt's Quay before my very eyes and immolating Mary and Charlie Backwell in Magee's boardinghouse, just as he had immolated Cousin Seamus and his housekeeper, Oonagh. Every one of those murders had occurred in plain sight. Yet there was not a soul, other than myself, who even began to suspect that these deaths were all related to each other, and to my father's death. Worst of all, each of these murders, and MacGowan's seeming propensity to pin the blame for them on me, added immeasurably to my ever-mounting despair and guilt, and they and my fear had propelled me along the path taken by my great uncle, joining yet another generation of Wild Geese, this time in service to Uncle Sam.

What happened next, in those shallow waters of Corpus Christi Bay, was equally as tragic as all of these awful assassinations. It also changed my life just as profoundly. There was one key difference, though. The Irishman had nothing to do with it. He was two thousand miles away and unlikely to find me ever again, for which I was thankful. Hoggs was enemy enough for me. Whether I or anyone else involved died or lived was as random as life itself.

⁓

Two days after I was bucked and gagged, the regiment began moving south from St. Joseph's Island to the army's main camp at Corpus Christi. I was still a little rocky on my feet and the back of my neck and almost my entire head (even through my hair) had blistered in the sun. I didn't dare see Dr. Crittenden, the regimental surgeon—not after being bucked and gagged. He would have put me into the hospital, and the good Sergeant Hoggs—God damn his nativist soul—would have seized the opportunity to convince Lieutenant LeFort to have me flogged for shirking my duty, regardless of the merits of the situation. Hoggs had threatened as much any number of times, and I had no reason to believe that C Company's commanding officer, an unknown God sequestered in his tent named

Captain McCall, would have done anything other than go right along with the two of them.

Hermann was a godsend. Army regulations mandated that I could not be left bucked and gagged once the sun had set. So he cut me loose just as soon as the sun disappeared, and fed me water and soup until I fell asleep. Fortunately, the next day was Sunday, so there was no drill. There also wasn't any fatigue duty such as unloading baggage from *Suviah*, gathering firewood, or digging fresh latrines. I slept through the entire day, except when Hermann fed me some shellfish soup and a thick steak he had cut from a redfish which Corporal Finnegan had caught that morning. I finished that magnificent repast with some melon from the family living just north of us. It turned out that the boy whom I'd confronted—and to my mind, nearly killed—was their youngest son. They were so grateful that we'd found him that they gave the melon to Corporal Finnegan when he'd returned the wayward boy the next morning.

Save for the presence of the United States Army in general, and Sergeant Hoggs in particular, St. Joseph's Island was as near paradise as you could imagine. The bay and the ocean were veritably alive with all manner of fish and crabs and shellfish, all of which were there for the taking along the shoreline. Hunting was just as good. During the several days we sojourned on the island, some of the officers from the Fourth went north on horseback a few miles to where the island broadened out in order to find game. Hermann and a couple of other privates went with them to act as bearers. Hermann told me that, to catch a deer, all you had to do was to sit by one of the fresh water ponds that abounded in the center of the island and wait for one to come to drink. The deer were so unused to humans that they hardly noticed the officers standing as close as thirty yards away, raising their rifles to their shoulders and shooting them dead. One officer had shot a deer while riding his horse at full chisel. Another officer tried to emulate that equestrian triumph. But he never bagged his deer. His horse threw him, and he died of a broken neck.

The only difficulty to be found on the island was in obtaining fresh water anywhere near where our company was bivouacked. Some companies were lucky enough to have bivouacked next to one of the numerous fresh water ponds. C Company had the bad luck of having camped next to a very large and inviting pond that appeared identical to the fresh water ponds, except to the disgust of all concerned, its water was brackish and undrinkable. So we tried to sink a well to find fresh water. But it also turned out to be brackish—as did the next couple of wells we dug. Fortunately, wiser heads decided that we should not try to dig any more wells. Of course, it would have been simpler to have allowed the company to move closer to an untainted water supply, but some shoulder strap decided that such was not prudent military policy. So we ended up hauling most of our fresh water from ponds and wells that were in some cases quite a distance away.

But stay on St. Joseph's we could not. On Monday morning, at sunrise, we mustered and began shifting baggage and cargo onto a tiny steam-driven lighter called *Undine*, which drew about four feet, which was apparently as deep a draft as could be used in the shallow Aransas Bay. The owner, scion of one of the St. Joseph's Island families, was earning a pretty penny moving the Fourth Infantry down to Corpus Christi, just as he had a few weeks earlier with the Third Infantry and Lieutenant Bragg's company of new-fangled flying artillery (the guns for which had yet to arrive, God bless the Washington City big bugs and their inefficiency). I was busy loading bags onto the deck when I heard the owner chewing someone's ear about another lighter, *Dayton*, coming down from Galveston in a few days on account of it being bigger than *Undine*—and cheaper. The owner was quite unhappy that he wasn't going to able to mint as much brass as he had during these past few weeks.

We finally got *Undine* loaded with as much as she could carry, and she chugged south for several hours at a snail's pace, towing six boats full of C Company's soldiers, including Hermann and me. To our east was Mustang Island, a long barrier island seemingly identical to St. Joseph's, with high sand dunes sloping gradually to the bay in a broad plain. To our west beneath the cloudless sky and in the shimmering heat and humidity of a late September day in Texas was low-lying scrubland, protected by a formidable series of mud flats. I was indifferent to the scenery, preferring to sleep most of the way in the shade of a canvas tent half that we rigged over our boat to shelter us from the relentless sun. I stirred only when Corporal Finnegan shook me awake and told me to get off my keister.

*Undine* was sitting motionless twenty yards in front of us, chugging disconsolately. She had run aground. So we were going to have to lighten her so that she could be taken off the mudflat. Into the waist-deep water we went, slogging our way to the lighter, where the water was only thigh deep. The men on *Undine* were shoving baggage to us, which we loaded painstakingly into the six boats. When we finished loading the boats, they were almost resting on the bottom from their burden of every imaginable type of ammunition, supplies, stores, and everything else needed to keep an army in the field—including mounds of the shoulder straps' baggage, the most precious cargo of all.

But *Undine* was once again afloat now that she had been freed of her burden. She steamed off with half of C Company in search of somewhat deeper water. If she ran aground again, those men were going to have to drag her across the shallows. The rest of us had to pull and shove the six boats about a mile across the mudflats to the southern part of the bay, which led south to the Nueces River and Corpus Christi.

Hermann and I were busy pulling on one line attached to the boat we had been riding in, while about ten feet away three other men were pulling on a second line attached to the boat. Another three or so were pushing and shoving the boat through the thigh-high deep water and over the muddy bottom that seemed to want to suck the boat in. We were all stumbling at almost every step. Every so often one of us sank thigh-deep into a soft spot, which sucked the victim completely under the water. Our mates would have to pull the victim free, choking and spitting out the bay's salt water.

It was grueling work, and it was hard to lose myself in it as we struggled and stumbled with the boat inching along behind us. I had nonetheless achieved a certain detachment for a few minutes at least, when the boat suddenly lurched free of the mudbank where we were standing and caromed away. Hermann and I let go of the line just before it forcibly pitched us into the water. I looked up as I regained my footing, and realized that the three men pulling on the other line were in the water, trying laboriously to swim to shallower water. They must have fallen off the edge of the mudflat, pulling the boat with them, for it now bore down on them like a bullet to its target. Two of the struggling swimmers were able to dodge the runaway boat. The third could not. The boat struck his head, and he disappeared beneath the water. He did not resurface.

Hermann peeled off his blouse and kicked off his brogans and handed them to me, saying, "I'll be right back."

As Hermann launched himself into the water, Hoggs appeared from nowhere, screaming at us to take a round turn on the line and haul the boat in. I knotted the laces of Hermann's brogans together, slung them and his blouse over my shoulder, grabbed the line again and began helping to haul the boat back towards us. Hermann was vigorously stroking towards where the man had disappeared.

"Wurster!" Hoggs bellowed as he clumsily waded towards us through the thigh-deep water. "Get back here and help haul the boat in."

Hermann waved back to Hoggs in acknowledgment and shouted, "There's a man in the water, drowning. The boat hit him."

Hoggs screamed at Hermann, "Wurster, get your ass back here or ..."

"Sergeant." Corporal Finnegan, who had been following behind Hoggs, interceded. "Wurster's right, Sergeant. The boat hit O'Leary, and he disappeared. He'll drown."

Hoggs turned towards Finnegan and hissed venomously. "I don't give a good goddam who's drowning out there. Wurster ... and you ... will both do what I fucking well tell you."

"Yes, Sergeant."

"Put that Dutchy shit on report."

Finnegan hesitated and then said, "Yes, Sergeant."

By this time, O'Leary's two companions had successfully made their way to us, and we hauled them out of the water and deposited them on the mudbank, gasping for air, and shoeless and shirtless from having shed their clothing in order to stay afloat.

As we recovered the boat, we riveted our attention on Hermann, who had just reached the spot where O'Leary had disappeared. He dove beneath the water and then surfaced. Nothing. He dove again, and once more he surfaced empty-handed. Hermann dove a third time. A minute passed, maybe more, before Hermann finally resurfaced. This time, he held O'Leary's head above the water. Everyone cheered and two of our party jumped into the water to help Hermann bring O'Leary over to the boat.

Hermann gasped for air and waved us to put O'Leary into the boat. We all heaved away and he fairly erupted from the water and landed none too gently atop the baggage in the boat. I reached down and hauled Hermann out of the water.

"We've got to get the water out of his lungs and get him breathing." The words came out in short bursts as Hermann gulped convulsively for air. "Get him on his stomach and push the water out of his lungs ... gently ... let me do it."

"Wurster," Hoggs snapped. "Stand fast."

Hermann remonstrated with Hoggs, "Sergeant, O'Leary's not breathing. We can save him if we can get the water out of his lungs."

"You stand fast, Wurster." Hoggs put his hand on Hermann's chest, daring Hermann to push it away. Hermann flinched involuntarily and then stood at attention. "Finnegan, attend to O'Leary."

I waded to Finnegan's side. "I think I know what Hermann wants us to do."

"Good," Finnegan grunted. "I sure as hell don't. I can't even swim."

As Hoggs began to dress down Hermann for having disobeyed orders, Finnegan and I were heaved into the boat like two sacks of potatoes, where O'Leary lay over the baggage.

"Get him on his stomach," I said. I could hear Hoggs dressing down Hermann, and then I heard the savage slap of Hoggs's starter. I looked up to see a nasty weal on Hermann's cheekbone. I wordlessly looked back down at O'Leary and gently pressed on his back. A little water spewed from his lips, which were already starting to turn blue. Finnegan helped me pull O'Leary over onto his side, and then rolled him back onto his stomach. I prayed that I was correctly remembering what Hermann had told me some weeks earlier about how years ago back in Prussia his father had saved Hermann's brother like this. I was beginning to give up hope when O'Leary coughed and began breathing. Once we had him conscious and sitting up, I climbed down off the boat and slid wearily into the water. As I did, I saw Hoggs cuff Hermann with his starter one last time, leaving a second bloody weal across Hermann's cheek. I wondered tiredly how long that evil bastard, Hoggs, had been beating Hermann.

<hr>

It must have been long enough, because Hermann never did end up on report. I'm also pretty sure that Finnegan did not remind Hoggs to put Hermann on report, either. Hermann never spoke of the incident or the humiliation. When I asked, he simply gave me a look that told me to shut pan.

We spent the rest of the day and well into the night helping haul the boats to the deeper water on the south side of the mud flats. We then went back and helped haul *Undine* over the mud flats, reloaded her, and then dropped, exhausted, into our boats while *Undine* chugged the last three or four miles to the camp. We spent several more hours unloading *Undine*, before we were allowed to drop to the sand at the water's edge and sleep until reveille.

We were a ragged lot at parade the next morning. LeFort was apoplectic over the fact that half the company didn't even have brogans to wear. The rest of us had brogans encased in slowly drying mud. Even worse to LeFort's mind, as he lectured us, was the fact that some of the men had actually had the temerity to fall into formation without their blouses on—those three poor coves being O'Leary and his two companions. Somebody up the line must have said something to LeFort, because we were never punished for our sorry appearance. Instead, we received new brogans and blouses, the cost of which, of course, was deducted from our already miserly pay. But even colder comfort than that was spending the next week in the broiling sun digging trenches and building parapets and glacises around the camp's perimeter, along with every other manjack whom the Army of Observation could muster.

A rumor had come up from Matamoros via Colonel Kinney, the man who had founded the little village of Corpus Christi and who was now General Taylor's chief scout on account of him being the only brother Jonathan around who could speak Spanish. Apparently, the Mexican general, Mejia, was about to march north with his whole army to exfluncticate us. This wasn't the first time that rumors had flown about predicting an imminent attack by the Mexican army, and everyone was pretty jumpy. In August, a couple of weeks before we of the Fourth Infantry had arrived, a terrible thunderstorm had struck camp. Lightning killed one of Lieutenant Bragg's Negro slaves, and the wind destroyed tents and damaged stores and supplies. When the storm struck, Colonel Twiggs and the Second Dragoons had been resting at the town of San Patricio, on the Nueces River some twenty miles west. They were at the end of a grueling, 500-mile journey to join the army, and were preparing to ride into camp the next day. The cavalry regiment mistook the thunder for Mexican artillery, and they rode hell for leather all the way to camp to "relieve" the Army of Observation from "attack."

After about a week of digging trenches, hauling dirt from one point to the next for glacises, and building parapets for our non-existent artillery, the grapevine quivered with another rumor from Colonel Kinney. This time the grapevine proclaimed that there was no big Mexican army poised to destroy us. In fact, General Mejia had only five hundred men with him in Matamoros, down on the Rio Grande, 130 miles to our south. Better yet, held the grapevine, the Mexican troops were months in arrears in their pay and thus not inclined to be adventuresome. Moreover, the Mexicans who lived in the five *villas del norte* along the Rio Grande didn't want war with the *gringos*. So they were refusing to help the Mexican army build fortifications to defend Matamoros. It was on the basis of the second rumor that the next day all 1,500 of us bluebellies abandoned construction of the nascent fortifications. We instead spent the next two and half weeks clearing chaparral, mesquite trees, and other scrub from a huge parade ground where the army was supposed to begin drilling. We also had to dig wells, which were a lot deeper than the ones we dug on St. Joseph's Island on account of the fresh water being harder to find. Finally, like every other army in history, or so Hermann told me, we dug latrines and still found time to perform myriad other fatigue duties.

After many days of such hard labor, Hermann and I were mighty glad to be detailed to go back up north to St. Joseph's Island on some errand or another to haul yet more supplies south—even though Hoggs was the sergeant commanding the work party. O'Leary chaffed us because he had been detailed to dig yet another well in the blazing late-September heat.

We weren't on *Undine* for this journey. True to her owner's prediction, *Undine* had been discharged from her duties and replaced by the larger *Dayton*, which was an ancient wreck of a side-wheeler. So dilapidated was she that some wag had snidely suggested that she was fifty years old. I didn't believe him, because steam had only been used in ships these last twenty years or so. But decrepit *Dayton* was.

Hermann and I didn't really care about her decrepitude, for we weren't digging wells or latrines or clearing scrub from the parade ground. Even better, we were sunning ourselves in the mild breeze generated by *Dayton* as she chugged north, side-wheels thrashing. The bay was a veritable millpond under the cloudless sky, and the shoreline was hardly visible on either side. Best of all, *Dayton* was passing well away from the mudflats across which we had hauled the boats and *Undine*. I don't know whether the army had dug another channel or whether a better route had been found, but we had been told that we were not going to have to drag *Dayton* across the mud-flats in either direction.

Hoggs was sprawled on the fo'scle a few feet away from Hermann and me and the other half a dozen other C Company soldiers who were also coming along for the fatigue duty—whatever it was. We were giving him as wide a berth as possible. Another detachment of bluebellies was lazing back aft. Just before I put my cap over my eyes and went to sleep, I remember seeing several officers, including Lieutenant Higgins and Lieutenant LeFort, sitting in wooden chairs in the shade on the port side of the pilot house, gossiping with each other and making room for the regimental surgeon, Dr. Crittenden, to sit with them. They were as happy to be away from the camp on a skylark as we bluebellies were.

I woke up with my ears ringing. I was floating on my back in the water, thirty feet from *Dayton's* starboard side. The lighter was ablaze virtually from stem to stern. Somebody told me later that one of the boilers had exploded. A second explosion rocked *Dayton*, and she rolled over to her port side, barely afloat and listing badly. The explosion seemed oddly muffled to me, and I realized that the noise of the first explosion must have deafened me. It didn't occur to me how lucky I was to be alive. In fact, I was quite upset that my forage cap was nowhere to be found, because it was going to be yet another charge against my pay when a new one was eventually issued to me. I cursed again when I touched the muddy bottom in the chest-high water and realized that one of my newly-issued brogans must have come off when I had been hurled overboard.

My good fortune at still being alive only slowly dawned on me as I looked around and saw not a soul moving about. I kept looking for what seemed to be many minutes, as I gradually regained my hearing and lost the overwhelming sense of isolation that my temporary deaf-ness had produced. Only then did I see a body bobbing, face-down in the water just a few feet from me, amidst a carpet of wreckage from the explosion. I waded over to it, hardly knowing what to think. I rolled the body over. It was a private from C Company whom I'd known slightly, and whose name I could not remember. He had been notable to me chiefly for his slowness of thought and his ability to attract a good deal of Hoggs's ire when Hoggs ran out of nasty things to say about Irishmen and Dutchies. There was hardly a mark on the poor bastard's face, and I wouldn't have known for certain that he was dead except for the fact that his neck had been horribly broken.

I waded to the next body, which was lying face up in the water. It was Lieutenant Higgins, a young fellow who had just been commissioned out of the military academy that the Americans had established up at West Point, just north of Gotham. He had been widely seen as still pissing out the water he'd imbibed during his four years at the 'Point. Higgins's face was half gone, and his skull had been crushed. I gathered the two bodies and began to walk them laboriously towards *Dayton*, stumbling on the uneven bottom every couple of steps. I couldn't think of anything better to do. It seemed that I was the only man left alive in the world, and I had to take care of the dead.

"Billy!" I snapped out of my reverie. It was Hermann. "It's Lieutenant LeFort. He's burned. Badly. Help me."

I pulled Lieutenant Higgins and the private whose name I could not remember along with me as I waded over to Hermann.

"You okay?" I asked.

"Sure," he replied. "Better shape than you—and better looking."

"Yeah."

"Seriously. You don't have a left eyebrow anymore." I felt my forehead, and then jerked my hand away as the salt water from my hand stung some cut or gash.

"I'm all right. How's the lieutenant?"

"He's unconscious. He might even be dead by now."

LeFort's face was almost unrecognizable. What little flesh remained was scalded and blistering, and white bone peeked out from under charred skin that covered much of the rest of his face.

"We ought to get him back to *Dayton*. There is nothing much else floating out here." Hermann pointed to the lighter, which was now only smoldering as she listed heavily to port, down by the stern.

"I think she's going to sink."

"Oh." Hermann didn't look very happy.

We both looked around for any other signs of life. I thought I saw somebody wade through the water about twenty or thirty yards away and disappear behind *Dayton*'s smoldering hulk. Before I could point him out to Hermann, LeFort started thrashing and writhing. I didn't think anybody could have lived with such hideous burns to his face and God knows where else. But LeFort was more than merely alive. He began screaming, gargling the bay's salt water as he thrashed from side to side. He screamed even louder as the salt water washed over his burns. I let my two dead bodies drift for the moment, and I grabbed one of LeFort's arms to help Hermann steady him. As I did, I felt the flesh peel away under LeFort's blouse, which was scorched and blackened from the explosion. The poor man thrashed still harder at this fresh insult.

"Lieutenant … Lieutenant, hold still. We're getting you out of the water," Hermann said gently as he leaned over the struggling man. Then Hermann nodded to me, and we began floating LeFort toward *Dayton* for lack of a better place to take him. LeFort thrashed once more, gave a final whimper, and was still. He was dead.

"I'll go back and get the other two."

Hermann nodded. "I will see you at the boat."

I retrieved the private whose name came to me now. Philips, it was. Joe Philips had come from up Poughkeepsie way when his father had given the family farm to his elder brother and told Joe that he would have to find his own way in the world. I corralled Lieutenant Higgins and began moving the two corpses towards *Dayton*, which rolled over completely on its port side with a hiss of extinguishing fire and slid into the water until only the broken mast and funnel were visible. There was hardly a wisp of smoke rising from the wreck, now that the water had gotten to the fire, and for the first time, I noticed the low shoreline past the wreck. It seemed very far away.

Hermann was stopped a few feet in front of me. "Do not come closer."

"Why not?"

"The water is really deep here."

I looked around, wondering with a cold chill whether we were the only ones left alive, and wondering as well how we were to be rescued. Then I remembered the figure I'd seen disappear behind *Dayton* and looked around to find him. He and a small group of survivors were visible now, huddled on the far side of where *Dayton* had sunk. They were only about fifty yards away from us. I pointed to them.

Hermann nodded. "They have a raft or something."

"You want to swim for it or should I?" I asked.

"You are fit to swim?" Hermann looked at me with concern.

"Yeah. Exercise'll do me some good."

With that, I left Hermann with the three bodies and a promise that I'd be back as soon as I could.

Half an hour later, one of *Dayton*'s crew and I were on a small raft fashioned from the debris, paddling back to Hermann with instructions to pick up all the bodies we could find. Judging by the very small size of the raft and the potential number of bodies, I figured that, before all was said and done, we'd be swimming back to where the score or so survivors had gathered on the mudbank. Almost every survivor was injured to one degree or another. The really badly injured were on a makeshift raft, and everyone else was standing or crouching in the thigh-deep water. Doctor Crittenden was miraculously uninjured. He was busy tending the wounded as best he could with what little laudanum and few bandages he had in his bag—good Lord knows how he managed to hang onto that when he'd been flung overboard.

When I told Dr. Crittenden that Lieutenant LeFort and Lieutenant Higgins were dead, he said nothing about LeFort. He instead replied, "That's most unaccountable, son, about poor Thaddeus. He and I were sitting talking together when the boat exploded. He was so happy that he was going to be able to send his letters to Mrs. Higgins and Sam Grant's letters along to that sweetheart of his. What's her name? Delightful young creature. Colonel Dent's daughter. Fine family. Aah, that's it. Julia. Fine girl." A look of distress crossed Crittenden's face.

"Captain Morrison is Mrs. Higgins's father, you know. He will be most distressed to learn that Thaddeus is killed. Did you see any letters, son?"

I told him no, I hadn't, but that I had not searched for them, either.

"Well you take a moment to find them," he said. "Sam will be most gratified, as will Captain Morrison."

"Yes sir."

When we got back to Hermann, we hauled the three dead men aboard the raft and paddled back to the other survivors. As we did, I checked Lieutenant Higgins's blouse, and found an oilskin pouch with a dozen letters inside. I gave the pouch to Dr. Crittenden when we returned. He told me to keep it and give it to Lieutenant Grant myself when we returned to camp, as he was sure that Lieutenant Grant would be able to arrange to return Lieutenant Higgins's letters to Captain Morrison.

A few hours later, a yawl from the camp picked us up, news of the explosion having been sent back via one of the few uninjured officers, who had been accompanied by Sergeant Hoggs and another uninjured soldier. Curiously, Hoggs did not make the return trip. Hermann and I spent our time making rounds with Dr. Crittenden, tending the wounded. Dr. Crittenden ran out of laudanum after a while. Fortunately, most of the wounded were still sleeping when the yawl picked us up.

⌒

We were introduced to our new lieutenant at formation the next morning. It was Grant, the shavetail I'd helped fish out of the water when we were unloading *Suviah*. It was only then that I remembered I had to give Lieutenant Higgins's letters to him. They were still wrapped in the oilskin, and stuffed into my belt.

I made my way over to his tent as soon as I could steal away. I handed the letters to him, explaining where I had found them. He gave me a sad look and thanked me for returning the letters, saying that he would arrange to have Lieutenant Higgins's letters given to Captain Morrison.

The entire Fourth Infantry Regiment paraded at sunset a day or two later for the funerals of the officers and enlisted men who had died on *Dayton*. We presented arms to the beat of muffled drums and the plaintive wail of three or four fifes as the funeral cortege passed in order of seniority in rank of the dead, each coffin in a separate wagon drawn by four horses draped in funeral crepes. The coffins were each covered with a pall and accompanied by a stand of colors. An old man in a captain's uniform, stooped and haggard in his grief, marched a few paces behind the first wagon, and I realized that he must be Lieutenant Higgins's father-in-law, Captain Morrison. I thought briefly of my own father in the instant and then of poor, dead Mary and Father O'Muirhily and the others close to me who'd been so foully murdered by MacGowan, and tears came to my eyes.

CHAPTER 4

# Zach Taylor Makes
# an Army Out of Us

⌒

"SERGEANT, THERE'S A CATHOLIC PRIEST holding services in town this Sunday."

Hoggs didn't reply. He sat on a small camp stool outside his tent, head down, whittling a small piece of wood.

I waited a moment. "Sergeant …"

"I heard you, Gogan. I ain't deaf. And, no, you ain't going to no mackerel-snatcher church on Sunday."

"Lieutenant Grant …"

"… Be damned. You ain't going."

"It's not me I'm necessarily concerned about," I said. "There're other Catholics in the company, and some of them …"

"Well, they ain't going neither. Now get out of it. I don't want to hear no more about it … understand?" Hoggs looked up at me.

"Yes, Sergeant."

Now the hook was set. I'd done precisely what Grant had told me to do—talk to the company first sergeant about us Catholics in C Company going to Mass in town. In other words, he wanted me to follow the chain of command, just as I was supposed to. Grant said he'd take care of the rest of it.

I'd surely knap a hot one from Hoggs over it, though, and I was just a little scarified by the thought of it. But I figured that I was going to have to go the whole hog if I was going to first discredit Hoggs and then eventually destroy him. My hatred for the man had slowly waxed ever since the first time I laid eyes on him on Governors Island, and that hatred had finally coalesced into a desire to destroy the man the day that *Dayton* blew up and he had not returned with the yawl to take care of his men, injured as they were. It didn't matter whether his failure to do so arose from cowardice, incompetence, or callousness. His behavior crystalized my desire to do something. God knows I'd run from MacGowan, and I was going to be damned if I was going to run again. But I had told no one about it, not even Hermann, if only to avoid his trying to talk me out of it.

Putting Hoggs on the spot with Grant was merely the first step in my campaign. The opportunity had arisen when a couple of days earlier Hermann and I had been on a work party with Grant, clearing an oyster bed and other underwater junk so that boats coming from St. Joseph's Island and other points north could land on the beach, instead of beaching on the oyster beds a hundred yards from shore, in calf-deep water.

Hoggs was in the water, ineffectually trying to organize us to clear some boulders and rotting tree trunks before we got to clearing the oyster bed itself. It was funny how Hoggs, as good as he was on the drill ground, was manifestly incompetent away from it. So he'd learned to make himself scarce whenever he could. Every so often, though, he couldn't disappear. Today was one of those occasions. Grant was on the shore, looking increasingly exasperated with Hoggs's ineptitude. With a final look of irritation, Grant stripped off his blouse and sacrificed another pair of boots—every bit as nice as the ones he'd ruined in his dive from *Suviah*—as he plunged into the waist-deep water and took charge from Hoggs. The latter promptly waded off—to the vast, if suppressed amusement of every doughboy on the work detail. He eventually ended up at the perimeter of the group, full of the wounded pride of a sergeant who had been wronged by his pumpkin rind. He had been rendered a mere spectator to, and absolved of all blame for, whatever debacle was about to unfold now that the pumpkin rind had taken charge.

Grant did not let Hoggs slip away so easily. He directed Hoggs to take charge of three men whose sole job was to move a single pile of debris. Hermann and I had circled well away from Hoggs during this face-off to avoid any entanglement with him. Kenny O'Leary had been neither as fleet-footed nor as fortunate. He had caught Grant's eye, and Grant included him in the work party he had detailed for Hoggs. There was no way to rescue Kenny from his fate, so Hermann and I turned back to the boulder that we had been worrying loose from its resting place in the mud. As Hermann and I worked, we watched covertly from our vantage point. Grant almost instantaneously transformed the work party from a shambles into a smoothly and efficiently operating bit of machinery that was methodically clearing the mud bottom of debris and hacking away at the oyster beds to clear a deeper channel to the water's edge.

Hermann and I worked steadily, exchanging few words until he stopped, wiped his brow, and said in his formal Dutchy fashion, "I have not been to confession since I left Hoboken, and if I do not go on Sunday, only Sam Hill knows when a priest will once again be in Corpus Christi. I must find a way to go—come hell or high water."

"Hermann, one day you're going to sound like a reg'lar downeaster, ya keep talkin' that way."

I earned a reproving glance from him.

"Anyway," I continued. "Hoggs isn't going to let us go. He hates us mackerel-snappers more than some of those bible-thumping Methodies I ran into back in the 'Points. And even if he didn't, he's just plain mean enough to stop us from going out of pure spite."

"*Ich weiß.*" Hermann grunted with effort as he worked the boulder a little looser from the grasping suction of the mud. "But I have heard that, over in the Fifth, they are permitting their Catholics to attend Mass on Sundays. No questions asked, and no answers given."

"Maybe we ought to do that too … Just go."

"If we do, we will catch it something awful from Hoggs."

I did not react to Hermann's fresh use of an American colloquialism. Instead, I said, "Hermann, to hell with Hoggs. Do you want to go to confession or not?"

"I do." Hermann stood up. "There. It is loose. Let us lift it up." Before I could respond, Hermann looked at me speculatively. "You should confess yourself as well. It would do your soul some good."

I didn't reply. I merely flushed from the unshriven guilt. Mary—and everyone else who had died as a result of my mere existence—weighed upon my soul. To hide my discomfiture, I stooped to help Hermann, and he did not press me further. We instead lifted the heavy rock and began staggering with it towards the beach some thirty yards away.

"Let me help you." A third set of hands lightened our load. It was Grant.

Hermann and I chorused—surprised, but highly gratified, "Thank you, sir."

"My pleasure," Grant grunted with the effort. As we began staggering—more easily, now—Grant said, "I couldn't help overhearing you, Wurster. You should go to church on Sunday."

"We are both Catholic, sir," Hermann replied. I remained silent, utterly indifferent to the prospect of going to church, but excited about the prospect of my first leave from camp since being rowed to Governors Island those many weeks ago.

"I don't give a hang about what church you go to, whether you're Catholic or Methodist. Captain McCall doesn't either." Ever since Grant had taken over for poor LeFort, Captain McCall, our company commander, had practically disappeared from view, seemingly content to leave most of the company's day-to-day operations to Grant. "So go—if you want. If not, don't, Go fishing instead. That's what I'm planning on doing." Grant chewed his unlit cigar for a moment as we moved steadily to shore. "But you should talk to First Sergeant Hoggs so that you're on the up and up."

Hermann and I looked at each other, and Hermann said, "Yes sir."

As we approached shore, three officers stood, watching us. They seemed unaware that Old Zach had sidled up behind them, accompanied by a single shavetail aide-de-camp and mounted on Old Whitey, one leg crooked around the pommel of his saddle, the other firmly in the stirrup. Taylor looked for all the world like what he was: a prosperous—if somewhat elderly and slightly gone to seed—plantation owner overseeing his fields of cotton and his Negro slaves, clad as he was in a loose brown frock coat over a fine linen waistcoat, with an enormous, battered straw sombrero planted firmly on his pate. There wasn't a single item about his person to distinguish him as the second-most senior officer in the entire United States Army.

Grant, Hermann, and I staggered out of the water with the misshapen rock, its barnacles cutting our hands. Water streamed from our sodden pantaloons and ruined brogans.

One of the officers, Lieutenant Porter, who had just been assigned to C Company and who was one of Grant's best friends and a scion of an old naval family (his father was a distinguished naval hero and his brother was destined for high rank in the Navy), called out to Grant, "Why, Sam, you're naught but a common laborer. You ain't Country Sam no more, back at the 'Point. Leave those men to it, and come hunting with us."

Another lieutenant—whom I didn't recognize—extracted a cigar from his mouth, exhaled a cloud of smoke and called out, "Sam, you'll give us shoulder straps a bad name with that sort of thing … manual labor." He spat a bit of something to the ground and turned away to see General Taylor clear his throat and say to no one in particular, "By God, I do wish I had more officers like Grant. Officers," he paused, "who stand ready to set a personal example when needed."

With that, Old Zach rode off, his aide-de-camp in tow.

A day or two later, the army began to drill in earnest, as the regimental and brigade parade grounds had been finally cleared. On that first day, Old Zach issued an order written in fair hand by Captain W. S. Bliss. Known universally as "Perfect" Bliss, he was at once the Old Man's adjutant-general, chief of staff, future son-in-law, and general dog's body who made the army operate as clockwork as it did. Taylor's order made it clear to every manjack that we were now an Army of Occupation, on account of our old moniker of the "Army of Observation" having been deemed by the Washington City as insufficiently warlike, and that we were going to fight as a single army of highly trained regulars. Everyone knew that the Army of Occupation was perhaps the largest concentration of regular troops anywhere on American soil since the War of 1812, and we were training for the sort of battle that the American army hadn't seen since then, when Major-General Winfield S. Scott, who was known as Old Fuss and Feathers on account of his liking pomp and circumstance and who was the only officer in the army senior to the Old Man, gave the *Sassenagh* a bloody nose in Canada at a place called Lundy's Lane nearly twenty years before I was born.

One evening, Corporal Finnegan told Hermann, Kenny O'Leary, and me as we peaceably smoked our pipes by the fire waiting for taps to be called, that he had it from the most reliable of sources— Lieutenant Grant and Captain McCall, themselves—that the Fourth Infantry had never fought as a single unit since it had been splashing through the swamps with Old Hickory, chasing the Spanish and Indians in Florida. Not even during the Seminole Wars back in the '30s, when the army had bloodily extirpated Osceola and his noble Seminole from the swamps of Florida for the grave crime of giving shelter to runaway Negro slaves—a state of affairs that rich, white cotton and tobacco planters from Virginia and the Carolinas to Georgia, Alabama, and Mississippi had found intolerable.

Hermann snorted derisively, "When I was in the Prussian army, the generals drilled entire divisions together. And we fought that way, too, even when we were putting down riots in the streets of Berlin."

Finnegan asked, "How long did you serve?"

"Three years. Then I came here to America and did what I was trained to do as a child—be a kinker." Either Kenny or Finnegan must have looked askance, because Hermann explained. "An acrobat. The prospects for a circus acrobat are better here in America than in Prussia. But even here, circuses go out of business. So I found myself on the streets of Hoboken, with two dollars in my pocket and owed a month's wages. That is why I joined the American army. I had not eaten for nearly a week when I found the recruiting station—not that

I had a square meal in the army until we caught that fish up at St. Joseph's Island. The food of the American army is worse than what they throw away in the Prussian army."

"Too right," Finnegan agreed. "Even army java's no good. And that's funny. Because when I joined three years ago, it was for the same reason. I hadn't eaten a decent meal in I don't know how long. I was a weaver down in Philadelphia, making six bucks a week. Then the looms shut down, and it was a case of "no Irish need apply." Nativist no-accounts. While I still had a bit of a grubstake, I should've simply headed west like a lot of folks were doing. But I hung on, looking for work, until I was about down to my last shilling. A recruiting sergeant found me and filled me with whiskey. The next thing you know, I'm standing at attention with a serious case of the jim-jams, listening to a Dutchy corporal screaming at me."

I thought about how effortlessly I had found work in Gotham, and how lucky I'd been to run into a few people who looked out for me. At least they did until MacGowan came around. But I didn't say anything. I also didn't want to discuss why I too was a proud member of C Company of the Fourth Infantry. Hermann knew. But no one else did, which was the way it was going to stay.

So I asked Hermann, "What do you mean when you said entire divisions drilled together?"

"Very simple. The drills we do now with our company? My entire battalion drilled like that nearly every day, and entire brigades and divisions—six or eight or ten regiments at a time—drilled as if they were a single company of infantry nearly as often."

"That's more regiments than there are in the entire U. S. Army," Finnegan said glumly. "Them *Sassenagh* drill like that too. God help us if Old Man Hitchcock over in the Third is right that we're going to have to fight them before it's all said and done."

Hermann didn't seem to hear Finnegan, and murmured, "But we did so much more, particularly those of us in the light infantry. We trained to operate in skirmish lines and small units. Wars are not always fought in lockstep like they want to teach us here."

"Who's Hitchcock?" O'Leary interrupted.

Hermann smiled, and Finnegan answered. "He's the colonel of the Third Infantry. I heard from a corporal I know over there that Hitchcock thinks he's the only big bug here in Corpus Christi who can drill anything larger than a platoon without making a royal hash of it—and this includes Old Zach, mind you. And he says that there isn't a battalion in our army that can form a square properly, which will mean the death of us all at the hands of the Mexican cavalry."

Hermann smirked. "Judging by how we drilled today, I understand his sentiment."

The sun had just started to hang low that afternoon. C Company had been marching in a column, right behind B Company and right in front of D Company. Lieutenant Porter was our company commander for the day. The command was given via drum and screeching fife for the regiment to form a line. But matters did not proceed quite so clinically. Porter didn't give us the proper command. If he said anything at all, it was lost to me, and I was in the second rank of the column, not twenty feet from him. C Company marched off a good hundred yards before Captain McCall halted us, called "about face," marched us back to where we were supposed to go, pivoted us to the left and stopped us right next to B Company. The captain was not pleased, particularly when as the dust cleared we saw Old Zach watching us. He was, as usual, perched on Old Whitey with one foot in the stirrup and the other knee crooked about the pommel, his expression inscrutable beneath the wide brim of his straw sombrero.

That would've been okay by us doughboys, because we were anticipating having a good chuckle over Porter's boggle-de-botch once we'd settled around our fires for the evening to enjoy a pipeful or two of tobacco. But the good Sergeant Hoggs robbed us of our treat. The son of a bitch blamed us for Porter's faux pas. He punished us by holding an impromptu inspection after the shoulder straps had retired for the day to the regimental mess tent for dinner and further jolliment and diversion—although God knows there was precious little diversion to be found in Corpus Christi that September. Hoggs spent two hours inspecting every one of us before we were allowed to fall out, gigging us left and right for dirty muskets and dusty uniforms (he cut us some slack on our brogans for some reason)—this after seven hours of drilling in the summer heat of mid-day in South Texas. As he dismissed us, Hoggs warned that he would be inspecting us again before reveille, and we'd better be ready by God or he'd run every one of us worthless fuckers out into the wilderness on a twenty-mile quick time march after tomorrow's drill. We all groaned inwardly at the thought of having to fall into ranks thirty minutes before reveille, which meant that we would have to be finished with our regular two hours or so of pre-dawn fatigue duties that much earlier—and which also meant that we were also going to have to make ready for inspection—and then ruin those inspection-ready uniforms in tomorrow's drill because we would be hustled directly from the inspection to the parade ground. Needless to say, few of us doughboys were entirely happy that evening, as we sat smoking our pipes—although we did chuckle about poor old Porter as we were all bound and determined not to let Hoggs win on that point.

Once we had our chuckle, I said, "Well, after today, I reckon we're lucky we're down here in Texas and not out in the Oregon territories fixing to fight the *Sassenagh*. The only enemy down here are the Mexicans. If, indeed, we fight at all."

"You'd better hope we don't fight," replied Finnegan.

"We will get better," Hermann said. "Anyway, I was told by this Texian covey that the Mexican army cannot fight. As he told it, they got 'whupped' at San Jacinto by Sam Houston back in 1836."

"'Whupped'?" This earned me another reproving glance from Hermann. "Did he say why?"

"Old Santa Anna," Hermann began. "He was the Mexican general, and he was taking a siesta. You know, a nap. Snoring away, he apparently was, in the middle of the afternoon."

That provoked laughter, as none of us could imagine being left to sleep in the afternoon like that by anybody in power, whether it was Sergeant Hoggs, Lieutenant Grant, Captain McCall, or Old Zach himself—unless, of course, it was a Sunday in camp.

Hermann continued his story. "So everyone else in the Mexican army took a siesta as well. As this Texian tells the story, Sam Houston was 'a crafty feller'." Hermann sounded positively Texian for just a moment. "And he knew that Santa Anna liked to take a nap. So he attacked the Mexican army while they were sleeping at 4:30 in the afternoon and whupped 'em but good." Hermann glared at me preemptively before I could even think to tease him. "He captured Santa Anna in his tent, and then he forced him to grant Texas her independence."

O'Leary observed, "I hear tell that Mexicans ain't reg'lar white folks, an' that's why they can't fight. They're mongrels, 'cuz the coloreds, the Indians, and the Spanish? They all marry each other down here. So they can't be as good as honest Irishmen and Dutchies."

"You hardly even know what a Mexican looks like, Kenny O'Leary," I retorted. "You haven't even ventured into town yet, because you've been too busy chasing Jenny ... although, Kenny, I do have to tell you, Jenny sure is a reg'lar fine white ewe."

Finnegan laughed. "Jenny the washerwoman?"

Jenny Billings was a washerwoman who earned her keep by charging bluebellies four bits for cleaning a dozen articles of clothing. Jenny and other women like her also did much of the cooking and otherwise made life bearable for us all. Every company was authorized four washerwomen to follow the company. Camp followers, if you will. In reality, there were usually more. Many of the men had wives who were understandably loth to let their husbands leave for far-flung duty posts for years at a time. So they followed their husbands, with kids, kinchins, and urchins in tow. Other doughboys had less formal arrangements, often with as many children as their more formally hitched-up brethren. Some officers' wives also followed their husbands. But officers' wives were an entirely different kettle of fish, and it truly was a case of "ne'er the twain shall meet"—that is until necessity forced them to, a situation not dissimilar to that onboard the fair barky *Maryann*.

Jenny had appeared one day not long after we arrived in Corpus Christi, replacing a woman who had run off God knows where deep into the desolate wastes west of the River Nueces. But sweet Jenny

58

was no ordinary washerwoman. Anything but. She was sixteen and just about the freshest cherry pie I'd ever met since leaving Ireland—memories of a sultry afternoon spent with the delectable Brannagh O'Marran in the upstairs parlor of her mother's goosing slum not-withstanding. To find such an innocent in an army encampment truly was akin to finding the proverbial nun in the knocking shop. Fortunately for Jenny, she had been befriended by Sarah Langwell, a laundress and cook over in the Seventh Infantry and mother hen to all the Cottonbalers' camp followers—and whoever else fell within her ambit.

Sarah was known to the entire army as "the Great Western." She was a magnificent and lusty woman of six feet and two inches in her stocking feet and possessed of the finest milk shop west of the Sabine. As the story goes, the last man to stare openly at her décolletage (and to have had the additional poor taste to loudly whistle his admiration) had earned a hard glare from Sarah. That would have been the end of it, but the fool stupidly whistled again. Sarah reached him in two mighty strides, hoisted him straight up into the air and pinned him against the nearest wall, which fittingly happened to be a bordello somewhere in the tent city, so that she could look him in the eye. Her victim's feet dangled a clean foot or more into the air, and his mouth moved soundlessly. Sarah stared hard at the poor unfortunate for a moment and then released him, whereupon he crumpled to the ground. She strode off without muttering so much as a single word. After that, no one in the entire Army of Occupation even began to think about getting in her way—nor were they likely to get in the way of a young lady under her wing (and all of the camp followers under her protection were young ladies, thank you very much).

Hermann smiled. "Kenny is very sweet on our Jenny, and she is very sweet on him, too. She keeps his uniforms very clean … and she doesn't even charge him a hard time token."

I grumbled, "Well that's about all any of us have … hard time tokens, Jackson cents. We haven't been paid since we left Governors Island."

Nobody paid any attention to my beefing. Every manjack in the Army of Occupation was either broke or perilously close to it, and many were up to their eyeballs in IOU's issued by the camp sutlers—civilian merchants licensed by the army to grievously overcharge us for everything from salt and tobacco to coffee and decent food, such as sausages, fruit, smoked hams, and sutler's pies, which were, as one wag put it, "moist and indigestible below, tough, and indestructible above, with untold horrors within."

"Hoggs is sniffing around her, Kenny. So watch yourself," Finnegan warned. "That bastard. Makes my life hell."

"She's my girl," Kenny declared. "She's said so."

He picked at the fire, and Finnegan, Hermann, and I all exchanged glances.

All through late September and into October, Old Zach kept the entire Army of Occupation drilling all day, six days a week, with fatigue duties being completed before the sun had hardly even poked above the horizon in the morning. At night, we were bushed. But we were getting better. Even Lieutenant Porter was leading the company with confidence now, moving from column to line and back again—first with C Company itself, then as part of the battalion, and later the entire regiment—all of it post-haste, lickety-split, and in a right soldierly fashion. Then we began to do more, far, far more. All of this drill welded Old Zach's tiny army into a formidable—if untested by fire—fighting machine. I say this despite Hitchcock's well-known (and in my view ill-deserved) words about Zach not being able to maneuver a platoon out of a wet paper bag, let alone even a tiny army such as ours.

One day, Lieutenant Colonel Garland, the regimental executive officer, was at the head of the regiment. Only the good Lord knew where Colonel Whistler, our commanding officer, was. Rumor had it that he was lying either drunk or ill in his tent. He was 60 years old, worn out, and fond of his whiskey. He had been an officer since 1801. Officers couldn't retire in those days without losing their pay, so they stayed on active duty until they died. As usual, I was marching in the second rank of C Company, next to Hermann and right behind Finnegan, who was marking time for the company. Hoggs was company first sergeant, making life hell for us all. Grant was commanding C Company that day, marching alongside me, a couple of paces away, sweat streaming from his face and pooling in his nascent beard. He seemed to be doing his best to ignore Hoggs.

It was 100 degrees under a cloudless blue sky, and the choking dust raised by 450 men marching in formation made it difficult to see more than twenty or thirty feet. The dust coated everything—faces, ears, eyes, and every nook, cranny, and crevice in one's clothing. The beat of the drums and the piercing twitter of the flutes of the regimental band, which accompanied us relentlessly and virtually wherever we went, steadily assaulted my ears. It also kept us all marching in lockstep at 90 steps a minute. We had been marching and countermarching all day in single columns and double columns, forming lines, wheeling the lines and columns, marching at the oblique, and advancing and retreating—all at the whim of one shoulder strap or another. Now the sun was hanging low in the sky. Every manjack of us was choking with thirst and faint with hunger, and we were more than ready to bivouac for the day and quietly smoke a pipe before taps.

But we weren't done yet. Far from it.

I saw the last rank of B Company pivot to the left and made ready for C Company to follow suit, figuring that we were once again going to form a line and dry fire our muskets for perhaps the thirtieth time. But we didn't.

Instead, Grant roared, red-faced in the heat, "Company, to the left oblique, DOUBLE QUICK TIME, MARCH!"

At 165 steps per minute, we were essentially running. We quickly slipped alongside B Company. As the first rank drew even with the first rank of B Company, Grant commanded, "Company, HALT! Right, FACE!

We now formed a single division in line, four ranks deep. C Company formed the first two ranks, and B Company formed the rear two ranks. There was only one circumstance that we would form four ranks like this. We were forming a square to resist a cavalry charge. The other six companies were forming the other three sides of the square, each face of the square comprising two companies and stacked four ranks deep. The officers, the regimental flutes and drums, and the regimental colors were all ensconced safely inside the square. As every schoolboy in England, and perforce Ireland, well knew, Wellington had deployed his battalions of lobsterbacks in squares at Waterloo and broken Napoleon's regiments of infantry and cavalry before sending Boney back into exile.

The American army had never used a square in battle—ever. It hadn't needed to. Cavalry wasn't very useful in the heavily wooded eastern United States and Upper Canada, where the American Revolution and the War of 1812 had been fought. But here, in the open plains of Texas and northern Mexico, where horses were essential to travel, we just might need to use the square to protect ourselves. Mexican cavalry was renowned for its ferocity and skill with the lance, and they were equally notorious for not giving quarter to a defeated enemy.

At least that's what Grant had told Hermann and me and a couple of other doughboys one day while we were on fatigue duty gathering ever more scarce firewood, a task that was daily becoming more time-consuming and onerous. The army had stripped all of the available mesquite and cottonwood trees for two or three miles in every direction for firewood. A fatigue party could spend all day marching several miles straight west to where the Comanche still patrolled just to find enough for the company's cooking fires for a day or two. I shuddered to think what the winter was going to be like, and I hoped that it would be nothing like Gotham in January.

The regiment settled into place, and the dust cleared. I was standing at attention in the first rank on the right-hand side of the square, near its apex. Out of the corner of my left eye, I could see the entire Second Dragoons, who were some three hundred yards away. They were charging right at us, sabers drawn and riding hell for leather. The ground seemed to vibrate from the thundering hooves of 450 horses. They were our own, these dragoons, and this was drill. But I nonetheless felt my gorge rise with fear at the thought of them riding us down.

Behind me, I heard Captain McCall's bawling command, "Division, Fix Bayonets."

As one, nearly a hundred of us doughboys unshipped our muskets from our shoulders as one and rested them on the ground—as we had done a hundred times before. We drew our toad-stickers, their 18 inches of razor-sharp steel flashing in the sun, and fixed them on our muskets, which we then reshouldered. We stood motionless once more. The dragoons were accelerating towards us.

"Division ... Ready."

We held our muskets at the ready, vertically at arm's length.

"Division ... Left oblique."

We turned ourselves a half turn to the left. We were now directly facing the onslaught. I thought I could hear the horses snorting as the dragoons stormed towards us, now a mere 150 yards away—the maximum effective range of the model 1835, . 69 caliber flintlock musket when fired in a volley.

"First rank ... Kneeling and Ready!"

I was a mere automaton. I moved three paces forward, knelt in unison with every manjack in the first rank, and raised my musket to fire, peering down the top of the barrel. My arms began instantly to burn because the bayonet unbalanced the already heavy musket.

"First rank ... Fire! Second rank ... Ready!"

As the second rank raised their muskets to their shoulders, we in the first rank cocked the hammers to our muskets and fired, our flintlocks clicking as they fell on the empty flash pans.

"Second rank ... Fire."

There was a clicking of flintlocks beside my head as the second rank fired, their muskets and bayonets sticking out over our shoulders.

"First and second ranks ... Charge Bayonets!"

Each man in the second rank had the butt of his musket against his hip, musket and bayonet pointing out at a 45 degree angle. Those

of us in the first rank—still kneeling—thrust our muskets and bayonets up at a similar 45 degree angle. We had all the hostile intent of a
hedgehog with its quills bristling.

"Third rank …"

The command was lost in the din of the dragoons descending
upon us. Instead of riding us down and either crushing us under hoof
or skewering themselves on our bayonets, the dragoons split into two
streams like rushing water diverted by a great boulder, with half passing to the left of the apex of the square and half down the right side,
men and horses thundering past, just inches away from the tips of our
bayonets. I suppressed the mad notion of reaching out and touching the boots and stirrups whipping past me. Then the dragoons were
gone, and the dust settled once more.

The entire regiment stood stock still in the sudden quiet. Behind
me, I could hear Captain McCall swearing softly about the third and
fourth ranks not having fired a volley before the dragoons reached
us, and how that failure could have been the death of us all had the
dragoons been Mexican lancers.

⌒

The long-awaited Sunday service in town could not have been more
different than the last time I took communion—which had been
with Mary, back in Gotham. There was no church in Corpus Christi,
merely twenty-seven single story adobe buildings with flat roofs strung
along a single unpaved street. The best buildings, a dozen of them,
were clustered together at one end of the street, forming Colonel
Kinney's compound, which could be closed up and fortified against
Comanche or Apache raids if need be. The exterior walls of Kinney's
ranch buildings had no windows, just narrow slits through which to
poke a rifle or a musket to defend against marauding Indians. Another
main point of defense was the top of the main building, which was
crenellated with an effect not dissimilar to a medieval castle in min-
iature, although the parapets (if you could call them that) were no
more than a couple of feet high, and the buildings but a single story.

The entrance to the compound had a stout wooden gate that could be swung closed and high stone and adobe walls connected each of the buildings in the compound to the building next to it.

The rest of the little village's adobe buildings were strung irregularly down the street, each more tumbledown the further down the street one went until it petered out at a huddled mass of several dozen wooden shacks, which the locals called *jacales*. Their roofs were thatched with a kind of long grass called *tula*, found in the marshes bordering the bay and the Nueces River. These huts differed from an Irish peasant's hovel only in locale and type of building materials. Despite their wretched poverty, Mexican peasants in Corpus Christi seemed to live much better than most *spalpeen* in County Cork. The climate was beautifully temperate here compared to the damp chill of an Irish summer, let alone an Irish winter. Better yet, food here was varied and bountiful, with as much fish and game as a mortal soul could wish for (all without a single potato in sight). The cluster of *jacales* was flanked by several freshly erected pens, which held hundreds of horses and mules that enterprising Mexican wranglers had been bringing to Corpus Christi ever since the army first hove into view back in July. Such was the town of Corpus Christi when the Army of Occupation arrived in the late summer of 1845.

Now, some weeks later, as October was about to pass into November, the permanent buildings and *jacales* had changed hardly a whit. But the stock pens had multiplied several-fold in number and size. They all fairly bulged at the seams with an evergrowing herd of mules and horses gathered by Colonel Kinney on the notion that the army was going to need every one of them and many, many more, besides—which we did when we eventually marched south. To the west and the south of the permanent buildings and well away from the *jacal* ghetto and the stink of the stock pens, a tent city had sprung up out of nothing, and grew daily by leaps and bounds. It was populated by an ever-burgeoning stream of card sharps running crooked tables at faro and bluff, confidence men running some scam or another, knights of the gusset with strumpets in tow (although, compared to Gotham, most of these clapped out old cows didn't deserve such a lofty title as "strumpet"), and adventurers of every other stripe imaginable. They had been arriving since August by way of boats down from St. Joseph's Island or, with increasing frequency, from Padre Island. Ships anchored briefly on the latter island's seaward side when the seas weren't running too badly, hurriedly debarked their human and other cargoes on the beach, and promptly disappeared back to New Orleans for another lucrative run.

These adventurers were, man and woman alike, intent on servicing the three thousand priapic young denizens of the Army of Occupation. Virtually all of us, other than our supremely fortunate Kenny O'Leary and others whose wives and doxies had found sinecures as regimental washerwomen, had been deprived of the companionship of the fairer sex ever since we enlisted—and certainly since lighting upon the shores of South Texas. We also had all too little to do on Sundays and in the evenings of the other six days of the week when drill had ceased for the day and after-hours duties such as standing post or fatigue parties did not beckon.

The grapevine was delighted when, a couple of weeks after the *Dayton* disaster and while the Army was virtually bereft of dedicated transport on the Aransas Bay, the arrival of the first great wave of adventurers had caused Old Zach to suffer the god-awfullest conniption fit. The owners of the boats and various other transports that the army had requisitioned began refusing to transport supplies down from St. Joseph's Island to the encampment because they could charge triple the rate to transport cows, zuckes, liquor, and other sundries down the bay. So, to the considerable disgust of the transports' owners, Perfect Bliss, Old Zach's chief of staff, promptly issued a general order—enforced with great satisfaction by the quartermasters—that promptly brought the various transports on the bay under the army's control. It was an exercise of martial authority that in turn caused the displaced civilians to scream blue murder and mutter darkly of penny-ante Napoleons and tinhorn despots from perfidious Albion.

Hermann and I learned that we were going to be permitted to attend church services in town early one Sunday, when Hoggs had routed us from our slumber (no reveille on Sundays, thank you very much), curtly snapping at us, "Quit your gawping. You're off to some mackerel-snatching, I reckon."

Hermann and I shrugged at each other and fell out.

As we snapped to attention outside our tent, Hoggs said to us in a fine stage-Irish tone, "Before ye be goin' an' mixin' with the upper tendom of Kinney's Ranch and consumin' the Almighty Host itself, I'm going to inspect yers, an' if ye ain't as sharp as tacks, I'll be finding yers something useful to do this fine Sunday." Hoggs abruptly shifted his tone, imitating the whine of an entitled shavetail still pissing his West Point water, "Mayhaps a little drill at the water's edge?" Hoggs sneered derisively. "You remember, Gogan. Don't you? Your introduction to Governors Island. Two or three hours with your musket above your head, marching up and down the beach? Do you a bit of good, I should think."

This last bit of formal speech was accompanied by a hot blast of Hoggs's fetid breath as he leered at me, inches from my nose.

Ten minutes later, Hermann and I were ready for inspection by the Old Man himself. Our blouses had nary a speck of dust on them, our brogans were brushed and blackened—and Hermann had shaved. (I did not need to.) We stood at attention outside Hoggs's tent and rustled conspicuously to alert him to our presence. Hoggs took his time emerging and walked around us very slowly, dogging us to his heart's content. But Hermann and I remained motionless.

Hoggs leaned into my ear and whispered, "I'm going to have your arse for this, Gogan. It'll be the death of you. West Point pumpkin rinds be damned." He stepped back. "Dismissed."

Hermann and I skittered as quickly as we could out of Hoggs's line of sight, ducking through a couple of rows of tents before we slowed our pace.

"What was that all about?" Hermann asked.

"Nothing."

"What?" Hermann persisted.

"I think that Hoggs just declared war on me."

"Why?"

"Apparently, wangling this pass from him under duress from Grant is to be the death of me," I replied pompously.

Hermann didn't say anything and we once again quickened our step towards town. We were already going to be a little late.

The service was being held in the open courtyard in the center of Kinney's compound. Kinney may not have been Catholic, but he was keen to honor the Mexicans who made it possible for him to maintain his outpost here on the fringe of the American frontier—and, yes, this was the American frontier, notwithstanding it still being the final days of the Republic of Texas. Everyone saw the formal admission of Texas into the Union as a foregone conclusion, even though the final act had yet to be played out. The people of Texas certainly did. Word of their having approved a new state constitution—the last step before Congress formally admitted Texas to the Union—had just reached us here in Corpus Christi, quickening the pulses of all concerned for a few days such that it seemed as if war with Mexico was going to commence at virtually any minute—notwithstanding Colonel Kinney's well-known advice to General Taylor that there were no significant Mexican forces in Matamoros or anywhere else near the Rio Grande.

No officer would willingly admit to being a Catholic in those days, so I wasn't surprised that we didn't see any. But there were a dozen or so "Other Ranks" attending along with Hermann and me, none of whom we knew. We were apparently the Fourth's only representatives, despite my having quietly passed the word around that those who asked to attend would be given permission to do so. We bluebellies all sat quietly on rough benches in the back, approaching the altar only to take Communion. The altar was a beautiful—and temporary—display placed under a shade tree, consisting of brightly colored shawls draped over a table and topped by a magnificent silver cross. In front of us sat what appeared to be the muckety-mucks of Corpus Christi.

Behind us stood the Mexican peons, bareheaded in the hot sun, their leather *huaraches* shuffling in the dirt and their peaked straw sombreros rotating on nervous fingers. The priest, a Spaniard by all accounts, came down from San Antonio de Béxar every month or so to administer to the souls of the faithful here at the mouth of the River Nueces. He spoke excellent English and broke from his Latin service to give an impassioned homily—in both Spanish and English—urging peace between Mexico and her neighbors to the north. He also welcomed us Irish and Dutchy Catholics to the fold and said that he would be hearing confessions after the service.

When the service broke, Hermann made a beeline to the impromptu confessional, and he was the first to be shriven of his sins. I was in no mood to confess my sins to a priest whom I didn't know. They were my burden, and no one else's. So I leaned up against a wall and closed my eyes for a moment, as I enjoyed the sun and the breeze. It was the first blessedly cooler day we'd had since arriving at St. Joseph's Island. I also enjoyed the momentary solitude, as most of the rest of the other doughboys attending the service had quietly vanished as soon as they were released. I supposed they were in no more of a mood to be shriven than I was.

I opened my eyes to the sight of two very pretty young Mexican ladies—hardly more than girls, by the look of them. They were walking in the company of a striking older woman towards the entrance to Colonel Kinney's compound, their parasols twirling as delicately as those of any fine uptown Gotham bleak mort. Yet as much as they looked like charter members of Gotham's upper tendom, the two girls (sisters, I imagined) were pretty in an exotic way I had never before experienced, with liquid black eyes, dusky skin, and jet black hair shining like silk in the bright sun (at least from what I could see of it tucked modestly under beautiful lace mantillas).

The girls had arrived at the service along with the striking older woman after Hermann and I had arrived and been seated. They had swept past us and our fellow bluebellies as if we didn't exist, leaving a faint, but intoxicating fragrance in their wake. They'd evoked an instant and quite profound hunger and longing in me, which until then I had thought died back in Gotham. By the time I leaned up against the wall to enjoy the sun and breeze, the girls and the feelings they had evoked had begun to recede into pleasant memory. But when I opened my eyes and once more saw them, I was enraptured all over again.

One of the girls looked my way and smiled, until the older woman caught her out and shooed her into Colonel Kinney's main hall. There were quite a few other people, American and Mexican alike, making their way into the main hall, all of them very obviously in their Sunday best. Invited by Kinney to post-church Sunday dinner, I reckoned.

"Ready to do some fishing this afternoon?" Hermann looked as rested and at peace with himself as I'd ever seen him. He caught me looking at him quizzically. "Something on your mind?"

I gave Hermann a slantendicular glance.

"Well, perhaps you should take the opportunity to confess your sins—particularly that of your unrequited lust."

"Not to a Spaniard."

"Why not? He is a priest of the Church. It does not matter where he was born. Anyway, his English is better than mine."

"Not for me."

Hermann shrugged. "I find it interesting that you should be so prejudiced about a Spanish priest, when you feel the way you do about how the coloreds are treated back in Uncle Sam."

"It's different."

"Is it?"

"Yes."

"Okay." Hermann shrugged. "So let us go fishing, my buddy."

I loved Hermann's endearing attempts to use slang.

"*Señores.*" A small man with a slightly supplicating air stood next to us, gesturing towards the front door to the main house. "*Por favor.*" He gestured again to the front door. Hermann and I exchanged a brief glance and followed the man.

As we entered the door, the man announced to us, "Don Guillermo Ñíguez Rodríguez." He then vanished without a trace.

A dignified man of middle age and middling height—clearly a Mexican—was standing just inside the front door, looking expectantly at Hermann and me.

"Very nice to meet you, sir. I am Billy Gogan, late of Gotham and Cork, Ireland." I reached out to shake the gentleman's hand. He goggled briefly and took my hand. "May I name my esteemed friend, Hermann Wurster?"

Hermann clicked his heels and bowed slightly. The gentleman gallantly bowed to Hermann in return. I caught an amused twinkle in the eye of each man and only then realized that perhaps not all folks were like us Americans and Irishmen (and, I hated to admit it, *Sassenagh*), for whom a handshake is a sign of respect upon meeting another gentleman.

"Colonel Kinney and I would be honored if you could join us for dinner."

Hermann and I gawped for just a split second. Why would anyone want to invite a couple of doughboys to Sunday dinner, let alone the founder of Corpus Christi and the Old Man's chief scout, honorary colonel notwithstanding?

I recovered first and replied without meeting Hermann's eye. "We are delighted to join you, sir." I wasn't quite sure which of his names was his proper family name. I had heard somewhere that it wasn't always the last name … and how to use this honorific, "don," was well beyond me.

The gentleman must have sensed my confusion, because he said, "You may call me don Guillermo. It is how we say it here in *Coahuila y Tejas*, señor Gogan."

Don Guillermo led us through the main house to an exterior courtyard in the rear, where a long table had been set for dinner with benches at the sides and two large carved wooden chairs, one at each end. It was paved in fine pebbled cement of some sort that I had never seen before and covered with a flat roof made of what looked to be sticks of mesquite woven together to filter the sun and break its hot glare without entirely blocking it. The paved area was surrounded by shade trees and fragrant with plants. One fragrance in particular virtually intoxicated me. The courtyard was perhaps the most utterly delightful spot I had ever been in, and it immediately banished the dreary reality of the camp of the Army of Occupation from my mind. I could have lingered there forever.

"Colonel Kinney," said don Guillermo, addressing a tall and broadly built man who was chatting with the two young ladies and the older woman I had seen earlier.

"Ah, yes."

"Our two guests, señor Wurster and señor Gogan."

Kinney shook hands with both Hermann and me, and said, "Henry Kinney. *Bienvenido a mi casa de sillar* ... welcome to my home. Don Guillermo's daughter, señorita Calandria, urged me to invite you. She said that you, señor Gogan, were looking very hungry, and that she could not enjoy her *merienda* if she knew that you were going hungry." Kinney smiled faintly. "But, gentlemen, as I am sure you are aware, señoritas Calandria y Serafina ... they are what they call in these here parts *mujeres decentes*."

This last admonition needed no interpretation.

"Sir, we thank you very much for inviting us," Hermann said gravely.

"You are not a *yanqui*, señor?" Don Guillermo asked. "Even though you are in ... what is the word ... *el ejército de coloso del norte*." He thought for a moment. "The army *de los norteamericanos?*"

"The army. Yes, sir. We are privates in the army. I was born in Prussia, sir. But I am an American now."

Don Guillermo turned to me. "And you, señor Gogan, you are *irlandés?* We have *irlandés* who are trying to settle in San Patricio, just west of here. They were having a terrible time with the Lipán Apache, so they withdrew themselves to San Antonio de Béxar. But they are back in San Patricio now. They hope that your army will protect them."

"I am sure that we will, sir. To answer your question, I was born in Cork. In Ireland. But I am also an American citizen now."

"And both of you serving *el coloso del norte*. For seven *yanqui* dollars a month." Don Guillermo shook his head in slight wonder.

"We volunteered, sir." I mustered as much dignity as I could to put a fine gloss over my shame at how I had become a stalwart member of the Fourth Infantry. "We are here to defend our country."

"I congratulate you on your … patriotism. We *méxicanos* have much to learn from you *norteamericanos* on this account."

I could barely resist asking why he felt that way. I could also feel Hermann's desire to give me a swift kick.

Kinney interceded. "Don Guillermo's cousin lost his rancho—and his life—in 1840, when he supported don Antonio Canales Rosillo in his bid to protect our lands between the Rio Grande and the Nueces from the depredations of the Comanche on one side and the Mexican army on the other side. Don Guillermo is a *méxicano* … a Mexican with a land grant from the Spanish king over a hundred years ago … but he is also a Texian, a *tejano*, if you will. And he is *mi compadre*. He did me the honor of inviting me to be *padrino*—sorry, godfather—to his two beautiful daughters all those years ago." Kinney gestured to the two young ladies, who whenever other eyes were not upon them looked to be appraising Hermann and me as so much prime stock. "Don Guillermo has made it possible for me to found this beautiful town of Corpus Christi, and to develop trade routes between here and Matamoros, west to *las villas del norte* … the towns on the Rio Grande and then as far south as Monterrey." Either Hermann or I must have looked at Kinney oddly, for he explained. "Monterrey is the biggest Mexican city north of the capital, Mexico City. It is three hundred leagues south of here, at the foot of what the Mexicans call the *Sierra Madre Oriental*. It is the gateway to Mexico City and the silver mines to the south."

Don Guillermo bowed slightly in acknowledgement of Kinney's praise. "Colonel Kinney is too kind. It is he who granted me the honor of being *padrina a mis hijas*. He is as much a father to *sus ahijadas* as I am."

With that, we sat for a dinner unlike any I had ever had. First came a tart and delightfully chilled fish stew—a *ceviche*, explained doña Alandra, the gravely handsome woman who was indeed the mother of the two *mujeres decentes* and matriarch of don Guillermo's sprawling hacienda. But we did not use forks to eat the *ceviche*. Doña Alandra instead showed me how to wrap the *ceviche* in what she called a *tortilla*, a thin, unleavened bread made from pulverized corn. It was sublime, and as unlike the meat and potatoes of New York and Ireland as food could be. (Comparison to our daily bluebelly's rations simply did not signify.) I was also served a small glass of *pulque*, a milky-white, fermented drink that came from the *maguey* plant, a type of cactus. Doña Alandra said that *"pulque sólo le falta un grado para ser carne,"* translating for me that pulque is only one grade shy of being meat, itself. In other words, she explained, it is very nutritious indeed, good for pregnant women and nursing mothers. But only one small glass, mind you ... on account of the fermentation. I prudently complied with doña Alandra's wishes and did not ask for a second glass. Blessedly, though, a servant did fill my glass two or three more times on the sly.

The second course I braved as any polite man would do, for it was *menudo*, a spicy soup of cow tripe, hominy, and plenty of hot *chiles* that sent me looking for several glasses of water to the amusement of señorita Calandria, whom doña Alandra had wisely sat across the table from me so that we could converse at a proper distance and no more. Serafina had been seated further down the table, near Hermann.

The main course comprised corn, every bit as delicious as the best hot buttered corn purchased from the prettiest girl on Broadway back in Gotham, and beef. But the beef was no mere roast of beef. It was the tenderest I had ever eaten, and not plain as we do in Uncle Sam or Ireland. It instead took the form of *tamales*, the meat shredded by its own tenderness and then encased in a cornmeal bread, which was then wrapped in corn husks. The beef, doña Alandra told me, came from a *barbacoa de cabeza*—the head of a steer that had been baked over mesquite coals in a deep covered pit since the previous evening.

Our dessert, or *postre*, was another *tejano* favorite: *buñuelos*, a tortilla dough fried in hot fat until it was crispy, and then covered with powdered sugar, cinnamon, and honey. It was simply sublime, particularly as I was able to wash it down with the strongest and most flavorful coffee I had imbibed in months. I was a well-fed and very happy fellow that afternoon.

During the meal, doña Alandra told me the story of how both her family and her husband's family had once been ranchers near San Antonio de Béxar. Both families still held title to thousands of acres in South Texas between the Nueces and Rio Grande, which had been given to them in the middle of the last century in the form of land grants from the King of Spain. "But the War of Independence against the *gachupine* took a terrible toll." Doña Alandra stopped, with a slightly embarrassed expression. I looked blankly at her. She apologized for using such an impolite term, explaining that it fit the hated Spanish to perfection, on account of the word referring to the spurs the Spanish wore when they first came to the New World, and which they used to torture the Indian and Mestizo.

She continued, explaining that the War of Independence and then, later, the influx of *norteamericanos* and the Texas War in which Texas broke away from Mexico, had done much to destroy the *bexareño* haciendas and businesses, and in many cases, families who held such title from the King of Spain no longer occupied their land. Indeed, doña Alandra sighed, her parents and her brother had abandoned their hacienda near San Antonio de Béxar and now made their living from a small hacienda south of the Rio Grande, which had been in their family even longer. Don Guillermo also had abandoned his hacienda on the outskirts of San Antonio de Béxar, but he and doña Alandra and their daughters had been able to retreat to their even more beautiful hacienda some leagues west of Corpus Christi, along the banks of the Nueces.

I asked her why the Americans who emigrated to San Antonio de Béxar had been so hard to deal with. Doña Alandra smiled sadly and said that a polite young man such as myself was an entirely different person than the *animales* who manned *los rinches* (that's how she referred to the hated Texas Rangers. I later heard them referred to as *los diablos rinches*, but doña Alandra was much too much the proper lady to use such language) and other filibusters who murdered *los tejanos y méxicanos* merely for having darker skin and speaking Spanish … and for being Catholic. I said that I thought I understood, and I told her a (properly edited) bit about my erstwhile lover, Brannagh O'Marran. She was the daughter of a free Negro who owned Gotham's spiffest stepping ken and an Irish woman he met on the streets. Her father was murdered by a redneck slave-catcher, and her mother later became madam of a brothel catering to Gotham's upper tendom. Doña Alandra told me that it was rare for any *norteamericano* to look past the color of a *tejano's* skin and really see one's true prestige within the community, which she said was the only real source of one's social standing. "But here, in *Coahuila y Tejas*," she said proudly, "Don Guillermo and I can both trace our lineage back to the Spanish *conquistadores*, the Spanish warriors who came with Hernan Cortés to conquer Mexico in the sixteenth century. My family can also trace our lineage back to the native Indians who lived in Mexico before the white man came. My family is mestizo, and thus truly *méxicano*. Don Guillermo's family has very little mestizo blood," she told me. "They are an old creole family whose *patrones* used to govern *Coahuila y Tejas* before *los norteamericanos* came twenty years ago.

"But even though we are no longer *bexareños*," doña Alandra said, "We are happy in our hacienda, *nuestro Casa de Las Corrientes de Golondrinas*, which is 'our house of the flow of the swallows.' You may think it silly, señor Gogan, but every spring the mud swallows nest in the great beams of our *casa de sillar*. I think don Guillermo would prefer that we call our hacienda *el Rodriguista* to honor his family, but he is a good man, and he understands why my daughters and I prefer to think of the swallows. They are as much a part of our hacienda as we are, and this hacienda is our life's work. We have a duty to pass it on to the next generation, but don Guillermo and I have only our two daughters. We were not blessed with sons who lived. So we will have to find *buenos maridos para nuestras hijas* … good husbands for our daughters," she translated with a quick apology. "Perhaps we will have to ally ourselves with a good *norteño* family. It is too bad that Colonel Kinney is not of suitable age," she said. "He would make a fine husband to carry on *el Rodriguista* for another generation. But we will find *los jóvenes de buena familia.*" Doña Alandra sighed with more than a trace of melancholy and translated: "young men from good families who can marry my daughters."

She shook off her melancholy with a radiant smile that lit the table. Señorita Calandria smiled back at doña Alandra with such a look of devotion and respect that I thought it could only have come from a lifetime of knowing who you were and who your parents were, and your parents having devoted their lives to you. A good thing, I thought, and all the more so given what the four of them had lived through in the last twenty years: drought and endless raids by marauding *bárbaros* (the Comanches and Lipán Apache, she explained) and Texian filibusters, not to mention countless predations by their own government's army.

As doña Alandra and I talked, I covertly studied Calandria when she wasn't still sneaking glances my way. As she gradually became detached from conversation with her two middle-aged *tejano* neighbors, she sat quietly listening to us. I couldn't see Hermann, but I suspected that, with a little luck, he was able to chat at least a little bit with Serafina—safely away from doña Alandra's watchful eye.

As our conversation lulled at one point, I asked doña Alandra, "What is the beautiful fragrance?"

Calandria quickly interjected before her mother could answer. "I think you are smelling *el jazmin*, señor Gogan. It is a flowering tree. We have them at *la Casa de las Corrientes de Golondrinas*. I water them every day." She batted her eyes at me (I did not look to see doña Alandra's reaction), adding softly, "The flower can be made into a … perfume."

"That must be perfectly intoxicating …"

Doña Alandra interceded. "Colonel Kinney also has the *anacahuita*," pointing to a gnarled tree with what appeared to be olives hanging from it.

"And *los frijolillos*." Calandria pointed to a shrub with large, bright red beans hanging from it. "They say that *los flores violetas* from *los frijolillos* can ensure the success of a suitor who gives them to his ..."

Doña Alandra interceded once again. "Yes, Calandria. But they are not in bloom now, are they?"

"*No, mamá*. They are not." Calandria sneaked a conspiratorial glance at me.

Later, when the women had retired for their siestas, Hermann and I were invited to share cigars and Kentucky bourbon whiskey (a very pleasant substitute for Irish whiskey). Colonel Kinney held forth, at first probing Hermann's and my bona fides, and then turning to the more serious subject of why the Army of Occupation was here. Hermann and I were glued to our perches on a rough wooden bench to the side of the half-dozen wooden chairs of varying degrees of fit and finish, the grandest of which was occupied by don Guillermo as Kinney's chief guest and the second grandest by Kinney himself. The remaining chairs were occupied by *tejano* gentlemen who said little, and who listened as hard as Hermann and I did. One of them stood out by his mere presence, unprepossessing as it was. A swarthy little man who looked as tough as nails. He took great care to carefully study everyone else sitting in the cooling shade of *el portal* as the conversation swirled about.

Kinney changed the direction of the conversation. "With respect, don Guillermo, and you and I have spoken many times of this subject. I cannot see your native country of Mexico ever controlling *Coahuila y Tejas* again. It is the Republic of Texas now, and soon it will be admitted as a state into the Union."

Don Guillermo shook his head sadly. "I am afraid, *mi compadre*, that it is not about whether *México* can control *Coahuila y Tejas*. It is about the belief of *México* and every *méxicano* that *la patria* will reconquer *Coahuila y Tejas* one day ... maybe a hundred years from now. Two hundred years." He looked around seriously at his audience. "*México* also believes that if *los norteamericanos* have the gall to attack south of the Nueces, *México* shall win a glorious victory." Don Guillermo crossed himself. "I do not wish to see that day happen. For if it does, we *tejanos* will be forced to choose. Do we align ourselves with *la patria* … the land of our forefathers? Or do we align ourselves with *Tejas* as *tejanos*? And does that mean we will become Americans? I do not know that all *tejanos* will make wise decisions, Colonel Kinney. I fear for the future."

Don Guillermo stopped, and we all sat quietly as a breath of air swirled and cooled us under *el portal*. Presently, he broke the silence. "Perhaps your business partner has the right idea, señor Kinney."

Kinney raised an eyebrow. "You mean señor Cazneau?"

"That's right, *mi compadre*, señor Cazneau. He has his heart in the right place in wanting to avoid war. But he wants to do it by negotiating with *México* for the establishment of a republic of the río Bravo to control both sides of the river, south into Tamaulipas and all the way north to the Nueces as a buffer between our two countries. If that could avoid war, I would give my life for it, because it would secure the future for my two beautiful daughters in my hacienda. But I do not see the Texians, as they like to call themselves, being particularly enthusiastic about abandoning their claims south of the Nueces. I likewise cannot see *México* allowing a republic of the río Bravo to come into being, thereby slicing yet another piece from *la patria*. Colonel Canales tried that in 1840. He is very lucky to be alive today after *México* came after him with all her might."

"Well, don Guillermo, both señor Cazneau and I … and you, *mi compadre*, as well, we all wish to avoid war so that we can all become rich by trading across the Rio Grande from north to south and from south to north. Whether that happens with yet another new republic or whether it happens because cooler heads prevail, it does not matter to me." Kinney rumbled to his feet and raised his glass. "So I offer a toast to peace among our peoples."

Hermann and I rose to our feet with the other four gentlemen, chairs scraping on the pebbled cement, along with don Guillermo and Colonel Kinney. "To peace."

Kinney motioned to us to sit once more. "But regardless of what the future holds, you and I will make the right choices. Of that, don Guillermo, I have no doubt."

Don Guillermo nodded thoughtfully, his eyes never leaving those of Colonel Kinney. Kinney rumbled to his feet once more. "I would be remiss if I didn't offer another toast. This time to General Taylor. A toast, gentlemen, to General Taylor and the Army of Occupation. May fortune smile brightly upon you."

Hermann and I leapt to our feet with alacrity. The other four gentlemen were noticeably slower in rising from their chairs for this toast. As we raised our glasses once more, Colonel Kinney said, "To General Taylor." As the chorus of "hear, hear," died away, Kinney continued. "Thank you, gentlemen. As I was saying, General Taylor has asked me, and I have asked don Guillermo to assist me, in gathering pack and draught animals for a baggage train. He has also ..." His voice lowered and we all instinctively gathered closer. "Asked me, and keep this confidential, mind you, to obtain intelligence down south. And as you know, don Guillermo, Chapita and I have been doing just that."

I glanced at don Guillermo, but his face was unreadable. The swarthy man I had noticed earlier stirred, perhaps at the mention of his name, Chapita. I then thought of the unfinished trenches some half a mile south of us and hoped fondly that the Colonel was not about to tell us that we would have to start digging again.

Kinney said, "General Taylor tells me that President Polk is even now planning to send a minister plenipotentiary south to Mexico City to negotiate a treaty whereby the United States will indemnify Mexico for the loss of Texas as it is admitted into the Union, and perhaps this minister can even settle the question of what is to happen to *Alto California*."

Don Guillermo shook his head. "God only hopes that such a minister succeeds in his mission, *mi compadre*. But I am fearful that *el presidente*, don José Joaquin de Herrera, will not be able to receive a minister plenipotentiary."

"Why is that?" Kinney's tone was suddenly sharp.

"*Mi compadre*. No *méxicano* can ever be seen trading away even *una pulgada de la Patria*." A twinkle appeared in don Guillermo's eye as he translated the last phrase as "an inch of our homeland." He continued. "What's more, *México* cannot accept a *norteamericano* minister plenipotentiary because to do so would be tantamount to restoring normal relations. Our two governments are not talking to each other, because *los norteamericanos* are annexing *Tejas y Coahuila. El presidente* would be attacked for allowing such diplomatic recognition without first extracting concessions from *los norteamericanos.*"

Kinney shook his head sadly. "Then, don Guillermo, it shall be war. If not this year, then next. And if not next year, then the year after that. The United States will not stand for Mexico retaining any land north of the Rio Grande. And I am sorry for it all, because you and I, don Guillermo … we have friends and *compadres* on both sides of the Nueces and on both sides of the Rio Grande. And I do not want to see those friendships tested by war. So, gentlemen, I offer another toast … to an amicable end to the dispute between the two lands of our births, and may cooler heads prevail."

Later still, Hermann and I departed after having offered our respects to don Guillermo and our thanks to Colonel Kinney. We also asked don Guillermo to convey our respects to doña Alandra and their daughters.

We did not see the three ladies again that day.

⌒

"That was the first time I've been treated like a real human being since I put on the uniform."

We were fishing and enjoying the sun setting over the Nueces. Neither of had caught anything, but I didn't care. Lunch had been magnificent, and we had met more of the leading lights of Corpus Christi and the Texian frontier than any other bluebelly would ever likely meet. I was content to smoke a pipe, cast my line into the water, and feel the cool and damp sand at the water's edge between my toes.

Hermann replied after a moment. "Do not get used to being treated that way, my friend. Tomorrow morning, we will be back to gathering wood, digging latrines, standing post, avoiding that *verdamt* Sergeant Hoggs, and drilling in squares with the Second Dragoons riding us down. Good Lord, I have never found that pleasant, experiencing the charge of the heavy cavalry. Not even standing with my old regiment."

"I'm going to savor every second of that lunch. It was magnificent. The food, doña Alandra ..."

"And her daughters, Calandria and Serafina." Hermann smiled devilishly. "Especially Calandria. She was making eyes at you. Measuring your ability to furnish her trousseau for the wedding, no doubt."

I laughed. "Yes, well, that's not likely to happen. And who are you to chaff me? Serafina was batting those gorgeous eyes of hers at you. Anyway, we'll be shipping out somewhere soon enough—whether to Mexico proper if we're going to war, or back to Jefferson Barracks in St. Louis, or Fort Jesup or some such place if we don't. And if that isn't enough, my friend, doña Alandra made damn sure to inform me of Mexican customs regarding the suitability of matches with daughters of *hacendados*. Apparently, I won't make the grade. Me, the scion of an old and distinguished Irish family of Catholic revolutionaries and the product of Ireland's finest public school ... and a private in the United States Army. Go figure ..."

"Doña Alandra is merely an excellent judge of human character, Private Gogan."

I ignored Hermann and said, "Did you know that don Guillermo is one of the largest landowners between here and the Rio Grande? They call their estates *latifundia*. Goes back to the old days when Spain ruled Mexico and these parts. Don Guillermo's grandfather had to wait twenty years to get his claims for his lands north of the Rio Grande, and they've been defending it ever since, against the Comanche and Lipán Apache, Santa Anna and the *centralistas* from Mexico City, and now from *los norteamericanos*. Doña Alandra told me that's what they call all us Yankees. Doña Alandra said that even the Texians have been marauding and stealing their cattle—and that's after they stole all their land near San Antonio."

"Where you come up with this *scheiße*, I will never know." Hermann shook his head. "You have spent far too long in school, my friend. Your head is filled with ... I do not know the right word in English."

I didn't reply, for there was something nibbling at the bait on my hook, which perhaps meant fresh fish for breakfast.

Presently, Hermann said to me quietly, "We have a problem with Sergeant Hoggs."

"Yep."

"What exactly did he say to you?"

"I told you. He said that today's pass to church will be the death of me."

"He is being literal."

I stayed silent so as not to be melodramatic.

"Billy, we cannot avoid this conclusion."

"I know."

"We have to do something about it."

"I provoked him, you know. I deliberately went to him to ask for a pass to church after what Grant told us about observing the chain of command. I knew that Hoggs would refuse. Just like I knew that Grant would countermand that refusal, once we'd alerted him to the issue. He's that kind of officer."

Hermann didn't reply right away. After a while, he said, "We have no choice but to destroy him. To kill him."

"You mean I don't have a choice. You're right. I don't have a choice. I decided that a while back. I'm going to have to finish it, one way or t'other. But you can stay out of it. He's not after you."

Hermann smiled at me. "*Wie Sie sagen, die Engländern.*"

"English, my friend?" This was an old game between us. We had played it ever since he genuinely confused the *Sassenagh* and the Irish when we first met back on Governors Island. He told me that no Irishman could be as educated as I was. We were all peasants in his mind. I'd apparently since disabused him of this strange notion, although he often saw fit to deliberately conflate the two races so as to rile me up.

"What is the phrase *sagen Sie Engländern*? 'Hanged for a sheep as for a lamb'?" Hermann added in a sober tone, "He will come after me and any other man whom he does not like. I would rather be hanged for doing something about that *böse bastard* than let him grind me into dust under his heel."

"I don't want that god-damned turdball to get to us, either. I've got him off balance. I made him look bad to Lieutenant Grant, and maybe even to Captain McCall. That's a good start."

"No it is not. All you have done is to put Hoggs on notice that you can fight back. Now he is wary. Like a spooked wolf."

I assented reluctantly, upset with myself for having been so foolish.

"We must kill him." Hermann pursed his lips. His eyes were hard.

"We'll hang for it." Curious, this, my being the cautious one— after all of my brave declarations to myself.

"Not if we are very careful. We will have our opportunities. I am sure of it."

"I don't want his death on my conscience." I surprised myself when I said it. "I'd be happy to see him lose his stripes. That would be a punishment enough to fit his crime."

"It would be dangerous to leave such an enemy alive."

"One step at a time."

"As you *Engländern* say."

"Quite …"

⌐

"Kenny."

O'Leary's tentmate, a sallow and slow fellow named Gaff, rolled over and said querulously, "He ain't here." Gaff was asleep again before I dropped the tent flap back into place.

It was two hours before reveille, and Hoggs was mustering our work party in ten minutes. We were to find wood for the cooking fires, and we expected the detail to last all day. Hence the early start. I didn't want to catch hell right out of the box for not finding O'Leary and, just as bad, not making muster on time. That would make for a long day. Hermann was marching post somewhere, and so he was going to be spared the joy of a ten-mile jaunt into the bush to gather firewood and a further ten-mile jaunt back to camp. It would have been nice to have known about the work detail before Hoggs had kicked me awake with a sneer, making it my duty to rouse the other fifteen doughboys in less than ten minutes, and holding me responsible if they were not all present and accounted for on time. But that was typical Hoggs, giving that extra turn of the knife. Kenny was the last one I had to find. Then I remembered where he was likely to be.

I skittered over to the C Company laundresses' bivouac, trying to remember which tent was Jenny's. Much to my relief, Jenny was already up and serving O'Leary a cup of hot, steaming java when I hove into view. She clearly was tied into the grapevine far better than I, for she'd already roused her man and gotten him ready for the work party. She offered me a cup of java as Kenny was sipping his, looking at his girl with the grateful eyes of a puppy being given a treat. I wavered for a moment on account of the time, then muttered "what the devil" and drank off the coffee as quickly as you please.

O'Leary and I stepped into line for muster just as Hoggs was beginning to cut his eyes at us. Fortunately, though, Hoggs didn't seem to be inclined to mess about at this early hour. I had heard that he had been out and about almost every night in the tent city springing up outside Corpus Christi, so I figured that he was likely quite fagged out. Perhaps that might bespeak a relatively quiet day of gathering wood without any untoward adventures with Hoggs. Although, I thought, Hoggs could have easily avoided the fatigue duty. He was C Company first sergeant, and he could have easily detailed Sergeant Larkin to take his place. Too bad, too. With Larkin, it would have been a very pleasant day for us all—ten-mile jaunt notwithstanding.

The fifteen of us marched out, muskets shouldered, followed by five empty wagons for us to load the wood onto. It was typical of Hoggs to make us march when we could have ridden in wagons, and I groaned once more when I saw how many there were, for that meant we were in for a very long day. But Hoggs didn't dog us as badly as he could have. For once we were out of sight of the encampment and the pickets patrolling some hundreds of yards away from the camp in the dark, challenging every snap of a twig, he quickly dispensed with the fife and drum, which meant that we could shamble along, carrying our muskets at the trail, or better, any old which way we wanted to.

As we passed the sentries shadowed in the pre-dawn gloom, I wondered why there hadn't been a shooting yet. Every picket and sentry carried a loaded and primed musket and spent half his time being spooked by tiny noises in the impenetrable dark, just as I had that day up at St. Joseph's Island when I'd nearly killed that little boy. You didn't know whether the sound was a rabbit or a squirrel, a wolf desperate for a meal, a Lipán Apache looking to count coup with a quick scalp, a scout presaging the unannounced arrival on our door-step of the entire Mexican army, or merely your imagination playing tricks on you.

It was still well within the forenoon when we stopped in a promis-ing copse of cottonwood and mesquite, where there was a sweet water spring. We drank our fill, topped off our canteens and set to work gathering wood. I wandered off alone to an untouched portion of the copse, breaking off dead cottonwood branches and slashing mesquite with my bayonet. I figured that it was better to use my bayonet and then spend an hour putting a new edge on it than struggling with green branches all day long.

I stood straight with a large load in my arms, ready to walk back to the wagons when I heard a rustling in the underbrush. Probably a rabbit, I thought.

"Sweet dreams, you stupid fucker. You're lucky I'm not going to douse your glim today. I'm just going to knock you cold, and let you die out here alone, iff'n you're too stupid to find your way back."

I felt a blinding pain in the back of my head, and then the black-ness came.

# CHAPTER 5

# Mules for Desdemona

⌒

I OPENED MY EYES TO A BILLION STARS blazed across half the sky. The other half of the Milky Way was oddly obscured, and I wondered why. It was only then that I realized I was lying on my back under a tree. Slowly, I began to recollect where I was, and what I had been doing: collecting firewood near a tall tree, hearing Hoggs's voice, smelling his fetid breath over my shoulder, and then, nothing. A wolf howled, and I shivered involuntarily. At least I thought it was a wolf. They'd been extinct in Ireland for fifty years or more. And they had been powerfully scarce in lower Manhattan for centuries. Then another one howled—or was it the same one? The ungodly sound got me to jump to my feet. I felt a stabbing pain at the base of my skull and top of my neck, and I touched it instinctively. My hand came away sticky. Blood, I assumed. I couldn't see it. I wiped my hand on the back of my trousers, but it was still sticky. But why was there blood? Then I remembered. Hoggs. The bastard. He had exacted a handsome fee for my delightful Sunday dinner with Calandria and her mother.

The wolf howled again, but seemingly from a different direction. Christ, was there more than one? A shiver of real fear gripped my bowels. I had never before been in the middle of nowhere, without a single sign of human habitation. It was as if I was the only human left on earth. The wolf howled, more insistently this time.

Where was my musket? I dropped to my knees to search the long grass for it and earned another stabbing pain at the base of my skull as my knees hit the ground. Panic rose in my gorge as I felt around like a blind man in the inky darkness. I couldn't find it. That didn't mean it wasn't lying next to me. I simply couldn't find it. Once more, the wolf howled.

At least I had my bayonet. It was still in its scabbard, attached to my waistbelt. I lurched to the tree and grasped its trunk. Actually, I grasped only a portion of its circumference, for it was a mighty thing, massive in girth and stretching many tens of feet into the air. Wolves didn't climb, did they? No. They were like dogs and foxes. They couldn't climb trees. So up the tree I would go. I ran my hand over the bark, which crumbled away in places to reveal a smoother, softer bark underneath. A *mesquite*. Even in the dark, I could tell that it was a right proper shade tree, just like the one on that beautiful, peaceful knoll near Corpus Christi Bay, under which Lieutenant Higgins and Lieutenant LeFort and the rest of the victims of *Dayton's* boiler explosion had been buried, along with others who had died of sickness and accident and even a murder, shoulder strap and Other Ranks alike, to the grumbling disdain of the inevitable sticklers for rank and privilege. As I crept around, feeling my way, a branch poked me sharply in my chest. I quietly thanked God that the branch had not been at eye level. I hoisted myself up, climbed up far enough where I felt safe from the wolves and settled myself down to wait until dawn.

I awoke with a start to the sun having just risen. I swung myself down from the tree and felt the blood pounding in the back of my head where Hoggs had clubbed me. I was in for a vicious headache. But that was manageable. Better yet, I knew generally where I was, somewhere north of the Nueces. If I walked long enough towards the rising sun and didn't walk in a circle once it was overhead, then I would eventually walk as far as the bay. Then I could turn south and hug the water until I finally ran into camp. Or at least, that was what I fondly hoped. How far the bay was, I hadn't the foggiest.

As my head cleared, I again searched for my musket. But it simply was not to be found. Hoggs must have taken it. God knows what he did with it. So I began walking. As I did, I remembered my canteen. It had been full. It still was. Hoggs may have been vicious, vengeful, and spiteful, but he had not been thorough, the dumb ... My throat was parched, but I resolved not to take a drink until the sun was directly overhead. I had marched for hours in formation desperate for a drink, so I figured that it would be easy to walk east without a musket for the same number of hours without taking a sip of water.

When the sun was almost directly overhead, I was passing a small copse of trees, which offered a modicum of shade. I sat and took a mouthful of water. It only made my thirst worse. After a few minutes, I lurched to my feet, mindful that I couldn't risk falling asleep and losing track of the time of day and position of the sun. Off I traipsed, trying not to think about how far away the coast must be.

After an hour or two, a little voice told me to stop and look north. There were two horsemen. One was leading a spare horse. A mirage? If it were, it was a damnably real one. Anyway, there was no shimmering surface in front of me like there was supposed to be when you see a mirage. There were just the two horsemen and a third horse trailing behind. I just hoped that they were friendly, and not Lipán Apache out for mischief or … the good Lord knows what or who else … My bayonet would not do me much good if they weren't friendly. But I saw no palatable alternative, so I waved my forage cap and my bayonet, on the principle that the sun might catch its shiny surface. It must have worked because the riders changed direction and headed toward me. As they drew closer, I realized who they were: Lieutenant Grant and another officer, a lieutenant named Benjamin, on their way back from leave in San Antonio de Béxar.

"Private Gogan, what on earth are you doing here?" Grant looked at me incredulously.

"Got separated from my wood-gathering detail, sir."

"Can you ride a horse?"

"Practically born on one, sir."

"Well, jump aboard. You're in luck. She has a saddle." Grant shook his head. "We almost left her in Refugio. Unaccountable … quite unaccountable."

⌒

89

"Sir. Private Gogan is a deserter. He deliberately separated himself from the fatigue detail and hid until we left." Hoggs was incensed that the veracity of his account was being questioned. "He even abandoned his musket."

Captain McCall was sitting on his campstool in front of his tent on officers' row, staring first at me, then Hoggs, and then Grant, all of us rigid puppets in a row in front of him. "Lieutenant, what do you make of it?"

"A strange matter, sir. Private Gogan was heading in the direction of Corpus Christi and the camp when Benjamin and I found him. He was alone. Without his musket, just as Sergeant Hoggs said." Grant paused and thought for a moment. "But he was definitely headed in the general direction of camp when we found him. No question." Grant blinked, and then met McCall's steady gaze. "I believe, sir, that the most unaccountable fact in this matter is the nasty gash across the back of Private Gogan's skull. Almost if someone smashed him over the head. Which, sir, I might point out, completely dovetails with Private Gogan's account of suddenly losing consciousness."

I hadn't told Lieutenant Grant about Hoggs's fetid breath, nor about what the bastard had said to me—words that I remembered all too clearly. But I still didn't quite fathom why Hoggs hadn't simply put the kibosh on me when he had the chance. Then everyone would have believed his story. I'd have simply disappeared, never to be heard from again—until someone ran across my bleached bones lying under that huge mesquite tree. There'd been a couple of desertions already. A few weeks back, Colonel Kinney had reported to General Taylor—the grapevine sending the intelligence around camp within twenty minutes thereafter—that a couple of deserters had shown up in Matamoros and had been sent along to Mexico City, where Kinney was told, they were to be deposited at the doorstep of the American consul's office. But nobody had heard anything further on the matter. But Hoggs hadn't doused my glim ... why not? Almost as if he were the cat playing with the proverbial mouse. The sick bastard. Almost as bad as MacGowan, for the love of Christ.

"You're right, Grant. It is unaccountable." McCall turned to me and asked, "What do you have to say for yourself, young man?"

"Sir. As I told Lieutenant Grant, one minute I'm gathering fire-wood as I was told to do by Sergeant Hoggs, and the next I'm waking up in the middle of the night. I don't know how I injured myself. I must've hit my head on something. Perhaps I fell. I simply don't know."

McCall frowned and thought for a moment. Then he said, "You are a lucky young man, Private Gogan, on a couple of counts. First, you didn't die of thirst in the wilds. And second, I'm not going to have you flogged and branded for desertion. Unlike Sergeant Hoggs, I think that the good lieutenant is entirely correct. You clearly had the good intention of trying to make it back to the encampment, which is more than I'd say for most of our doughboys. Particularly the Irish ones. The dumb, vexatious … intractable … You're Irish, aren't you, Private Gogan?" He didn't wait for an answer. "You seem to be truthful enough, though. And intelligent. Not like the Paddies I used to recruit …" He snorted derisively. "Telling me they were born in New York when they were born in County Tyrone. Where were you born, Gogan?"

"Cork, sir."

"Where'd you live before you enlisted?"

"New York, sir."

McCall looked at me suspiciously. "You twenty-one?"

"Yes sir. At least, that's what the recruiting sergeant said, sir, when I enlisted. He was a Corkman as well, sir."

"Quite." McCall looked up at Grant. "You see, Grant? That's what I mean. If there's a Paddy involved, there's always a story. And half of it will be true. The other half … well, you can see for yourself. So if you ever find yourself on recruiting duty in Philadelphia or New York or some such place, you should never recruit an Irishman—not even a smart one like Gogan, here. I was given that very commend-able advice when I was back in Philadelphia in the '30s. Always better to recruit a Dutchy than a Paddy. The Dutchmen're much more solid. And they're liable to be Prussian army veterans who actually know what they are doing … Gogan's sidekick is a Dutchy, ain't he? What's his name?"

"Wurster, sir."

"That's right. Wurster. Good soldier. Just the type we need. If he were a native American, I'd have him rated as first sergeant quicker than you can say Jack Robinson. Good, smart, and dependable." McCall glared at Hoggs, who winced visibly. "As I was saying, Gogan, I commend you for trying to make it back to camp. The average blue-belly would've headed due west, right into a Comanche village and gotten himself scalped for his pains. Just to see the back of us. And you didn't." He shook his head just like Grant had. "Unaccountable. Simply unaccountable."

"Sir." It was Hoggs. "What about his musket, sir? I must report it to the quartermaster as missing so that he can be issued another one. He'll have to be charged for it sir. $25."

Three and half months' pay. I winced inwardly.

"Yes, Sergeant. Have another musket issued to Private Gogan. And no, don't charge him for it. Lost in the line of duty." McCall looked at me severely. "But don't let it happen again, Gogan, or I will have the cost deducted from your wages … and I'll have you flogged. For stupidity in making the same mistake twice, if for no other reason. Dismissed."

I saluted, pivoted, and skedaddled before Hoggs could follow. The bastard.

⁓

"How is he?"

I was visiting Hermann at the camp hospital. He had been there since the day I got back to camp, with a desperately high fever that began after a blue norther had soaked the camp, while it had left me bone-dry hardly a score of miles away. Blue northers were a bane of our existence in south Texas. Rattlesnakes were another. Corporal Finnegan once told me he had counted 117 in a single day, and I never doubted him. The mosquitoes at sunset were worse, although not quite on par with finding poisonous scorpions in your brogans in the morning. But blue northers were in a class of their own as a form of south Texas torture. The air could drop in half an hour or less from a stiflingly humid 90 degrees in the shade under hazy blue skies to 50 or 60 degrees under lowering blue-black and gray clouds. The howling gusts of wind that came with the clouds would not have been shy about being compared to a North Atlantic gale. Then came the rain. Freezing-cold, driving sheets of it that instantly soaked you to the bone if you were caught without shelter. Yet a man standing ten miles away might be hardly aware of the storm. Then, as the worst of the storm passed, the temperature would drop even further. In the wintertime, ice can form an inch thick in buckets, and you might awaken to the thin muslin of your tent frozen stiff and the sand and grass and mesquite bushes whitened with frozen sleet. On days like that, I never got warm again until the sun came out, which was precisely when the mosquitoes came out to feast, hungrier and meaner than before. Some of the officers had decent slickers—purchased at their own expense of course. But the rest of us, and this included all the Other Ranks and the camp followers alike, couldn't have mustered a single piece of proper foul weather gear among us. It was during these storms, sitting in our leaky tent, when I missed my father's slicker the most. But it was gone. Most likely burned up in the fire or gracing the back of some needy soul in Gotham.

The downpour had not only sickened Hermann, but it had also ruined our tent, along with most of our possessions. We weren't alone in our misery, for virtually every bluebelly in camp had lost possessions and many had become sick. Fortunately, not quite all of our possessions had been irretrievably lost, because I'd somehow been able to rescue one of my uniform blouses and restore it to some degree of respectability for my audience with Captain McCall. Hoggs had remonstrated with me about my brogans as he inspected me before I was ushered into McCall for office hours—that endearing term of art in this man's army for when an officer considers your case before deciding whether to buck and gag you, flog you, or have you ride the horse. But Hoggs hadn't been able to exact any further vengeance for the sad state of my brogans, as McCall and Grant had been waiting for us.

Fortunately, nobody had drowned when the rain hit and the torrents of water that seemed to appear out of nowhere washed away so many of the tents—and their occupants. But the deluge had left hundreds sick and the sawbones and their meager skills overwhelmed. The maladies ranged from diarrhea to jaundice to a simple fever, which merely wracked its victim, leaving him exhausted, soaking wet, and desperately thirsty—if it didn't kill him in the meantime. Doc Crittenden reckoned that as many as two in five of the Army of Encampment had been laid low at one point or another in the week after the storm.

The doc was standing at my shoulder as I gazed at Hermann sleeping fitfully on a cot in the hospital. "Wurster will be okay, Gogan, the good Lord willing. He's not jaundiced, so that's good. You just keep some water in him, and he'll most likely live."

So I sat with Hermann for two days—Hoggs having seemingly made himself scarce since the contretemps at McCall's office hours. Corporal Finnegan had been decent enough to see me off any fatigue duties, and there weren't enough fit doughboys in the entire army to hold a decent close order drill. So there was little to do during the day. I sat, wiping Hermann's brow, forcing a sip or two of water into his mouth every time he roused from his tortured slumber, and holding him still when he thrashed in the throes of some fever-driven nightmare. Hermann's fever broke at dawn on the third day, and he asked me why the hell I hadn't come back with the wood-gathering detail.

I told him, and he growled something or other in German. Then he told me to watch out for Kenny, because Hoggs was going to go after him next.

⌒

"Hermann, dear, would you like some more java?" Jenny hovered solicitously over Hermann. He sat wrapped disconsolately in his blanket, refusing even his pipe, which he normally puffed in a state of relaxed satisfaction at this point in the evening. His fever had set back in this afternoon, and he looked tired and drawn. Jenny, bless her heart, had become his nurse-in-chief as well as the domestic mistress for our mess, which comprised Finnegan, Hermann, Gaff, Kenny O'Leary, and myself. Kenny's eyes followed Jenny around our mess with that slightly stupid, bovine gaze reserved for those few who are blessed with being truly and hopelessly in love. She fluttered about, seemingly obliviously, serving us first coffee, then biscuits, and finally a bit of melon, which we had gathered a couple of days before on a Sunday afternoon expedition to Padre Island. The rest of us were puffing on our pipes, warmed by our evening fire and rendered very nearly catatonic by Jenny's good cooking. Our conversation had been desultory at best for the better part of the hour since we had eaten.

Finnegan was bitching to no one in particular about the high cost of wood in town—$60 a board foot for sawn planks, fifty times what it would cost in the Five Points. Highway robbery, it was, he said. Me? I was pleasantly surprised that sawn planks were even available, imported as they were from New Orleans to St. Joseph's Island and then barged south to Kinney's ranch at an astronomical cost (which was not to excuse shameless war profiteering—of which there was altogether far too much). Of the four of us, Finnegan was the only one who could have possibly afforded to pay for enough sawn planks to floor his tent. He had some blunt saved from the last time he had been paid, and as a corporal, he made a princely nine dollars a month, two dollars more than we privates. Most everyone else was dead broke, as the Fourth had last been paid in New Orleans, before Hermann and I joined the regiment. Hermann, Kenny O'Leary, and I had not been paid since we had enlisted in August—despite Army regulations requiring our being paid monthly. I was beginning to think that I was going to have to run a scam to gather a grubstake. I did have standards, I told myself, and I resolved to target only the right sort of people with the divers card tricks and other various skills and bits of skulduggery I had learned from Magee, Charlie Backwell, and a dozen others during my sojourn in the 'Points. Penury was not a condition to which I aspired—not that I had confided even in Hermann about this nascent intent to rectify my destitution (and his, if I had anything to do about it).

Finnegan apparently wasn't quite finished with his bitching, for he was now noting the high price of everything else imported from New Orleans. Potatoes were five dollars per barrel. Butter was six bits—a princely 75 cents—per pound. Milk was four bits a quart, and corn and sweet potatoes were $1.50 a bushel. That is, unless you knew that the Mexicans living over in their *jacales* were happy to sell you corn, squashes, and every other type of fruit and vegetable imaginable at a tiny fraction of that amount (which is precisely where the profiteers were buying their corn and squashes). Hermann and I had learned that little insight at dinner with doña Alandra and Colonel Kinney the other week and had kept it a well-guarded secret for fear of ruining the arbitrage opportunity—a technique as easily applied to corn in Corpus Christi as to penny stocks on the New York Stock Exchange. We were quite content to allow the sutlers and other profiteers to gouge the ordinary bluebelly (not to mention the officers) as long as we were not burdened with having to pay such exorbitant prices.

Finnegan had moved along to still another topic: the Military Retreat, a full-on ten pin bowling alley that some wag had imported. It was now safely ensconced in a wooden frame tent complex that also contained a small, but highly profitable brothel in the back—for those lucky few who could afford it. I waxed eloquent for a moment about the many different scams that a crooked bowling alley operator could run. But Hermann quickly told me to just shut up and quit being a bore—which I did as a courtesy on account of his feeling so poorly. Kenny remarked that he'd heard through the grapevine that some associate of Hoggs actually owned the joint. He also cracked that Hoggs was rumored to be entertaining camp followers and other dells he fancied there as well. How Hoggs could afford to do so was something of a mystery, Kenny observed, blithely unaware that Jenny seemed to flinch ever so slightly when he mentioned Hoggs. I wondered if I'd imagined it. But I knew, with a sinking feeling, that I had not.

Hermann croaked that he would be happy to see the last of Hoggs, because a more tolerant—or even a merely not so unthinkingly sadistic—top sergeant would mean that we wouldn't constantly face the minute-by-minute risk of bucking and gagging or the lash for some undetectable transgression.

Finnegan replied disgustedly, "Just because we see the back of Hoggs don't mean that we're home free, there, bucko. Just open your eyes, fer Chrissakes. We've had doughboys so sick in this man's army that they're at death's door, and they've been put on report for missing duty. And some of them have even been flogged for it, particularly if they were micks."

"Not in C Company." Hermann looked irritated. He clearly wasn't at his best.

Finnegan explained patiently. "That's only because Grant somehow keeps McCall from giving full rein to his worst side. And Grant, bless his heart, has also figured out what our good friend Mr. Hoggs is all about. But it's happening in other companies and in other regiments. And every manjack in our little army knows about Bragg's artillery. There, you'd better be measured for your pine box 'afore them poxed redleg bastards will give you light duty. Simply being up at the camp hospital ain't enough."

"That Bragg ... he is a right bastard, ain't he?" Kenny interjected. "That giving his trooper the flat of his sword in front of the entire army as his battery pranced about. What did that poor devil of a redleg do wrong? Them six-pounders went bang right quick, didn't they?"

"Those six-pounders will save us, Kenny O'Leary, you mark my words." Hermann coughed. "They will break a full regiment of hussars ... if they can be deployed in time."

"Kinda like us ... deploying ... in a square and getting all four ranks to volley 'afore the *méxicano* cavalry gets to us." I drawled as lazily as possible. But poking at Hermann's ponderous formality today was about as much sport as pinching pennies from a dead man's eyes. It simply wasn't proper. So I once again resolved to be nice.

Hermann refused to engage me. "As you would say, Billy: 'Yep.' It is the same. And when we find the Mexican army, we will see how good they are. I am not sanguine about the prospect. The Mexican cavalry is supposed to be excellent, particularly their lancers."

"You are dreary, aren't you, old man?" I forgot my resolve.

"Merely realistic, my friend."

"You two are like a durn hitch-up gone wrong," Finnegan complained. "Worse than our young Kenny with his beautiful Jenny."

Jenny curtsied as she flitted by, filling Kenny's cup of java without him moving so much as a muscle, and then disappearing back into the dark in a simple, but elegant bourrée. Quite the lady, she was. I liked her.

"Anyways," Finnegan said, "I wasn't meaning to bring up the ... what was that fancy word you used the other day, Gogan? Eso ...?"

"Esoterica?"

"Yeah, that's it. I got to get me a proper education, just like Mr. Gogan here. I wasn't meaning to bring up the ... esoterica ... of military tactics. I'm more interested in why bastards like Lieutenant Bragg can do the things they do."

"Actually," I observed. "It wasn't Bragg who beat that redleg. It was his pumpkin rind—the prick is so new to this man's army that he's still pissing water from the 'Point."

"I'll bet that he jumps at the flick of Bragg's aristocratical, slave-owning wrist and then asks how high on the way up." Finnegan was quite indignant.

"True enough," I replied. "And he sure does have a fine teacher."

Finnegan ignored me. "That poor devil's scalp was laid open to the bone. He'll never be the same, even if ol' Doc Crittenden himself stitches him up. No wonder good, solid Irishmen and Dutchies are slipping away from camp and walking a hundred and fifty miles south to Mexico. Native Americans, too. Some of them ain't so thrilled about five years working for Uncle Sam for seven bucks a month when they see their mates being treated such-like, even them mates what was born Paddies and Dutchies."

"I heard worse than that," Kenny said. "I heard that over in the Seventh, some shoulder strap had one o' them Cottonbalers branded on the cheek—just like they does for deserters. 'Cept the poor fucker waren't no deserter. The officer had him branded with a 'W' simply because he thought the poor bastard was worthless."

We all shook our heads over that story, one which we had heard many times. I had been told by the Great Western that the officer in question had at Major Brown's direct order been given leave and sent back to New Orleans in disgrace. The galoot was not expected to return.

"Hermann and I have talked about this ..." Hermann nodded in agreement with me, knowing what I was about to say. "The funny thing is, as loathsome a man as Bragg is, and he surely is loathsome, his outfit is the best trained in our little army. Right now, that's saying something given all the drilling we've been doing. So in a curious way, we have to give him his due."

"*Cia baois!*" I looked up with a start. It was the first time that Finnegan had ever spoken Irish in my hearing, and it was clear that he was having none of my argument. "You don't need to half kill a man to shoot your six-pounder popguns quickly and accurately. Bucking and gagging and laying a man open to the skull with your saber ain't any way to get an army to win on the battlefield. I'll drill in the line until my legs fall off, and I'll drill my detail until theirs fall off. That's one thing. What you had to go through up on St. Joseph's Island, and what five hundred men have gone through in this army since then is an entirely different kettle of fish ... and rotten fish at that. Particularly as 'most every manjack who gets punished is a Dutchy or a Paddy."

Kenny piped in. "'T'ain't right. I'll kill the man who tries to buck and gag me."

I looked at him coolly and said, "No you won't. You'll do what I did. You'll take it like a man and get on with your life."

Hermann added, "Billy is right, Kenny."

Finnegan nodded his support. Kenny just poked at the fire without acknowledging us.

Then Finnegan asked, "Have you heard this little ditty?" He began singing in a fine, clear voice:

> Come, all Yankee soldiers, give ear to my song,
> It is a short ditty, 'twill not keep you long;
> It's of no use to fret on account of our luck,
> We can laugh, drink, and sing yet in spite of the back.
> Derry down, derry down, derry down.
>
> "Sergeant, buck him, and gag him," our officers cry,
> For each trifling offence which they happen to spy;
> Till with bucking and gagging of Dick, Tom, and Bill,
> Faith, the Mexican ranks they have helped to fill.
> Derry down, derry down, derry down.
>
> The treatment they give us, as all of us know,
> Is bucking and gagging for whipping the foe;
> They buck us and gag us for malice or spite,
> But they're glad to release us when going to fight.
> Derry down, derry down, derry down.
>
> A poor soldier's tied up in the sun or the rain,
> With a gag in his mouth till he's tortured with pain;
> Why I'm bless'd, if the eagle we wear on our flag,
> In its claws shouldn't carry a buck and a gag.

A few days later, Grant and I became mule-skinners. Not willingly, or at least not willingly on Grant's part. I on the other hand was more than happy to be relieved of all manner of tiresome fatigue duties (including collecting firewood, which I seemed to have lost my enthusiasm for, particularly when Hoggs was around). But Grant had just been promoted to be C Company's executive officer, after Captain McCall had been kicked upstairs to serve on Perfect Bliss's staff in some function or other, and Grant's great friend, Theodric Porter, had been placed in temporary command. Hoggs had been as quiet as a church mouse ever since the change in leadership, and as virtuous as a choir boy to boot—mostly, I reckoned, because of the dim view that both Porter and Grant took of some of Hoggs's more brutal disciplinary methods. My messmates and I—and every other doughboy in the company—had been as pleased as punch with these developments.

Then the word came down that Grant was to put together the regimental mule train for our eventual march south. Colonel Garland was then commanding the Fourth, with the good drunk Colonel Whistler having been given other duties. Garland had detailed Grant to take charge of the Fourth Infantry's mule-skinning operations on the strength of his prowess with breaking horses. In so doing, Garland had assumed, in typically military fashion, that breaking a horse and mule-skinning were one and the same. After all, Garland pointed out to Grant, "you need a horse as dam to carry a mule, don't you? So how different can they be from each other? And you, sir, can break a horse as well as any man in our little army, so I can entirely trust you to break mules for service."

Garland had caught wind of Grant's equestrian prowess from a story on the grapevine. Grant had wandered down one day to the *corrales* with his great friend Lieutenant James Longstreet to have a look-see at a score or more unbroken mustangs that a *tejano manzeador* was selling for two or three dollars apiece—or more if the *manzeador* saddle broke the mustang for the buyer. There were several other shoulder straps present, all of whom had bought one or more horses. The *manzeador* was looking pretty pleased with his day's work, but he had not been able to sell one particularly high-spirited animal, which had skittishly avoided all human contact and, when touched, had lashed out viciously. Finnegan heard tell that Grant leaned over and with a bit of a smile said to Longstreet that he was determined to buy the horse and break it or break his own neck in the trying of it.

So Grant paid over the princely sum of $12 to the *manzeador* for the horse (still unbroken, mind you). The *manzeador* was smiling even more broadly now at his day's work, and was more than happy to comply with Grant's desire to have the horse blindfolded, bridled, and saddled. Grant climbed into the saddle and guided the horse to the middle of a half-circle of curious onlookers, whereupon he sank his spurs deep into the horse's flanks. Horse and rider shot like a cannon ball due west over the horizon. About three hours later, after everyone, Longstreet included, had long since figured him for a goner, Grant rode back into camp with the horse perfectly trained, to offers of $30 or more for the magnificent steed from the likes of Captain May over in the Second Dragoons, who declared Grant the best horseman in the army.

Grant knew better than Garland, of course, about the entirely different sets of skills required for breaking horses as compared to those required for mule-skinning. But Grant was a good officer, and having been given the assignment, he made the best of it and called me into his tent to tell me that I was his assistant, because I could at least ride a horse. He noted a bit sourly to me that virtually all the Other Ranks in the army in those days were foreign-born city-dwellers, none of whom knew a saddle from a tramp. He told me that if tempted he might be willing to bargain his soul away for a competent drayman, who were even rarer in the ranks than literate (let alone well-read) men.

It was then that I suggested to Grant for the first time, "Wurster would be an outstanding choice, sir. So would O'Leary. He's a smart guy, too."

"Wurster's on light duty. Has O'Leary ever been on a horse?"

"He's an Irishman, sir, just like me."

"You'll prove Captain McCall right regarding the nature of Irishmen if you keep that nonsense up."

"Sir."

"So you're elected. Ever seen a mule?"

102

"No sir."

"Stubborn things." Grant re-lit a half-smoked cheroot and puffed on it for a moment. "Know any Spanish?"

"A little, sir. I met some real nice *tejano* folks that day I went to church in town. They taught me a bit." This was thankfully not a complete lie, as the Latin I'd studied had so far been of enormous help in communicating in a doggerel fashion with every *tejano* with whom I'd come into contact.

Grant looked at me skeptically. "Well, learn some more. You and I are going to have to start learning the finer points of mule-skinning from these Mexicans. Apparently, they're the only ones who know what they are doing."

"Sounds fantastic, sir."

Grant looked at me a bit slantendicular. "Get out of here, and report back at 0500 tomorrow morning."

"Yes sir."

So here Grant and I were about a week later, standing outside one of the fifty or so *corrales* bordering the *jacales*, with half a dozen *arrieros* and *carreteros* and about a hundred of the unruliest mules ever seen in south Texas. We had to train the mules for one of two tasks—either for mule trains of twenty-five or more mules led by a single *arriero* or as part of a five or six mule team pulling a Conestoga wagon handled either by a *carretero* or a doughboy playing at being a drayman. The Conestoga wagons were being built for the army in New Orleans and shipped to Corpus Christi at exorbitant cost. (Jesus wept, you could have had the crown jewels of Spain for the rates that wagon wrights were charging the United States Army that fall. I only wish I had learned the lesson better. For if I had, I would have spent the entire American Civil War supplying transport to the Union Army and retired thereafter, richer than Boss Tweed and John D. Rockefeller combined.)

Grant relied upon me to do the translating with our *arrieros* and *carreteros* on the strength of the few words of Spanish I had learned during that afternoon I had spent with Calandria and doña Alandra.

All I can report from that first day is that by the end of it I could speak a little more Spanish (again, thank God for the Latin that Father O'Muirhily strapped into me at St. Patrick's), and that both Grant and I had come to know as a moral fact that mules are alien creatures as unrelated to horses as men are to the great apes.

Grant was smart in relying on the *arrieros* and *carreteros*. The Third Infantry did not utilize the *méxicanos*, figuring that as white Americans they were better than any dirty Mexican at mule-skinning. They instead used bluebellies who had volunteered for the task on the theory that they, like I, could avoid some unpleasant fatigue duty or another. The results were disastrous.

As Grant observed to me, the Third relied on sheer numbers to overcome complete incompetence. Early one hot and sultry morning, as I was finishing up some task or another, I happened to watch the sergeant in charge of the Third's "teamsters," if one could call them that (not a drayman or horseman among them, as I later learned), select five mules based upon uniformity of color from the score or so mules tied to a picket rope. He intended to hitch them to a Conestoga wagon that was waiting at the ready, with two drivers sitting patiently. The sergeant directed two of his teamsters, by now stripped to the waist and glistening with sweat, to cut out one of the mules and attach it to the traces of the waiting Conestoga wagon. The two men cautiously approached the mule from the front, rightfully mindful of its hind legs, and each attempted to slip a lasso over the mule's neck.

The mule bucked and kicked, which encouraged the rest of the mules to begin similarly kicking and bucking. The sergeant and two other men wisely withdrew until the mules once again stood submissively at their picket rope. With the two men holding their lassoes at the slack, the sergeant slipped the line securing the mule to the picket rope. The two men then took the slack out of their lassoes and manhandled the poor mule over to the wagon. Carefully, they secured the mule in its traces and repeated the process with the remaining four mules. Once the five mules were in place, the leading mule, lassoes still around its neck, was encouraged to begin walking, apparently on the theory that where the lead mule went the others would follow—not a bad theory insofar as it went.

At first, the lead mule refused take even a step, and nothing happened other than that the mule simply planted its hoofs firmly in the dirt. When the two "teamsters" renewed their efforts, the mule began bucking and kicking, and the four other mules joined in complete unison. The wagon began rocking, gently at first, and then bouncing from one side to other until it violently careened to one side. Two teamsters, who had been sitting patiently in the wagon's seat, were sent flying into several nearby century plants, cruelly spiked cactuses each standing five or six feet tall. The wagon needed to be rebuilt completely because the body itself was oddly twisted, one of the axles and the tongue had snapped, and the white twill of its cover had been torn and the bows holding up the cover crushed. I think that the two putative teamsters were fine once the spiked aloe needles had been extracted from their hides.

Our *arrieros* and *carreteros* were far more competent than the Third's bluebellies, to say the least. As I learned from the *caporal* of the *corrida* of *arrieros* and *carreteros* that Grant hired, a wonderful fellow called Juan Pablo Delgado, there were two ways to move goods before *los norteamericanos* showed up with their great big Conestoga wagons. *Carreteros* driving two-wheeled carts called *carretos*, and pack mules. They both plied every trail in *Coahuila y Tejas* and ventured across the Rio Grande as far south as Monterrey with trade goods, with the *arrieros* going places that the *carretos* couldn't go. As word of the army's need for mules and muleteers spread, scores of *méxicanos* had shown up in Corpus Christi, one or two at a time, all of them hoping that *los norteamericanos* would hire them on at the exorbitant rates *los norteamericano* big bugs were wont to pay.

Many were disappointed, because most units did what the Third Infantry did—rely on their own (mostly inept) skills. Grant somehow wheedled the money out of the regimental quartermaster to pay for our *corrida*. The investment paid off, for it turned out that Grant was a born mule-skinner, and he learned his craft from Juan Pablo. As good as Grant was with a horse, Grant learned from Juan Pablo how to coax a mule—or a team of mules hauling a Conestoga wagon about—to do what it was bid, all without so much as raising his voice. Within the matter of a week, word of his prowess had spread through the army.

Grant's hiring of Juan Pablo and his *corrida* also allowed me to take my first steps in learning to speak Spanish like a native. I became the go-between for Grant and Juan Pablo as Grant slowly mastered the art of mule-skinning. Even better, Juan Pablo taught me so much more about Mexico than just how to speak Spanish like an *arriero*, which I can tell you, is quite a different language than the Castilian Spanish spoken by the *hacendados* and *hombres de bien* who rule the country.

⌒

"What are you reading?" It was Lieutenant Grant.

I was leaning against the corral containing the regiment's pack mules, taking a break, reading the only book in my possession—my much battered copy of *The Last of the Mohicans* that Mary had bought me in Galway. Mrs. Shipley had rescued it from Mary's ruined belongings in our burnt-out lodgings and given it to Hermann the day he went to the 'Points and the Bowery to see her and Fíona. Hermann had, oddly enough, held onto the book for a few weeks and had only given it to me when we were onboard *Suviah*, on the way from New Orleans to St. Joseph's Island.

Every so often, I pulled out the book and read a bit. Today I was rereading the very beginning, one of my very favorite bits, where Cooper was describing Cora's tresses, and I was letting my mind wander between sweet memories of Brannagh and more recently of that beautiful *tejana* I had met at Sunday dinner, Calandria—each of whom in her own way had equally as beautiful tresses. Then I woolgathered a little more, this time about golden ringlets, and I wondered if I would ever hear from Evelyn again.

"What are you reading, there, Gogan?" It was Grant again.

I snapped to attention. "Sorry, sir. Lost in the forests somewhere." I held my battered book up with a bit of crooked grin. "*The Last of the Mohicans*, sir. The only book I have with me."

"At ease, soldier. That was my favorite book when I was at West Point. Great description of a siege by a man who, by all accounts, served ten minutes as a midshipman and has spent the rest of his days since then scrivening to his heart's content. Never a day in the army, though."

"Yes sir. I love the descriptions of the forests, as well. So unlike Ireland. Or here, for that matter. My father first bought me the book a few years ago, and I dreamt of coming to America and exploring such wildernesses."

"Well, in joining the army, you surely chose an odd way to explore the wilderness."

"There were, shall we say sir, exigent circumstances at play."

"Yes, there often are. You and Wurster are a strange pair. We're lucky to have you both in the company. He was in the Prussian army, wasn't he?

"Yes, sir. And he's a circus performer, a trapeze artist."

"Strong."

"And he reads and writes as well as I do, sir. He'd be a great addition to our team."

"So you've mentioned once or twice." Grant peered at me a little more closely. "You are a persistent devil, aren't you?"

There are times when one—particularly an Other Ranks—must recognize the rhetorical nature of a superior officer's question.

"Well, you can rest assured, my good Private Gogan, that your continued requests to have Wurster join us have not fallen on entirely deaf ears."

I perked up a bit.

"Just not in the way you intended."

"Sir?"

"Your good friend is now a corporal."

"Fantastic, sir."

"And your other messmate, Finnegan, is no longer a corporal."
Grant paused for dramatic effect. I did not react, so he continued,
"He is now a sergeant. We've been short this past few weeks since
Larkin died of the bloody flux, and more to the point, we've a fresh
draft of men coming in from New Orleans. I cannot imagine a better pair to whip those hay foot, straw foot, tenderfoots into shape
lickety-split."

"That is outstanding, sir."

"Don't be disappointed. Your time will come. You're young yet."

"Sir?" It had genuinely not occurred to me to be upset at not having been considered for promotion. I wondered daily whether I should
even be here, wearing the blue blouse. Although, that said, no viable,
let alone honorable, alternative had as yet come to mind.

"How old are you?"

"Twenty-one, sir."

"Don't give me that nonsense you gave Captain McCall. He no
more believed you than I did. But ..." Grant seemed to want to say
something else, but said instead, "How old are you, really?"

"You'll not send me back to New York?"

"Do I look that dull to you, Gogan?"

Another one of those rhetorical questions.

"Sixteen, sir, this past August."

"Those must have been quite exceptional circumstances to com-
pel you to join this man's army. Your father still alive?"

"No sir."

"If you don't mind, when did he die?" Grant was surprisingly
gentle.

Dear sweet Lord above, tears nearly came to my eyes. "About a
year and a half ago."

"I'm sorry. Here in America?"

"No sir. In Ireland."

"Dear God, you came over by yourself? You were what? Fourteen?"

"Just turned fifteen, sir."

"You were in school in Ireland?"

"Yes sir. A little boarding school called St. Patrick's. It was idyllic, really," I mused. "Cricket, prayers in Latin, and just a smattering of Greek, sir."

"A perfect education for a young Irishman, it would seem. What did you want to do with yourself back then?"

"Not sure I ever really thought about it." I smiled in recollection. "My father wanted me to go to Oxford or Cambridge. To be as well educated as any fine *Sassenagh* grandee. No Trinity College for me, so he said. But at the same time, we would tell each other stories about the American frontier. He once told me just before he was arrested by the *Sassenagh* that Ireland was done as a place to live and grow, and that it was high time for the two of us to strike out over the Western Ocean to seek our fortunes in America."

"Your father was arrested?" Grant sounded incredulous. "What did your mother think?"

"My mother died when I was born, sir." Grant made motions to say something, what I don't know. I uncharitably thought it would be along the lines of, "sorry for your loss," one of those oft-said, trite statements that costs the speaker nothing and delivers less to the listener. So I waved him off and said, "And my father? Well, he died in prison, sir. Alone and at the hands of the *Sassenagh*."

Grant seemed to take my cue, and asked, "Who are they, Gogan? These *Sassenagh*?"

"Sorry, sir. The English. The word means outsider. It's what we Irish call the English. Bit of an insult really. But what else can you say and do about your overlords when you were born on an island that is the cornerstone of the greatest empire since Rome?"

"The *Sassenagh*." Grant seemed to chew on the word for a moment. "So what did your father do to earn himself a trip to prison? That is if you don't mind my asking."

"Not at all sir. My father was a great patriot." My eyes began to mist involuntarily and I stopped for a moment. "A great patriot. He was the right hand man to the Great Liberator, himself, Daniel O'Connell. Perhaps the greatest man in Irish history since Brian

Boru died eight hundred years ago at Clontarf, freeing the Irish from another oppressor—the Vikings. O'Connell was the man who brought Catholic Emancipation to Ireland, which meant that Catholic Irishmen could sit in Parliament. First time in a hundred years. That was all before I was born, though, and all of Ireland thought that Daniel O'Connell was done as a political force. Then came the Repeal Year in 1843."

"Good Lord, Gogan, you're making my head spin with it all."

"Sorry, sir, but this is all about why there are so many Irishmen here in the New World."

"Yes, I quite appreciate that. I do apologize for the interruption. Please ..." Grant gestured.

I resumed my story. "I don't really know whose idea it was. I'd like to think it was my father's, though I suspect the history books will not remember it that way. The thought was that if O'Connell could harness the will of the people, sir, then perhaps the English yoke could be lifted from Ireland. Maybe not entirely, but just a little bit."

"Since we Jonathans still see Ireland as part of the United Kingdom, I take it that matters did not work out."

"No sir, they did not. But the Irish were mobilized, that is for certain. Why, at the royal hill at Tara, there were 750,000 who gathered to listen to the Great Liberator. My father was the one who organized it all. Behind the scenes, mind you. Ruined his health. Destroyed our family fortune, or so I was told by my cousin, Seamus. It all came to an end at Clontarf, just outside Dublin. That's where Brian Boru died fighting the Viking invaders 800 years ago, funny enough. An almost sacred place in Irish history. They say that there were to be a million people there that Saturday in October 1843. Imagine that, sir, a million people in a country of hardly five million. All in one place. Well, it wasn't to be. The English proscribed the meeting, and O'Connell gave in rather than risk open rebellion against the most powerful empire on earth."

"That when the arrest came?"

I nodded. "They took him away while I was at school, and I never saw him again. The English eventually let O'Connell and the others go. Health broken and any hope of Irish freedom shattered. My father died in prison, though." I smiled crookedly. "When word came, I was immediately sent down from school." I sped to the conclusion, afraid that my emotions would overwhelm me. "My cousin, Seamus O'Creagh, was afraid—or unwilling—to keep me, and there was no money left for me to continue my education." I forebore from mentioning what Seamus had hissed at me about his fears for his dear, sweet daughter, Evelyn, who would always remain my first boyhood love. I also did not mention Seamus's ghastly death by fire at the hands of that murdering Fenian bastard, MacGowan. Not to mention poor, innocent Oonagh's death, or Father O'Muirhily's murder, for that matter. "So off across the Western Ocean it was for me." I smiled again, less crookedly. "New York is a hard place, and so here I am, a private in Uncle Sam's army here on the Nueces."

"An amazing story." Grant looked thoughtful.

"Yes sir." And I left it at that, unwilling to plunge into my torment at the hands of MacGowan. I only thanked my lucky stars that I seemed to be rid of the man, for we had been here for months in Corpus Christi and there was not a sign of him. Not, I reasoned, that he could have begun to know what happened to me after the fire that killed poor Mary Skiddy and burned half of New York to a cinder. Perhaps I really had made a new start, after all.

◦—

"Son, I am going to have to get you a proper *sombrero galoneando*, some *chaparreras* and a proper pair of boots and spurs if you're going to be wrangling mules. Then maybe we can promote you to be a proper *caporal* in charge of this here outfit instead of being *segundo* to that officer pal 'o' yours."

I looked up from where I had been (ineffectually to be sure) helping our *arrieros* brand a mule with the Fourth Infantry's brand—a large and lopsided "4"—to see Colonel Kinney sitting on his horse, watching the goings-on. He was every bit as hale-fellow and well-met as he had been at Sunday dinner once he'd figured out that Hermann and I were square and fit company for *las mujeres decentes*. But his eyes were tense and perhaps a bit sadder than I remembered.

"*¡Hola, señor!*" I said, proud of my newly acquired Spanish skills.

"*¡Hola*, señor Gogan!" Kinney chuckled. "You're speaking pretty good Mexican for a gringo."

I shrugged and grinned. "What brings you out to the *corrales*, Colonel?"

"I was just returning from down south. Picked up a New Orleans newspaper down in Matamoros. Thought you and Mr. Wurster might like to read it."

"Thanks very much, Colonel. I will definitely pass it around. With any luck, just about everyone in the company will read it—leastways, those who can read."

"There is one article you may want to read very closely. It is a report that *el presidente* Herrera has agreed to receive an American minister plenipotentiary. You can read all about it."

"Then it's peace?"

"Not so fast, young man. A lot can go wrong. But there's a chance. Just a chance … and that's only if the Mexicans agree to sell *Alto California* to *los norteamericanos* and agree to let Texas join the Union. And you heard what don Guillermo said about the chances of that happening …"

Grant was suddenly at my elbow, and I introduced the two men. Grant looked vaguely surprised at my knowing—and his meeting—such an illustrious fellow as Kinney until I explained that Hermann and I had attended the Catholic service at Kinney's casa. Kinney said to me that doña Alandra and don Guillermo would very much like Hermann and me to ride out and visit them at their *casa de sillar* next Sunday if we could find horses. He then mischievously said that las señoritas would also be most gratified if we were to make an appearance. With that and a raised eyebrow of interest from Grant at the exchange, Kinney rode off to his casa. I offered the newspaper to Grant, who declined, saying that our mess should read it first, but that he'd appreciate a gander at it afterwards. In the exchange, I mentioned what Kinney had told me about the possibility of peace.

Grant replied almost formally, as if it were something he'd thought about long and hard. "That would be a good thing, Private Gogan. Then we could all go home and see our ladies instead of fighting some unholy war in a foreign country we have no business invading."

We looked at each other, each of us a little surprised, both at what Grant had said and the fact that he had said it to me. I saluted Grant without a word. I finished branding mules for the day and made may way back to camp with the newspaper, looking forward to a little coffee, some *cecinas* (dried beef jerky) and *frijoles* (Mexican beans), which the *cocinero de corrida* had showed Jenny and me how to make. With a little luck, I would also be able to enjoy a puff or two on my pipe before turning in.

I was sitting alone that evening, warming myself at our mess's firepit in front of a small blaze that warded off the autumn chill. Rónán Finnegan and Hermann were off somewhere with a baker's dozen of recruits who were every bit as hay foot, straw foot, tenderfoot as Grant had feared. But there had been no beatings. A bit of impatient yelling, yes. But no beatings, and the recruits could now hold their muskets properly and not run into each other—much, that is—when they marched. Jenny and O'Leary weren't about either, so I was left to shift for myself for dinner, which I did not mind, as it would give me time to read the newspaper.

Just as I settled down to tuck into my *cecinas* and *frijoles*, Kenny O'Leary hove into camp looking extremely agitated. I asked him what was wrong, and he said something about Jenny having "disappeared" and how he had spent the whole night wandering through the tent city over by town, hoping to find her. He said that this wasn't the first time she'd gone off somewhere, and when he asked her where she'd disappeared to, she either said she was visiting with the Great

Western or that it was none of his business, and he didn't own her like some Negro slave. They'd quarreled the last time Kenny saw her, and he was "feeling mighty low" as a result.

I consoled O'Leary until a very weary Rónán and Hermann tumbled to the ground next to us and gratefully partook of the *cecinas* and *frijoles* I'd put aside for them. We turned in shortly after that, and just before going to sleep I resolved to chat with Hermann about Kenny and Jenny—well away from camp and prying ears.

The next Sunday, Hermann and I borrowed a couple of horses, one from a friend of Grant's and the other from my *caporal*, and ridden out to *la Casa de las Corrientes de Golondrinas* for a delightful Sunday visit with *las mujeres decentes*, Calandria and Serafina, and I had started to think that Hermann was falling in love. On the ride back to the encampment, he didn't tease me even once about Calandria batting her eyelashes at me nor my responding to her, and he seemed unusually preoccupied and happy. So we ended up not talking about the brewing issue of what to do about Jenny. As to Calandria and myself, I thought it rather more like a fencing match back at school. As smitten as I was with her dark beauty, I was rather more interested in remaining unventilated by her rapier-wit. I would otherwise have been a leaky fellow indeed by the end of the day.

Not long after that, Grant told me that he was getting into yet another new line of work during his evenings—acting.

"Acting, sir?"

"Yes." Grant scowled and looked up at me. There was a pained silence, which I filled.

"The role, sir?"

"Desdemona."

"Othello. That seems a bit Elizabethan, sir."

"You know the play? What do you mean, 'Elizabethan'?" Grant merely glared at me this time.

"Well, sir. It is a play that every schoolboy in Ireland reads ... notwithstanding its *Sassenagh* author. Anyway, sir, Shakespeare was probably a Paddy. Had to be. No Englishman could write like that. And women didn't act on stage in those days. It was considered indecent. So young men played the female roles."

"I see."

"You don't seem entirely happy, sir."

"Well Longstreet was going to have the part."

"He's six foot and some tall, sir."

"Yes, that's what Prince John said. He said he couldn't bear the thought of poor Porter having to look up at Longstreet and still give a convincing performance as the Moor declaring his undying love for Desdemona. And of course, Longstreet won't shave his beard." Grant rubbed his own beard, now just starting to grow in. "And I'll be damned if I do, even if Prince John says I should."

Prince John Magruder was an artillery captain well known for his elegant uniforms, his flamboyance, and his eye for the bleak morts. And he was man enough (and big enough in stature) never to be teased for his lisp, which disappeared only when he sang a beautiful tenor or when he declaimed in the lead part of an amateur theatrical production behind which he, like as not, had been the driving force.

"I understand, sir."

"Do you? Yes, I suppose you do." Grant chewed his unlit cheroot. "Here's the thing. I'll need some assistance ..."

"Sir?"

"Learning the part."

"Happy to help, sir."

# CHAPTER 6

# Rescuing Jenny and Losing Desdemona

∽

I NEVER DID GET A CHANCE TO TALK with Hermann privately. About three or four nights later, I saw Hoggs leaving camp, and I decided to follow him. It wasn't the first time. I'd been following the bastard every time he left camp when I was not otherwise occupied. His departures had grown more frequent, as his curious sense of detachment from the day-to-day running of the company intensified in the wake of Rónán Finnegan's promotion to sergeant. As Rónán, Hermann, and I had discussed many times, a good first sergeant should run all the company's affairs insofar as the Other Ranks are concerned and leave the officers to worrying about other, more important matters, such as when dinner was coming and whether the week's mail delivery had brought letters from their sweethearts. Yet Hoggs was steadily abdicating that role to Rónán, and none of us knew why.

The sense of torpor that had overcome the Army of Occupation's encampment after the first blue norther deepened dramatically in the intervening weeks. Drill among us old hands was now restricted to platoons led by sergeants—if it occurred at all. Lieutenant Porter made only occasional appearances to lead the entire company in the most rudimentary of drill, and then only for an hour or so. The company's only bright spots were Rónán's and Hermann's labors with the recruits, and Grant's efforts with the mules. Rónán and Hermann were both full of the energy of their late promotions and were ambitious to whip the recruits, whose numbers had swollen by a further dozen or so, into as good a shape as the rest of the company and put to shame even the most experienced of doughboys in the rest of the regiment.

C Company's general air of torpor was only a little better than the outright sloth of most of the rest of the regiment, and my sense was that the Fourth differed little from any of the other infantry regiments. Even the cavalry seemed to have succumbed. The Second Dragoons only occasionally sallied forth to exercise their mounts and little more. The only impetus for their extra spark of energy was maintaining their mounts, for the last thing the cavalry wanted was mounts unable to handle the march south. That left the flying artillery. Major Ringgold, the father of flying of artillery himself, and his principal officers, Ridgely and Bragg, were still pushing the artillery batteries hard. Bragg was still as savage as ever enforcing discipline in pursuit of perfection. God knows where the powder and ball came from. We often speculated that Bragg might just diminish the army's entire supply of powder as a prelude to our heading north when (many of us continued to hope) Mexico agreed to sell its lands north of the Rio Grande to the United States.

I thought that, if peace were indeed to break out, I could perhaps contrive to stay down here, south of the Nueces. I might even try my hand at a little ranching when the rest of the Fourth headed north to St. Louis or some other locale to resume its frontier duties. I resolutely did not want to drown in what veterans such as Rónán told me was the dreary and mean life of an enlisted man in a small frontier fort for the remaining years of my enlistment (and of my youth). This fantasy was as tender and nascent as could be, but I nursed it along on the memory of the fluttering eyelashes and foining wit of the alluring Calandria and a beautiful casa near a big mesquite shade tree named for the swallows nesting in its joists. It was also quite detached from my sense of the near inevitability of war with Mexico—a view informed by my occasional talks with Colonel Kinney. Curiously, I was also quite ambivalent about the fantasy itself, into which the silent (for more than a year, now) Evelyn seemed to intrude at the most unseemly of moments. I wasn't quite sure what drove my ambivalence. But I did know that I wanted to be careful of what I asked for, because it might just come to pass.

Hermann had guard duty that evening, and Rónán Finnegan was nowhere to be found. O'Leary and Jenny were similarly absent. So I trailed after Hoggs alone as he made his way over to the tent city. I stayed a good fifty yards behind him, ready to look as if I were heading the opposite direction if Hoggs were to turn around. As I reached the edge of the encampment, Rónán—I had come to think of him by his first name, our difference in rank notwithstanding—caught up with me.

"Headed into town?"

"Yep."

"Good. I'll join you. We can have a cider and a pipe of tobacco together."

We sauntered along for a couple of minutes, and Rónán asked, "That Hoggs up there?"

"Yep."

He looked at me strangely. "You following him?"

"Yep."

"Why?"

I didn't enlighten him, but he didn't press me either, and we both continued to walk up the well-beaten path towards the tent city, gossiping in a desultory fashion about the day's doings.

When Hoggs reached the tent city, still some fifty yards or so ahead of us, he disappeared behind a row of tent and frame buildings. We picked up our pace a little as I cracked to Rónán that we would make a lousy pair of spies. We rounded the corner, and Hoggs was nowhere to be found. I was a little upset at losing him like that, because I'd always been able to keep an eye on him until he was eventually safely ensconced in the tent brothel next to the Military Retreat. Nonetheless, I wasn't inclined to go crashing about the tent city looking for him. I figured that I could surreptitiously look in on him at the Military Retreat before I went back to camp, and maybe this time I could figure out who the girl was whom Hoggs was more and more frequently entertaining in one of the brothel's tent rooms. So I suggested to Rónán that we find a hard cider for two bits, wander around, look at the sights, and call it a night after we looked in on the Military Retreat. There were only few doughboys about, because most were still dead broke for the want of a payday.

"Don't even think about turning around, you dumb plugs. What are you doing following me?"

It was Hoggs, and he was behind us.

I replied first. "We aren't following you, Sergeant."

"Don't feed me that load of old wank, Gogan."

Rónán said patiently, as if talking to a slightly stupid recruit, "All we're doing, Sergeant, is finding a hard cider. Assuming, of course, that there is some to be found in this dusty pesthole. Then it's home to bed, just like Momma taught me to do."

"Knock it off, Finnegan," Hoggs barked. Then he cautioned, "And don't turn around."

"Oh, Hoggs, don't be such a jerk," Rónán replied, conversationally. I remained shut pan. "What are you doing?" I heard a contemptuous note in Rónán's voice that I'd never heard before in his dealings with Hoggs. "Running a dead game of faro and planking dear little Jenny under poor O'Leary's nose?"

Hoggs was dead silent, and I knew I had been right to suspect the bastard—not that I imagined Jenny could have possibly submitted to him willingly. I couldn't see Hoggs standing in the darkness behind us, but I could feel him wanting to explode. But he could do nothing to either of us here. Too many people about, even if we were momentarily alone in this little alley of the tent city. Anyway, there were two of us. He wouldn't dare take us both on unless he had one of Sam Colt's Paterson repeating pistols, and I didn't think that anyone in the army had one, outside a few officers who had purchased them at their own vast expense, and Captain Walker and his Texas Rangers, and they weren't in camp anymore.

"Follow me again, and I'll kill you both. And you, Gogan, you stupid little Paddy get. You're a dustman next time. I am going to douse your glim, come hell or high water."

I could feel Rónán wanting to look at me. There was a rustle, and we both knew that Hoggs had disappeared.

Rónán said to me, "What the Sam Hill was that all about?"

"How much do you want to know? Not even Hermann knows it all."

"Tell me. But first, let's get clear of this place. I'm no longer in the mood for some cider."

⌒

"You, Billy, are every bit as impetuous and silly as I have warned you about." Hermann was highly displeased. "And you, Sergeant Rónán, you are nearly as impetuous and silly."

Rónán silently acknowledged the rebuke.

"Hoggs is dangerous," Hermann said. "And he knows he let something slip to the two of you. The question is whether he cares. Or is he so arrogant and stupid as to believe that he is impervious? But the really important problem we have is that Hoggs has a friend somewhere out there, and we do not know who he is. This is not the end of it. Has anyone seen Jenny?"

"No," Rónán and I spoke in unison.

Kenny was in his tent, probably lying sleepless next to Gaff.

"We must talk to Miss Sarah," Hermann said.

"The Great Western?" I asked.

"Yes. We must have a plan about what to do with Jenny. That beast cannot be permitted to have his way with her. And Kenny is not to know any of this. He is far too distraught. *Scheißdreck!*"

⌒

"I haven't seen Jenny." Sarah Langwell said to Hermann and me. She was busy shuttling between the laundry pot, which was just beginning to steam over one fire and breakfast for her mess, which was sizzling on another. She stood and straightened up to her full six foot two inches after flipping over a slab of unidentifiable meat on a skillet to cook the other side, wiped the sweat from her brow, and arched her back. Her breasts strained against the thin fabric as she did. I tried not to stare, ever mindful of the consequences.

Hermann furrowed his brow. "We have not seen Jenny either. This is not like her."

"I know. Jenny told me that she was shot of that Hoggs character, because he quit coming around once he realized that you lot were her friends. She first told me about Hoggs the night that half-baked ding left Billy-boy, here, drifting about in the wastelands as bait for the Comanche." Sarah looked at me and smirked. "I heard tell that Hoggs was fit to kill after Captain McCall let you off so easy. Not, mind you, that anyone had the gumption to tease ol' Hoggs over the humiliation of it all. It's a wonder he ain't hushed you yet, Billy-boy."

"Well, he's made it pretty clear that he intends to, shall we say, rectify his mistake," I said.

"Well, lad-de-da, my lad. That shore sounds high-falutin' to me." Sarah gave me another smirk. "But I reckon you're right, Billy-boy. He will be after you again, one day, and he won't be merciful when he does. You can be sure of that, my sugar."

It was at times like these that I felt as if she thought me to be a mere toy, and I thanked heaven that she was damn near old enough to be my mother. She regarded Hermann in an entirely different light, and on more than one occasion in the past couple of months since she and Jenny had come into our lives, Hermann had gallantly evaded Sarah's grasp, pleading the presence of her erstwhile husband. Unfortunately, Hermann no longer had that excuse. The poor man had expired in the camp hospital a few weeks back, victim of a fever contracted in the wake yet another abominable blue norther. The grapevine discounted the blue norther as the source of the poor deceased's demise, insisting instead that his fatal fever was entirely the result of over-exertion in the discharge of his marital duties. Whatever the cause of his demise, Sarah had once again made it quite evident to Hermann that she was on the prowl for a new lover. Apparently, she believed that a couple of weeks was a sufficiently respectable period of mourning.

"O'Leary is beside himself about this. He is ready to murder Hoggs in his tracks." Hermann was pacing back and forth in front of Sarah, oblivious to her hungrily following his movements.

"That won't do any good," Sarah said. "You really think that Hoggs has her somewhere?"

"I cannot imagine where else she could be, not after what Hoggs let slip to Rónán and Billy. In any case, we have not seen her for three days. But what I do not understand is why she would have gone with Hoggs willingly." Hermann paced some more, and Sarah looked at him again with ill-disguised lust. It was almost as if she were challenging me to make some comment. I did not.

"That's easy, my pet." She touched Hermann on the shoulder, and he looked at her. "She must be terrified of him doing something to Kenny. There can be no other reason."

"That she would willingly ...?"

Sarah looked at me. "You have never known love, have you, my sugar? Real love. You do what's necessary. That is what you do when you love a man."

"Even ..."

"Yes. Even that. Willingly." Sarah's face softened. "And such an innocent lamb."

"Let us stop with the morality play," Hermann snapped testily. "What do we do now to find her?"

"We put a spy inside."

"Who? Inside where?" I didn't want to sound sharp, but I was confused.

"Me. Inside the Military Retreat."

Hermann said nothing.

I said, "You'd go there on the strength of my having followed Hoggs there once or twice, and no more?"

Sarah nodded.

"But how do we know ..."

"It's got the only knocking shop worthy of the name in those tents out back." Both Hermann and I forebore from inquiring as to how Sarah came upon this precious bit of knowledge. She explained, "It caters to shoulder straps, mostly. Nobody else has got the chink. And I happen to know a couple of shoulder straps who frequent the joint." She smirked again.

Hermann ruminated as I remonstrated with Sarah. "But Hoggs knows you. So, too, presumably, will his confederate."

"Of course they do. They also know that I just lost my man ... and they know that half the army wants ... Well, you know what I mean. And to hell with the other half. I'd be the draw from heaven for any knocking shop worth its salt." Sarah thought for a moment. "There might be another way, but let me think on it a spell."

Sarah and I waited for Hermann to say something. But he remained silent, and the three of us looked at each other until Sarah stood up and began bustling about, sparing us only the most occasional glance, tending first to the laundry and then to breakfast. Finally, Sarah told us that we weren't going to have any privacy in a moment as her doughboys were beginning to rumble out of their tents looking for their coffee. Then she asked Hermann to come by later in the morning. I was distinctly not invited.

⌒

Hermann told me that evening that Sarah "had a good plan" to rescue Jenny. He didn't tell me what Sarah intended to do, but he did reveal, almost shyly, that Sarah had out-and-out propositioned him. Those were not Hermann's words, for he had been less blunt in his description. But I understood Sarah's intent perhaps better than he did. Her proposition had not merely been sexual. She had almost certainly proffered some vision of one business opportunity or another to him, leaning into him suggestively and painting a rosy picture of a bright and wealthy future. Sarah was not being meretricious, though. She was a thoroughly practical—and commercially-minded—being. I admired her.

I almost said something about her magnificent milk shop. And about the convenient location of her nipples for a man just under six foot. But the look on Hermann's face dissuaded me. I contented myself with, "So, is it true love?"

This bit of cheek earned me a disdainful look and something of an explanation. "Her life is not for me. I cannot see myself scraping a living as a parasite on the army. And her business ideas …"

I refrained from asking about the particulars of Sarah's latest business notions, and contented myself with a different question. "Serafina more your *métier*?"

Hermann looked at me petulantly. "What is '*métier*'?"

I grinned at him. "What I mean is that Serafina is more your kind of girl, isn't she? *Una mujer decente*?"

"She is a lady. A young lady. But a lady."

"Your lady?"

"Billy," Hermann explained to me in his patient and slightly Teutonic manner. "I am a corporal in the United States Army, and I have years before I am a free man. Anyway, she is a lady whom I have met only a few times, and I will almost certainly not have the opportunity to come to know her well enough to think like that before the regiment moves on to wherever it is going to go next."

"Of course you can."

"I am not a deserter. Not in the face of war. And that is no way to … how do you say? *Eine junge Dame den Hof machen*?"

Something about courting young Serafina, I thought he meant. But I did not reply to him, and we both let his question linger. Unlike Hermann, I was becoming increasingly resolute about eventually taking a bit of French leave. It was simply a matter of waiting until I believed that I would be much better off for having done so. I simply did not see a happy outcome to my deserting before the army left Texas and went back up north. If the army went south to war, then any thought of desertion would have to be postponed, for there was no way I was going to brave the hangman's noose. Anyway, going south to war might provide some adventure that I wouldn't want to miss. But perhaps my procrastination simply meant that I simply lacked the courage to desert.

Or maybe I was not ready to risk all for the delectable Calandria and her mordant wit. I had met her only a few times—enough to burn her image into my mind's eye, but like Hermann had said about Serafina, hardly enough to come to know her. And in any case, I was beginning to think that even if I did come to know her better, I would end up feeling about her much as I had felt about Brannagh. I hadn't had the desire ... or the courage ... to follow Brannagh to Canada or wherever the devil her mother, Black Muireann O'Marran, had sent her. Mary, on the other hand, had been a different matter, I declared to myself. I had committed myself to her and to Fíona, and I would therefore have stood by her until the end of time. Of course, Mary was dead—very convenient for me in the sense that it allowed me to believe in the strength of my commitment to her without it ever having been tested. It was a corollary to my commitment to Mary, I constantly told myself, that I was continuing to stand by Fíona—as best I could under the circumstances, of course—simply because I had given to Mrs. Shipley far more than enough money to pay for Fíona's keep and schooling for a very long time.

It also occurred to me that my ambivalence about Calandria and *la Casa de las Corrientes de Golondrinas* was being reinforced by Hermann's increasingly apparent desire for Serafina—and by this nagging feeling that the house of flowing swallows was Hermann's future and not mine. What really shook me as Hermann and I had talked that day was that I could not envision Hermann and me together after the war, carving out a living under the hot south Texas sun.

It wasn't until later that I realized that neither Evelyn nor the lingering mystery of that evil bastard, MacGowan, had entered into my calculus.

The next night, as Hermann, Rónán, and I sat at our fire and puffed on our pipes, Sarah told us that there was no need for any further planning, because it was all over. The whole affair had been absurdly simple. Sarah had marched into the Military Retreat and loudly demanded to see the proprietor of that fine establishment, as she had a proposition for him. The announcement had stopped the entire bowling alley cold as the score or so bowlers and gamblers idling away the evening stared openly and appraisingly at the six-foot something Amazon beauty to see what would happen next. A man who called himself the proprietor appeared almost instantly and introduced himself as Captain Antoine "Carambole" Rouquette, late of the Louisiana Volunteers.

As Sarah told it to us, Captain Rouquette was apparently a gambler well known on various Mississippi riverboats. He was taking advantage of the business opportunity afforded by the Army of Occupation's sojourn in Corpus Christi to give tempers raised by some incident on one of those riverboats time to cool. For reasons unclear to Sarah, the captain and a business associate apparently had the makings of a ten-pin alley on hand this past summer and no clear idea of what to do with them, until Taylor and the first elements of the Third Infantry departed New Orleans for Corpus Christi back in July. They recognized the opportunity and found a ship bound for Corpus Christi that was rapidly filling with like-minded adventurers and a small number of women. The two of them were also foresighted enough to ship enough lumber and canvas with them to set up their ten-pin alley, which they called the Military Retreat, and a small brothel right behind it—thereby establishing the premier den of iniquity in all of Corpus Christi.

Captain Rouquette immediately invited Sarah to retire with him to one of the brothel's small tent rooms (the only place where he could offer even a modicum of privacy for their interview)—with a bottle of whiskey, a couple of shot glasses of indifferent cleanliness, and a bit of a leer on the good captain's face—to discuss Sarah's proposition. On account of the small size of the tent room, they sat on the cot, knee to knee, but not quite touching.

Sarah observed to Captain Rouquette that the tent room really didn't need to be any larger to discharge the sort of business for which it was normally used. She did allow, though, that her proposition was of an entirely different nature, and one that held the promise of far greater profit for the both of them. Sarah then apologized for interrupting the good captain, as she was most interested in learning how he had acquired his unusual nickname.

Captain Rouquette happily answered that his nickname, "Carambole," arose from the aftermath of a duel a few years back. Sarah simpered that she would love to hear Rouqette's story, which was surely fascinating and romantical, as befit such a gentleman adventurer. Rouquette almost bowed at the compliment. He prefaced his story by saying that he was a peaceable man. But unfortunately some years ago, some embarrassment stemmed from the salacious nature of the rumored details of a matter involving Captain Rouquette, a young man, and the young man's wife. The young man and his wife, as did their friends and closest allies, all vehemently denied the salacious details to anyone who would listen, details that involved midnight carriage rides and stories of deshabille at particularly inconvenient moments. But the denials seemed merely to fan the flames of curiosity. Rouquette told Sarah that he remained silent as a matter of honor. He also tried to avoid the man, so as not to give undue offense. Sarah agreed whole-heartedly with Rouquette's sentiments on that point, and he once again contemplated Sarah's suddenly quivering bosom before clearing his throat and continuing his tale.

The young man was more intemperate, the captain said, and chose an unfortunately public moment to confront him. One fine spring morning, the young man was passing through the French Market, just outside the Café du Monde when he stumbled over three Indian women sitting cross-legged in the middle of the thoroughfare and noisily hawking gumbo to passersby. He recovered himself and was preparing to walk on his way, when he locked eyes with Captain Rouquette, who was breakfasting with a dozen of his closest associates at the Café du Monde on the finest fresh beignets in the city, washed down by a gallon or two of fine café au lait. The captain and a couple of his associates were doing their best to hide their amusement over the poor man's momentary discombobulation, but he was not to be mollified. He strode over to Captain Rouquette and struck him across the face with his kid gloves and demanded satisfaction. For what wasn't entirely clear, whether for the perceived rude display of hilarity or for the rumors swirling about the young man's wife and his reputed cuckoldry at Rouquette's hands.

The young man, who by now had reconciled with his wife, instantly regretted his angry confrontation with Rouquette, and was anxious for the whole matter to be forgotten as quickly as possible. Carambole once again emphasized to Sarah that he, too, wished for no blood to be spilled. But he was afraid of what price would be demanded by honor now that the young man had so publicly demanded satisfaction from Captain Rouquette. Sarah sympathized with Carambole over what should have been no more than an innocent misunderstanding regarding the young man's unfortunate encounter with the squaws hawking gumbo in such an inconvenient spot so near a busy establishment such as the Café du Monde. It was an embarrassment, Sarah said, that was much like the one involving his hand, which had just alighted upon her knee—a hand which Captain Rouquette hastily withdrew with an effusive apology before continuing his story.

Rouquette said that he merely wanted to teach the young unfortunate a small lesson in decorum while still preserving his own honor as a proper Creole gentleman who considered himself equal to any gentleman born and raised south of the Mason-Dixon line. (There unfortunately was no such thing as a true Yankee gentleman, he confided to Sarah. They were far too preoccupied with the mundane concerns of commerce to be proper gentlemen.) But he was afraid that the young innocent would not have a sporting chance in a duel. Carambole told Sarah that he did not want to boast, but he reluctantly acknowledged that he had been elected this past year by general acclaim as captain of his company of Louisiana Volunteers for the duration of a recent campaign chasing a small band of Indians up on the Red River. And this was not to mention his well-known—among the right sort of gentlemen of New Orleans and the community of riverboat gamblers—prowess with the *pistolet*, again something that

129

he preferred others to talk about on account of his view that modesty does so become a proper gentleman.

Sarah nodded sympathetically at Carambole's predicament, and she was positively effusive in approving of his ingenious solution to that predicament in light of his having the choice of weapon, on account of his having been the one who had been challenged to a duel. Rouquette chose billiard balls to be thrown at a distance of 10 paces as the weapons with which the duel would be fought. At first, Captain Rouquette's second was a little unsure of the propriety of the captain's choice of weapons, but he was quickly persuaded when Captain Rouquette informed him of a Parisian duel some years earlier where each combatant fought from a hot air balloon, which created quite an enthusiastic stir because hot air balloons were then very much in fashion. (Admittedly, the Parisian duel itself had been fought with *pistolets*, but Captain Rouquette did not emphasize the point to his second.) The Parisian balloon duel had apparently ended abruptly, when one of the duelists unaccountably fell out of his balloon and plunged to his death.

The young man and his second were likewise nonplussed at first. But they quickly recognized the wisdom of Captain Rouquette's ingenious solution to an affair that was quickly becoming embarrassing to all parties concerned (other than Captain Rouquette himself, who was unflappable). The young man was heard to say on more than one occasion that he believed the novel and unorthodox nature of the duel—which could hardly end in death—would communicate to observers that he and the captain had resolved their differences while allowing them to both retain their honor by neither of them having to publicly apologize to the other over the affair. So the thinking went, this would encourage the wagging tongues to conclude that the salacious rumors must be without merit, because otherwise how on earth would the two putative duelists have been able to apparently resolve their differences without one of them dying in the event? Captain Rouquette was indifferent as to whether his opponent was right or merely thinking wishfully.

The duel took place at dawn, the traditional time for such matters, the captain airily allowed to Sarah, with seconds and a doctor in place—the seconds deemed this last detail to be very wise in view of the potentially dangerous, if surely nonfatal, nature of the chosen weapons. The two duelists stood back to back in their shirtsleeves (collars loosened for quick access by the surgeon, if necessary), and they marched off five paces each to the cadence of Captain Rouquette's second. They turned to face each other at the command, and after what seemed to be an intolerably long time, the second for the captain's opponent let his handkerchief flutter to the ground. Captain Rouquette was happy to report to Sarah that he did not flinch, not even a bit, when his opponent threw his ball first. The ball flew wide of the mark by a considerable distance. Captain Rouquette was saddened to learn afterwards that his opponent was completely unfamiliar with the principles of throwing such a small and hard object. Had he known of this deficiency beforehand, Rouquette assured Sarah, he would never have chosen this particular weapon.

As Captain Rouquette made ready to throw his billiard ball, his opponent stood tall and as steady as the captain had. Captain Rouquette was spot on the mark with his throw, and the hard wooden ball cannoned off the side of his opponent's head and promptly struck his opponent's second in the head as well. It was a banked shot, a "carambole," someone said later that morning amidst the gaiety of the captain's supporters congratulating him on such a successful duel. The captain did not report how his opponent fared after the duel, nor did he report what became of his opponent's second or his opponent's wife. Sarah thought it proper not to inquire further.

But she did allow to Carambole that she was mighty amused at the story and she surely did not want another such misunderstanding, so would the good captain be so kind as to once more remove his hand 'afore she broke it for him. Carambole blanched slightly and asked Sarah about her business proposition. Sarah smiled daintily at Captain Rouquette, tossed her long red hair (it having been specially combed out and primped for the occasion) and heaved her bosom in a very pretty fashion as she slid a few inches further away from him. Sarah told us that she moved away from Captain Rouquette to reduce the poor captain's increasing distraction from the task at hand by making him realize that, on this night at least—one should never vouchsafe for the future—she was quite unattainable.

Sarah then began to tell Captain Rouquette about her business proposition. He interrupted with "call me Carambole." She smiled appreciatively and said that she was a mighty good hand at this new-fangled game called poker, or bluff as it was called up in Gotham, and she thought that she and the captain could profit mightily if she were to run a table. The only difficulty was that she'd need a stake to get started with drawing in all the simkins and suckers to be found in the tent city. As Sarah made her pitch, the captain's eyes kept wandering down to her bosom pressing against her thin white blouse (which I noticed, as she was telling the story, she was still wearing). As a basis for further negotiation, Sarah mentioned some very favorable (to herself) numbers in terms of how the proposed joint venture's future profits might be split between them. But Carambole did not seem inclined to negotiate. Indeed, he agreed quite readily to Sarah's view of the arrangements. After their negotiations concluded, Sarah rose and reached out to shake Carambole's hand to seal their bargain. Carambole, his eyes hardly rising above Sarah's milkshop—Sarah's words, not mine—raised her hand and grazed it most delicately with his lips as he murmured that she had thoroughly enchanted him. He said that he was already longing for their next appointment, which Sarah fixed then and there for the very next day. She had yet to see hide or hair of any of the dells and cows, and she needed to talk to them to have any chance of finding Jenny.

Sarah departed much as she arrived, with a booming *buenas noches* to the two or three stalwarts still occupying the Military Retreat as she paraded through the swinging doors and disappeared into the night. She had gone hardly thirty paces when a mere chit of a girl, pretty in a slatternly sort of way, tugged at Sarah's sleeve. She told Sarah that Jenny had sent her, and that Jenny was in the tent room right next to where Sarah and Carambole had negotiated the terms of their joint venture.

Sarah thanked the dell and asked her whether she could arrange to leave open the wooden back door to the brothel, which normally was barred shut. Sarah also suggested to the young slattern that she make herself scarce—and to make sure that she had a story to tell about where she had been in case she was ever asked. The girl looked at her quizzically. So Sarah explained that in ten minutes she intended to barge through that back door, find Jenny, and take her away. The slattern said that would be a good thing 'cause the poor thing warn't no kinchin mort, born and raised to the life. Anyhow, she said, that Sergeant Hoggs was an evil man, and all the girls were terrified of him.

Sarah was good to her word. Just ten minutes later, having meanwhile procured a stout wooden staff some four feet long, she slipped in through the unbarred door and opened the canvas door to the tent where the slattern had said Jenny was being kept. And there Jenny was, just as the slattern promised, naked from the waist down. Hoggs was there as well, with his uniform trousers about his ankles. He rolled off Jenny, stood up, pulled his trousers up, and snarled that he was not going to brook being interrupted like this. Hoggs lunged at Sarah, but his timing was off. He had also disregarded Sarah's staff, and Sarah rewarded him by poking him with it very hard in his bread basket. When he doubled over, she smashed him over the head with it. As he tumbled down face first, Sarah kicked him very hard. He grunted with pain, although she was not sure where she had struck him. Sarah gave Hoggs another stab in each kidney with her staff for good measure as she stepped over his prone body. Jenny had by now covered herself and was crouching with her knees drawn to her chest and her face virtually buried. Sarah sized her by the wrist and pulled her from the tent.

The tented hallway was crowded with dells curious about the commotion. At the other end of the hallway, at the entrance from the Military Retreat, two young toughs appeared and began pushing through the girls crowding the corridor between them and Sarah and Jenny. The two women turned and ran to the back door as Hoggs staggered from the tent room, his head bleeding profusely.

Hoggs yelled, "Stop that bitch."

Sarah put Jenny behind her, turned and said loudly, "Any man-jack who touches me will answer to Old Zach himself. Him'n'me are sweethearts, and he likes his milkshop nice and fresh. And it so happens, Sergeant Hoggs, that I'm just going to see him now. I do apologize for drawing a little claret, Sergeant. But you were being most indecent with this young girl, who is pledged to another—a member of your very own company."

The girls tittered, and the toughs stopped. Hoggs stared incredulously. In the ensuing silence Sarah burst through the brothel's back door hand-in-hand with Jenny, and they ran into the night as hard and fast as Jenny would allow. They did not stop moving until they were on the outskirts of the encampment.

Only then did Sarah stop Jenny and pull her close. "Let me see you." The moonlight revealed that the sparkle that had once animated Jenny's eyes was gone without a trace. It also revealed the physical damage Hoggs had wrought: An ugly blackened eye, a bruised cheek, and still more painful-looking bruises on Jenny's neck that stretched below her blouse.

Jenny recoiled a bit as Sarah spat, "The bastard."

The two of them then fairly flew the remaining few score yards to the Seventh's digs.

⌒

The next morning, Kenny stared Sarah in the face and refused to see Jenny—this after Sarah had reported to him (her own voice audibly catching in her telling of it) that Jenny had asked for him in a small and tremulous voice. Hermann, Rónán, and I looked on with dismayed bemusement.

Sarah's voice strengthened when she asked, "Why not, Kenny? Why not?"

"She's impure. She lay with him. That makes her a whore in the eyes of God."

Sarah glared at him. "The bastard kidnapped her and raped her."

"What about before? She came and went for weeks. She never resisted him then, an' he got in her beef, didn't he?" Kenny's voice broke with the grief of a man who'd irretrievably lost someone dear to him.

"She did it to save your life." Sarah's tone was blunt.

"It makes no difference. I fight my own fights. I'm a man. I'll hide behind no woman's skirts. I'll kill Hoggs." Kenny lunged incoherently. Rónán and Hermann restrained him.

"You'll do no such thing, lad," Rónán said in a calm voice. "For if you do, Hoggs will still be alive and you will be dead. He'll whip you as sure as the sun will set tonight. Even if you did live through it, no court martial would hesitate even a second to sentence you to hang. It wouldn't matter a whit to them what Hoggs did to Jenny … or to you. He's your first sergeant, and you'll have tried to kill him."

Kenny sagged against Rónán and Hermann, and they released him. Kenny sank to his knees, weeping, "She should have let me handle Hoggs. I'm a man who fights his own fights."

We three men stood silently. Who were we to object to such sentiments? All I could think about was how thankful I was that I was not in Kenny's shoes. It didn't bear thinking about what I would have found myself compelled to do.

There was little more to be said, and so Sarah left presently, but only after securing pledges from the three of us that we would watch Kenny like hawks—if only for Jenny's sake. Her parting words to us were that Jenny wouldn't bear Kenny dying stupidly over all of this. Time enough to sort out what was to become of the two of them and to see whether Kenny could see past his cuckolding.

Kenny finished the morning in fine form when he retired to his tent and for good measure kicked Gaff, who had soundly slept through what Hermann called *der stürm und drang*. I allowed to Hermann that Kenny's reaction seemed a little overmuch. Hermann replied that

Kenny's volte-face over Jenny had been coming for a while. I then thought back over the past few weeks and realized that Hermann was probably right.

In the days that followed, we learned that Jenny's injuries, both physical and psychic, were far, far worse than the black eye and tremulous voice reported that first night by Sarah. There were bruises, cuts, and welts all over her body and other damage that went far beyond such mere transitory wounds. Jenny kept to the tent she now shared with the Great Western, rocking gently and otherwise hardly stirring. Little by little, Sarah coaxed the ghastly story from Jenny. She relayed it to Hermann when they saw each other from time to time, and Hermann gave Rónán and me his terse synopsis.

Hoggs must have followed Jenny into town one day as she was making her way over to the *jacales* to buy some corn. He accosted her, demanding that she come with him right then and there. Otherwise, Hoggs snarled at her, he would buck and gag Kenny and force him to ride the horse until he died under the hot Texas sun. She tearfully surrendered, not knowing what else to do. Hoggs took her to the Military Retreat, where he seemed to know Captain Rouquette and the two toughs who minded the place. She crawled away when Hoggs was finished with her and hid until her tears were done. Only then did she return to camp.

At first, Hoggs only occasionally forced her to be with him, and she learned to stoically hide her revulsion at herself when she returned to camp. After a few weeks, Hoggs's demands began increasing, and he became more abusive, particularly if she struggled. In fact, her struggling only seemed to intensify his pleasure, so she stopped resisting at all and lay inert. This enraged Hoggs, who began beating her. Once he had left a mark on her face, he refused to let her return to camp. The beatings intensified until Sarah miraculously appeared one day and rescued her.

As she recovered, Jenny stayed with the Seventh's camp followers, where neither Hoggs nor the toughs employed at the Military Retreat dared to venture. Kenny deserted our mess, and spent days walking about in a haze. None of us knew where he found his food, and his laundry surely wasn't getting done because Hoggs erupted in rage at the poor state of Kenny's uniform during an inspection about a week later. The entire company paid for Kenny's slovenliness with two hours of drill before we secured for the evening. To my chagrin, I could not avoid the drill since Hoggs had cleared the punishment with Grant, and I saw the look in Grant's eye, which told me not even to begin to funk it. Hermann and Rónán promptly cornered Kenny and persuaded him to rejoin our mess and square away his uniform so that we could avoid another tirade by Hoggs.

The next day, with Rónán's and Hermann's blessing, I went down to the *jacales* and talked to the old woman who sold us our corn. Within fifteen minutes, I had secured a Mexican woman to work for us until we could make more permanent arrangements. She was married, with children, and was as unappealing to Hoggs as she could possibly be, which suited us just fine. Rónán, bless his heart, agreed to pay her wages until payday, when we could reimburse him.

About two weeks later, Sarah reported to us that Jenny was pregnant. Jenny was adamant that the child was Kenny's. Rónán gave Kenny the good news. But Kenny refused to believe that the child was his, and he spluttered through his tears that Jenny was "unclean" and thus unfit to be his wife because she had caught the oyster from Hoggs. Kenny remained obdurate on the point, and no amount of persuasion, remonstration, or argument moved him one iota off it.

Over the next several weeks, Rónán, Hermann, and I took care never to be caught alone outside the regimental digs when we were off duty, particularly at night. We continued to watch Kenny like hawks, lest he succumb to some suicidal impulse or another. Jenny remained with the Great Western, secluded and unapproachable among the women of the Seventh. I caught a glimpse of her one day. Her belly had just begun to swell, or so I thought, and her cheeks remained hollow and her eyes terribly haunted. Hermann and Rónán both shook their heads sadly, when I told them that just glimpsing her tore my heart out. But we all agreed there was naught to be done about it for now, so we contented ourselves with remaining on guard for the revenge that Hoggs would inevitably exact.

I was the luckiest of the four of us. I spent hours each day away from the company, either down at the *corrales* or with Grant, rehearsing Desdemona's protestations and dramaturgies until I once again knew the Moor's play from stem to stern. All of this rehearsing raised a question for me, which I asked Grant in the most innocent way possible.

"Sir, how is Lieutenant Porter playing the Moor?"

"Eh?" Grant's eyes were closed as he silently mouthed some passage or another of Desdemona's—probably the one where she defends the Moor even as he so tragically kills her. "What's that?"

"How does Lieutenant Porter play the Moor?"

"Why, as a Moor, of course."

"I understand, sir, but is the Moor an Arab or a Negro in the Lieutenant's eyes?" I kept my tone as noncommittal as I could.

Grant stared at me as if I were quite mad. I probably was, but …

"I haven't a clue. I hadn't thought of the matter. But I'm sure Prince John'll have a view. He always does."

"Of course, sir."

I spent many an hour playing opposite Grant, variously as Othello, the evil Iago, the besotted Cassio, the bamboozled Emilia, and others—not that I minded it at all. During those couple of weeks, we talked about everything under the sun—except Hoggs and Jenny, of course. One day, he even told me that he had an offer in hand to teach mathematics at a well-endowed college at some place called Hillsboro, Ohio. If Julia were willing, Grant said, he would resign his commission in a minute, race to St. Louis, marry her, and carry her off to Ohio and live out the rest of his days as a professor of mathematics.

Grant made Hillsboro sound like a wonderful corner of God's green earth—wherever Ohio was—and I often wondered over the next several years why in the Sam Hill Grant hadn't resigned his commission right then and there and taken the job. It would have saved him a tolerable amount of heartache if he had done so.

Moreover, helping Grant rehearse his lines as Desdemona, which he delivered in a wonderful falsetto to great effect, assuaged the growing hunger I had for the world of books and learning. My dog-eared copy of *The Last of the Mohicans* and an occasional newspaper were nowhere near enough to satisfy me.

It was a frosty and brilliantly clear Sunday morning just before Christmas when Hermann and I once again borrowed a pair of horses from our *caporal*'s friend and made our way to *la Casa de Las Corrientes de Golondrinas*. Pedro, the same retainer who had first summoned Hermann and me to Sunday dinner with Colonel Kinney and don Guillermo those many weeks ago, greeted us at the entrance to the casa. *Las dos señoritas* had detailed him nearly two hours ago, Pedro told us, to wait for us by the main gate to the casa and greet us the very instant that we arrived. He smiled indulgently when he said that he had known *las señoritas* since they were born, and he had known doña Alandra since they were both small children. His father and mother had served doña Alandra's parents' family as loyal retainers since before he and doña Alandra was born. Pedro and his wife Maria came with doña Alandra to *la Casa de Las Corrientes de Golondrinas* when doña Alandra married don Guillermo.

Doña Alandra greeted Hermann and me warmly at the entrance to her casa by offering us a cool drink of water from the *tinaja* hanging from the *portal*. Despite the chill of the early morning, the sun had grown hot during our transit. We were both dusty and thirsty, and glad to wet our whistles. Señoritas Calandria and Serafina made their appearance within a minute or two. During the meal, Serafina took advantage of every opportunity to lovingly make eyes at Hermann whenever doña Alandra's attention was drawn away, which it was in turn by the conspiratorial Calandria and dealing with her servants who kept bringing course after magnificent course. I was amused to see that despite the intense attraction between the two of them, Serafina was still very much *una mujer decente*, for she was not so brazen as to actually meet Hermann's eye. Hermann was similarly circumspect. Calandria did not make such eyes anywhere in my direction. Indeed, when she wasn't providing distraction for her sister, she kept me off balance with small jabs of her wit, each of which was inevitably followed closely by flirtatious remark that threatened to, but never quite did, transgress into a physical invitation I would likely have taken, all caution to the wind.

It was a happy meal until Calandria mentioned that her *papá* was due home within the week, just in time to celebrate *la Natividad* with the family. As Calandria cheerfully prattled on, a cloud of pain—or was it anxiety—passed across doña Alandra's brow, and she silently crossed herself. I thought little enough of it at the time. After dinner, doña Alandra allowed Calandria and me to walk alone through the courtyard and out beyond the *corrales* to a huge mesquite tree. As we approached, we heard a girl's giggle and a man's laugh. Calandria put her hand to her mouth as we caught sight of Hermann and Serafina kissing—an unheard of liberty, she later told me. But she was happy for her sister, she said, because her sister was very deeply in love with Hermann.

Later, as we rode back to the encampment and reality, Hermann once again had a dreamy look to his eye, much as he did when we had last ridden back. He spoke of how a man could make a living in this dry and forbidding land if he had *eine starke Dame*—a good, strong woman, he translated—at his side. I remained as ambivalent as ever about Calandria, at once lusting after her and yet, paradoxically, cool to her charms.

⌒

Christmas passed quickly, and there were horse races on New Year's Day. The touts made a tidy killing on the races from the army's doughboys, whose pockets were full from a pre-Christmas payday. It had been the first payday for Hermann and me since we'd signed up in Gotham back in August, and we'd paid Rónán back for our share of our mess cook's wages. As December began to slide into January, Hermann and I kept our heads low to avoid Hoggs. I spent most of my days very pleasantly indeed, with our *corrida*, training mules and working on the Conestoga wagons. My Spanish grew better by leaps and bounds, and I learned to appreciate mules as a species unto themselves, although my knowledge of such matters paled before Grant's skills. Mules are as tough (and stubborn) as donkeys, virtually as big as horses and seemingly stronger—howbeit with none of the common equine frailties, for they were able to haul great loads over long distances, whether by pack or as part of a team hauling a Conestoga wagon.

It was funny to see the differences between how we Americans thought and how our Mexican *arrieros* and *carreteros* thought. One day, at Grant's direction, I greased the axles to the Conestoga wagons to make the wheels turn more easily. Juan Pablo looked on the greasing process with ill-concealed horror, saying that the grease looked positively poisonous, and even if it was not poisonous, it was not necessary to lubricate the *carretos*, which made them far more practical than the Conestoga wagon in the wastelands of south Texas. I reflected to myself afterwards that Juan Pablo was probably right about *los carretos* being better suited to the exigencies of the trans-Nueces. But it was a lot easier on the ears to be driving a Conestoga wagon than a *carreta* because the wheels did not harshly squeal with every turn as they rumbled over the prairie.

It was over this Christmas period that, after several weeks of Grant rehearsing with me in private, the day came for him to don crinolines and a dress to play the part of Desdemona on the newly erected stage of the Army Theater, opposite his good friend, Theodric Porter, who was to play the great Othello himself (his face suitably blackened for an effect not dissimilar to that of a minstrel pacing the boards at the old Bowery Theater). When I walked into the half-finished theater, there were two officers whom I did not know on stage rehearsing their lines as Cassio and Iago. Grant, who was in a gingham dress (presumably his costume), sans his wig and (incongruously) smoking a cigar through several days growth of beard, sat on a stool in the wings watching Cassio and Iago sing the praises of Desdemona:

CAS.

Welcome, Iago; we must to the watch.

IAGO.

Not this hour, lieutenant; 'tis not yet ten o'clock. Our general cast us thus early, for the love of his Desdemona; whom let us not therefore blame; he hath not yet made wanton the night with her; and she is sport for Jove.

With seemingly every man in the theater looking at him, Grant pulled the cigar from his mouth and rolled his eyes coquettishly at the praise.

CAS.

She's a most exquisite lady.

IAGO.

And, I'll warrant her, full of game.

Longstreet, who had been watching from the audience, jumped up onto the stage, slid onto a stool next to Grant, elbowed him in the ribs and whispered into his ear. Grant almost coughed his cheroot out with laughter and turned beet red.

CAS.

Indeed, she is a most fresh and delicate creature.

Grant rose briefly as Longstreet began guffawing, and he curtsied to the rows of empty benches in the audience. Prince John, who as the director, was sitting in the center of the front bench, positively bit his lip in an effort not to laugh.

IAGO.

What an eye she has! Methinks it sounds a parley of provocation.

Grant waved at the imaginary audience in mock disapproval of Iago's sentiment.

CAS.

An inviting eye; and yet, methinks, right modest.

Grant pretended to hide his face.

IAGO.

And, when she speaks, is it not an alarm to love?

CAS.

She is, indeed, perfection.

Longstreet threw a lady's fan to Grant, who promptly began fanning himself.

IAGO.

Well, happiness to their sheets!

Iago stopped for effect, and everyone in the theater clapped. Grant rose in response to the applause and curtsied in a most pretty fashion that would have been creditable in the finest of girls' finishing schools. Porter appeared out of the wings at all the commotion, his mouth a grinning rictus through the ridiculous blackface. He stood next to Grant, and turned positively green about the gills at the prospect of even a theatrical coupling between Othello and the fair Desdemona.

It was a couple of days before I saw Grant again. He had gone off to our supply depot at St. Joseph's Island to see about uniforms for us bluebellies. We were starting to look a little threadbare, and Garland looked askance at us at parade every morning. Grant had loafed around to the *corrales* to see how Juan Pablo and I were coming along with the mules and repairs to one of the wagons. I asked him how rehearsals were going.

Grant chewed on his unlit cheroot, and said, "Well, Gogan, I've been fired." He raised his hand before I could say anything. "It wasn't because I didn't know my lines. You drilled them into my skull in a right fine fashion. Prince John told me that it was Porter. Apparently, my good friend Teddy Porter protested that a male heroine, even as one as comely as I, could not properly support the character. He protested to Prince John that he could not feel the proper sentiment from me in his development of Othello's character."

I did my best to look as serious as possible.

"Well, apparently," Grant continued, oblivious to me, "they've sent to New Orleans for a Mrs. Hart, who's played the part before, in the Indian Wars in Florida." Grant lit his cheroot and said, "Just think, Gogan. You've lost all hope of ever seeing your lieutenant in crinolines."

With a smile and twinkle in his eye, Grant departed. I never did bother to correct his misapprehension of the facts.

⌒

# CHAPTER 7

# Bucking the Tiger

SOME WAG TOLD ME LATER THAT Grant's selection to play Desdemona was a put-up job. Prince John wanted to engender support from fellow officers reluctant to bear the inevitable tab for an invitation to Mrs. Hart. I didn't believe it. Grant was too good an actor and more than sufficiently believable as the tragic heroine (even if he occasionally did need a shave).

That said, Mrs. Hart was an actress of great beauty and virtue who had appeared in many productions in lonely army encampments in Florida during the '30s, when she was hardly more than a debutante, as well as in a wonderful set of performances at Fort Jesup a couple of winters back, or so the grapevine maintained. She had been sojourning in New Orleans, between engagements, so she was very pleased to accept Prince John's invitation. Moreover, it was said, she had played the part of Desdemona in her youth and was well-suited for the part— for an older woman, so the Great Western sniffed. Within a couple of weeks Mrs. Hart had arrived, and she was despite her years immediately the toast of the officers of the Army of Occupation, in great demand for dinner in the various regimental messes. Mrs. Hart had earned her status in no small part because as a widow she was quite literally the only "respectable" unmarried lady this side of New Orleans. There were a few officers' wives in camp. But there was not a single eligible lady insofar as the pumpkin rinds were concerned. Virtually none of them would deign to look twice at a *tejana*, no matter how beautiful she was. Too bad for them, I thought, fixing Calandria's seductive look in my mind's eye.

All this was discussed in a rather salacious and tittering conversation with the Great Western one evening as I was visiting her and taking a look-see at how Jenny was doing. Jenny was still not talking much. But she smiled a little, now, and the pain in her eyes had seemed to ease markedly, a view that Sarah confirmed once Jenny had disappeared out of apparent earshot. There was little I could do about Hoggs, who without being obvious about it was thankfully keeping a wary distance from the members of our mess as we discharged our various fatigue details and participated in the few parades and drills being held now that the holidays had passed.

Of far more interest to me was Rouquette's purse. The grapevine had been buzzing for weeks about it overflowing with all the honey he'd been reaping from his various crooked faro and dice games. Every time I'd brought up the notion of easing the covey of his riches, both Hermann and Sarah had cut me dead. When I raised the topic this time, as polite as could be, Sarah smiled as prettily as she must have for Rouquette (I couldn't bring myself to think of him by his self-proclaimed moniker of "Carambole"), and I once again understood why the poor man had been so distracted. Sarah saved me from my own distraction by sharply telling me to "pay attention or I'll knock you in the chatterers." She sniffed, "Anyways, you'd hardly know what to do if you was to try to roll me … you're a regular Doctor Green, you are … Too green for the likes of me."

"So you say."

"Well, even if you did know what to do …" Sarah tossed her head. "I'm saving myself for our good friend Mr. Wurster. It just wouldn't be proper for you'n'me to …"

"A very good reason to stay friends." And an equally good reason not to peach to the Western about Serafina, although given Hermann's being such a square cove, I was sure that the Western already knew all about the beautiful *tejana*. If she did, I mused, high marks to her for not asking me about it as I gossiped to her about Calandria.

"True enough," she replied archly. "If only to draw a little sweet honey from Carambole's roll."

"Why now?" I asked suspiciously.

"We need the rhino," she replied flatly. "For Jenny."

"So we do. What about Hermann?"

She looked at me with tolerant glint in her eye. "Don't you trouble yourself on that account. You just be a good little confidence man and help me draw some of that sweet honey from Carambole's roll."

"Well, that's the issue, isn't it? Hitting on a con."

"Hitting on a con?" Sarah asked drily. She occasionally failed to appreciate my Big Onion patter. I couldn't imagine why.

I translated for her. "Running a confidence game of our own that wins." She didn't reply. "I won't be able to simply buck the tiger with Rouquette." Sarah looked at me blankly. "He runs a skinning," I explained patiently. "A sure game … for the sharper, that is. In other words, I can't buck the odds on an already crooked game—not with any hope of succeeding."

"Then you'll just have to think of something else, won't you, my little confidence man."

Sarah must have said something to Hermann, for she sent us both to the tent city the very next Sunday afternoon to have a look-see at what Rouquette might be doing, and to formulate something of a plan to ease the poor cove of all that burdensome honey. Hoggs was apparently otherwise occupied with supervising sentries or some other such bit of military nonsense. We found Rouquette preparing to bank a faro game in the shade of an open-sided tent set up alongside the Military Retreat. He looked cool and unruffled in the shade, occasionally quaffing a drink from a tall earthenware cup as his assistants set up the faro table. Rouquette was at first glance just as Sarah had described him: an elegant man with a deportment and display of finery to match—a very baroque diamond stick pin displayed prominently above an equally fine and expensive brocaded silk waistcoat which covered a well-starched white shirt of the finest cambric sporting cufflinks that matched his diamond stick pin. He also had a quite distinguished handlebar moustache, waxed such that each long hair of it lay precisely in harmony with every other hair, all of them building to a magnificent whole that swept boldly across his face and terminated in a rakish upward curl. He was elegant at a glance. Then I looked more closely and observed a certain coarseness underneath. You could tell that the cove was a regular knight of the barrow pigs, jumped up from nowhere and aping the manners of his betters. What particular quality exuded the coarseness, I couldn't quite say. Perhaps it was his reddened forehead. (Everybody was sunburned to a deep mahogany in these parts. But Rouquette was merely red-faced—notwithstanding his unruffled demeanor—rather than tanned.) Perhaps it was his manner, which was too refined by half—except when it wasn't. I couldn't quite figure it. But the coarseness was there as surely as the sun will set in the evening. And there was another, malign quality to him, one that I couldn't quite define.

Hermann and I stood for a few minutes, studying Rouquette through the thicket of simkins gathering around the faro table and fairly straining to fling their brass on the green baize tablecloth—on which were emblazoned representations of the thirteen playing cards, where coins and markers were to be dropped indicating the cards on which a punter was betting. The punters were mostly regulars leavened by a civilian or two. They were rough-looking characters who, I imagined, might have been Texas Rangers armed with Colt's Paterson repeating pistols and giant Arkansas toothpicks. You'd have thought that they would have been familiar enough with New Orleans and riverboat gambling to have steered a wide berth around Rouquette's little den of iniquity. But I won't admit that I was at all surprised by the ruck in front of Rouquette's table. If my months in Gotham had taught me anything, it was that as a general proposition, Americans— rich, poor, native, Irish, colored, or German—were always ready to be skinned of their children's milk money at dice and cards in return for a moment's thrill in some gambling hell.

Rouquette's assistants finished their preparations by placing a silver-plated faro spring box on the table, directly in front of an elaborately carved oak chair cushioned on the back and seat with red velvet. It was probably the only chair like it west of the Sabine River, and certainly the only chair like it in Corpus Christi. With a bit of a flourish, Rouquette opened a polished wooden box handed to him by one of his assistants and placed it next to the faro box. Inside was Rouquette's bank, heavy with gold eagles, double eagles, and myriad smaller coins. The crowd gasped at the richness of it.

I leaned over to Hermann and said quietly, "That's for show. His purse'll either be in his inside coat pocket ... or more likely it'll be tied around his waist, under his vest."

Hermann didn't answer as he continued to survey the goings-on.

Rouquette raised his hand and everyone became still.

"My bene culls." Rouquette gestured theatrically at the faro box. "I am very proud to announce the arrival of the latest improvements to the well-known 'Fair Dealer of Charae Lusoriae,' the squarest faro-dealing box in these here United States. Why, Uncle Sam himself, all the way up in Washington City on the Potomac, he's granted the inventor a fresh patent on these improvements." Rouquette took a sip from his earthenware cup, surveyed the crowd, and then pointed to the bank. "Boys, there can be no question about it. This is the richest bank west of the Sabine. Who wants a bit of it?"

The ruck of doughboys boiled with enthusiasm and surged towards the table, only to be pushed back by a couple of well-worn looking milling coves, likely the toughs Sarah had mentioned.

Rouquette concluded his speech. "It's a square game, boys. You can bank on it."

The crowd cheered and strained once more against the milling coves. Rouquette raised his hand one more time. "But this ain't no 'summer game' played with ma and pa or your best girl. Yes sir, my bene coves, you can make a month's pay with a single turn of a card ... two months, maybe ... So, who's ready to play?"

Rouquette pointed to four men, three of them regular army and the fourth a Texas Ranger by the outlandish look of him. Suffice it to say that the Texian would never have passed a uniform inspection by any regular army sergeant I'd ever known. The four punters sat without further ado and placed their markers on the cloth representations of the cards they were betting on.

Faro is a simple game, which is why it is so easy to cheat—as either a punter or a dealer. Punters may bet on any one of the thirteen cards painted on the baize tablecloth. When all bets have been placed, the dealer draws off the top card face up off a shuffled deck. When a faro box is used, the shuffled deck is placed face up in the faro box, which is then closed. The dealer slides the top card out through an opening in the side of the box—ostensibly to render cheating impossible. If a punter bet on that card, then he wins from the bank an amount equal to his bet. The dealer then draws a second card. Any punter betting on that card loses unless the second card is the same as the first card, in which case the dealer calls a split, and the bank takes only half the money bet on that card. The dealer then calls for fresh bets to be placed, and the process begins anew. It is a fast-paced game, and a flat can find himself broke in just a few minutes—even if he is betting only a penny or nickel at a time.

The Texian seemed to be doing pretty well. He survived three rounds of bluebellies, all of whom lost their stakes within a few minutes, only to be promptly replaced by new simkins eager to lose their chink. I began to think that the Texian might be a capper, because he was running quite a shoestring. In other words, I thought that he might be in league with Rouquette, allowed to win simply to encourage the other simkins, who to a man were still fairly straining to bet their money at the faro table.

But I was wrong about the Texian. The cards turned, and he began to lose badly, doubling down on his bets until he had lost to Rouquette's bank all that he had won and then quite a bit more. By this time, Hermann and I had worked our way through the press of flats so that I was standing hardly more than a foot or so from the Texian's shoulder. Hermann brushed past me.

I murmured, "Watch the play. Something's going to break here."

Hermann nodded and stopped a couple of feet away from me. I looked over the Texian's shoulder at the table with what I hoped was an expression of unconcerned bemusement. As I did, I caught a whiff of cheap whiskey on the breath of some cove who pushed past me. It smelled every bit as toxic as the "aged Binghamton whiskey" flogged by Con Donoho in his Five Points lushery. And then I smelled the liquor on the Texian. Someone must have been operating an impromptu boozing ken somewhere, which at least partly accounted for why the mobocracy was as game as pebbles to lose their chink.

The Texian rumbled to his feet. As I danced clear, I could feel him vibrating with booze-fueled rage. The Texian fixed his eyes on Rouquette, and announced to the ruck of doughboys, "This here scalawag's been skinning us."

Someone behind me cried, "Is he on the mace?"

You could have heard a pin drop in the sudden silence.

Then came scattered howls of rage, "A sharper, is he? Scrag the fucker. There's a tree around here somewhere."

There was a rustle of support for the proposition, and a shadow crossed Rouquette's eyes. But it was gone quicker than it appeared as he rose to his feet. "Boys, he's just sore. Look at the poor wretch ... He's been losing steady. If you can't stand the heat ..."

There were a couple of laughs, but the mood of the ruck remained surly.

Rouquette coolly searched the crowd and alighted on me. "Say, boys, let's have this kinchin cove here look at the box." Rouquette pointed directly at me. "He can tell us that it ain't no sharper's tool."

Someone in the ruck shouted, "How do we know he ain't no capper?"

I heard Hermann bellow in a thick Dutchy accent, "I know him. He is just a kid over in the Fourth. He does not know anything. He is a duncehead. A dumb mick."

The crowd laughed and then cheered, while I bowed as grandiloquently as I could.

"Come on over here, kid." Rouquette beckoned me to his red velvet cushioned chair.

"I gotta operate this thing?" I gawped at the ruck and blinked slowly. Inwardly, I thanked Charlie Backwell, God rest his soul or wherever he was, for my education.

"Sure, kid. It's simple. Just slip the card through here." Rouquette slipped a card out. "But, first, let's use a fresh history of the four kings." Rouquette pulled a second deck of playing cards from a tray next to the faro box and shuffled them. He was very good, and he impressed the bluebellies with his show. I could feel their surliness begin to dissipate as Rouquette smiled and said, "You can't cheat with a shuffle like this, boys."

He nonchalantly opened the box to put the shuffled cards inside.

"Say there, bub," I exclaimed.

"Who you calling …?" Rouquette snapped straight and glared at me.

I looked him in the eye. It had probably been years since someone had addressed him thusly. The crowd tittered. But I knew I had Rouquette. I had recognized the trick in the box as soon as he had opened it, because Charlie had once shown me a box exactly like it.

"What's this here?" I grabbed the faro box and slid loose the safety catch on the inside of the lid, all the while staring Rouquette in the eye.

A fifty-third card fluttered out and dropped onto the baize tablecloth. There was a brief instant of quiet, as Hermann sidled up next to Rouquette. Hermann broke the silence, yelling, "That *verdammt* scalawag is cheating."

The ruck exploded in rage, instantly swallowing the two milling coves who had been edging around to support Rouquette. Hermann flung himself onto Rouquette, who crumpled to the ground under the onslaught.

I shouted, "Here boys," as I grabbed the bank and flung the reservoir of eagles and double eagles high into the air. Everyone—except Hermann, who was busy smothering Rouquette, and the doughboys busy pummeling the milling coves—was instantly captivated by the spectacle of a couple score of gold coins flying through the air.

I turned away from the sudden rush of the falling coins to see Hermann motion Rouquette to his feet and say in what must have been nearly a bellow, but instead sounded like mere *sotto voce*, "Get moving. And get out of town … unless you do want to be scragged …"

Rouquette looked at Hermann strangely, muttered "Thanks," and absquatulated without giving a second look at his milling coves, who were drowning under a hail of fists, brick bats, and cudgels that included the splintered remains of Rouquette's carved oak chair.

I looked at Hermann, who nodded very slightly, and I yelled, "Hey, boys! The sharper! He's getting away! He's taken a read and write!" Hermann looked at me oddly. "He's escaping!" I repeated. "Thataway!" I pointed about 90 degrees away from the direction in which Rouquette had fled.

"Let's go." Hermann grabbed my elbow and guided me from the tent. We had gone hardly ten paces, when Hermann pushed me roughly out of the way of a horse and rider thundering due west, into the prairie. I glanced up to see Rouquette accelerating away from the hue and cry of the ruck that was now boiling out of the tent into the dusty street.

I looked at Hermann and said, "I sure hope for his sake that the fellow doesn't have a queer prancer."

Hermann looked at me impatiently.

"A bad horse."

Hermann and I slipped away as quietly as we could from the bedlam (which was quelled only when the officer of the day turned out the guard—fifty men from the Third Infantry—who had to drive the rioting bluebellies at bayonet point from the tent city into the mesquite brush before they calmed down.) We wandered about seemingly aimlessly until I realized that Hermann had guided us to a deserted bit of beach. As we stood beside the water lapping gently at the white sand, Hermann handed me a purse. I stared at it in shock until I realized that Hermann must have reefed Rouquette's leather when he fell on him.

The purse contained a cool $200. If the truth were to be known, I wouldn't have minded trying to steal the bank itself, but that would have been impossible—and greedy. Anyway, I took quite a bit of pride in having distributed so much wealth to so many bluebellies.

The next day, *Othello* opened at the Army Theater to general acclaim. Gone of course was Grant from the part of Desdemona, having been replaced by Mrs. Hart. Gone also was Porter as Othello, replaced by a fellow rendered unrecognizable by his cork-blackened face. What part the Immortal Bard may have had in writing this play was a complete mystery to me, for there was nary a line I recognized.

Indeed, Brabantio challenged Othello:

> O you black thief! Where have you hid my daughter?
> Damn'd as thou art, to whose house have you brought
> her? Where are your love-powders? How dare you use
> 'em to coax my Desdy to your sooty bosom!

Othello sang his defense of courting and marrying Desdemona before the Duke and Senate to the tune of *Yankee Doodle*:

> Potent, grave, and rev'rend sir,
>     Very noble massa—
> When de maid a man prefer
>     Den him no can pass her.
> Yes, it is most werry true,
>     Him take dis old man's daughter;
> But no by spell, him promise you,
>     But by fair means him caught her.
>
> 'Tis true she lub him berry much,
>     'Tis true dat off him carry her,
> And dat him lub for her is such,
>     'Tis werry true him marry her.
> All dis be true—and till him dead,
>     Him lub her widout ending—
> And dis, my massa, is the head
>     And tail of him offending.

When Mrs. Hart took the stage as "Desdy" later in the same scene, the applause was so thunderous and the audience of two hundred men were so besotted with Mrs. Hart's décolletage that I doubt anyone (save perhaps Grant, whom I could see from my vantage point puffing on a cigar) heard Brabantio's challenge to her:

*Come here, you slut; don't you know white from black?*

Mrs. Hart gave Branbantio a winning smile and a wiggle, winked elaborately to the audience, and sang in reply:

*You bought respect from me by many a whack;*
*But as mama loved you before her grand-father,*
*So do I better love my husband than you, father.*

I don't recall much after that, and mercifully, the play was concluded in under an hour, to five separate curtain calls, each one more thunderous than the last, as Mrs. Hart curtsied as deeply and prettily as you please. Had she been so inclined, Mrs. Hart could have set up shop backstage after the play was over and retired on the proceeds.

I ran into Colonel Kinney about a week later. He did not look happy. Instead of greeting me, he waved what appeared to be a letter in my face before stuffing it into his vest pocket.

"It is from *mi compadre*, don Guillermo." His countenance darkened with the effort of his speech. "He has chosen another path now that war is coming."

"What do you mean?"

"Chapita Sandoval brought this to me. You remember him, don't you? From dinner when we met. He was that swarthy little fellow sitting next to you."

I remembered the man, and how he had studied everyone on the shaded and fragrant *patio*, particularly don Guillermo, as Kinney and don Guillermo spoke their minds about the coming scrimmage between Mexico and Uncle Sam.

"The latest news to reach Matamoros from Mexico City is not good," Kinney told me. "There is a new *presidente*. Some fellow named Paredes. An army general. He's refused to see the American minister plenipotentiary."

"So what will happen?"

"General Taylor expects that he will be ordered south, to the Rio Grande."

So much for hopes of the army going back north. Then I remembered the letter Kinney had waved at me and asked him about it.

Kinney's face fell. "I am afraid that my old friend don Guillermo has obeyed the call of his ancestors to protect *la patria*. He has joined Juan Seguin and some of the other *tejanos* who have thrown their lot in with Canales and *los méxicanos*. Not that I can blame them for what they've done. Seguin was mayor of San Antonio de Béxar a few years back, and the Texians chased him from the home of his ancestors with death threats ... not only against him, which he could have borne, but against his family. Disgusting. Don Guillermo never forgot that, nor did he forget losing his own lands. I think that this has all eaten at him for years." Kinney shook his head. "Chapita was right. He told me weeks ago that don Guillermo was not going to come back north after he sold his sheep and wool down in Matamoros.

"My only hope for *mi compadre* is that Arista will revolt and declare *Coahuila y Tejas* south of the Nueces an independent state— and that Uncle Sam respects it as such. But that's a forlorn hope at best. Arista was the head Mexican general who captured Canales and Zapata when they tried to do just that back in '40. He had Zapata's head cut off and stuck on a pole outside his home as a warning to anyone else who tried to revolt. And after he cut off Zapata's head? Well, he offered Canales a commission in the Mexican army to buy off him and the rest of the rancheros. Canales took the commission, and he and Arista have been great pals ever since—even though Canales is a *tejano* with haciendas north of the Rio Grande and Arista is an old-style *caudillo* from central Mexico."

"If Arista doesn't revolt," I asked, "then what will become of doña Alandra and her daughters? And of *la Casa de Las Corrientes de Golondrinas?*"

"I don't know. Seguin and his boys will likely throw their lot in with *los méxicanos*. So they will rise or fall with Mexico … on the opposite side of the war from us." Kinney shook his head again. "But what I can tell you, young feller, is that you've made a mighty good impression on the Rodriguez family, particularly on doña Alandra. Both you and your compatriot …"

"Hermann," I said. "Hermann Wurster."

"Yes. Mr. Wurster. Like I said, you boys have made a mighty fine impression on them. In fact, you two ought to ride out and see doña Alandra. Your visit would be mighty appreciated."

Hermann and I sent a message to *la Casa de Las Corrientes de Golondrinas* via one of Kinney's men that we would be out there a week from the following Sunday. In the interim, General Taylor received his orders from the Washington City big bugs. We were to march south to the Rio Grande. The orders were supposed to be a secret. But everyone in camp knew within the day. Kinney sent for me and told me himself. And he made sure that Hermann and I were heading out to the house of the flow of the swallows at least once more before we made the trek south to the Rio Grande.

The day after the grapevine reported that we were to be moving south, Grant told me that he was no longer attached to the regimental quartermaster and no longer responsible for our mule teams. This meant, he said with a ghost of a smile, that I wasn't going to be riding south on a Conestoga wagon pulled by one of the teams of our mules. I was going to have to march, just like every other manjack of C Company.

The army didn't head south for another month, and Old Zach was heavily criticized after the war for not having moved faster than he did. The grapevine fairly crackled with the notion that the Old Man dithered because he didn't know the route south and hadn't planned how to get the army south to the Rio Grande. I had no truck with the notion. I always thought that he was rightly waiting for the roads to dry after the winter rains. Whatever the truth of the matter, it gave Hermann and me one more chance to visit *la Casa de Las Corrientes de Golondrinas*.

The Sunday we went was beautifully hot and dry, with nary a lick of wind. The silence of the prairie weighed heavily on us both as we rode out at dawn and began to sweat as the sun rose on our backs. Pedro once again met us at the gate to the hacienda, and we were greeted by doña Alandra at the front door just as three of the mud swallows darted past us from their nest in the beams of the house and into the bright sunlight. Calandria and Serafina joined us a couple of minutes later. They sat across the table from Hermann and me. Doña Alandra sat at one end of the table and don Guillermo's chair at the other end remained empty, although a place was set for him. It was as if he had been unaccountably delayed in the paddock and was expected to join us at any moment.

Lunch was a curiously subdued affair, and the conversation desultory. As soon as coffee had been served, doña Alandra withdrew, complaining of a headache. The omnipresent Pedro and his wife Maria (who normally seemed to hover silently in the background making sure that every function in the casa ran smoothly) also took a powder once the remains of lunch had disappeared. The four of us were left with our earthenware mugs of cool water and the soft fluttering of the swallows in the rafters.

Serafina whispered something into Hermann's ear. He smiled and said airily (or as airily as he could manage) that he and Serafina were going for a walk.

I drank off the water in my mug in a fit of compulsiveness that momentarily filled the sudden intimacy between Calandria and me— it being the first time that we had ever been in a room alone together.

Calandria soundlessly stood up from her chair across the table, refilled my mug and then sat in the chair next to me and turned towards me, our knees all but touching—as if it were the most natural thing to do. A wave of jasmine perfume rolled gently over me, and I then and there conceived a violent desire to make love to Calandria.

She smiled at me. I swallowed.

"Let's walk out to the stables." Calandria took my hand.

The cicadas buzzed loudly in my ears as we walked hand-in-hand through the deserted courtyard and out the gate and over to the stable, past the paddock where Hermann's and my horses stood with the Rodriguez horses, baking under the hot sun and lazily snapping their tails at the horseflies and bluebottles. Calandria and I swept around into the cool interior of the stable. We were suddenly very close. I could feel her slightness in my arms. The buzzing grew louder in my ears, and we kissed.

After an exquisite moment, I drew back and looked Calandria in the eye. "You are ..."

She touched her finger to my lips. "Shh."

I began again, this time in Spanish. "I have to say this ... you are *una mujer decente*. There are things you shouldn't be doing. This is one of them."

She returned my look, penetrating me to my very core. "These are changing times."

"But ..."

"I have had my *quince años*."

I must have looked at her quizzically.

"I am a woman now."

She shivered slightly in my arms, and I kissed her again until she was still once more, leaning gently into me.

"You are a good man," Calandria said in Spanish. "*Mamá* and *papá* say that you will make *un buen marido*."

"Your parents are wrong. I'm a soldier. A doughboy making seven dollars a month." I grimaced. "I'm not fit for polite company. Not now. Maybe never."

"You are wrong. You told *mamá* and me about yourself and your family. *Tu mamá*, taken so young ... *y tu papá* ... such a brave man to stand up to those wicked ... what did you call them?"

"*Sassenagh.*"

"And you are no mere doughboy, as you call yourself. You are so much more. *Un hombre de bien. Papá* says that's what you were in *Irelanda*. And that's what you can be here. A *hacendado*."

Quite a compliment, that. Doña Alandra had explained to me one afternoon that *los hombres de bien* were the backbone of Mexican society. Men of education, "virtue," and "honor," who governed *la patria* for the benefit of the poorer masses. At least that's what she told me.

Calandria was speaking again in Spanish. Her tone was so soft as to be almost a whisper. "*Papá* has no sons to protect *la Casa de Las Corrientes de Golondrinas* for the next generation. You can be that man. A *norteamericano* who can beat the *rinches* and the Texians at their own game. You can protect our hacienda."

"You hardly know me."

"Let me finish. I know you well enough. *Papá* may never come home. He may die at the hands of *los norteamericanos*. We need you." Tears glistened in her eyes. "I need you."

I kissed her again, and she yielded to my touch. I knew then as a moral certainty that she was giving herself to me, and that she was mine to do with as I pleased. But I could not have her that way. Not now ... Not yet.

"I have to go away ... with the army."

She cut me off before I could say anymore. "I know. But you will come back." Stated as fact, and not as a question.

"Yes, I will." All doubt was gone, and I could now see myself—and Hermann, too—passing the rest of our days as *hacendados* here on the south bank of the Nueces River. Dear God, I was happy.

CHAPTER 8

# My Aching Feet

⌐

[Editor's note: The original manuscript contains two letters as part of this chapter, one from Billy to Calandria and another to Evelyn. Both letters were dated the same day and had been edited to be virtually identical.]

April 10, 1846

Dear [Evelyn] [Calandria]:

My apologies for not writing earlier, but the army has been on the march. We are now presently encamped on the north bank of the Rio Grande, just across from the Mexican city of Matamoros. We arrived yesterday and raised Old Glory on the bank of the Rio Grande for the very first time, as the band of the 8th Infantry Regiment played *Yankee Doodle*. I heard one of the officers grumbling that the entire army should have paraded in a formal pass in review in honor of the occasion. But I was happy to avoid several hours of preparing for such a parade, not to mention the several more hours that we doughboys would have had to have spent in formation while the army's big bugs attended to all of the formal military niceties that inevitably accompany such an occasion.

That said, the Mexican civilians on the other side of the river seem as friendly and as unwarlike as could be. We are safe for now, and many of us still hope that there will be no war. But if there is to be war, I shall do my duty and see myself safely through until …

The army left Corpus Christi in early March in a grand style. The fifes and drums played *The Girl I Left Behind Me*, and every manjack sang the lyrics. As we marched off, I thought of you:

> *I'm lonesome since I crossed the hill*
> *And o'er the hill and valley*
> *Such heavy thoughts my heart do fill*
> *since parting from Sally*
> *I seek no more the fine and gay*
> *For each but does remind me*
> *How swift the hours did pass with—*
> *The girl I left behind me.*

Our regiment, the Fourth Infantry, was among the last to leave. As we marched away, I took a glance back at the field where the white tents housing four thousand American soldiers had been pitched until so recently. The plain was utterly bereft of any hint that humans had ever visited—except for the complete lack of any vegetation. The dust swirled where the grass had been beaten away by marching men, and every lick of mesquite for as far as you could see had vanished into our campfires over the winter (other than the magnificent old tree sheltering the graves of those who had died of disease and misadventure in the months since *Dayton* exploded and sank). Somebody calculated that the army had been encamped along the bay for seven months and eleven days. As much as many of us are ambivalent—to say the least—about the prospect of war, few of us were sorry to see the last of the camp, if only because leaving it will bring us home to our families and loved ones that much sooner.

It had not rained for more than a month when we left, and the prairie was choked with dust as we marched. There wasn't much water for the first several days, and we suffered mightily with thirst as the sun rose to broil us in our dark blue uniforms. On the second or third morning, we started marching before dawn. As the sun rose, we saw what we thought could have been ranges of blue mountains and lakes fringed with trees along the far-off horizon. But this beautiful and exceedingly alluring vista was nothing but a mirage that vanished as the sun rose higher, leaving the harsh and flat prairie for as far as the eye could see, leavened only by occasional ponds—which were not fresh water, but instead an alkali soup that burned the mouth of more than one doughboy who fell out of ranks (much to the dismay of the sergeants involved) to slake his thirst and replenish his canteen.

One afternoon, a herd of thousands of horses appeared from the west. We could see the dust and hear the thundering of hooves long before we could see the horses. Some big bug thought that the entire Mexican cavalry had come to attack us. We stopped marching and formed lines to meet the charge. In the end, though, we stood at attention, frozen in our two slender ranks of blue, watching the herd slip past us, led by a magnificent white stallion that snorted in sympathy with the suddenly restive horses ridden by our officers.

Lieutenant Grant, who as I've mentioned before, is a magnificent horseman, kept his mount under control. But one or two others had to lay the spurs and crops onto their mounts to break the spell cast by the stallion as he vanished across the prairie, followed by a thousand equally free mustangs. One of the camp followers fell from her horse, which ran off to join the herd, its saddle slowly slipping off. The woman had been carrying all of her worldly possessions in a pair of big saddle bags, and they had slowly spilled onto the south Texas prairie as the horse vanished over the horizon, dragging the saddle and bags as it went. As we started marching again, the woman was helped into a wagon. She sat next to the teamster, sobbing at her loss, as the wagon resumed its southward journey.

⌒

# CHAPTER 9

# The Patrol

⌒

WHAT I DIDN'T TELL EITHER Evelyn or Calandria was that it took three weeks marching in the choking alkali dust of an early south Texas spring to reach the Rio Grande, sweltering every step of the way in heavy woolen blouses buttoned up over our leather stocks. We carried everything we owned on our backs save for our muskets. We marched with that ten pounds of wood and iron at shoulder arms, as there were far too many big bugs about for us to carry them at the trail. On long marches such as this, a good company first sergeant or company commander should curry favor with the regimental quartermaster for a bit of room in one of the supply wagons for the knapsacks, each of which weighed about sixty pounds. But there was no such luck on this trek south. The army was so short of Conestoga wagons that we bluebellies did not get our usual allotment of space, on account of it all having been taken up with food for the march, ammunition, and our shoulder straps' baggage. Although we had some mule trains driven mostly by *norteños*, there were nowhere near enough. There were, however, enough *carreteros* and *arrieros* in and around Corpus Christi to have given all of us a ride down south to the río Bravo and saved us the long, hot march. But the big bugs were leery of using *carretos méxicanos* to supplement the wagon trains. Rónán, ever the contrarian, maintained that he'd rather carry his knapsack than hear that dreadful squealing of unlubricated wheels all the way from the Nueces to the Rio Grande. He then complained in almost the same breath that we doughboys were bound up like barrels while we marched south, unable to breathe from the straps of our knapsacks and haversacks, and smelling of wet wool soaked with rancid sweat.

Actually, if the truth be known, we didn't march. We walked. It would have been the death of every manjack in the army, other than the shoulder straps and the Second Dragoons, who had the luxury of being on horseback, to have marched in lockstep at 90 steps per minute to a monotonous drum and a shrill fife, carrying all that weight in the heat and the dust. But walking was bad enough. Our misery was compounded by a virtually complete lack of fresh water along the way. The only water we received from the time we left Corpus Christi until we reached the Arroyo Colorado, nearly 150 miles south, was from water barrels transported all the way from Corpus Christi in some of the Conestoga wagons, which meant that we were only able to replenish our canteens once a day. Indeed, I remember there being more than one day on the march when we never saw a single water wagon.

Notwithstanding the almost constant thirst, the march nonetheless gave me a lot of time to think. Mostly I contemplated the pleasant fantasy of that pretty *tejana* who had seemingly pledged herself to me. But as I did, Evelyn kept coming to mind, rather like Banquo to Macbeth's feast. I temporarily resolved my dilemma by sending letters to both Evelyn and Calandria once we had pitched our tents in the muddy cornfields overlooking the Rio Grande.

But Calandria and Evelyn were not the sole tenants of my thoughts. As unwelcome as it was, I also spent a lot of time contemplating Hoggs's newly reinvigorated persecution of me—and of Kenny O'Leary. Hermann and Rónán did their best to shield the two of us, but with only limited success. My first contretemps with Hoggs occurred early in the march as I gathered firewood one evening, just out of earshot of our encampment. During these past weeks of Hoggs's curious passivity I had grown slack (as had Rónán and Hermann) about keeping a watchful eye on Hoggs's whereabouts.

"Hey, turdball ..."

I whipped around, on guard for a sudden assault. Hoggs smiled grimly at me, but did nothing more. When I realized that I was not about to be attacked, I groaned audibly, at once irritated with myself and disappointed with Hoggs's renewed in interest in me.

"Yes, Sergeant?" I made sure that I sounded long-suffering in my patience at having to deal with this slightly deficient non-commissioned officer.

Hoggs got close enough for me to receive a blast of his sour breath. "You're naught but a walking stiff, Gogan. One day, I'm going to quash you just as sure as God makes little yellow daisies."

I replied sarcastically, if conversationally, so that no one else but Hoggs could hear me, "Pray tell me, Sergeant, why would you want to murder me?"

"You know ..."

"I'm quite sure I don't know, Sergeant."

Hoggs's face twisted with exasperation and mounting rage. "The leather."

"Sergeant?"

"Rouquette's leather ..." Hoggs seemed to extrude the hissed words as if he were some sort of industrial machine.

"Rouquette, did you say?" I replied. "Don't know the cove, Sergeant." I shook my head. "No, I don't know him. Don't know anything about a leather, either, Sergeant. Did it have any chink in it?" I made to turn away as if I were dismissing the exchange as an odd one about a subject of absolutely no importance to me.

Hoggs grabbed my elbow. "Do not fash me, Gogan. I want the money you stole."

"I really can't help you, Sergeant. I can't give you what I don't have ... and what I didn't steal." I blandly looked him in the eye.

Hoggs grabbed my blouse.

I hissed at him. "You will fucking well lose your stripes for this, Hoggs. Grant'll see to it."

Hoggs tightened his grip and smiled viciously. "Or you'll be scragged for trying to tip me the jordan. 'Course, ye'd never take a swing at me, would you? You really are naught but a chicken-hearted turdball. Aren't you, Paddy? Yellow about the gills?"

"You want to give it whirl, me bucko?"

We glared at each other. Then it was over, and Hoggs disappeared into the gloom. When Hermann and I spoke of it later, I don't think I hid the shaking in my voice very well.

A couple of days later, the heat was particularly brutal, and our canteens had been dry since the day before. As we marched, we kept passing small pools of brackish water that advertised themselves with deceptively luscious green cattails. More than one man, heedless of the cries of his sergeants and corporals, broke ranks and ran over to one or another of these brackish pools and drank urgently, only to writhe in agony as the alkali water burned its way through him. Usually, the poor fool would promptly puke up his toes as his body tried desperately to expel the poison. As the day wore on and the heat became even worse, we grew almost punch drunk from thirst, and doughboys began to drop out in numbers. Those whom the sergeants and corporals could not kick back to their feet were left to lie semi-conscious in the dust until they were scooped up later into a few Conestoga wagons that had been pressed into emergency duty after being emptied of their water barrels. (The sudden lack of wagons carrying water accounted for why we weren't getting much to drink as we marched, which of course caused still more men to fall out as we went …)

The rest of us marched on.

Kenny O'Leary was the first in our company to fall by the wayside. We had been marching for only two or three hours when Kenny began stumbling. His face was already caked with dust and he was muttering gibberish to himself through cracked and bleeding lips. Hermann and I each grabbed him by the elbow before he could drop, and we steadied him on his feet to march along until the company was halted for a precious ten minutes or so. Kenny was still in very bad shape when we began marching again. After another hour or so, he simply gave up and sat stupidly in the dust, unresponsive to Hermann's and my trying to hoist him back to his feet. Hoggs came over and laid his switch on my shoulders. Thank God I was carrying so much equipment that he hardly touched me.

"Back in ranks, you filthy bog trotter. Wurster, leave O'Leary if he don't get up."

I looked back from where I'd rejoined the ranks. Hermann made a final effort to drag Kenny to his feet. Hoggs said something to Hermann, who promptly let Kenny slump back onto the dirt. Hermann then jogged back and fell in beside me and resumed marching, all without saying a word. I looked back again and saw Hoggs kicking Kenny and then cruelly flogging him about his head and unprotected arms with his switch. Kenny rolled away from the blows and into the underbrush by the side of the road. Hoggs walked over to where Kenny had disappeared and gave what appeared to be three or four vicious kicks, after which he walked off with a satisfied grin on his face. I quickly faced forward before Hoggs could look up to see if either Hermann or I had been watching.

That night, a wagon with full water barrels showed up, so we were able to drink a bit and refill our canteens for the next morning's march. As we lay next to our flickering campfires, shivering in sweat-sodden uniforms from the sudden cold that had come with the setting sun, Rónán let Hermann slip away from the bivouac on some trumped up fatigue detail or another, which allowed him to search for Kenny. When Hermann found the sorry procession of wagons carrying scores of heat exhaustion victims, Hoggs was already on the scene with several other sergeants from the regiment. They were busy kicking their doughboys out of the wagons and leading them off into the dark. There was nary a doctor or an officer to be found. Hermann slipped back to our bivouac and told us what he had seen.

About half an hour later, Hoggs unceremoniously dumped Kenny back by our campfire with a curt, "He's marching in the morning, the damned deadbeat."

We made sure that Kenny's canteen was full and his lips wetted, and then we rolled him in his blanket so that he wouldn't freeze in the sudden cold. We awoke the next morning to the beautiful mirage that

I wrote about in my letters to Calandria and Evelyn. But we knew of the false nature of this seeming utopia of far-off mountains and shimmering pools of water, and quite frankly paid it little mind.

At muster, Hoggs loudly told Rónán that he, Hoggs, would see Kenny ride the horse or be bucked and gagged for malingering if he fell out again today. The look in Kenny's eyes was anything but rage or even frustration. It was abject defeat. I think Hermann saw the defeat in Kenny's eyes as well. We both kept the closest eye on Kenny that we could. One of us was within arm's-length of him the entire day we marched. But we could not stay that close to him when Hoggs took charge of setting the pickets that evening as C Company was the duty company for guard. (This instead of giving the detail to Rónán, who as the company's junior sergeant was the natural choice for such duty. Hell, even Hermann or another corporal would have been more natural choices for the assignment than Hoggs, the company first sergeant.) There was naught to be done except hope for the best as Hoggs tapped Kenny and a score of others for the picket duty. Hermann, Rónán, and I looked at each other and shrugged ineffectually.

Kenny told me on the march the next day that Hoggs had appeared out of the gloom while he was standing post. Kenny charged his bayonet and challenged Hoggs properly. But Hoggs violently shoved the bayonet aside, braced Kenny to attention and delivered his ugly message: Hoggs was going to corpse him, but not before Kenny got to watch Hoggs once again take his turn in Jenny's frills—and oh, by the way, the little get in Jenny's belly was Hoggs's, because Hoggs had been doing Jenny's job for her ever since the day that she'd hove into Corpus Christi—and she was eternally grateful to him for her pleasure, according to Hoggs. Hoggs had laughed as he walked away. He'd found a new victim to torment.

When the Fourth Infantry, which had been marching as part of the rear guard, arrived at the north bank of the Arroyo Colorado, the entire rest of the army was in line at the crest of the bluff overlooking the shallow blue water of the arroyo, ready to give battle. The water looked inviting until we learned that it was brackish to a fault. The infantry regiments were standing at attention, the artillery was at the center of the line with hammers cocked, the cavalry was in reserve, and the flags were flying and the fifes screeching. Some working parties had hacked the underbrush clear from the bluff down to the water to provide a field of fire several hundred yards wide, and they were just scuttling off to the side to rejoin their units as the Fourth arrived on the scene.

As our regiment maneuvered into our designated part of the line, I saw a small ostler's wagon career wildly through the gap we were about to fill. From my vantage point, it seemed hardly possible that the wagon did not smash right into A Company, so close was the head of our column to the gap. The wagon stopped right in front of where Old Zach was palavering with General Worth and the rest of the big bees about what in Sam Hill to do next. The Great Western jumped out of the wagon as it crashed to a halt. Jenny, her growing belly and all, was left at the reins, restraining the mules, which restively pawed the ground with the excitement of the moment. None of us saw what happened next, because the regimental column began to maneuver into the line. But Jenny related the story to us when she stopped by our campfire that night to say hello to us. Kenny had ostentatiously walked off the instant she arrived. But she paid him no heed and spoke breathlessly, still full of the excitement of the day and as full of life as I'd seen her in a very long time.

Jenny told us that Sarah bounded from their wagon towards General Taylor, who was astride Old Whitey with his back turned to her. Unaware that she was there, Old Zach leaned over and spoke to Perfect Bliss, who then held up his hand. The drums and fifes fell quiet.

"Good morning, General." Sarah's greeting thundered in the sudden quiet.

Taylor whirled Old Whitey around with a look of shock on his face to see Sarah standing there, hands on her hips and her bosom heaving from having driven her ostler's wagon hard for many miles and then having run to address the big bugs. The general and his staff all reflexively touched their caps and mumbled surprised greetings to Sarah, who smiled very prettily in acknowledgement. Their horses stirred with excitement at her arrival. Sarah then turned her attention back to the Old Man, who with his battered straw hat stirring in the afternoon breeze looked as always like a gentleman farmer gone slightly to seed.

"General," she declared. "If you would be so kind as to lend me a pair of tongs, I will wade over that little ditch yonder, and I will climb up onto that damned bluff and whip any scoundrel who dares to show himself to me."

As if on cue, several bugles sounded from across the arroyo, and half a dozen or so voices started shouting in Spanish, giving highly contradictory military commands.

Taylor looked at General Worth with an air of resignation. "The forlorn hope, if you please, General."

Worth saluted and turned to one of his aides, who galloped off, post-haste.

Old Zach then said, "Major Ringgold, please see to your guns."

Ringgold saluted and galloped off to his waiting battery of six-pounders.

"Mrs. Langwell," the Old Man said in a tone of long-suffering patience as he gave a slantendicular look at Sarah's still-heaving bosom. (Jenny tittered at this point, calling the General "a naughty man.")

"Yes, General?" Sarah positively simpered, her crush on Old Zach oozing from every pore.

"Thank you for your very kind offer, but I do believe that Captain Ford will be seeing to the matter in just a moment. So if you and your companion ..." Taylor looked at Jenny and tipped his cap. "Good morning to you, ma'am, and the best of health to you and ..." Old Whitey bridled a bit as his master surveyed Jenny's pregnant state and considered the presence of the Mexicans just across the arroyo. He whispered to his horse, which settled down, and then said to Sarah,

"Mrs. Langwell, would you and your lovely companion be so kind as to rejoin your compatriots?"

"I'd be delighted, General."

Sarah curtsied very prettily. Old Zach and his staff all tipped their hats to her, and bade her and Jenny a good morning as their wagon pulled away smartly, pots and pans clanging in the eerie quiet of the westerly breeze.

A few minutes later, the forlorn hope, comprising four companies of redleg infantry, hove into view. (We didn't have enough artillery to keep the redlegs properly entertained. So they had been transformed into doughboys for the duration.) They assembled at quick time into an assault column of eight files wide and forty men deep. Once the column formed, a bugle sounded. The column advanced at a double quick march into the arroyo and the men waded through the chest-high water to the other side, maintaining formation as they went—muskets and powder held high over their heads. The forlorn hope emerged from the water on the far side, scrambled through the brush up to the crest of the thirty-foot high bluff and lickety-split formed a skirmish line. A moment later, a couple squadrons of Second Dragoons splashed and swam across the arroyo to reinforce the forlorn hope. Nary a shot was fired, nor was a single Mexican soldier seen during the entire evolution.

It turned out later that only a company of Mexican cavalry had been there. As soon as the redlegs and the dragoons began crossing the river, they rode south at full chisel with the Second Dragoons and Walker's Texas Rangers snapping at their heels until dark, when the Americans turned back on account of not wanting to get bushwhacked.

A week or so later, after a great deal of marching between Point Isabel, the army's newly established port and supply depot on the coast, and the low-lying bluffs overlooking the Rio Grande opposite Matamoros, we found ourselves camped in muddy cornfields just north of the bluffs. The Old Man had summoned the owner and bade Perfect Bliss to pay him in gold specie for the damage to his crop. We passed our days digging trenches, drilling, and watching the Mexican girls. Each morning, they issued from the city with dirty laundry and traipsed to the river's edge, where they cleaned it (and themselves). None of us had seen anything like it before: The girls tied their skirts about their waists as they did their laundry. When they were done and had hung the laundry on every mesquite bush within reach to dry in the hot sun, they disrobed entirely and splashed about in the water for nearly an hour. Curiously, none of the *mujeres jovenes* ever ducked their faces into the water as they paddled about, with lustrous black hair piled on top of their heads.

We doughboys had ringside seats on the gentle bluffs, hardly a hundred and fifty feet from where the girls were frolicking on the south bank, and we quietly appreciated the show. Those who were inclined to disrupt the show with whistles and offers to go bed-pressing were quieted by the rest of us through various forms of soldierly moral opprobrium—and such more concrete measures as were infrequently required.

We also watched the Mexican army ostentatiously parade about every time some regiment or another arrived from deep in the interior of Mexico or a new commanding general hove onto the scene to supersede his predecessor—the latter of which happened three times in the month of April, as one faction or another either supported or actively worked against the current man in power. We came to know the individual regiments during their parades by their gaudy and wildly varying uniforms—blue coats with scarlet, white and green trim for one regiment of cavalry and white coats with sky blue and green trim for another cavalry regiment. Other cavalry looked a little more like the infantry, who were less colorful, with blue tunics and red facings, although the infantry often wore white pantaloons and sandals instead of the blackened boots and blue pantaloons of the cavalry. As I watched them, I remembered Kenny's sneering observation back in Corpus Christi about Mexican soldiers being "amalgamatin' mongrels." Most of the Mexican Other Ranks were Indians (or mostly Indian). There were also more than a few Negroes, quite a few of whom wore a sergeant's or corporal's chevrons, which drew many a scathing comment from our side, shoulder strap and Other Ranks alike. I saw hardly a creole among the Mexicans' Other Ranks. The officers, by contrast, all seemed to be *criollos*. They spent their days parading about importantly on horseback, often with their sabers drawn and held at shoulder-arms, each of them as haughty as the day is long.

The Mexicans did not content themselves with merely parading about. They were hard at work, soldiers and civilians alike, digging embrasures, fieldworks, and earthen forts all along the south bank of the Rio Grande, directly across from the peninsula where our army had encamped. As the various fortifications were completed, the cathedral bells would toll portentously and priests would parade forth to consecrate the finished fortification. I even caught a whiff of their incense once, when the wind veered around to the south.

We weren't idle either. For the first couple of weeks of April, every regiment spent some portion of the day digging trenches and starting a fort—provisionally known as Fort Texas—to secure the peninsula where we were camped. Just to the north of the fort, at the mouth of the peninsula, was a pond, or *resaca*, which we incorporated into our defense in case the Mexicans crossed the Rio Grande and attacked us from the north.

Hermann and Rónán both expressed their disgust at Old Zach's selection of our encampment site. Both of them sneered that, while it was true that the three sides of the peninsula formed by the bight of the river and the *resaca* to the north formed a natural fortification for the army, the little bight in the Rio Grande was just as much of a trap from which our army could not escape as it was a natural fort. I noted to them both that it could only be a trap if the Mexican army were ever to become energetic enough to cross the Rio Grande and invest us from the north.

Worse though, Hermann and Rónán said, such a siege would cut the army off from Point Isabel, our sole source of supply and reinforcement, and render it vulnerable to capture. Adding fresh injury to incompetence, Hermann snapped one night, was the failure to design the fort to provide enfilading fire against the newly built Mexican fortifications across the river—or against the main streets in the city proper, for that matter. When I asked what "enfilading fire" was, he replied impatiently that we were not going to be able to place our cannon on the parapets of Fort Texas so that they could put a raking fire lengthwise into the Mexican earthenworks and the streets of Matamoros without radically rebuilding the fort. In other words, the fort was useless as a means of investing the city of Matamoros. Hermann finished his diatribe by saying something nasty under his breath in German about the incompetence of our engineering officers in selecting the fort's placement and design.

As we labored in the hot sun (and in the cold rain every third day or so), doughboys began deserting. Desertion was not all that unusual in the peacetime army, given the poor pay, lousy food, worse living conditions, and the vicious discipline of misbegotten sergeants such as Hoggs and bloody-minded officers such as LeFort and Bragg. During any given year in peacetime, perhaps as many as one in ten bluebellies in a particular company or battalion might brave the lash and branding to cut short their enlistments and try their luck in some new line of work. What made this situation different—and all the more dangerous—was that the Old Man had issued orders to treat deserters as if it were wartime. Thus, instead of merely being subject to flogging, branding, and dismissal from the army in little more than one's underwear, deserters were now subject to being jerked to Jesus for their pains. The proximity of our prospective enemy (with whom deserters could find ready refuge), and the way our enemy tried to use our deserters against us, just made matters worse.

About a week after we arrived, some poor cove, I don't know who, took a powder in broad daylight (God knows what madness possessed him to do it then). He splashed into the Rio Grande at its narrowest point to swim across the 100 feet or so to the safety of Mexico. The sentries implored him to return to our bank, but he kept swimming towards the Mexican side, encouraged by a score or more laughing and gesticulating Mexican soldiers. The officer of the day ordered the sentries to shoot the swimming man. He sank without a trace under a hail of musketry. The Mexican soldiers fled, thinking that our sentries had fired upon them. Several companies of Mexican infantry mobilized and paraded along the riverfront just outside easy musket range, which caused the fifes and bugles and the duty drummer's long roll to raise the alarm in our camp. We grabbed our muskets and scrambled into formation in record time, whereupon we stood for about two hours in the broiling sun while the big bugs figured out whether our sentries had started a war by killing the deserter.

The killing didn't end the desertions. But it did cause the bathing Mexican beauties to disappear—not that we had much time by then to admire them. We were now working in twelve-hour shifts building Fort Texas. Fortunately for us, despite the half-finished and vulnerable nature of our defenses, the Mexican army did not stir even the least bit. Instead, they contented themselves with strewing leaflets about the camp urging us to desert. Presumably they were brought in by some of the Mexicans who flooded the camp every day, looking to sell us this or that or to sign on as wranglers or even day laborers building our walls. They were shooed away with great regularity, but they had the tenacity of flies about a pig farm.

One of the leaflets read:

> The Commander-in-Chief of the Mexican army
> to the English and Irish under the orders of the
> American General *Taylor*.
>
> KNOW YE—That the government of the United
> States is committing repeated acts of barbarous
> aggression against the magnanimous Mexican
> nation; that the government which exists under
> the flag of the stars is unworthy of the designa-
> tion of Christian. Recollect that you were born
> in Great Britain; that the American government

looks with coldness upon the powerful flag of St.
George, and is provoking to a rupture the warlike
people to whom it belongs, President Polk boldly
manifesting a desire to take possession of Oregon,
as he has already done of Texas. Now then come
with all confidence to the Mexican ranks; and I
guarantee to you upon my honor good treatment,
and that all your expenses shall be defrayed, until
your arrival in the beautiful capital of Mexico.

Germans, French, Poles, and individuals of other
nations! Separate yourselves from the Yankees,
and do not contribute to defend a robbery and
usurpation, which be assured, the civilized nations
of Europe look upon with the utmost indignation.
Come therefore and array yourselves under the
tri-colored flag; in the confidence that the God
of armies protects it, and that it will protect you
equally with the English.

Pedro De Ampudia.

The grapevine buzzed with the news that General Ampudia had
offered one of our Mexican agents a captain's commission if he would
raise a company of Irish and German deserters from our army. The
agent, liking his chink from Uncle Sam better than a fancy title, a
fancier uniform, and the prospect of uncertain pay, declined General
Ampudia's kind offer. He was reported to have said that he was very
highly honored that the general would think of him, but he wanted to
return to the bosom of his family and his hacienda, which lay closer to
the Nueces than to the río Bravo.

Despite this refusal to join the Mexican side, a score or more
deserters had made it to the other side over the next few days. A score
more had drowned in the attempt, swept away by the Rio Grande's
currents—which were as varied as a woman's moods: Sweet and placid

one night and on the next capable of carrying a strong swimmer to the bottom. Nearly as many more were shot in the attempt. The Irish and Germans—and even the occasional native American—were not alone in their desire to swim the river. More than one of the officers' Negro servants and slaves escaped, some never to be seen again. One slave, oddly enough, was reported by the grapevine to have returned from Matamoros after a few days, happy enough to resume his old role. The grapevine also maintained that the Negro did allow that he had been treated with the greatest consideration and given—for the first time in his life—the first seat at the table and a pretty señorita to keep him warm at night in the best bed in the house. Why he would have wanted to return from such nirvana was beyond me.

Different parts of the grapevine held that this was a pure cock and bull story. The Negro (and every other escaped Negro) was treated just as miserably in Matamoros as he would have been anywhere in America, so he returned because he had better prospects of being fed, even as a mere slave. I couldn't judge the truth of the matter, and I didn't foresee a time when I might be in a position to do so. I thus dismissed it from my mind until I also heard through the grapevine that Lieutenant Bragg lost two of his remaining three Negro slaves. Captain McCall had similar problems. He was heard to have remarked that, if this kept up, he'd need to hire a white man as his valet. He wouldn't have minded doing so, but there simply weren't any decent white men for hire here along the Rio Grande. The only ones available were Irish. And everyone knew that the Paddies were too stupid and smelled too much to warrant taking them on in such a personal capacity.

One night we sat at our mess's campfire, making a miserable time of dinner for ourselves. Our Mexican woman from the *jacales* of Corpus Christi had chosen not to make the trek south. Not that I blamed her under the circumstances. Kenny O'Leary remained obdurate that Jenny could not return to our mess, and he proved to be as poor a cook as the rest of us. Not that any of us had much enthusiasm foraging for our supper and preparing it. We either spent our days on guard waiting for an attack that fortunately never came, or we were digging trenches and hauling dirt from one location to another under the direction of anxious officers, most whom didn't seem to have the slightest idea of what a star redoubt was supposed to look like. I wondered what they must have learned in those endless engineering courses back at the 'Point, about which Grant had sung panegyrics to me back during those halcyon winter days when we had been mule-skinning and bronco busting, and when I'd had at least the prospect of seeing the fair Calandria on a Sunday afternoon. I supposed that the prospective shoulder straps who were later responsible for designing Fort Texas must have slept through their engineering classes in much the same way I'd slept through Greek when I was twelve years old. I wondered whether cadets at West Point were caned like we were at St. Patrick's for closing our eyes in class for even an instant.

After poking for a few minutes at the unappetizing product of our culinary efforts, we all picked up our pipes by unspoken agreement. As I lit my pipe and took the first couple of contented puffs of good Virginia tobacco, I heard someone far off howl something or other in Irish and then laugh mockingly. Rónán, Kenny, and I looked at each other to see who might have understood what had just been said. Hermann looked at us all quizzically. Then we heard the Irish again, "Come join us, Irishmen! Forsake your nativist tormentors. Come south to Catholic Mexico, and you can worship to your soul's content in a proper church—just like an honest Irishman should."

Then a second voice took up the call, again in the Gaelic of our forefathers, "There's mead and whiskey." The caller paused, almost as if he'd been elbowed in the ribs. "Well, not exactly mead and whiskey. It's ... *mescal*. But it tastes as good as whiskey, me cullies. And the *pulque*." There was a dramatic pause, the sounds of digging over at the fort ceased and every ear in the American encampment twitched in anticipation. (Even the ears of those who couldn't understand a word of the mother tongue twitched, so apparent was the subject-matter to every manjack within earshot.)

"The Mexican señoritas are beautiful." Another dramatic pause. "And they are bathing in the river just beyond the bend ... where they're safe from being shot down by your sentries. If you want to see them, me cullies, you must be on our side of the river, on the side with God, the Virgin Mary, and the One True Faith." There was still another pause. It was so quiet that I could have heard a musket being cocked at a thousand yards. Even the wind had died down to listen.

"Come south. You can have land. Become a ranchero. Find a señorita of your own, and live in the land of plenty."

Kenny muttered something under his breath.

"Not now, Kenny," Rónán commanded. "Not now."

Kenny querulously ignored him. "What is there for me here? Nothing. No faithful girl. No decent food. Just hard labor … just as if we were damned slaves on some plantation, with that jackbooted thug Bragg as our master and Hoggs as our overseer."

Hermann cleared his throat heavily. "You must honor your oath and remember your duty, my friend."

"To an army where you are bucked and gagged for doing your duty? Ask Billy boy about that." Kenny spat in disgust.

I said nothing.

Then the catcalls started on our side of the river, one or two at first, and then generally from every part of our encampment. Echoing across the river. Derisive. Scatological. In English. Castigating the manhood and honor of every Irishman ever born. A swell of Irish arose in response—again on our side of the river. Equally as derisive … of America, the *Sassenagh*, and our shoulder straps and sergeants, and roaring approval of all things Mexican, whether it was the *mescal* and *pulque* (which more than a few bluebellies had discovered while we were in Corpus Christi), the señoritas, or shriving oneself at confession to a proper Irish Catholic priest (never mind the impossibility of finding an Irish priest in Matamoros—or anywhere else in Mexico, for that matter). We could also hear a few German voices chime in, although I did not ask Hermann what they were saying. His expression said enough.

Kenny started to howl his support of the Irish, but Rónán harshly whispered, "Shut pan," and Kenny promptly complied, although a bit of a mad light lingered in his eye.

Bugles sounded and drums beat briefly, and top sergeants and officers boiled from their messes, harshly calling for silence, which slowly returned to both sides of the river.

⌒

The very next night, C Company was one of the duty companies, and so we stood picket duty along the bluff overlooking the river. Old Zach had been so incensed by the desertions and by last night's performance—on both sides of the river—that he had ordered that "none but Americans" be put on sentry duty. Hermann was the corporal of the watch. He told his squad (me included) to depart for the bluff to relieve the E Company sentries, who were due to come off their watch. Before we could leave, Hoggs stopped us.

"You heard the orders, Gogan. Down from on high, they are." Hoggs glared at me. "None but Americans tonight."

Hermann interceded. "Private Gogan is an American citizen, Sergeant."

"Wurster." Hoggs looked at Hermann venomously. "Hold your blow. I don't care whether Gogan is descended from General George Washington himself. He ain't no American. He's a lily-livered bog rat. Aren't you, Gogan?"

Hermann stood at attention, staring past Hoggs's shoulder, and spoke at Hoggs. (And through him and past him. Anything but to him.) "Then I shall send him back to camp, Sergeant, and we shall be one man shy, for I am just a Dutchy."

"You'll stand Gogan's post duty, Wurster, because you didn't muster enough Americans." Hoggs grimaced with pleasure as he stared at Hermann. "Anyways, you're more American than that Paddy whore's get." Hoggs turned his attention back to me, "But Gogan ain't going back to camp. No sir. He's going to stand sentry here. Right in front of the guard shack. All night until dawn. No one is to relieve him. Mutinous bastard. Am I being clear, Corporal?"

"Yes, Sergeant."

⤳

"C Company! PARADE ... REST!"

Hoggs sounded ever so slightly strained as he gave this final command after having had C Company fall into formation a full thirty minutes before the rest of the regiment. In the ensuing silence, broken only by the sounds of the rest of the army slowly moving about behind us on various fatigue details before morning formation, we stared at the gibbous moon, which cast a spectral glow as it set behind the muddy cornfield that served as the regiment's impromptu parade ground.

Lieutenant Porter fairly bounded over to Hoggs from the direction of the Old Man's tent. The grapevine had buzzed with anticipation over why he had been in close conference with Perfect Bliss for the past hour. Porter whispered in Hoggs's ear. I thought I detected a shadow pass over Hoggs's otherwise impassive countenance.

Porter dispensed with the preliminaries as he began to stride back and forth in front us, slapping his gloves from one hand to the other with evident relish. "Colonel Cross is missing." He paused and let the information pass over us and sink in, information that had been the single topic of conversation since yesterday. Colonel Cross was the army's quartermaster and the man who had so mercifully furnished the wagons that had collected those, including Kenny, who had fallen out from the heat during our march south. He had gone for his daily morning ride and had not returned by nightfall. Never ever mentioned by a single shoulder strap, but quite true according to the grapevine, Cross had intended to have more than one morning gallop when he left camp. His destination had apparently been a small rancho where a pretty señorita he had met some days earlier awaited him for a morning dalliance. I had my doubts about the grapevine's version of things on account of the good colonel being an old man of forty-seven. By contrast, I could understand the young lieutenant who had swum the river over to the Mexican side a few days earlier looking for a bit of fluff and been captured for his pains.

Porter spoke again with barely suppressed excitement. "It is feared that he may have met misfortune at the hands of that notorious Mexican bandit chief, Ramón Falcón."

When I last saw Colonel Kinney, he had told me that Falcón was one of the *tenientes* of Canales' group of *tejanos* from *las villas del norte* who had thrown their lot in with *los méxicanos* when Old Zach had refused to support them in their desire to free *las villas del norte* from both Mexican and *norteamericano* rule. Falcón was a *hacendado del norte* whose land lay north of the río Bravo, and was a feared fighter who had stood beside Canales and Zapata against Arista in 1840. As Colonel Kinney had told me, the *hacendados del norte* and *rancheros* had ridden against the Mexican army in 1840 to protect their lands from the army's depredation, and they had ridden against the Comanche and the Apache any number of times to protect their women, their children and their way of life. Now they were riding against *los norteamericanos*. I wondered whether don Guillermo was riding with them now—and whether he had been riding with Falcón when Falcón delivered the message to the Americans on the bank of the Arroyo Colorado that their march south would be met by war with Mexico. (It had been the receipt of this message that had precipitated Old Zach's decision to ready the army before it forded the Arroyo Colorado.)

Porter continued, "I have volunteered to lead a patrol to search for the colonel. First Sergeant Hoggs will be my second-in-command. Corporal Wurster will also accompany us, along with …"

Porter named eight privates, including Kenny. Neither Rónán nor I would be going. I was disappointed. I couldn't see Rónán, so I couldn't assess his reaction. But it struck me, as I stood there in formation, watching the patrol fall out and Hoggs take charge of them, that Hoggs was as disappointed as I was—but for exactly the opposite reason.

⌒

Just before he fell into formation to depart with the rest of the patrol, Hermann thrust a small package into my hands and looked me directly in the eye. It was Hermann's share of our spoils from Rouquette's leather and a couple of letters. As I looked dumbly at the package, Hermann touched me on the arm.

"Mail these letters for me?"

He left the rest unsaid, and with nary a glance back he joined the formation, which marched off forthwith (even Porter was on foot) without a fife or a drum to attend its departure. I stuffed the package into my blouse pocket and went about my business. When I looked at the letters more closely later that day, I saw that they were both addressed to Serafina.

When I saw him next, days later, Hermann wouldn't tell me much about what happened on the patrol, other than to confirm what everyone in camp already knew, which Sergeant Hoggs had reported when he crept into camp, alone, sporting a gash on his cheek and without his musket, more than a day before Hermann and the rest of the patrol. I was nonetheless able to piece together what happened from the other members of the patrol I knew, as well as from all the scuttlebutt emanating from various reports to Old Zach.

Two patrols had marched out of camp together, one of them under Porter's command. They soon separated, intending to meet the next day after searching for Cross in roughly adjacent areas. Porter marched his patrol upriver about twelve or fifteen miles. At first, Hoggs marched the ten enlisted men in formation at 90 steps per minute, with all of the noise and fuss that attends forcing ten men to march in lockstep over broken ground and through thick mesquite underbrush. To put a finer point on it, Hoggs's efforts lasted until Porter looked back at him with ill-concealed irritation.

For the next several hours, as the sun rose and the humidity and heat increased, there was no more marching, just walking. Porter led his patrol along an undulating ridgeline running roughly parallel to the riverbank, each man stumbling through the underbrush in only the most tenuous connection with the man in front of him and the man behind him. Hermann spent most of the time within elbow's reach of Porter, aching to tell Porter that the patrol was terribly vulnerable to ambush as it crashed through the underbrush with little regard for what might lie ahead. Hermann knew from his days as a light infantryman in the Prussian army that a small unit such as Porter's patrol could deploy in any one of several different ways to better protect itself as it stumbled through the mesquite. But Porter and Hoggs were not trained in such tactics, Hermann thought, and anyway, every time he worked up the nerve to say something about it to Porter, Hoggs seemed to magically appear from the rear of the column to give Porter some inconsequential report or another. Soon enough, Hermann's concerns were mooted.

By unspoken agreement with Porter, Hermann gradually had taken the lead, clearing the way through the insect-laden underbrush for Porter, who was now some yards behind him. As Hermann stood for a moment, wiping his brow clear of sweat and an errant fly, he heard a rustle in front of him. He signaled to Porter, who quietly stopped the column in its tracks.

"What …?"

Hermann put his finger to his lips, and quietly retreated to where Porter stood.

"I am not sure, sir," he whispered, *sotto voce*. "But I heard a horse … or something. It looks like there is a clearing up ahead."

Hoggs joined them, and Porter whispered to him, "Wurster and I are going to scout up ahead. Keep everyone out of sight. Fix bayonets as well."

Hoggs did not look very happy, but he saluted. "Yes sir."

Hermann led the way as he and Porter slowly crept to the edge of a clearing, where a dozen or so Mexican irregulars (maybe this was Ramón Falcón, himself?) drowsed in the noonday heat around a dying campfire and the remains of their mid-day meal. There were a dozen or more horses picketed on the far side of the clearing. Neither Hermann nor Porter saw any sentries.

Hermann muttered a couple of quiet suggestions in Porter's ear as they crept away. Porter deployed his little patrol on one side of the clearing, muskets charged and primed, bayonets fixed, with Hermann and Kenny detailed to secure the enemy horses when the excitement began. Porter drew his pistol—a Colt Paterson repeater that his father, Commodore Porter, had purchased for him at vast expense. He had shown it to both Hoggs and Hermann earlier in their march. Then, as cool as you please, he stepped out of from behind a mesquite bush into the clearing and loudly commanded the shocked Mexicans to surrender.

One *guerrillero* grabbed his short little *escopeta*, an old-fashioned blunderbuss from the seventeenth century that didn't even have a proper flintlock hammer and fired whatever was loaded into it. He snapped the trigger. But it did not fire, probably because its flash pan had not been freshly charged. Porter raised his pistol and shot the Mexican down. There was a ripple of musketry from the rest of the patrol, and the remaining dozen or so Mexican irregulars fled into the underbrush, leaving one or two of their brethren lying motionless on the ground. When the shooting began, Hermann bayoneted the Mexican guarding the horses and secured them, leaving them in Kenny's charge.

"Sir." Hermann tapped Porter on the shoulder, who was standing over the fallen Mexican with a slightly self-satisfied air.

"Yes, Corporal?"

"We should leave, sir."

Hoggs said, "That be …"

"It's all right, Sergeant. Corporal Wurster is right." Porter looked at the horses. "Well, this is a fine gift. Can the men ride, Sergeant?"

Hoggs goggled. "I …"

"Find out." Porter was curt. "Get everyone mounted up, and let's skedaddle." Porter thought for a second. "Oh, and make sure everyone's reloaded his musket before we leave."

"Yes, sir."

Everyone mounted—Kenny having whispered furiously to Hermann that he'd never been on horseback in his life. (Hermann whispered back that riding a horse was just like walking, and just as easy—except you didn't have to walk.) They'd hardly left the clearing and its dead Mexican *banditti* when the heavens opened, and the rain poured straight down, soaking everyone and everything almost instantaneously.

"Sir." Hermann said to Porter, who was busy calming his mount.

"Yes, Corporal?"

"We need to protect the powder, sir. Our Mexican friends ..." Hermann gestured in the direction in which the Mexicans had fled. "They will be back."

"Don't worry about it, Corporal. We'll be long gone before they've had a chance to find us. We've got their horses, remember?"

Hermann made to remonstrate, but Hoggs hissed at him. "Shut it, Wurster."

And off they rode, higglety, pigglety, and pop, Porter in the lead, and with Kenny, Hoggs, and two or three others barely staying in the saddle. They rode steadily eastward along a trail leading from the clearing for a couple of hours, until the sun was hanging low on the western horizon.

"¡Hola, señor!"

Porter swerved to a halt and stared, befuddled, down at the Mexican standing in the center of the trail. The Mexican moved his fingers, visibly counting the number of Americans who were bunching up behind Porter. Then, as quickly as he appeared, the Mexican vanished into the underbrush.

Porter shook himself from his momentary disbelieving reverie, but he was far too late in reacting. "Dismount. Take cover ..."

The patrol was no crack troop of the Second Dragoons. They tumbled untidily—and slowly—from their horses. Before Porter could say another word, and before the dismounted doughboys could retreat into the underbrush on the far side of the trail, a ripple of musketry came from near where the Mexican disappeared. Four horses dropped like stones, screaming in agony. Their respective doughboys, who had been struggling to dismount, fell with them. One unlucky doughboy was pinned beneath his dying mount. His luckier compatriots scrambled free and tumbled into the underbrush near Hermann, opposite from the Mexican ambuscade. Porter wheeled his mount and emptied his Paterson revolving pistol into the chaparral at three men who were rushing towards him. Then two more shots rang out. Porter sagged in the saddle and then fell to the ground, his viscera splattering across Kenny O'Leary's face. Porter's mortally wounded mount collapsed on top of him, and they both lay still. Blinded by Porter's gore, Kenny tumbled involuntarily from his horse, which galloped off down the trail.

Hermann reached out and pulled Kenny into his hidey-hole. Hoggs was now the only American still on horseback. As several Mexicans boiled out of the underbrush on foot, Hoggs spurred his horse and disappeared down the trail without so much as a fare thee well.

Hermann barked *sotto voce*, "Prime your muskets."

Then he looked at his own musket in dismay. It was useless. The powder in the flash pan had clogged from the rain, and it would need to be cleared. Hermann looked at the other men huddled in the underbrush. Kenny and two other men had lost their muskets. The remaining three still had theirs, but the crestfallen looks on their faces told Hermann that their muskets were as useless as his.

Kenny shivered beside Hermann, and huddled closer to him, as if he were a child seeking comfort from a parent. Hermann glanced at Porter and the private lying next to him, and he knew that they were both beyond mortal help, as was the poor cove who had been trapped beneath his dying horse. There were now a couple of dozen or more Mexican ambushers standing in the trail, laughing and talking excitedly about their defeat of *los gringos* and plundering Porter's Colt Paterson and pocket watch from him—after plunging a knife into him to confirm that he was indeed dead. Hermann motioned and mouthed to the others, "Back." Slowly, Hermann and the other seven remaining members of the patrol retreated further into the underbrush.

Hermann did not stop the patrol's quiet retreat until they were well out of earshot of the Mexican irregulars and night had fallen. There they stayed until first light, without food or water—all of which had been left with the horses—and precious little dry powder. Once the remaining muskets had been cleaned, and presumably made operable (Hermann was not about to fire one of them to see if it worked), Hermann led the little group through the underbrush towards the rising sun, staying well away from both the river and the trail on which they had been ambushed. They passed another night under the stars, hungry, thirsty, and miserable. About noon the next day, Hermann led his battered little patrol back into camp. He was immediately whisked away to an immediate audience with Perfect Bliss and Colonel Garland, where he was grilled for two hours about the debacle. During the entire journey back to camp, Kenny never uttered another word, moving only when Hermann led him by the hand.

Hoggs, who had returned to camp on foot a day earlier, never disclosed what had happened to his horse or his musket—or how he acquired the gash on his cheek. The grapevine buzzed with intimations that the big bugs viewed Hoggs as something of a coward, but nothing ever came of it. I wondered privately whether Captain McCall should have charged Hoggs for his missing musket.

At morning muster the next day, Grant publicly congratulated Hermann on his having safely returned the surviving members of the patrol to camp. He also choked a bit as he announced the "unfortunate passing" of his "great friend, Theodric Porter," who had "died so heroically at the hands of dastardly Mexican bandits who would not show themselves in a fair fight." Porter left behind a widow and a small child.

⌒

# CHAPTER 10

# Desertion to Utopia

HERMANN KNELT NEXT TO KENNY and gently turned Kenny's head so that he could look Kenny directly in the eye. "Kenny, stay here, near your tent. Don't go anywhere. Billy and I are standing sentry duty tonight. So you'll be alone. Sergeant Rónán will be in the guard shack if you need someone."

Kenny looked at Hermann a little blankly. He hadn't spoken more than a dozen words in the week since the patrol debacle, and between Hermann, Rónán, and myself, we'd hardly left him alone.

It was the final night of sentry duty along the Rio Grande. It had become all too clear in the week since Hermann's return to camp that war was nigh, no matter what happened. So at dawn the army was to be on the move to secure Point Isabel and resupply before the Mexican army could cross the Rio Grande in real force. At least, that was the official version coming across the grapevine. Rónán Finnegan had heard that the real reason we were heading to Point Isabel was not to resupply. Instead, the Old Man really wanted to provoke a fight with the much larger Mexican army and whip them with just the regulars before the volunteers, of which there were thousands coming from Texas and Louisiana, showed up here on the Rio Grande and took credit for the victory over the dagoes that was surely to come. That said, we all reckoned that we would be purchasing our victory with the blood of the regulars, regardless of whether the volunteers were already here or still sipping mint juleps in New Orleans while they awaited transport south.

Events had begun to spin out of control just two days after Hermann returned to camp. We had spent the entire day toiling on Fort Texas, building the ramparts ever higher, and readying it for something ... although none of us bluebellies knew quite what that "something" was. Our toils were leavened by the spectacle of what we later learned was the arrival of General Arista to take command of the Mexican army. And what a spectacle it was: The grandest review yet of their entire army—cavalry, infantry, and artillery, all of them wearing the same colorful riot of uniforms they had just a couple of weeks earlier. The bands played, the artillery boomed salutes, and the priests consecrated. We could hear the cheers of the townspeople. Within an hour of the last parading regiment having disappeared from view, the grapevine was electric with the news of the Mexicans having finally crossed the Rio Grande, although nobody quite knew whether they had crossed upriver or down, or even how many had crossed.

Upon receiving the news, Old Zach sent one squadron of the Second Dragoons downriver under the command of Captain Ker and sent two more squadrons upriver under the command of Captains Thornton and Hardee. Ker returned within a few hours, reporting that he had seen nothing. Of Thornton, we heard nothing until the middle of the next day, just as we were coming off our six-hour stint working on Fort Texas. The entire army was now divided into two sections, one of which worked on the fortifications while the other manned the trenches alongside the *resaca*, waiting for the Mexican army to come bursting out of the underbrush to the north. Every six hours, the two sections switched. Those who had been in the trenches labored on the fortifications, and those who had been laboring rested as well as they could in the trenches while they were guarding against a Mexican onslaught.

A Mexican *carretero* came into camp bearing a wounded dragoon in his two-wheeled cart with a note pinned to his *serape*, signed by the Mexican General Torrejon himself. (Upon hearing the news, Hermann asked how many Mexican generals there were. We had just one—General Taylor. He wasn't even a real general, just a colonel who had been brevetted to brigadier, which nonetheless made him the second-ranking officer in the entire army after Old Fuss and Feathers, himself. In other words, the Old Man was a mere colonel facing how many generals, only the good Lord knew. Our only other general (also a brevet brigadier), Worth, had gone back to Washington City in a huff because the lord high muck-a-mucks back in Washington had decided that Colonel Twiggs was senior to General Worth on account of Colonel Twiggs having received his commission as a colonel before General Worth, even though General Worth had been brevetted as a brigadier general and Colonel Twiggs had not.) General Torrejon's note contained a fulsome apology to General Taylor, saying that General Torrejon's forces were unable to care for the wounded trooper as General Torrejon had not brought a flying hospital with him. General Torrejon did allow that not all of Captain Thornton's eighty-man command were dead, for many of them were now prisoners of the Mexican army. General Torrejon further assured General Taylor that they would be accorded the treatment due prisoners of war.

The fuller story outed within the hour, to the fascinated horror of all, the loudly declaimed threats of revenge by many, and the snorting disgust of a few veterans of other armies and other wars, including Hermann and Rónán, over the amateurish showing by the best cavalry regiment in the entire U. S. Army—and the only cavalry regiment with Old Zach's little army. After leaving camp, Thornton had ridden west twenty-five miles or so, until his guide, Chapita Sandoval (Colonel Kinney's valued spy, Hermann and I remembered, whom we'd met at Sunday dinner after church), refused to ride any further, declaring that the entire Mexican army lay just a couple of miles away with General Torrejon. Chapita bluntly told Thornton that he could no longer accompany Thornton because his, Chapita's, life would certainly be forfeit if he were to be captured.

The grapevine steadfastly maintained that Captain Thornton had been as mad as a hatter ever since the explosion and sinking of the steamer *Pulaski* back in the '30s. He had been among the last to leave the ship, and then only after he had heroically ensured that dozens of women and children made it into the severely overcrowded lifeboats. As the ship slipped beneath the waves, Thornton lashed himself to a hen coop and rescued several other men who were swimming in the water. They floated along for days, crazed by thirst under the hot sun. One by one, his companions slipped into the sea, never to be seen again. By the time a passing ship had spotted Thornton and rescued him, the coop was breaking apart and sinking, and he'd been reduced to raving insanity. Thornton had always been slight of build, with a delicate constitution. But after the sinking, he grew even more gaunt and evermore easily affected by the emotions of others. Worse, the grapevine held, Thornton (who was universally praised for his unflagging bravery) had continually striven to overcome his physical delicacy, so as to become as pollrumptious a cavalryman as there was in the Second Dragoons—all damn your eyes and hell for leather.

Thornton refused to believe that General Torrejon and his troops were anywhere close by. So he summarily dismissed Chapita. He said to all within earshot that Chapita was being either an old woman who was afraid of his own shadow or he was an unreliable Mexican who was in the pay of the Mexican army. Colonel Kinney told me later that Chapita rode off muttering his disbelief under his breath, only to spend the next day and a half hiding from Mexican army patrols determined to find him before he could make his way back to our encampment.

After Chapita (quite sensibly) rode off in disgust, Thornton continued down the track that traced along the bluffs overlooking the river to their left. After about an hour or so, they hove onto a large hacienda that was fenced on three sides by mesquite and chaparral. The fourth side was a bluff overlooking the Rio Grande. Without any reconnoitering and without leaving a rear-guard on watch outside, Thornton led his entire command into the hacienda, which comprised a number of houses within the fenced perimeter. In fact, it did not occur to Thornton at any point that perhaps he should have kept his entire command, as little as it was, clear of the thorn-hedged hacienda, and simply sent a sergeant and a couple of troopers to roust the inhabitants. As the story goes, they had gone to the hacienda to look for some contact or another who might have had intelligence regarding Mexican bandits in the area (perhaps even the hated Ramón Falcón, whom Thornton was anxious to capture as a nice feather in his cap). Without ceremony, a number of troopers dismounted and began searching the houses for this contact. Unsurprisingly, there was no one in any of the houses.

But as with Porter, disaster struck before it dawned on Thornton that all was not well. He led his troopers back to the hacienda's gate—the only egress from the hacienda—where he found a company of Mexican infantry blocking his way. Hundreds more Mexican infantrymen were now seen to be sticking their muskets through the chaparral and mesquite fences. At a disembodied command emanating from outside the thorn bush fence, the infantry began shooting the Americans down in rippling volleys of musketry. Thornton led his men one way and then another, frantically looking for a bolt-hole. At some point, he found a weak place in the fence. After urging his men to follow him, he jumped it and disappeared from view, severely wounding his horse in the process. But his men couldn't follow him, as their horses shied away from the fence and the Mexican musketry. That left poor Captain Hardee in command.

The hacienda was now a killing field. The withering fire from the Mexican infantry was dropping troopers from their saddles. At the gate, there was hand-to-hand combat, during which Lieutenant Mason maimed Ramón Falcón, only to pay for this small victory with his own life. Hardee led the survivors in a desperate flight down to the river's edge, where they became mired in the mud and cattails along the shoreline, unable to reach the water. They turned around, only to find a couple of squadrons of Mexican lancers deployed in a line at the crest of the bluff, ready to ride them down. Hardee counted his men: He had only twenty-five or so effectives by now, and half of them had lost either their carbines or their sabers in the frantic effort to escape.

A Mexican officer approached under a flag of truce and gallantly offered Hardee terms of surrender, which Hardee unhappily accepted on the condition that he and his men were to be treated as prisoners of war as is the custom among civilized nations of the world. Hardee was heard to say at the time that, if the Mexican officer had been unprepared to accept Hardee's condition, then he and every surviving manjack was prepared to sell his life dearly in a forlorn hope. Fortunately, the Mexican officer acceded to Hardee's demand, assuring Hardee that General Arista was a gentleman.

I quite understood Hardee's concern. Arista, you will recall, had put down Canales' revolt back in '40 and executed Zapata for his pains in joining Canales, even as he pardoned Canales and joined him to his side as a loyal aide. Arista's predecessor, Ampudia, was no better: He had put down a revolt somewhere in the jungles of southern Mexico, and he was said to have boiled the rebel general's head in oil and stuck it on the gate to a local hacienda as a warning to all.

Captain Thornton, we learned a few days later, was subsequently captured by a Mexican cavalry patrol just a few miles from our encampment, having successfully evaded other patrols for the better part of two days.

The Thornton Affair (as the *casus belli* became known to the Washington City heavyweights when they declared war on Mexico) and the ambush of Lieutenant Porter's patrol, along with one or two other small disasters, had spooked Old Zach. He now realized what half the army had been talking about for two weeks: If the Mexican army cut the road to Point Isabel, we would be marooned. So here we were, packed up and ready to dash to Point Isabel the next morning to secure our supply line, and then dash back before the Mexicans could reduce Fort Texas—which Old Zach had garrisoned with the Seventh Infantry Cottonbalers (with Sarah Langwell and Jenny Billings and the one or two other intrepid camp followers who had come south with the regiment), Bragg's flying artillery, and a battery of two eighteen-pounders, along with enough powder, shot, food, and water to last them until we got back.

C Company was the duty company that night, and Grant was the officer of the day. He and Rónán Finnegan were sitting inside the old guard shack, whittling something or other, or perhaps Grant was writing a letter to that pretty young lady back in Missouri. Hermann was busy traipsing from one sentry to the next, making sure that everyone kept an eagle's eye peeled on the river now that dusk was beginning to fall. I was a sentry, Hoggs's accusation that I was not a true American having apparently been forgotten, and I had quickly fallen into a routine of 40 paces in one direction along the bluff overlooking the river, a pivot and a return journey of 40 paces, only to begin once again. By now, I had stood post so often that I was hardly even conscious of the weight of my musket on my shoulder. I viewed the next four hours of my life as a welcome interlude away from some noxious fatigue detail—such as hauling firewood and ammunition into the fort—as the army struck camp and readied for the march.

After a couple of hours and what seemed like two or three hundred identical laps along the well-worn sentry's path, I pivoted to commence yet one more such lap, only to almost run down Kenny, who looked me in the eye, lifted his finger to his lips, and then high-tailed it, full chisel, to the river's bank.

I responded automatically. "Halt, or I will shoot!" There was no response. "Halt! Corporal of the guard … Halt!"

"Shut it, turdball, and give me that thing." Hoggs roughly grabbed my musket from my hands. "Is it primed?"

Hoggs checked the flash pan, raised the musket, and to my instant horror, fired. Arms akimbo, Kenny fell face first into the water and did not move.

"Billy!" It was Hermann. "Do not say a word."

Hoggs lowered the musket with a look of satisfaction. "You see, turdball? Easy enough to shoot a bog trotter who's so stupid that he runs in a straight line." With that, he handed me back my musket. "You really ought to clean it," Hoggs said conversationally. "You never know when you'll be inspected." He turned to Hermann and said, "Corporal, you really should keep better track of the men in your own mess."

With that, Hoggs pivoted and marched smartly away. He saluted crisply as he marched past a shocked Grant who, accompanied by

197

Finnegan, had rushed from the guardhouse to see what the commotion was all about.

I cried when I told Jenny what had happened.

PART TWO

# I Met the Elephant

⌒

ALONG THE RÍO BRAVO
MAY 8, 1846–SEPTEMBER 1846

CHAPTER 11

# To Draw the Claret

"ORDER ARMS!" Grant's stentorian command rang out.

The butt stocks of thirty-six muskets dropped to the ground almost silently.

"REST."

Grant said more conversationally, "Stand easy, boys. We're going to be a while." He then nonchalantly took out a cheroot and went through the elaborate procedure of lighting it in the suddenly waxing breeze with one of those new-fangled safety matches as our little Army of Occupation stood, paraded in the gently swaying sawgrass of a vast open plain. Grant had told us it was called "*Palo Alto*"—the place of the tall trees. The sawgrass stretched under the cloudless blue sky as far as I could see except to our right, where it ended abruptly at a road. A great, low-lying forest of mesquite and chaparral lay on the other side of the road. I thought that the mesquite, which stood hardly twenty feet high at the highest down here in the Rio Grande valley halfway between Point Isabel and Fort Texas, must have qualified in these parts as the tall trees giving this place its name, for there was not a single proper tree that I could see.

Kenny had been dead and buried in his grave just north of the trenches that guarded the approaches to Fort Texas for a week now. His grave was unmarked as he had been lawfully slaughtered for desertion in a time of war. At dawn, I and a detail from our company under Hermann's direction buried poor Kenny, just as the army began marching to Point Isabel. Jenny was still weeping in the Western's comforting bosom when we marched away, and her sobs were still echoing in my ears all these days later. I shrugged my shoulders to ease the ache as we stood in our ranks under the punishing noonday sun, staring at our enemy across the windswept plain.

We'd marched eight miles that morning from Point Isabel back towards Fort Texas, full of knowledge that the Mexicans were waiting for us on this plain of sawgrass. We'd been burdened with both our 60-lb. knapsacks carrying all our belongings and our haversacks full with three rations of beans and moldy bacon meant to see us through the day and twenty extra rounds of shot and powder (in addition to our normal forty rounds). Thankfully, the big bugs had seen fit to allow us to shrug off our knapsacks half an hour ago and leave them near the wagon train that we had been escorting back to Fort Texas, and which had been circled up defensively behind us. This small courtesy only slightly eased our torment. The mid-day heat was frightful, tempered only fitfully by a sea breeze waning and waxing according to its own devices. Our suffering was made all the worse by the fact that our blouses were buttoned up tight and our leather stocks firmly in place as if we were about to parade in a grand review for Old Fuss and Feathers, himself.

Hermann smiled at me, bringing home to me how very fantastical it all was, and how curiously detached I was from the spectacle. Six thousand Mexican soldiers ready to do battle with us were in serried ranks in the waist-high sawgrass. The infantry, paraded by regiment in a long line, was fronted by a thin, shorter line of Mexican cavalry hardly more than a thousand yards away, their burnished lances glistening in the hot sun. The pennants hanging from their lances alternately drooped and flew bravely in the desultory sea breeze. I couldn't see the Mexican cannon, but they were surely there. On our side of the matter, hardly more than 2,200 of us bluebellies had departed from Point Isabel, and nearly a third of our number were in the rear, guarding the wagon train. It was only then that an electric shot of something twitched through my belly at the thought of being on the short end of the two seemingly unequal sides.

If we'd been sitting on the half-finished rampart of Fort Texas, looking at the Mexican army ensconced safely on the other side of the Rio Grande, Hermann and I would have made sport of trying to identify the different regiments by their riotously varying uniforms. To do so now, while in ranks, would have been an act of lèse-majesté that would surely have earned a swift rebuke from anyone who heard us. We simply had to stand there, whether at ease or at attention, and wait for a command telling us what to do. In any case, I had no appetite for it. Figuring out which regiments were fixing to kill me and my fellow doughboys didn't seem very important. More important was holding onto the thought of living through the day. Most important, though, was the realization that my forage cap was no longer absorbing my sweat, which was now streaming into my eyes and burning. I squinted through the tears, making it impossible to distinguish the little bits of color on the various uniforms that would tell me which units were opposite us.

The wind fell off again, and for a moment we heard cries of "¡Viva la República!" "¡Viva México!" A proud horseman pranced along the Mexican line towards our end of things with all his minions formed in a V behind him. As the procession passed, banners were tossed in the air and each of the Mexican regimental bands in turn struck up martial tunes to accompany the cheers.

"Must be Arista himself," Hermann murmured *sotto voce*, his lips not moving.

"Awfully proud-looking. Gives me the shivers ... all that hoopla and their brave show," I whispered as nonchalantly as I could.

"That is what those bastards want you to feel."

"They've succeeded."

"Do not let them bother you, my friend. We are going to ... how do you like to say, Billy? Yes. We are going to croak the bastards today." Hermann chanced a big grin at me. Hoggs's back was turned, and Grant, although he could probably hear us, was paying us no mind as he calmly puffed on his cheroot.

As I grinned back at him, a series of barked orders echoed up and down our line. Our fifes screeched and the drums sounded. In response, the regimental colors were unfurled. The sight of Old Glory flying behind each regiment ripped a deep-throated cheer from every manjack of us. It momentarily eased the cold feeling that had been growing inside me since before we left Point Isabel the previous afternoon. With our simple display, I thought that we had given the Mexicans more than a taste of their own medicine. Then the breeze freshened, whipping away our cheers as if they had never existed. We stood in silence once more, staring at our enemy.

⌇

We stood there for another hour or so, each of us lost in his own thoughts. I watched our new major, who had just taken over command of the regiment. He had been seconded from another regiment that was still up north somewhere, I think, on account of all our officers having seemingly vanished, what with Captain McCall now working directly for Old Zach, and Lieutenant Colonel Garland having taken command of the First Brigade ever since our very own Colonel Whistler had been ignominiously sent home for being drunk on duty. Our major cut quite an elegant figure in his calf-length, snow-white linen duster, which fluttered dramatically as the breeze took it. As he turned this way and that on his horse, moving along the regiment's front, I could see that he wore an open-collared blue and white checked gingham shirt underneath his duster, with a red bandanna tied around his neck. It all looked very comfortable, particularly as my forage cap was now thoroughly sodden and my leather stock slimy against my neck with the day's sweat. I could only begin to imagine if I reported to morning parade in such a fine duster as the major's with my only visible uniform item being my pantaloons. He wasn't even wearing a regulation forage cap, having instead equipped himself with a broad-brimmed, cream-colored slouch hat of a style that had been all the rage among gentlemen back in Ireland when they took to the countryside. Just another reminder, I suppose, that rank doth have its privileges.

I had heard the major in conversation with Grant a couple of nights back, while we were still at Point Isabel. I was standing post outside Grant's tent, a privilege he rated since he was now in acting command of C Company. Grant had been sitting behind me on his little campstool by the side of his tent, writing in the fading light. The major had cruised past me without so much as a "by your leave," which left me in the unenviable position of not having been able to warn Grant. I heard him leap to his feet behind me. It sounded as if Grant's little camp stool had gone flying into the side of his tent.

"Grant? Damned glad to meet you."

"Likewise, sir." Grant sounded flustered.

"Oh, please, I am so sorry to have disturbed you, Grant. Go right ahead and pick up your papers. Writing a letter?"

"Yes sir."

"Girl back home?"

"Yes sir. St. Louis."

"Harrison told me you've gotten yourself engaged."

"Yes sir."

"Harrison also tells me that back up in Fort Jesup he fined you a bottle of wine three times in a week for joining the mess late for dinner—after the soup had been served." He murmured, "That is quite late indeed. Harrison said that you were apparently spending a little too much time with your young lady and neglecting your duties to the mess."

I could almost hear Grant flush. "Yes sir. Mess rules. Bottle of wine each time an officer is late to mess. Captain Harrison had every right to enforce them."

"That's what he said to me as well. Curious that he should mention the incident, though. Said you were impertinent with him over the matter."

The major let Grant twist a little in the silence. Then he said, "Expensive way to court a young lady."

"I found a way to control the costs after that, sir." The grapevine held that Grant and Captain Harrison, who had been the president of the regimental officers' mess at the time, had positively loathed each other ever since Grant had replied to Harrison, "Yes sir, I understand. But if I am to be fined again this week, I shall be obliged to repudiate."

Known as "Captain Martinet" to doughboys and young pumpkin rinds alike, Captain Francis Marion Harrison acted true to type when he rebuked Grant quite harshly by replying in front of the entire mess, "Grant, young people should be seen and not heard." I had seen Porter, one day not long before his ill-fated patrol—God bless his soul—tease Grant about it. Grant didn't respond. He had merely studied his friend with a very cold eye.

The major—whose name I still hadn't heard—changed the subject. "You've seen General Taylor's orders?"

"Yes sir. Read them to the company this morning."

"Good." The major's voice deepened with anticipation. "Bayonets, Grant. We're to depend upon the bayonet. That's what the Old Man is telling us, and he's right. We'll show those damned papist dagoes a bit of cold steel, and then we'll throw them right back over the river whence they came. Draw a bit of claret, we will." I heard a gloved fist slap into a gloved palm. "That'll teach 'em to take on God-fearing white men."

"Yes sir."

"We've a fine army here, Grant. Professionals to a man. None of these damned volunteers. They were damn near the death of us back in the '30s when we were chasing that red bastard Seminole, Osceola, down in Florida. We'll show the country what its regular army can do—and lick those brown-skinned devils 'afore any of those damned buttermilk-fed volunteer regiments descend upon us." The major's voice took on a confidential tone, "You've done your part in getting this man's army ready. You've done an absolutely fine job with C Company, Colonel Garland tells me. It's as pretty a company as there is in the regiment. He thinks highly of you, Garland does."

"Thank you, sir. But Captain McCall bears most of the credit ..."

There was some rustling and murmuring. Then there was silence. The major must have departed because I heard Grant next to me. "You hear that, Gogan?"

I knew enough not to respond. One cannot talk to anyone outside the strict line of duty while standing post, you know.

"Your bayonet sharp?" Grant asked testily. I heard him pace back and forth once or twice. "Damn it, Gogan. There are times like these when I wonder whether I should have been a soldier at all. This simply is not a just war. Those poor Mexicans didn't ask us to come to the Rio Grande, and now we're fixing to thrash them, all because we came down here to them. And thrash them, we will, Gogan. For these Mexicans are good only for paper wars. Mark my words." He paused for a moment. "But … it's still a damned poor way to settle national grievances, this killing your fellow man who has picked no fight with you, and where you, yourself, have picked the fight with him."

Grant moved back and forth behind me a couple of more times.

"It ain't right, but we're going to follow our orders. We'll put them back on their side of the Rio Grande, and hopefully we'll stay on ours. With any luck, that'll be the end of it, and you'll be able to write to that pretty girl of yours back in Ireland to tell her that you're a hero and still alive."

Amen to that, Lieutenant, I thought. Amen to that. It was about then that the cold feeling began to grow inside me.

⌒

As we doughboys stood easy in our ranks in the sawgrass swaying in the fitful breeze, the shoulder strap aristocracy began paying social calls on one another. At first it was just the officers on horseback, the majors and an occasional captain (there not being enough colonels and generals in our little army to hold a decent high tea), riding over from one division or battalion to another. After an hour or so, even the shoulder straps on foot were visiting from one company to another and gossiping up a storm. As they did, May's dragoons, an entire squadron of them, issued from near the center of our line and thundered full chisel down the entire length of the Mexican line, staying just outside of easy musket shot, all the while looking as if they were on the parade ground. A very tempting target for the Mexican cavalry, infantry, and artillery alike, but nary a shot was fired, and May's dragoons eventually retired to our lines.

"Not likely to spot the Mexican artillery at that speed," Hermann growled to me *sotto voce* as May's dragoons thundered by. "Got to tempt them to shoot at you, to give their position away."

About twenty minutes later, two officers slowly rode out from somewhere down our lines to well within musket range of the Mexican line, much closer than May's dragoons had ventured. They dismounted as casual as you like and walked their mounts some fifty yards or so down the Mexican line towards our end of things, seemingly talking to one another and throwing only the briefest and most occasional of glances at the Mexican lines. After a few minutes, they mounted, rode a couple of hundred more yards and once again dismounted—all still within easy musket shot of the Mexicans. As with May's dragoons, they remained unmolested. After repeating this routine a couple of more times, they galloped back to our lines. I heard Captain Page say to Grant (Page having wandered over to socialize) that they were a damned sight more effective in looking for the Mexican artillery than May had been.

A few minutes later, the drums rolled and fifes screeched. Page skedaddled. Grant turned to face us. "C COMPANY! 'TEN ... SHUN!

We formed and marched towards the enemy. I could hear the fifes squealing out "*The Girl I Left Behind Me*" as encouragement. Its verse, "I'm lonesome since I crossed the hill," and refrain, "For each but does remind me, How swift the hours did pass with—the girl I left behind me," seemed to mock me and my fear. I repressed an overwhelming desire to scream. I sneaked a glance over my right shoulder and saw two regiments maneuvering across the road to face an indistinct mass forming in the chaparral. Mexican cavalry, I supposed. I gave it no further thought as Grant issued a couple of sharp commands, and the company once again stood at attention in line facing the Mexican lancers, who had just advanced some four hundred yards closer to us. I could now see individual troopers on horseback and make out the facings on their uniforms.

Grant told us to stand at rest, made ready to pivot around to face the enemy, stopped, turned back towards us and flashed a smile. "All right, boys. This is as easy as a day on the drill field, and you've been looking mighty pretty on the parade ground today."

Laughter rippled through the ranks, only to be cut short by a terrible sound slicing through the air, just like a steam locomotive going past one's ear, only much, much faster. I turned around instinctively to see where the noise went. A black blur bounced high out of the sawgrass and crashed into an artillery caisson from Churchill's Bull Battery, so-called because it comprised a pair of the biggest guns in our little army's meager artillery train, eighteen-pounder siege guns whose best use was to destroy forts and trenches, and an assortment of caissons and ammunition wagons, all of which had to be drawn by ponderous bull oxen. The battery had been lumbering from the road behind us and was now slowly making its way through the gap between us and the next regiment down the line to our left. Splintered wood flew from the caisson. The driver, who had been talking to his assistant next to him, flew over the back of the caisson like a rag doll flung by a disgruntled giant.

I snapped my eyes forward, realizing that I had just seen a man die in battle for the very first time. Kenny's death was murder in my eyes, as was poor Mary's. And God knows one couldn't have lived even a day in the Five Points without having seen death in all of its forms. This was profoundly different. I wondered if this was what everyone really meant when they talked about going to see the elephant. I had long since figured that I had already seen the elephant and gotten to know him tolerably well in the ten months since I'd landed at Governors Island, what with having been bucked and gagged by Hoggs and Hermann having nearly died from whatever it was that had griped his bowels. But I had been wrong. Perhaps it was what the major meant when he referred to the prospect of drawing a little claret from the Mexicans. He had sounded dispassionate, elegant even. But the death of the redleg catapulted from the artillery caisson had been neither dispassionate nor elegant.

I caught sight of Hoggs as he paced back and forth beside the two thin ranks of C Company. He looked quite green about the gills. I hoped I didn't look as ill as he, for I certainly felt that way. I saw a puff of smoke marking the Mexican battery, and another cannonball screamed overhead. A third one rocketed overhead shortly afterwards and crashed harmlessly behind us.

Gaff chirped, "My God, they're firing balls at us."

I laughed involuntarily, but I and every other manjack was deeply thankful that the Mexican artillery was firing mostly solid shot—brass and copper on account of iron being too expensive, so the grapevine maintained—and when they did fire explosive shells, they were also made of copper, which exploded with great sound and fury, but produced nary a scrap of shrapnel.

"Silence in the ranks." Hoggs slashed his starter on the hapless man next to him. Gaff was at the other end of the rank.

Grant affected not to hear us. He stood nonchalantly in front of us, facing forward, looking for the puffs of smoke that gave away the hidden Mexican artillery battery.

Each of the two guns of the Bull Battery was hauled by a team of ten ponderous oxen tended by a pair of patient Texian drover calling, "Haw, Brindle! Get along, Brandy!" Two separate coteries of redlegs, most of whom had stripped off their blouses in the heat of the day, rolled up the sleeves of their red flannel shirts above their elbows and tied their suspenders about their waists, hovered solicitously about their respective artillery pieces. This stately procession was closely followed by three or four ammunition wagons. One of the Texian drovers, a boy of no more than fourteen, yelled every so often as he helped drive the team hauling the lead ammunition wagon, "Go along, Buck!" At one point, I heard him declare, "Iffen you're killed, Buck, you'll make right fine beef, 'cuz you are fat … and slow." He hardly flinched as a cannonball skittered through the sawgrass less than a yard in front of him and past his wagon. The Mexicans were firing shorter now, and their shot was falling more towards the Bull Battery, as if they sensed its danger. We infantry were apparently not as much of a threat as the eighteen-pounders.

The Texian drovers were urging their oxen back from the two artillery pieces now and into relative safety. The two coteries of red-legs limbered their respective guns into position and sighted them towards the Mexican lines.

Grant turned to us, hand on the pommel of his saber and eyes burning intensely. "Boys, you make sure you scatter out of the way of these Mexican balls …" Gaff tittered. Grant ignored him. "And then reform ranks. We don't want to make their work any easier for them."

One of the eighteen-pounders barked deeply. We cheered once more as the redlegs jumped to reload—a rapid, well-drilled sequence carried out with almost machine-like precision. The shell from the eighteen-pounder exploded above a squadron of Mexican cavalry, and a couple of riders fell, their horses thrashing beneath them. Another shell fired by the second eighteen-pounder burst over a platoon of infantry, and several men dropped. The rank reformed instantly to cries of "*¡Viva México!*" that waxed and waned in the breeze that was now snapping around us with renewed vigor.

We could also hear snatches of music from the Mexican lines— very martial, with drums and trumpets and a cymbal crashing every now and then. We could just see the band as it played, positioned in front of the Mexican infantry line and partially obscured by a squadron of lancers busy controlling their mounts, which were becoming increasingly restive as the occasional shell from the Bull Battery exploded near them. The Bull Battery's artillery crews were so efficient that the two eighteen-pounders interrupted the music at almost perfectly regular, if syncopated intervals as they began to make hot work for the Mexican infantry and occasionally for the hidden Mexican battery. Smoke swirled about the sweating redlegs. Their faces were blackened from the powder, and their red flannel shirts and their relentless pace in sighting, firing, repositioning, and reloading their ordnance made them seem like demons hard at work in some godless factory located cheek by jowl with the very hinges of Hades. It was a feeling that seemed to blossom almost to reality when I tasted the acrid clouds of smoke drifting past us.

Hermann whispered, "It is 'Los Zapadores de Jalisco.' Commemorates one of their best battalions, their Zapadores. Sappers. But they're actually infantry most of the time. Saw them drilling in the square in Matamoros. Quite a sight. They know their business."

"What?"

"What the Mexican band is playing. I heard one of their regimental bands playing it one night."

I thought to ask Hermann how the Sam Hill he knew the name of the tune—and about the Zapadores themselves for that matter, but both eighteen-pounders barked at the same time—one had seemingly waited for the other, and a couple of seconds later two shells exploded simultaneously above the band. The shells must have been spherical case shot, each shell loaded with 120 musket balls, because the band disintegrated instantly into a pulp of smashed trumpets and drums and broken men writhing in the trampled sawgrass. Hardly a figure remained standing. In the place of the trumpets, I thought I could hear the screams of the wounded.

Hermann murmured, "I am going to miss the music."

⌒

About ten minutes later, we heard the higher-pitched bark of six-pounders. It sounded like our flying artillery. I couldn't see them, but it sounded as if a pair of guns were two or three hundred yards to our right, each banging out two or three rounds a minute in a sustained, duple rhythm. I could see the object of their anger, a great mass of Mexican cavalry, horses flinching as the brass shot from the flying artillery smashed into them. The Mexicans were preparing to charge at a hollow square of American infantry. The Fifth, I thought, by the look of her regimental banner stirring in the once-again fitful breeze alongside Old Glory in the very center of the hollow of the square, surrounded by the regiment's mounted shoulder strap aristocracy. I could see the heads and caps of the dismounted officers and sergeants as they swarmed about the hollow, dressing the ranks and readying their doughboys for the inevitable onslaught. The square bristled bayonets that flashed in the sunshine as the first rank in the side of the square facing the mass of cavalry knelt and leveled their muskets, presumably to fire a volley. But the muskets remained silent as the Mexican cavalry reined in their charge a hundred yards or more from the square, loosed an ineffectual volley from their *escopetas*, and wheeled about to regroup for another charge.

The charge of the Mexican cavalry against the Fifth had unfolded in pantomime, accompanied only by the six-pounders bombilating to our right and the deeper report of the Bull Battery to our left. None of it seemed very real. It was all so very far away, acted out with explosions that looked like cotton-puffs and doughboys and *presidiales* who looked like tiny mechanical dolls.

The Mexican cavalry gathered itself for another attack. This time they charged hell for leather towards the waiting square. A volley of smoke silently billowed from the muskets of the kneeling rank, and then there was a second silent volley of smoke. The cavalry charge broke as *presidiales* were swept to the ground. The survivors wavered uncertainly. A third volley, as soundless as its predecessors, put flight to the Mexican hesitancy. The *presidiales* began to retreat, slowly at first, and then pell-mell. The unseen pair of six-pounders banged again, and a few more Mexican cavalrymen at the rear of the retreating mass tumbled to the ground. Then Walker's Texas Rangers swept in behind the retreating Mexicans to cut down stragglers.

A cavalry charge against a square didn't seem so bad … from here, four or five hundred yards away, anyway.

"C Company!" Grant was facing us, and we were on the move once more.

The sun was hanging just above the western horizon now, luridly red through the smoke and haze and still hot on our faces as we advanced steadily in a line towards the enemy. Except for the initial Mexican artillery rounds that had passed overhead, we had been comfortably outside the line of fire since the battle had begun a couple of hours earlier. Since then, the Mexican artillery had fought a losing duel with Churchill's Bull Battery and Ringgold's flying artillery, which had reappeared after helping repel the charge of the *presidiales*. Ringgold's six-pounders were now almost directly in front of us, pouring a torrid fire into the Mexican infantry. I was very glad not to be standing in the Mexican line, on the receiving end of Ringgold's attention. The Mexican cavalry that had screened the infantry had long since vanished, and their artillery had been silent for a while.

Ringgold's six-pounders, which operated in pairs, did not remain in place for more than a couple or four rounds at a time. They dashed about in deliberate haste. The sequence was clockwork, if anything even more precise than it had been back up north on the drill ground at Corpus Christi. The horses were unhitched from the six-pounders, the sweating redlegs, stripped to their red flannel shirts just like their brethren in the Bull Battery, sighted the guns at one target or another—now a company of infantry, next an artillery battery and then a squadron of lancers—and fired several rounds with deadly accuracy. Then, before the Mexican counterbattery, which was so terribly slow by comparison, could find the range, they'd pack up and dash to a new spot. The cumulative effect of their peppering the Mexican lines, along with the deadly work of Churchill's eighteen-pounders, had torn some grievous holes in the luckless infantry regiment directly in front of us.

To our left, a few hundred yards away at the other end of our line, the sawgrass had caught fire. Only the good Lord knew what had started the blaze, but the dry grass was burning well, the flames licking well above the height of a tall man. A bluish-black pall of smoke, acrid and eye-watering, was beginning to obscure the view each side had of the other, and it brought a welcome cessation to both the Mexican and bluebelly artillery fire all along the line. The only other hitch in the entire matter was the fact that we of the Fourth—and also the Fifth to our right, now that they had unshipped themselves from their square since driving off the Mexican *presidiales*—were marching forward all in a great line, arms shouldered and all more or less in step

---

*To Draw the Claret*

to the incessant fifes and drums positioned safely behind us. Grant had drawn his sword and shouldered it as we marched—God knows why. There wasn't a Mexican in sight to be smote with the damned implement. But that was the way of it. Grant was a shoulder strap, notwithstanding his mighty decent manner, and shoulder straps could be mighty peculiar in their habits at times. Even the best of them.

During the lull, both Ringgold and Churchill's batteries had resupplied themselves with ammunition, made some running repairs, and quickly repositioned. (At least in Ringgold's case. The Bull Battery was somewhat more stately in its progress.) Ringgold was now on our left. Churchill was on our right, between us and the Fifth, sitting high on the dirt road that wound its way through the Mexican lines and then on towards Fort Texas. The smoke was clearing now, despite the desultory wind, and the blood-red sun had slid still lower in the sky. The air was oppressively hot and stuffy, and our canteens were preciously low. Every manjack I could see was red in the face, sweating. I licked my lips and realized that they were cracked and bleeding, like everyone else's.

"C COMPANY! HALT!" Grant had scabbarded his saber. "Remember boys, if their artillery starts firing at us, you get out of the way of the shot as they roll through the grass."

Captain Page tapped Grant on the shoulder. Grant saluted, and they once again began to pass the time of day. The shoulder strap aristocracy's social hour had apparently reconvened now that the Mexican artillery was no longer firing at us.

Within a minute of Page having joined Grant, the Mexican artillery began firing again. Ringgold's six-pounders and Churchill's Bull Battery replied almost immediately. The banging of the guns was almost continuous now. We were a lot closer to the Mexicans than we had been three hours earlier and the wind had died down almost completely. Thus we could hear the enemy's guns as they fired—that is when there was an odd lull in the almost continuous barking of Ringgold's six-pounders and the deeper reports of the Bull Battery's eighteen-pounders. Curiously, Captain Page tarried with Grant, even

215

though the artillery duel had recommenced with renewed vigor. Chatting about the weather, I suppose, or what the Fourth's regimental mess would be serving that evening—as if any one of us was likely to eat anytime soon. My stomach gurgled at the thought of a decent meal that didn't contain cold beans and moldy bacon.

"Stand aside!" Page jumped to the side, just in front of me. Our ranks parted like the Red Sea and then closed up just as quickly after a tiny greenish-black cannon ball bounced forlornly through the gap. Enough to take a man's leg away, nonetheless, Hermann said to me. Page turned to say something to Grant. But he never did, for another cannonball hit him in the face, caromed away and decapitated the man next to me, a slow Irish-hating farmer from New Jersey named Johnson. I was covered with the poor bastard's blood and brains.

I closed my eyes, repressing with all that I had in me my alternating and equally overwhelming desires to be physically sick or to simply run away. I cracked an eye and glanced almost involuntarily at Hoggs through the glutinous waste. Thanking God that his back was turned, I chanced a quick swipe to clear my eyes of Johnson's gore, the touch of which to my hand once again almost caused me to vomit. As the stickiness began to dry on my face and smell for all the world like a rancid charnel house, I chanced a look at Hermann. He was impassive, staring at the horizon, blood from either Page or the man who had once stood next to me rolling down his cheeks. I looked back at Page, and the horror of it all almost overwhelmed me for a third time. He was lying in the sawgrass. His lower jaw was gone, and I could see his tongue hanging from his mouth, moving wordlessly, as if it were a giant worm suddenly unearthed and fighting for its life. Save for his eyes, which were wide and unblinking—whether with pain or terror, I could not tell, for Page's face was masked with his arterial blood. But for his wordlessly moving tongue, I would have thought him dead. Grant detailed two men from the ranks, and they pulled Page through to the rear. We reformed again and closed ranks at Hoggs's barked command. The decapitated private lay where he fell, and we all took care not to trip over him as the Mexican artillery continued to fire at us.

Despite this most galling fire from the Mexicans, we did not move. Through clouds of smoke from both Ringgold's and Churchill's batteries, I could see movement along the Mexican lines. Hermann whispered something to me, but it was lost in a sudden tattoo from the drums and a renewed squealing of the fifes. We were to form a square. The Mexican cavalry had reappeared in front of us. I realized with a frisson of terror that this time we were not to be the mere spectators we had been when the Fifth had formed its square an hour ago.

We maneuvered in double quick time, 165, 33-inch steps per minute, banishing all thoughts of fatigue and disgust at the now-dried bloodied waste covering my face and blouse. But our pace was not so fast as we passed Ringgold's battery that I couldn't spare a moment to realize how badly the Mexican artillery had knocked them about since the smoke had cleared and the artillery duel had resumed. Although Ringgold's redlegs had out-dueled their Mexican counterparts, nimbly avoiding the plodding Mexican counterbattery, it was clear that the piper must eventually be paid his due and the butcher paid his bill. However you say it, men were going to die. Major Ringgold himself had just paid that price, lying there, trapped by his horse, which had been shot through. An officer, a lieutenant I think, was standing ineffectually over Ringgold, staring at the man's thigh, which had been visibly shredded to the bone. Ringgold's blood was mingling with the blood bubbling arterially from the withers of his horse. He wasn't dead, for I could see him weakly gesturing to the lieutenant from where he lay.

I lost sight of Ringgold and his lieutenant as C Company pivoted and raced into position in the front rank of the square. We turned, and there was a great gathering of cavalry in serried and impatiently pawing lines some hundreds of yards in front of us. This was no mere rabble of provincial *presidiales*, armed only with *escopetas* that were dangerous to a range of twenty or thirty yards—if they could be fired at all—and who had been press-ganged from the nearest *presidio* where they normally spent their years lazing in the sun and procreating when they were not being massacred by the very Comanche and Lipan Apache from whose depredations they were ostensibly protecting the local *rancheros*. Instead, these were squadrons of lancers. The best the Mexican army had to offer. And they were massing, lances lowered, ready to do to us in the Fourth what the *presidiales* could not do to the Fifth—break our square and turn the tide of battle.

The lancers began advancing deliberately, at little more than a walk. Then they broke into a canter. At two hundred yards, they were at full split, galloping hell for leather. Five lines of two ranks each, serried in front of the broad side of our square. The first rank of the first line crumpled as spherical canister rained a thousand musket balls down upon them. Likely from Churchill's battery. Ringgold's horse artillery were still maneuvering as they regrouped from the Mexican counterbattery fire, and Duncan was on the far left flank, a thousand yards from us. The Mexicans were not daunted, though. Onwards they charged, now at breakneck speed, straight over the ruins of their first line, desperate to reach us before Churchill's eighteen-pounders could rain death upon them once more, and before we infantry could try to break them with our musketry.

It all happened just like we had drilled so many times before, only so very much faster:

"First rank ... Kneeling and Ready!"

I peered down the barrel of my musket, unbalanced as it was by the bayonet, squinting through the sweat dripping from my soaked forage cap.

"First rank ... Fire! Second rank ... Ready!"

As the second rank raised their muskets to their shoulders, we in the first rank fired our muskets. Every musket in our rank fired—except mine. The flintlock clicked on the flash pan and nothing happened. I cursed inwardly and waited.

"Second rank ... Fire!"

The volley from above deafened me, but the combined effect of our two volleys crumpled the leading edge of the lancers, horses and riders tumbling into the sawgrass, broken lances sticking from the ground. The third and fourth volleys from the rear ranks and another canister shot From Churchill's Bull Battery stopped what was left of the Mexican lancers cold, less than a hundred yards from the promised land of our charged bayonets.

The Battle of Palo Alto was over. I stank of a dead man's remains and of the fear and the disquiet of having done sweet damn all on this day when so many of our enemy died.

# CHAPTER 12

# Go It Strong

⌒

As NIGHT FELL, we were ordered not to light any fires for fear of renewed bombardment by enemy artillery. So we ravenously ate the cold beans and moldy bacon from our haversacks and drank what little water we had. I used some to clean a little more of Johnson's remains from my face, resolutely ignoring the smell and stiffness of my blouse, which for now at least was beyond all cleaning. Neither the food nor the drink were nearly enough to sate us. Eventually, Rónán, looking harried and utterly weary and covering for Hoggs's unaccountable absence, detailed a couple of men to fetch more water and another cooking pot or two full of beans from the quartermaster's mess kitchens near the wagon train, which was under the protection of the Artillery Battalion in anticipation of tomorrow's expected renewal of today's unfinished battle.

The couple of mouthfuls of hot beans warmed me for a moment. But it wasn't nearly enough. Worse, the temperature had dropped precipitously since sunset, and every one of us was soaked to the bone in his own sweat from the day's exertions. No one had dry clothing, greatcoats, or blankets, because everything was with our knapsacks half a mile to the rear with the wagon train. So we lay shivering in the dark, exhausted from the day, with only our haversacks for pillows.

I took my mind off my misery for half an hour by taking advantage of the light, poor as it was, from the dying grassfire near out left flank, trying to figure out why my musket had misfired. I unloaded it carefully, mindful of keeping it pointed out into the blackness and the twinkling campfires of our enemy. Hermann nonetheless saw fit to chaff me in a particularly ponderous manner about not killing him or some unfortunate picket walking post two hundred yards from us in the dark as I fiddled with my weapon—although, he allowed, putting buck and ball into the good Sergeant Hoggs would not be an altogether untoward development. Finally, with Hermann having questioned me for a solid ten minutes about whether my native wit had deserted me all together, I found the cause of why my musket had misfired. A tiny bit of something had clogged the touchhole, a common enough problem that could cause one or two out of every ten muskets not to fire in a given volley. I swore at my ill-luck and cleaned my now-repaired musket as best I could. At the risk of a tongue-lashing from Hoggs for not stacking my musket with the rest of the company's muskets, I laid it carefully cross my pack beside me. (Normally, such a tongue-lashing would have been warranted because of the risk of accidental discharge from not stacking my musket. But I was damned if I was going to let my weapon out of my reach before tomorrow's battle. I had been lucky today, and I did not want to press that luck any more than I needed to in view of what tomorrow was likely to bring.) I lay down to doze, weary to the bone. Virtually everyone who was not on picket duty two hundred yards in front of us was now asleep, drowsy with that certain fractured and anxious ennui which, as Hermann told me, came over a man when the killing (or in my case, the busy task of spectating at the killing taking place some hundreds of yards away) was done.

"¡Hola! Mr. Billy and Mr. Hermann."

That was the last greeting I was expecting, and both Hermann and I were suddenly very awake.

"Chapita," I said involuntarily. That swarthy little man we'd met at Colonel Kinney's Sunday dinner, who had tried to dissuade Thornton from continuing his lunatic patrol into the teeth of the Mexican army, and who was still Kinney's chief scout, even in the face of withering criticism from some of the Army's finest over the Thornton Affair.

"It is indeed I." As I thought about it later, Chapita was quite perspicacious to speak in English. I shuddered to think what hearing

222

Spanish spoken might have done to my brethren doughboys as we lay less than half a mile from 6,000 Mexicans who were presumably still looking to kill every manjack of us.

"What are you doing here?"

An evasive shrug, and then, "Looking for Colonel Kinney. I have just been over yonder." He casually gestured to the Mexican lines. Chapita was as bilingual a *tejano* as I had ever met, right down to his colloquial use of our mother tongue.

Hermann and I looked at each other, wondering how in the Sam Hill he had slipped past our pickets. If they were that inattentive now, then God help us if the Mexicans were to get ambitious in the wee hours.

Chapita seemed to read my thoughts. "They are not very happy over there in the Mexican camp, and they will not be inclined to make mischief tonight." There was a glint in Chapita's eye that I couldn't quite read: Was he pleased or disappointed over the state of affairs in the Mexican camp? Chapita added, "Anyway, your pickets are awake enough. It is dark, and I am only one man."

"Do tell." Rónán had just joined us, and he was curiosity incarnate at our chatting with this raffish creature. Hermann hastily introduced them.

Chapita shrugged his acknowledgment, saying, "I just spent a couple of hours walking around their camp. They are very hungry, and they are not very happy about your exploding bombs that killed so many of them. What intrigues me, though, is that so many of them think that their generalissimo, Arista, is a traitor. These poor, misguided fools think that he has agreed to sell the army to *los gringos* for his thirty pieces of silver."

Hermann and I looked at each other in disbelief.

"It is crazy, is it not?" Chapita's eyes were hooded in the flickering light of the dying prairie fire. "There is great resentment that Arista took over command from Ampudia last month, and there are those who would destroy Arista by whatever means possible, even if it means the destruction of …" I thought he was going to say "our," but he seemed to correct himself before he said it. "The Mexican army. It is a sad testimony to the even sadder state of *la patria*. That we could be so busy fighting each other that we forget to fight the Northern Colossus. It is why I can no longer live in *México*, and I now live in *Tejas* and work with Colonel Kinney. It is sad but true."

I noted Chapita's unconscious lapse in the use of "we."

Rónán scoffed. "How'd you get there?"

Yet another shrug. "I have some friends who are with señor Canales."

I wondered again whether Thornton had been right to suspect Chapita. How could the man mingle with Canales's rancheros, when he had so feared for his life in the event of his capture by the Mexican cavalry with Torrejón that day he failed to dissuade Thornton from blundering into the ambush at *Rancho de Carricitos*?

Chapita continued, seemingly oblivious to my inner doubts, "I believe you may know one of them: don Guillermo Ñíguez Rodríguez."

Calandria's father. Serafina's as well. I stole a glance at Hermann. His face was inscrutable.

"Don Guillermo asked me to pass his regards along if I crossed paths with you two fine gentlemen."

Hermann nodded wordlessly. I think that I merely gaped at Chapita, so far from my consciousness had Calandria been—or anyone outside C Company and that damned horde of Mexicans on the ridge in front of us, for that matter. I dismissed her from mind just as quickly, as Chapita continued.

"So you see, I did spend a little time this evening visiting with some of my friends who were riding with Canales today. They were all lost up in the chaparral over there, some distance from General Torrejón and his lancers and *los presidiales*." Chapita gestured in the general direction of the road next to us. "They were very smart, being lost up there this afternoon. They didn't feel like facing your infantry square."

I wondered whether he meant the Fifth facing the *presidiales* or us of the Fourth facing the lancers later in the day.

Rónán gave voice to my earlier doubts in a shocked tone of voice. "Sweet Jesus, Chapita, you're going to get the firing squad yet. That's what that clown Thornton accused you of just before he got himself bushwhacked."

"*Mí amigos* were my passport into the Mexican camp, weren't they? Anyway, I did not go there for my health. I am doing exactly what Colonel Kinney and your general, Old Zach, have asked me to do. Anyway, Thornton is a fool."

"So, what did you learn?" Hermann had become impatient.

"They ran out of ... what do you call them? For their big guns."

"Artillery. Cannon. Ammunition. Shot. Shells. Powder." Hermann became even more impatient.

"Yes. Shot and powder. Their generalissimo, Arista. He said that his cannon needed only 650 cannon balls. So the Mexican cannon, they fired their 650 balls, and then they stopped firing. That is why the battle ended. And that is why General Arista and his men will not be over there in the morning." Chapita gestured towards the camp-fires. "No, they will wait for you somewhere else and try to destroy you there."

"You'd better go tell that to the Horse Marines, Chapita," I said. "Everybody here is figuring that we'll be showing them the cold steel up on that little ridge yonder as soon as the sun rises." I also pointed to the line of Mexican campfires.

Chapita shrugged for a fourth time and turned to Rónán. "Would you be so kind, Sergeant, as to escort me to General Taylor?" He gestured to his serape. "I fear that I might not be quite so welcome otherwise."

The two of them vanished into the gloom. Rónán said later that Perfect Bliss and Colonel Kinney greeted Chapita with open arms. He also observed drily that Colonel Twiggs confirmed the rumor that he was a great supporter of Captain Thornton when he glowered at Chapita.

⌒

We were kicked awake at dawn. The mist was so thick that we couldn't see fifty feet. I hoped that meant we were not going to form up for some precipitous, hell for leather assault against an army we couldn't see before they (or we, for that matter) had tasted some morning joe. God only knows I wanted a bottomless pot of it to shake away the ennui of fatigue that gripped me as I awoke. No early assault meant that we could enjoy breakfast—cold beans from last night and then later more bacon that had miraculously appeared with still more at least warmish pots of beans. Then I thought: Why wouldn't we sneak up on them and give them a little morning treat? They wouldn't be expecting it. I pushed the stray thought aside, not wanting to face combat again quite so soon. My hope was rewarded, for Old Zach seemed to have contracted a bad case of the slows. There seemed no rush to form us up as we set about the fresh waves of beans and bacon.

After about ten minutes, the cry came to form up, which caused a lurch in the pit of my stomach. It was a false alarm, for we were merely led over to the *resaca* across the road and allowed to refill our canteens. We moved slowly enough that I was able to drink deeply while at the water's edge and douse my head, my flannel shirt and my blouse in anticipation of the coming heat (not to mention scrubbing out some of the worst of the remains of poor Johnson's head). We could see the heat shimmering in the air as the sun rapidly burned away the mist to reveal a clear blue sky. My belly was as full as it was going to get with beans, bacon, coffee, and water, and both Hermann and I still had a little food left over for our next meal. Life was looking a little better than it had when we first woke up.

When we returned to our position in the line, I saw that Chapita's prediction that the Mexicans would be gone in the morning had come true. There wasn't a flag or a human to be seen when the mist had cleared sufficiently to see the little ridge where the enemy had set up camp the night before. All we could see was the rear guard of the Mexican army filing away down the Matamoros road like the hind end of some snake slithering back to its haunt. We knew, though, that the Mexicans still meant to do us some grievous harm on this side

226

of the río Bravo. Just as the last of the mist lifted, we heard far off in the distance the crump of the Mexican artillery as they had renewed their cannonade of Fort Texas. About an hour later, we saw Captain McCall and an advance guard of two companies of doughboys quick-march down the road that the retreating Mexicans had taken. The dragoons also were busy dashing about hither and yon, patrolling our flanks and keeping a north eye on our adversaries.

"Burial detail." That was the word down from on high. The big bugs wanted us to bury the Mexican dead. Thankfully, precious few Americans other than the luckless, decapitated Johnson had died, and none of them remained on the field. Almost as soon as the guns had stopped firing, we'd quickly scooped up our dead and those of our wounded who had not been as lucky as Captain Page to have been carted off during the battle itself. They went straight to the tender mercies of the sawbones operating by the light of candles and campfires near the wagon train. We'd all heard the occasional unearthly scream last night as the surgeons sawed off some limb or another lickety-split. As Dr. Crittenden had told Hermann and me all those months ago, when we were waiting in the middle of Aransas Bay to be rescued after the *Dayton* explosion, any surgeon worth his salt took pride in how fast he could whip a limb off and make ready for the next unfortunate. It was a good medical skill to have when you hadn't even a soupçon of ether or tincture of opium to dull a man's pain. I was happy that I had never been tasked with acting as a surgeon's orderly, which often happened when there were many casualties from a man's company or battalion. My one experience with a military hospital (or any hospital at all, for that matter) had been during Hermann's illness. That experience had been far more than enough for me, even though I hadn't witnessed even a single amputation. It might have been the viscera from Johnson that was making me particularly sensitive this morning, but I was happy nonetheless to be clear of such duties.

We made our way forward in parties of four or six or so, bayonets fixed in case some poor bastard who had been lying on the no man's land between us and the Mexicans still had the gumption to be disputatious. We didn't find any wounded. Instead we came upon clumps of dead Mexican soldiers once we began marching across where the enemy's lines had stood yesterday. Many of the corpses were grievously wounded in the head, which bore eloquent testimony to the deadly effect of the spherical case and shells flung at the enemy by Churchill's Bull Battery and Ringgold's (now Ridgeley's, we had heard, on account of Ringgold's wounds) and Duncan's flying artillery yesterday afternoon. Others were missing limbs and heads entirely, carried away by the solid shot that our artillery had also rained upon the Mexicans. We stopped to bury the dead of the band that had been playing "*Los Zapadores de Jalisco*" before being rudely cut down by the Bull Battery. Half our group began digging a mass grave for the two score or so dead musicians who lay amidst their shattered instruments, undisturbed since they'd died mid-note. The rest of us were detailed to pick up the poor bastards to the mournful clank of our brethren's shovels and spades. I could see shattered clarinets, trumpets, drums, and flutes amidst the carnage, and that foul odor of the not-so-freshly dead assaulted my senses. I turned away, suddenly very sick.

"Let us go it strong." Hermann was suddenly next to me. "Do not be yellow. These poor devils deserve a decent burial—or at least as decent a one as we can give them this morning." Hermann crossed himself—something I very rarely saw him do. He continued in a more practical vein, "Anyway, Hoggs is on a rampage."

He gestured to the bastard, who was cuffing a poor unfortunate about the head with his starter and knocking him to his knees for some imperceptible failing. Rónán quietly moved the rest of the company away and engaged them in various tasks to give them a better chance of avoiding Hoggs's ire—and to get the grisly task of burying the dead musicians over with as quickly as possible. Grant had a stony look fixed upon his face, so it was hard to figure out what he thought of Hoggs's display. He spoke only once, directing Rónán to have us shield our noses and mouths with our kerchiefs to mitigate the burgeoning stench.

I picked up my first corpse by the shoulders to drag him to the grave, and his cap fell off. Three or four letters fell out, and without thinking, I stuffed them into my pocket. The third or fourth corpse I dragged to the grave had a daguerreotype of his sister in his hand. He was an officer, and he must have been standing in front of the band when the shells exploded overhead. I stuffed the daguerreotype into my pocket, not wanting to bury it with its dead owner. After an hour's heavy labor, we were done, and the company was forming up, save for the two gravediggers who were going to fill in the last of the shallow grave. I happened upon the last corpse to be interred. I stopped cold, for the corpse was not a man, but that of what had once been a very pretty young woman. Her long black hair had spilled out from her cap, which must have jarred loose as she fell to the ground. I would have been inclined to believe her to be merely asleep, but for the two cymbals lying on top of her that had been riddled with half a dozen musket ball holes from the spherical case shells that had destroyed the band. I picked her up to carry her rather than merely dragging her to the grave. But I recoiled in horror and damn' near dropped her when I realized that the entire back of her head was missing. Her brains and clotted blood freshly stained my blouse as I carried her over to the open pit and placed her as gently as I could atop another dead Mexican soldier. I left the riddled cymbals on the ground. Nobody said a word to me when I rejoined the column, still stinking of the poor girl's blood and brains, and we marched off in pursuit of the Mexican army. It was during the march that I surreptitiously disposed of the daguerreotype and letters I had purloined. I suddenly did not want to know anything about my enemy as we marched towards him once more, as he waited at a dry riverbed called Resaca de la Palma.

~

# CHAPTER 13

# We Will Depend Upon It

⌒

UNTIL THE DAY HE DIED, Grant was always very reticent—humble, even—about his exploits saving the lives of so many of us in C Company during the Battle of Resaca de la Palma, which we fought just a few hours after the burial detail. Grant always maintained later that C Company charged over ground that had already been taken by other American doughboys. He claimed that his exploit—and hence ours—was equivalent to the soldier who'd boasted that he had cut off the leg of an enemy. As Grant tells the story, the soldier was asked why he hadn't cut off his enemy's head. The soldier replied that he would have, but someone had gotten there before him. Grant concluded that nothing would have turned out differently at the Battle of Resaca de la Palma had he (and presumably the rest of C Company, Fourth Infantry) not been there. I recollect the afternoon of the 9th of May, 1846, a little differently.

The sun was well past its prime by the time we had deployed into a line and had promptly gotten lost in a seven- or eight-foot-high forest of chaparral that abruptly terminated the sawgrass through which we had been marching for a couple of hours. During a brief break, just as we entered the bantam forest, Grant had briefed us that somewhere up ahead of us was an old, dry riverbed laden with *resacas*. (Apparently the Rio Grande had once meandered through the area.) And somewhere beyond that, on a small bluff overlooking the far side of the riverbed, the Mexicans had dug themselves in, and they were patiently waiting for us.

For about ten or fifteen minutes now, starting just after we entered the chaparral forest, musketry and cannonades had commenced to our left and had steadily increased in intensity such that it was now virtually nonstop. The engagement was utterly invisible to us, and it sounded strangely disembodied and unreal, rather like hearing Hephaestus hammering at his forge. I had no concept of who was doing what to whom. For all we knew, the Mexicans could be crushing the bluebellies' line to our left, turning our flank and descending upon us at any moment. To our right, there was an occasional—and equally invisible—ripple of musketry as some company or platoon on one side or the other fired upon his enemy.

We eventually lined up in a small clearing in the midst of the diminutive forest. Grant had us standing easy while he conferred with Hoggs about something or other, pointing at the brush in front of us. Grant was good that way. He had also allowed us to pass the time of day in the softest of whispers (as long as he couldn't hear us, he said). This magnanimous gesture must have stuck in Hoggs's craw. Rónán Finnegan passed in front of us with his fingers to his lips and his sergeant's chevrons oddly prominent on his arm. When he reached the end of the line, he opened his haversack, again pressed his fingers to his lips, pulled out a canteen and mouthed the words "mountain dew." The company's discipline in the face of the prospect of a mouthful of whiskey was magnificent. You could have heard a pin drop as the canteen silently passed down the line. Grant and Hoggs continued to talk, both of them staring intently at the wall of chaparral in front of us. Rónán passed by Hermann and me and winked deliberately at us. When he reached the end of the line, he scooped up his canteen from the last man and took one last taste. When he turned around to face forward after having placed his canteen back in his haversack, both Grant and Hoggs were staring at him.

"Just making sure the lads had one last mouthful of water, sir," he whispered. "It be a powerful hot and thirsty day today."

Grant ignored him, and we doughboys of C Company were impassive. Hoggs scowled.

Grant spoke *sotto voce*. "They're up there, boys. Just ahead of us." He pointed to the thicket in front of us. "So be very quiet. We're going to creep up on them and give them a taste of this." He grabbed Hermann's musket and emphasized the bayonet. "Old Zach told us that we may depend upon it." Grant grinned. "So, boys, let there be no doubt that we shall depend upon it up there." He pointed at the thicket again. "Follow me, and stick together as best you can. If we get separated, it's every man for himself, and we'll meet on the other side."

With that, he led us into the thicket as the unseen battle howled about us in an ever-increasing frenzy. After about five minutes, we approached the far edge of the thicket where the chaparral abruptly ended at a muddy expanse that gave way to a gentle incline thirty yards away on the far side. To our left was a *resaca* with cattails growing at its borders. To our right, the mud dried out to sandy ridges and the open expanse widened to a hundred yards or more. Grant pointed upwards, and I followed his hand. At the crest of the gentle rise, a company of Mexican infantry reinforced by a small cannon had dug in behind an impromptu breastwork of half a dozen dead mules. The company was in the process of shouldering arms, and the rammer was being withdrawn from the cannon.

"EVERYBODY! DOWN!" We hardly needed Grant's stentorian command as we flattened ourselves as low as we could go. The Mexican cannon boomed and the Mexican infantry's muskets cracked in a ragged volley. I swear that cannon ball howled past not a foot above my head before it crashed harmlessly into the chaparral behind us. The musket balls sounded like angry hornets as they snapped twigs and small branches and scattered leaves overhead.

Still a little stunned by the Mexican volley, I heard a man start swearing on my left. His cartridge box was burning hotly, and his blouse smoldering. He shrieked in panic, and his companions next to him rolled him in the sand and smothered the flames. I wondered how in the name of Old Scratch his cartridge box could have caught fire. Then I realized that the box, which was full of powder in little wax paper cartridges, must have been struck by a musket ball and ignited.

"CHARGE BAYONETS, BOYS! CHARGE! Run as if your lives depended upon it!" Grant scrambled to his feet, waved his sword and ran out of the thicket without a backward glance.

I lurched to my feet and followed him as fast as I could. Thorny branches of the chaparral seemed to grab at me, but I stumbled my way clear and joined the rest of the company in roaring "Give 'em Zach!" as we clambered up the incline, bayonets leveled, and then jumped on and stumbled over the dead mules at the incline's crest. I glimpsed terrified faces gathered about the cannon as I fell to my knees and then scrambled back to my feet. The ramrod hung crookedly from the mouth of the cannon. Before I could level my musket, the cannon's crew turned and ran. Out of the corner of my eye, I saw Hoggs slide out of sight down the incline we had just climbed. I couldn't tell if he had been shot.

To my right, Hermann remorselessly bayoneted two Mexican infantrymen who had tarried too long. He speared the first one like a fish, and then pirouetting like a dancer, he slashed across the chest of the second unfortunate. I ran towards him. I looked around and only Hermann, Gaff, one or two others, and I were there with the cannon. I didn't see Grant or the rest of the company. Where the devil had they gotten to? We hadn't gone that far astray in fifty yards. Or had we? I looked around again. The Mexicans who had fled the top of the bluff as we'd charged up and over it were no longer retreating. They'd stopped in an untidy mob, fifty or a hundred strong, and an officer was exhorting them to turn and face us. I could see him waving his sword and shaking his fist. If he succeeded in rallying his men, we were too few—seven of us, I counted—to stop them. They would almost certainly sweep us from the gun and back down into the *resaca* from whence we had come, where they could slaughter us with volleys of disciplined musketry. Either that or they'd kill us outright where we stood.

"Quick! Help me turn this thing around." Hermann gestured to the Mexican cannon.

"Do you know how to shoot it?" I asked.

"It's a big musket," Hermann snapped. "It's already loaded! At least I hope to God it is." He pulled the ramrod out.

I helped Gaff and the others lift the box trail of the gun carriage—my God, it was heavy, even with the leverage. So old-fashioned compared to our modern six-pounders.

Hermann ordered, "Heave 'round, boys!" We pushed the gun carriage clockwise, and the gun pivoted on its wheels.

"Stop." Hermann pointed to the mass of Mexicans who had after what seemed to be many moments formed into two irregular ranks. They were fixing bayonets, and were about to charge us. "Bring it back just a bit. There. Drop the trail. Billy, find the match. And the pricker. And the priming powder."

"What's a pricker?"

"To poke the cartridge through the hole on the top. The quill's got the priming powder in it." He turned to the rest of our little group. "The rest of you: FORM A LINE! IN YOUR OWN TIME, LOAD MUSKETS!"

I fumbled about and found implements vaguely resembling what Hermann had described. My hands shook from the rush of having to quickly—without error—complete a task I had never before undertaken, when my life and those of my friends depended upon it. I leapt to my feet and jabbed the pricker through the touchhole.

"KNEEL!" Hermann then called back to me, "Billy, prime it. Put the quill into the touchhole. Tell me when you are ready."

A few more seconds of fumbling about. I willed myself to focus on priming this gun and not to look up at what was about to come down upon us.

"Billy ..." Hermann hissed urgently.

"Ready!" I snapped as I looked up. The Mexicans were now charging, bayonets leveled, running full chisel right for us. Their numbers had grown. I figured that there must be a hundred or more of them by now. And they would be on us in seconds.

"Billy, fire only on my command. PLATOON! READY! FIRE!"

The paltry six muskets spat. Three charging Mexicans stumbled and fell. The rest of the attacking mass kept coming, for they knew that there was no second rank of muskets to protect us and our enemy wanted to exact revenge upon us for all that had happened these past two days.

"Billy! FIRE!"

I leaned over the wheel of the gun, which was almost to the middle of my chest, taking care to keep as clear of it as I could in case the gun actually went off. I touched the match to the touchhole and then jumped back. For an instant—which seemed to last an eternity—nothing happened. Then the gun bellowed and kicked back, missing my feet by barely an inch. The gun must have been double-shotted, because half a dozen Mexican soldiers tumbled to the ground, one of them spraying blood everywhere. The men around him wavered, but the rest, still far too many for us, kept coming. We were dead men, I thought wildly.

"PLATOON! CHARGE BAYONETS!" As the platoon rose to their feet, bayoneted muskets at their hips, I suddenly remembered that my musket was lying against the match tub. I lunged for it and joined the tiny line of our makeshift platoon. Really more of a squad, I thought wildly, and not even a full squad of a dozen. Hermann really was getting grand in his ideas by calling us a platoon.

"PLATOON! CHARGE!"

We sprinted forward. I wanted to close my eyes and wish it all away. There was hardly ten yards between us and the Mexicans who were still charging us. Then a miracle occurred: a volley of musketry. I flung myself to the ground, not knowing where it was coming from or from whom. Then there was a second volley and a third. I looked up. Hermann had landed next to me and Gaff on his far side from me. I couldn't see anyone else. In front us, hardly more than three or four or seven yards away, Mexican soldiers were tumbling to the ground. Those who were still on their feet were starting to run away. The officer—a lieutenant—who had been rallying his troops just a moment before, was kneeling and blankly staring at me. He was bleeding from his mouth. I watched him slowly slump to one side. He did not move again.

Hermann tapped my arm, and we scrambled to our feet. Hermann hauled Gaff up, and the three of us, joined by the rest of our impromptu platoon, instinctively ran towards the fleeing enemy. I looked to my right, and an entire company ... more ... too many to count, were madly charging at right angles to us, Grant in the lead, brandishing his saber above his head, a rictus grimace on his bearded face. Where they had come from, I hadn't a clue. We joined in the mad rush. I had no idea where we were going—or why.

⌒

Every so often, it occurs to me that I do not easily remember the lessons of life. The moments after Grant saved us was one such occasion. When I finally stopped running madly in a blood lust ready to spear any living creature with my bayonet just as Old Zach had ordered us to do, I was once again separated from the sweet safety of C Company. I was alone, although being alone in the midst of the Mexican army's camp was a relative term. All around me were small groups of doughboys, some led by officers, although most were not. All were chasing cowed Mexican soldiers fleeing for their lives.

"What do we do with them?"

I whirled around in shock. It was Gaff. Kneeling in front him, Gaff's bayonet at her throat and tears brimming in eyes wide with terror, was a *soldadera*, a woman who had accompanied her husband on campaign. His head lay in her lap, and I suspected that he was not long for this mortal coil.

"Leave them."

"Billy." Gaff whined like a petulant little boy denied his dessert.

"For the love of Moses. Leave the poor woman alone. He's going to die ... and then where will she be?" I closed my eyes for moment, thinking of Mary, who had died in my lap not so very long ago.

"I want to capture a prisoner and take him to Lieutenant Grant."

I stared at Gaff. He lowered his bayonet from the *soldadera's* throat. She was crying now. Her man had closed his eyes. I shut the image out of my mind and instead stared at a giant kettle of beans simmering over a fire next to the *soldadera*. I picked up a ladle that had been dropped onto the ground, wiped it on the seat of my pantaloons, and scooped out some beans. I ate hungrily and then offered the ladle to Gaff. He took it and ate as greedily as I did.

"Do what you want," I said to him. "I'm going to look around."

Gaff waved at me as he stuffed his mouth. As I turned away, I saw him kneel down next to the crying *soldadera* and gently remove the dead man's head from her lap.

In front of me was a roaring fire consuming a stack of papers. Just behind it was a magnificent tent surrounded by a number of other, smaller and slightly less grand tents. I slipped past the fire, which blasted me with its heat, and warily approached the big tent. I poked my bayonet through the curtain across the entrance and swept it aside. Inside, bent over an enormous, ornate desk in the center of the tent, were two Mexican officers, both resplendent in blue uniforms bedecked with gold braid. (I couldn't have told you the ranks, but these coves were really quite splendiferous.) They were gathering papers to burn in the fire.

"¡*Señores!*"

They both stood upright and stared at me wide-eyed.

"Please put down the papers and show me your hands," I said in Spanish in as conversational a tone as I could manage, pointing my (still-unloaded, I suddenly realized) musket at them. "Turn around." I gestured to the beautiful carpet in front of the desk, on which I stood in my muddy brogans. "Kneel here. Hands behind your heads."

The two officers complied wordlessly.

"Keep still, gentlemen." I exchanged places with them, burning with curiosity over what was on the desk—and whose desk it was. "Don't move."

I looked at one of the stacks of paper. The top document was a letter in beautifully elaborate Spanish from the Mexican president himself, Mariano Paredes, to General Arista. The letter left no doubt that *el presidente* expected *el general* to win a great victory and to capture Old Zach and the entire *yanqui* Army of Occupation (not how either term was referred to in the letter). The letter went on to instruct Arista to send Old Zach and the other captured American shoulder straps to Mexico City lickety-split. The letter further admonished Arista to treat them with all the care and attention as became the magnanimity of the great nation of Mexico. I was a little miffed to note that *el presidente* had failed to mention anything about the care and feeding of us mere bluebellies once Arista had us safely in captivity. I pointed out this lapse in the Mexican president's courtesy to the two officers kneeling on the carpet in front of me. They were not amused. One of them scowled. The other remained impassive.

Next to the pile of papers was a magnificent pistol in a plain leather holster. A repeating pistol of the revolving type. A Colt Paterson, to be more precise. I had never seen one up close before. Brannagh had told me about her father's repeating pistol. I had seen Texas Rangers such as Captain Walker swaggering about with them casually belted and holstered and slung low at their hips. And I remembered that poor Lieutenant Porter had one in his hand when he died, a gift from his father, the commodore. But I had never held one in my hands. I wondered where in the Old Scratch this had come from. Then I remembered that Captain Walker's camp had been overrun by Torrejón's and Canales's cavalry several days before, while the rest of the army was up at Point Isabel, and a number of these remarkable weapons had been captured. I supposed that it was not surprising that one of the captured repeating pistols—there being none like them in the entire Mexican army—would have been presented in triumph to the army's commanding general. I wondered briefly where the other dozen or so captured Colt Patersons had disappeared to. I put my musket down on the desk, bayonet pointed threateningly at my two prisoners. I politely admonished them not to move. I pulled out the gun and saw that it was loaded. I smiled at my prisoners, as I stuffed it into my belt and the holster and loading equipment into my haversack. I gathered up my musket and motioned my prisoners to their feet. We then proceeded out of the tent, my bayonet in the small of the back of one of them.

I suggested to his companion that if he ran, it would cost his friend his life and cost him his manhood. What's more, I allowed to him, I'd take great pleasure in hunting him down and exfluncticating him for being a pusillanimous little shit. We were immediately confronted by a wild-eyed lieutenant running through the tent complex with a rabble of doughboys behind him, bayonets fixed and all of them to a man breathing hard.

"A couple of prisoners, sir."

The lieutenant stopped with a lurch hardly more than a yard or two in front of my prisoners, whose faces had blanched even further at the sight. They raised their hands even higher over their heads as the lieutenant appraised them with a bemused detachment.

The lieutenant recovered himself and said to me, without saluting (since I could not salute him, what with being somewhat otherwise preoccupied). "Very good, Private. Your name?"

"Gogan, sir. Billy Gogan. C Company, Fourth Infantry. There's a lot of important papers in that tent over yonder, sir. These coves were trying to burn them all up 'afore we caught up with them."

"Well done. Who is your company officer?"

"Lieutenant Grant, sir."

"I shall look him up and tell him of your initiative. Carry on."

Which I did after I left the prisoners with the lieutenant and his men. As soon as I had a moment's privacy, behind one of the lesser tents, I slipped the repeating pistol unobtrusively out of my belt and into my haversack. Then I headed back in the direction of where I thought C Company might be. As I did, I fell in with a couple of fellows from the Fourth's F Company, including a corporal named Reeves. They'd had a far tougher day than C Company on account of their having to take the battery of Mexican guns controlling the Matamoros road as it crossed the old riverbed. Reeves was positively outraged about one of the dragoon shoulder straps, Captain May, having taken the credit for the capture of a Mexican general whom the Fourth had nabbed as they and the Fifth took the battery. To hear Reeves tell it, May had been commanded by the Old Man to capture the Mexican battery, which would allow the Americans to attack the center of the Mexican line without fear of being torn to pieces.

May stood six-foot-four and sported flowing shoulder-length hair, a magnificent beard, and an even better moustache. According to the grapevine, he really was every bit as pollrumptious as Thornton aspired to be. May was ready to attack the Mexican battery without further ado or thought, when Ridgely suggested to him mildly that he might want to wait until the flying artillery had drawn the Mexican fire, it being quite a bit safer to charge a battery while it's reloading than when it's ready to pump you full of grape, canister, and whatever else they might have at hand to greet you. May wisely acceded. Ridgely forthwith fired his four six-pounders, and the Mexicans duly replied. May and his bowlegs rode at the Mexicans like a pack of hounds after a hare, with nary a shot fired at them.

"But," Reeves sniffed contemptuously, "May was a right daft bottle-head. He and his bowlegs overran the battery, all right. But they charged so hard that they didn't stop for a clean quarter of a mile after that. They had to ride back to the battery through a hail of musketry from several companies of Mexican infantry supporting the battery. Not surprisingly, a whole raft of bowlegs got themselves croaked on the ride back to the battery.

"Worse, when May and his bowlegs finally made it back to the battery, they couldn't hold it against a counter-attack by the Mexican infantry." Reeves spat in disgust. "That's when we boys of the Fourth and the Fifth was ordered to take the battery and hold it, by God! Well," he continued, "take it, we did, although Ridgely's guns did kill several of us as we took the first gun, on account of some big bug not having told them about the Old Man's orders."

"The Mexicans fought like devils," Reeves murmured. "And we killed them for it." Reeves told me that the Mexican dead and wounded piled up around their abandoned artillery pieces. The general, a fellow named de la Vega, was standing alone among his dead and dying soldiers, swearing in Spanish when half a dozen doughboys leveled their bayonets at him and threatened to run the cove through if he didn't shut pan forthwith and surrender right quick. Well, General de la Vega haughtily refused to surrender to mere bluebelly peons. He insisted instead upon yielding his sword to a proper officer, and not to a mere corporal such as Reeves, the senior non-commissioned officer on the scene, because he obviously was not a sufficiently magnificent fellow to receive the little dago's sword.

Before Reeves and his companions could find Lieutenant Hays, their company commander, May rode up. De la Vega promptly offered up his sword to May, on account of his being a fellow member in good standing of the shoulder strap aristocracy. Reeves finished his story by complaining that he'd heard tell that May had taken the Mexican general all a' helitywoop and without delay right up to Old Zach and presented de la Vega's sword to the Old Man as if he'd captured the damned dago all by himself.

I allowed that there were some powerfully bad shoulder straps running around, and we parted ways.

It was later that night when I finally found Hermann, who warned me to stay out of Hoggs's way. I asked him why, and Hermann replied that Hoggs was on a rampage after me, because I had been missing for a couple of hours. Hermann suggested that I instead report in with Grant and explain myself.

Before I left, he said, "Rónán was shot."

"What happened?"

Hermann shrugged. "He caught one when we came out of the chaparral and got ourselves all split up. I found him after you disappeared."

I shrugged in return.

"I don't think he is going to go home yet, though."

"Thank God. Where is he?"

"Back with the sawbones at the wagon train. They're going to ship him and the other wounded up to Point Isabel in the morning.

I am going to go see him as soon as we are finished up here and the company is bivouacked." Hermann looked at me peculiarly. "Yes, well you had better look lively, there, Private Gogan."

I gave him a slightly mystified look and replied to him in kind, "Yes, Corporal."

I found Grant a couple of minutes later. He was giving Hoggs instructions on gathering the wounded—doughboys and Mexicans alike—and getting them to the field hospitals. Hoggs shot me a most venomous look as I walked up and saluted Grant.

"Ah, Gogan. The prodigal private returneth."

"Yes, sir."

Grant turned to Hoggs. "Sergeant, that's all for now." Hoggs saluted, and Grant turned back to me. "So, where have you been these past hours?"

"Gaff and I got separated from the rest of the Company when you rescued us, sir."

"Well, Gaff made it back much faster than you did, and with a crying Mexican woman in tow, no less. Know anything about it?"

"A little, sir."

Grant didn't press me on the matter. Instead, he said, "Now that you're back, report to Sergeant Wurster. I think you'll find he has something for you to do."

"Sergeant, sir?"

"Well, I needed someone with poor Finnegan all but gone home. Hasn't he sewn on his stripes yet?"

I furrowed my brow, but for the life of me I couldn't remember.

Grant smiled. "You should be more observant, Corporal."

"Sir?"

⌒

About a week later, I learned that Grant was just about the only second lieutenant in the Fourth Infantry not to have been brevetted to first lieutenant for bravery during the Battle of Resaca de la

Palma. According to the grapevine, Captain Harrison—who himself had been brevetted to major on account of the day's doings—had berated Grant for not having captured more prisoners when C Company charged the Mexican gun and infantry on that little bluff overlooking the *resaca*. Harrison also saw fit to neglect mentioning Grant in the despatches.

# CHAPTER 14

# Matamoros

⌒

*[Editor's note: The original manuscript contains two letters as part of this chapter, one from Billy to Calandria and a second, also from Billy, to Evelyn. Both letters were dated the same day and had been edited to be virtually identical. The elided letters are reproduced below with the differences noted in brackets.]*

June 19, 1846

Dear [Evelyn] [Calandria]

You may have heard that the war between America and Mexico has started. We fought two battles in early May and sent the Mexican army back over the Rio Grande, as we Jonathans call it. The Mexicans call it the río Bravo or río del Norte. A couple of weeks ago, the Army of Invasion (which is what we call ourselves nowadays) finally crossed the river and occupied Matamoros, which is the capital city of this part of Mexico. There was a lot of palaver about how Old Zach did not immediately cross the river and deliver a *coup de grâce* to the Mexicans. Perhaps we should have, but then again, no one had thought to build the components and boats necessary for a bridge across the river.

Hermann and I are safe and sound. He is sitting next to me on the south bank of the Rio Grande in the shade of a mesquite tree, *[Editor's Note: the following clause appears only in the letter to Calandria.]* writing letters to Serafina.

I am sorry to report that our great friend, Sergeant Rónán Finnegan, was shot through by a Mexican musket ball. We all pray that he will live. He is in hospital up at Point Isabel with the rest of our wounded. Hermann and I are hoping to visit him soon. Lieutenant Grant has promised to take the two of us along in a fatigue detail which is going up to Point Isabel in the next day or two. The good lieutenant apparently convinced Major Allen, who now commands the Fourth Infantry, that the future well-being of the regiment lies in the balance of our being permitted to go.

So here I am in Matamoros, Mexico, a city—and a country—that twelve months ago I didn't even know existed. Someone recently said to me that Matamoros is a handsome place, and I have to agree, although there is great poverty here as well as great wealth.

Matamoros is on the south bank of the Rio Grande. The valley is fit for kings despite it being in the midst of a broiling desert. The rich soil and bountiful water from the river have allowed a tropical jungle to spring up in a welter of shrubs intertwined with vines and creepers, creating places where the sun's rays never penetrate. Had the Egyptians been here three thousand years ago, they would have excelled even more than they did on the River Nile.

[*Editor's note: This paragraph appears only in the letter to Evelyn.*] Dearest Evelyn, there are birds here that defy an Irishman's imagination, with herons and egrets that render pallid those that you may see on Ireland's rocky shores. The valley teems with birds of iridescent plumage that I cannot begin to identify. I suspect that there are scores of species whose taxonomy has yet to be described, so backward are the Mexican people in this district.

I would have described the public square in Matamoros as beautiful, and perhaps even magnificent, if only the cathedral were completed and the adobe freshly painted. Apparently, the city fathers and the church ran out of money a few years ago, and they were able to erect only the walls and towers, which grandly cast shadows over the square that rotate through the day like twin hands of a clock. The cathedral lies virtually empty and unusable, without even a roof save

for that over a pretty nave graced by only a single stained glass window. But what a window. It catches the morning light and illuminates
a blood-red image of Jesus Christ on the cross from sunrise until the
sun is high overhead. [*Editor's note: This last parenthetical appears only
in the letter to Calandria.*] My dear Calandria, the altar in the nave
compares quite unfavorably to the altar placed beneath that great
mesquite tree outside Colonel Kinney's home the day we met. It con-
sists only of a big silver cross placed on a crisp white tablecloth covering a rude bench, and it is taken down after each service, leaving the
nave rather bereft.

The bishop and his priests finished their residences, which are
next to the cathedral, before the money ran out. I suppose that is to
be expected. But it does jar one's sensibilities when the bishop's residence, a quite fine place, is cheek by jowl with the outward skeleton
of the unfinished cathedral.

The military governor installed by the Old Man has occupied the
former mayor's palace, a two-story, whitewashed adobe affair on the
western side of the square, directly across from the cathedral and right
next to the "calaboose," which is what the Texians call the city jail.
The jail is a mean affair on the inside for all of its exterior grandeur
and beauty, and I should not care to be one of its denizens. When the
Mexican civil authority controlled the prison before we arrived, the
half-dozen prisoners or so held inside were a sorry lot, barefoot and on
starvation's edge, so the grapevine insisted.

These days, the calaboose's principal residents are not Mexican
wrongdoers, nor do many of us doughboys occupy its filthy cells, for we
have rid ourselves of our miscreants, either through dismissal from the
service for misconduct or through desertion to the Mexicans (there
having been quite a few disaffected fellows who believed that a better life beckoned in the uniform of the Mexican soldier). The jail is
instead occupied almost entirely by a never-ending parade of volunteers recently arrived from Louisiana.

Matamoros is a poor town in many ways, mostly because the
Mexican government, the *centralistas*, they are called, imposed so

many rules on trade as to make it virtually impossible for merchants to carry on profitable businesses. For example, the *centralistas* granted a monopoly on the sale of tobacco, which means that it is normally very expensive—even though there was a huge warehouse full of it. The Old Man took possession of the warehouse, and passed the cigars out to us regulars as a bit of reward for our success and for our troubles since we have not been paid since we left Corpus Christi. Not a few coves, particularly those who are not addicted to the evil weed, have used it as a sort of currency to barter with the local Mexican populace for food, drink, and a variety of services.

The warehouse is on the eastern side of town, where many of the poorer inhabitants live in *jacales* very much like those up in Corpus Christi. The ferryboat landing is right next to the warehouse, and I was up there helping distribute tobacco when *Neva* landed and disgorged four companies of Louisiana volunteers. It seemed as if the whole town of Matamoros turned out to see *Neva*, for she was apparently the first steamboat ever to proceed the 100 miles of the Rio Grande up to Matamoros. None of the Mexican populace had ever seen a steamship before, and they all jumped ten feet into the air when *Neva* blew her whistle.

We now have a functioning post office up at Point Isabel, and many are starting to receive letters. I dearly look forward to hearing from you.

I am your devoted,

CHAPTER 15

# We're in Business, Now

⌒

"HOW MUCH DO WE HAVE BETWEEN US?" I asked.

"$164.78, including Jenny's $4.52. She is so anxious to invest with us." Sarah smiled at Jenny and patted the money belt secured deep underneath her petticoats. At least that's where I assumed it was, having neither the temerity nor the desire to test the proposition. She'd held Hermann's and my shares for safekeeping ever since the army marched to Point Isabel, leaving her, Jenny, and the Cottonbalers to defend Fort Texas. Neither of us had asked for them back. Sarah's person was as safe a bank as any place in the Rio Grande valley.

"That's all?" I asked, thinking about how so much of Hermann's and my haul of just over $200 from Rouquette's leather had slowly melted away like the snow in the spring after a hard winter. Ninepence here, a couple of picayune there, for the myriad things a soldier needs to survive, not the least of it being for decent food and new shoes that the army seemed so loth to furnish. It had become apparent over many weeks of conversation prior to the army occupying Matamoros that we were going to have to do something to repair our fortunes. Sarah and Jenny frequently joined our talks, and we slowly began formulating proposals, with Sarah and myself being the primary sources of ideas, the best of which seemed to be a cavaulting house.

"It's enough," Sarah replied primly.

"How much is the house?"

"Fifty dollars for a year."

Sarah, Hermann, Jenny, and I were standing in the cool, shaded courtyard of an eight-foot-high walled casa that was forbidding on the street side of the stout wooden double door. Inside the wall was completely the opposite, a perfect refuge from the heat of the day and the bustle and dirt of the street. It was the perfect venue for a goosing slum, rivaled only by Black Muireann's Church Street cavaulting house. The casa had fifteen rooms in the two floors, with a small garret above a nicely-sized parlor in which we—more correctly Sarah and Jenny—could entertain the shoulder strap aristocracy before they retired upstairs to conduct their business. A back entrance led to a kitchen that we could convert into a slightly less comfortable parlor well away from the shoulder straps, in which we could entertain the Other Ranks. The casa was also blessedly free of damage from Fort Texas's 18-pounders. A couple of buildings a few doors up the street had been quite badly damaged. One of them was completely abandoned. A cannonball had plowed right through the roof and landed in the middle of the floor of the great room, where it still lay.

Just the day before, the casa's owner, a local merchant and quondam *hacendado* of a now-abandoned spread on the north bank of the río Bravo, had deserted his home and fled for his life to Tamaulipas. Foolishly in my view. Not only was he not in any danger, but he was missing the biggest commercial opportunity he was ever likely to see in Matamoros. Now that Uncle Sam had rumbled across the Rio Grande and set up camp just to the west of town, anyone with even a modicum of wits about him could make chink by the bucketful in the nascent boomtown that was threatening to put the Corpus Christi of last winter to shame. Indeed, the same confidence men, card sharps, and knights of the gusset, the latter with their clapped-out cows toddling behind them, who had decamped from Corpus Christi when the army left, were beginning to flood into Matamoros to service the Army of Invasion in its new digs. Moreover, commerce of all stripes between Matamoros and Texas was just beginning to explode. Over the past twenty years, smuggling operations had evolved to avoid onerous Mexican customs duties and to enrich the likes of Colonel Kinney and others like him. Now the Northern Colossus actively encouraged the now-legitimate trade, and turned a blind eye to the other sorts of commerce attendant to any occupation.

The merchant had left his majordomo behind as a forlorn hope to protect his property against the anticipated depredations of the conquering *gringos*. Unlike his employer, the majordomo, a sallow-faced and charmlessly obsequious fellow named Luis (I never learned his surname), had at least some appreciation of the commercial opportunities, for he had contrived to make himself and the availability of the casa known to Sarah. As we toured the casa, Luis expressed to us that his master's beloved casa would be all the better protected if two such distinguished *norteamericanos* as Hermann and me occupied it. (He couldn't distinguish officer from Other Ranks, and we were not disposed to enlighten him.) I suspected that Sarah's cooing in his ear that she was Old Zach's favorite courtesan was what actually persuaded him. No matter, for Sarah and I both recognized that we'd found a gold mine—as long as we secured our title to the house lickety-split. The price in a week's time would surely be ten times what Luis was asking today—and impossible for us to afford. Worse, there would be a score of other brothels in business by then, all catering to the flood of volunteers rushing from Louisiana to join the fray before all the Mexicans were killed.

Within a fortnight after Resaca de la Palma, 1,500 volunteers had made their way, first to Point Isabel and then to Matamoros. Hundreds more were expected to arrive every day for many weeks from virtually every state except New England (the citizens of which according to the grapevine remained resolutely opposed to a war of conquest that promised to add an untold vastness of slaveholding states to the Union). Most arrived hot, thirsty, and footsore from the thirty-odd mile march from Point Isabel. The luckier ones were disgorged from *Neva* or one of the two or three other sternwheel riverboats that had been plying the Mississippi before they were pressed into service by the army at a fabulous day rate. To a man, the volunteers were rumbustious with the excitement of being away from the strictures of home for the very first time. It was on the strength of such freedom the vast majority of them were peloothered within hours of arriving.

Sarah and I may have disagreed on the details, but we knew a business opportunity when we saw one. Even Jenny, bless her heart, was enthusiastic, even if she was a bit unclear on the finer points of prostitution as a money-making proposition. Hermann merely glowered at Sarah and me as we discussed the logistics involved in opening up a better class goosing slum—a parlor house, if you will. Sarah had secured a supply of ice from New Orleans, which seemed utterly fantastical. Apparently mint juleps were undrinkable without ice, and they were currently all the rage in New Orleans. So mint juleps were part of what we planned to give the punters.

I tore myself away from such thoughts by running down my own mental checklist of what we needed to do to open our doors in a couple of days' time. "French letters?"

"Too expensive, Billy." Sarah glared at me. "Safes just ain't worth it. The cullies don't like 'em, and who cares about the dollies? They ain't white. They're Mexican."

"It doesn't matter. We'll not burden these little Indian maidens with whelps born of their labors with the Louisiana volunteers," I said in a toploftical tone. "It's cruel and it's wrong."

"I don't see it, Billy boy. They ain't American, so nobody cares. Anyways, them knights of the gusset, as you so gallantly call them back up north … They don't care a whit about their doxies—even ones as Uncle Sam as Jenny and me and as bleak as driven snow. So why should we care about a bunch of savage Indians?"

"It's bad business to have your dells getting knocked up the instant they start spreading their legs. The minute their bellies swell, you've got to replace them. That's expensive, and it makes it harder to recruit the really bleak morts, if they think they're going to be saddled with by-blows. And the bleaker the mort, the more we can charge for her. That's why we make the cullies use French letters. It's about the chink. Beginning, middle, and end of it."

"You and your bleak morts ... always pining for the dell who's as pale as death," Sarah snapped. Jenny sniggered, and Sarah smiled appreciatively at her. "Them Indians we're hiring are hardly going to be pale like the cullies want them up north. One darkie looks like another to Uncle Sam. And to me, for that matter." Sarah looked thoughtful. "Although, now that you mention it, I have seen a number of nice-looking white girls running around. If they didn't open their mouths, you'd think that some of them were Black Irish or even high-falutin' downeasters—that is, if you dressed 'em right. I'll make sure we have some o' them on staff. Find some proper gowns ... charge a premium for a 'back home' experience ... The dusky ones, they can smoke their cigarillos while they entertain their customers, and we'll charge the simkins extra for the novelty."

"Now you're thinking," I replied to a warning glower from Sarah. "We're going to run a parlor house and charge premium prices for a top-notch flutter. This ain't going to be some hog ranch that'll attract all the wrong sort of attention ... And, worse, get Hermann and me flogged or scragged for our pains."

"I couldn't agree more, Billy m'boy. But safes ain't our problem. We've already got more than enough pretty morts to choose from, bleak, brown, black as death itself, and every shade in between, and I can find a hundred more at the snap of a finger. My God, if you offered the bleakest mort in town two bits to lie with a bluebelly for twenty minutes, she'd act as if she'd found the entrance to the Seven Cities of Gold themselves." Jenny looked quizzically at Sarah. "You know, dearie," Sarah explained. "That mythical, lost goldmine from the olden times that's supposedly up north somewhere in a place called Colorado, which all them señoritas keep jabbering on about. So I just don't understand why we have to worry so much about them molleys."

"Doesn't matter, even if you are right, Sarah. We still don't want them getting knocked up. It's bad business. You're forgetting that French letters'll keep the girls clean, and we can sell clean dells at a premium—a big premium. Flats appreciate it when they've got comfort that they won't be pissing from a dozen holes at the end of the night." I warmed to my sales effort. "Do you know what else? It'll save us lots of chink, because we won't be needing the services of the local Madame Restelle—even if we could find one."

"Is that the Gotham abortionist you were telling me about?" She waved her hand dismissively. "We could find one easily enough. Where there's a midwife, there's an abortionist, and every one of them'll run for two bits damn near as fast as the girls. Anyway, it seems a waste to have to train the girls to use French letters. They won't even know what the Sam Hill they are." She shrugged. "I'm through arguing. Hell, I even did as you asked already, and I wrote away to New Orleans for ten gross of them. Just like you wanted. That took our first $50."

Hermann winced.

"And we'll put another order in the minute we're in business," I said, careful to keep the triumph out of my voice.

"Hmmph." Sarah rolled her eyes at me.

I didn't push my luck with my idea of putting a sawbones on retainer and having the girls checked every day. Black Muireann had done that, and I saw no reason to deviate from the practice. Even the dells who had initially resisted Black Muireann's insistence on the sawbone's daily visits, which they characterized as "unladylike" and "immoral," very quickly came to expect—and even demand—such services as they watched the competition in other brothels become pregnant or rattletrap, while they didn't. Nonetheless, I wasn't going to push Sarah any further just now. Anyway, I wanted to find the doctor myself. American or Mexican, it didn't matter a whit to me. I wanted to make damned sure that he was a reliable cove.

"This is all quite fantastical," Hermann finally snorted. "I cannot believe that an honest woman and a well-educated boy who cannot grow much of a beard ..." He stopped as I glared at him. "My apologies, Billy. You are anything but a boy nowadays."

I gave a mock bow. "Apology accepted. Anyway, if I'm not a boy, it's due only to my knowledge of the 'fore and after,' I can quite assure you."

Jenny looked quizzically at me and then Sarah. We both declined to explain.

"Billy, you are both ..." Hermann searched for the words in English.

"Pompous and incorrigible?" I asked helpfully.

Hermann shot me a glance. "Yes. Incorrigible." Jenny giggled. Hermann ignored her and turned to Sarah. "And you, Sarah. An honest heroine of the siege of Fort Texas ... even that mad slaver, Bragg, cannot stop singing your praises. To hear him tell it, you single-handedly stopped the Mexicans from taking the fort, and dared those damned deserters to come and get you and the Cottonbalers."

"Oh pshaww." Sarah positively blushed.

Bragg and others had indeed sung praises about Sarah's obdurate refusal to seek shelter during the siege, when the Mexican artillery had bombarded Fort Texas fifteen hours a day, from before dawn until after dusk for a solid week until the army chased them away after the Battle of Resaca de la Palma. Their praise had spread across the grapevine long before she, Hermann, Jenny, and I had reunited. What had gone unremarked upon was Jenny's bravery during the siege—and her being with child, no less. When the Seventh Infantry went into Fort Texas, Jenny joined Sarah and one or two other washerwomen, each of whom had vowed to stay with their men come what may, refusing to go to Point Isabel in the baggage train with the five or six score other camp followers from other regiments who had come down from Corpus Christi during those anxious weeks in April, when we didn't quite know what was going to happen.

During the siege, both Sarah and Jenny had continued to operate the mess virtually around the clock, even during the heaviest bombardment. When Major Brown, the commanding officer of the Seventh, had been struck in the leg by a cannonball, Jenny comforted the poor man until he bled to death nearly three days later. After the major died in her arms, Jenny closed his eyes and wrapped him in his winding sheet. After she had wiped her hands on her bloodstained skirt, she went back to serving beans and bacon to the grateful doughboys—right alongside Sarah, who continued periodically to climb the ramparts during lulls in the bombardment to hurl invective at the deserters who had joined the Mexican army and were now fighting against us.

The turncoats were reputed to be led by some dastard named Riley, who had deserted from the Fifth just as he had deserted from the *Sassenagh* army up in Canada a few years earlier. No coincidence there, in my view—not that I had any more use for the *Sassenagh* now than when I lived in Ireland. But by their actions, Riley and his brethren had blackened the name of every God-fearing, decent Irishman in the Army of Invasion, for half the shoulder strap aristocracy believed that every Irishman in the army was ready at the drop of a hat to desert to serve the papist Mexicans. I asked Grant one day about why that was, when we all knew that, Riley notwithstanding, the deserters who fled—or tried to flee before they drowned or were shot down— were just as likely to be native Americans and Dutchies as they were to be Irishmen. We also all knew that thirty-six dragoons, native Americans to the man, had deserted last summer during the Second Dragoons' overland journey from the Sabine River to Corpus Christi. Of course, that didn't stop the nativist shoulder straps or the newspapers back home from believing otherwise. The Mexicans themselves added fresh fuel to the fire with their encouragements—letters and bills to that effect had been found in Arista's tent, where I had found the Colt Paterson. As some wag put it, the Mexicans were so wrapped up in the effort that some of them must have been expecting Old Zach himself to desert.

Grant demurred on the point. It wouldn't have done for him to peach on his fellow shoulder straps. But what he did tell me shocked me: Desertion since the army first descended upon Corpus Christi had been lower than it normally was during peacetime—even taking into account those few mad weeks in April along the Rio Grande. Grant said that the numbers had surprised him as well, particularly when one considered the fact that half our casualties at Resaca de la Palma and Palo Alto had been immigrants—English, German, and Irish alike. Finally, hardly a man had skedaddled since we crossed the

Rio Grande. Grant said wryly, that was probably on account of the long, hot walk to Monterrey, where the Mexican army had holed up to await us.

Hermann was speaking again. "I am quite serious. Both of you. Why don't we run a numbers game instead?" He nodded to me.

"Hermann, you know I'd rather run a numbers game. But we can't."

I could not devote the time and energy required to make a success of it. Running a profitable numbers game required a non-stop, loving devotion to the odds, plenty of chink, and putting the fear of God into one's runners. Charlie Backwell, God rest his soul, had taught me that. It was too bad. A good square numbers game here in Matamoros would be as near to being money in the Bowery Savings Bank as having made the very deposit itself. The same yahoos fresh from the cotton plantations by the Mississippi and the hardscrabble farms further east who were eager to get to know pliant dells were also spending most of their waking hours as drunk as David's sow and as eager as you please to gamble away their last half cent. I liked the idea of a numbers game. It didn't have the varied and sundry complications sure to arise from establishing and maintaining a house of ill repute, not the least of which was a visitation from the army. Indeed, we stood to knap the almighty Tartar if Perfect Bliss or the Old Man or some other big bug turned out to be offended by the prospect of providing a safe outlet for the overweening lusts of yobs away from the strictures of home for the first time.

But I simply could not devote that kind of time, for I was, after all, a doughboy. And being a newly minted corporal did not mean that I could come and go as I pleased. Worse, Hoggs would have loved to find a way to take away my chevrons, and I was not about to allow him to do that. If anything, I wanted a third chevron, so that I could be that much closer to being on an equal footing with the bastard, who as company first sergeant, had a lozenge underneath his three chevrons.

Sarah had the sauce to pull off running a numbers game. But she had proven hopeless in learning the finer points of probabilities.

The good Lord only knows how hard I had tried to teach her during the long nights back in Corpus Christi. She had the native wit to master the rackets, but not the least desire to do so. Sarah liked to do what she knew how to do—and no more—and she knew molleys and the running of them. Hermann could be taught—and indeed he'd grasped the basic concepts in seconds—but he had as little freedom as I did. Jenny was quite the mathematical prodigy, and running a numbers racket and figuring other ways to fleece the flats tickled her fancy. But she was gravid in her sixth month and a pretty young thing to boot.

I continued, "What else do we know how to do that'll make us buckets of lucre here, in Matamoros? This is staring us in the face. We're going to give these volunteers exactly what they want. And we're going to be as decent as we can about doing it."

"It is morally ... what is the word?" Hermann paused.

"Oh bollocks," Sarah snorted in disgust.

Hermann flushed, and Jenny tried to hide her amusement.

"Hermann, "I said, "I've got to say I agree with Sarah. We've got a golden opportunity. We'll be the first to be in business. We've got enough chink to get us going, and ... best of all ... we'll be offering a product no one else will—a high-end, Church Street cavaulting house, or least as close as can be down here on the río Bravo. The army's going to be here for a while unless the Mexicans beat us on the battlefield—and that ain't going to happen anytime soon. There are going to be thousands of these volunteers pouring into Matamoros in the next few weeks, according to the grapevine. Better yet, they simply are not under the same restrictions we regulars are, nor do they spend any time drilling. That means they'll have a lot of time on their hands."

Sarah broke in dryly. "And idle hands are the devil's playground. Men away from home need to be entertained. That's a fact. We're in the perfect position to make a mint. Billy here has had a brilliant education in the finer knocking shops in Gotham, and me ...?" She looked at Hermann and me. "I have spent far too much time doing the flat not to know my way about." She looked evenly at Jenny. "An experience I fondly hope you will never have, dearie."

"We need the chink, Hermann. We can't leave this opportunity alone," I said. "We've Jenny to consider, and her baby. And I have my obligations to Fíona. We cannot let any of them want for anything." Hermann nodded his assent, but I was not yet done. "We … all three of us: you, Sarah, myself … we need a bit of blunt ourselves. None of us knows what's going to happen, and we need to have some options. Who knows what the future will bring? And options require blunt."

"We are not going to desert, Billy. So I am not sure …"

"I'm not talking about skedaddling on a bit of French leave and then being branded and drummed out or, God forbid, scragged for my pains, damn it." Hermann looked a little affronted. So I softened my tone, although I was not going to yield my point. "Hermann, I'm not going to skedaddle until we're through with this little war of ours. So there's time enough to think about our next act …"

Hermann opened his mouth and then thought the better of it. The timing of our respective departures from the service of Uncle Sam continued to be an item of periodic discussion between the two of us.

"… After we leave this man's army—and leave it we will, for I will not spend thirty years as a bluebelly. I am also not absquatulating without a plugged nickel to my name." I stared Hermann in the eye. "To run a goosing slum here in Matamoros is to practice the art of the possible in acquiring the chink we need, my friend. No more." I looked equally hard at Sarah. "And if we are going to have such a goosing slum, I want to run it the right way, as a parlor house where the huckleberry is as far above the persimmon as we can get it … which is why I want French letters."

Sarah stuck her tongue out at me.

Hermann eventually gave in, and within the week Sarah had resigned her position as laundress to the Cottonbalers, installed Jenny in the best bedroom of the house—"We can do no less for the expectant mother," she snapped at me when I asked why she didn't take the room herself—and given herself over to running the finest parlor house in northern Mexico. It may have been a role in life akin to being a tall man among pygmies, but it was a good enough niche in the Matamoros flesh trade such that, when combined with Sarah's popularity among the shoulder straps for her showing at the Little Colorado and later at Fort Texas, our little cavaulting house drew just the right sort of customers. Indeed, we were able to entirely dispense with the need to cater at all to the Other Ranks, which we agreed saved us all manner of complication.

Even Bragg's pumpkin rind—the same one who had laid open that poor redleg's scalp right in front us on the parade ground back in Corpus Christi for some perceived inadequacy—patronized Sarah's academy, as it had affectionately become known among the more frequent punters. It turned out, Sarah told me one evening as I took my ease smoking my pipe in the kitchen, that this young lieutenant was a scion of a venerable Virginia planter's family. Curiously for a man whose father owned three score or more darkies, the young shavetail showed a distinct preference for the darker meat. Sarah was happy to indulge him—at a handsome and happily paid premium, of course— even though every other punter paid for the very same dark meat less than half what the bleak morts commanded.

Colonel Kinney also visited our establishment late on a Saturday night not long after we opened our doors. He came through from the parlor to the kitchen, where Hermann and I were gossiping with Jenny and counting our blunt. For some reason I could not discern, the colonel made a point of congratulating me (as opposed to both Hermann and me) on the new business venture and my perspicacity in becoming partners with two wonderful women such as Sarah and Jenny (the latter curtseying elegantly in her seat). I caught sight of Hermann smiling to himself as Colonel Kinney offered me a job when I "mustered out after the war."

On the other hand, Perfect Bliss did not frequent the academy. He was kept far too busy writing the Old Man's despatches, according

to the grapevine. But even if he had not been so busy, he probably would have avoided us like the plague on account of his being
betrothed to the Old Man's daughter, Miss Betty, who was back in
Virginia, presumably pining for him. Anyway, Bliss was reputed to
live up to every inch of his moniker of "Perfect"—although I couldn't
say myself whether he really did live up to it. I'd never met the man,
and knew him only by reputation. Grant and others who sought to be
faithful to their sweethearts also didn't sample our wares (or anyone
else's, for that matter). Bragg and others of his ilk, who just didn't
seem to be inclined to partake, were not to be seen darkening our door
either. But their absence did not noticeably dent our business.

The newly-minted brigadier general of Louisiana volunteers was
a nightly client. He was a toploftical ass of a former lieutenant governor with a letch for fresh (each evening) pairs of virgin Negresses
whom he instructed to vigorously apply the switch to him. He meant
well, though, and paid better. So Sarah catered to his every whim
to the extent of reserving a chamber especially for his use. The general had only the kindest words for the quality of our clovens (girls
who could "pass" as virgin. Understandably being rare commodity in
a whorehouse, such ripe cherries were quietly recycled from one cove
to another. Sarah—at my insistence—took particular care to freshly
equip every one of them each night with the proper bona fides to
demonstrate their virginity, including blood from chickens who had
lately given their all for the stew we fed our girls for supper just before
the rush started). The brigadier general's kind words spread far and
wide among the Louisiana volunteer shoulder straps, attracting all
manner of them to our doorstep, which allowed us to be very selec-
tive in our clientele. This air of exclusivity tempered the likelihood
that one of our customers would become unruly. But it did not quite
eliminate the risk.

Within the week, we had our first incident. Hermann and I
weren't at the knocking shop. We had been tied to quarters by some
task that had come down from on high to Hoggs, who in turn before
disappearing into town had deposited it in Hermann's lap with dark,

muttered imprecations of what would come to pass if the task were not to have been discharged to perfection. (Hoggs had reverted to his old ways of staying conspicuously absent from virtually every evolution undertaken by C Company, and mysteriously showing up only when Grant or some other shoulder strap showed interest.) So I heard the story many days later from Sarah and Jenny.

A drunken captain of Louisiana volunteers had begun his evening at one of the newly-established gambling kens located just off the main square by playing away his entire grubstake (save a single half-eagle) on an anti-goss—a card that had turned against him three times in a single hand. A card he swore would go his way on the fourth turn. It didn't. Busted, he noisily sought solace in Sarah's academy on the strength of his last half-eagle and the recommendation of the brigadier general of Louisiana volunteers, who had just recently ensconced his head on Sarah's milkshop as he did most nights before finding his way up to his chamber, where that night's pair of cloven Negresses were waiting patiently, switches at the ready. Against her better judgment and after she had separated him from his half-eagle, Sarah sent the captain upstairs with a particularly talented young señorita named Adabelita, who had taken his fancy. The chamber where the beguiling young señorita had led him was right next door to Jenny's bedroom. Jenny had taken to bed early that evening, feeling poorly as the baby was beginning to kick. Eddie Rocheron, Sarah's new factotum, had just looked in on her and caught her giggling at the thumps and moans emanating through the wall.

Sarah had wisely (and entirely without the benefit of counsel from either Hermann or me) hired Eddie as her factotum after Jenny had met him on one of the walks she had started taking each morning, before the sun rose too high in the sky. On the first morning or two, Jenny walked with Sarah. Within a few days, Sarah began begging off to indulge her new-found love of sleeping in as late as she pleased. The maid Sarah had hired to share with Jenny now that the cavaulting house was open for business and generating cash accompanied Jenny wherever she went. That day, Jenny went first to the market, twirling her parasol as she studied the chickens, eggs, vegetables, fruit, and trinkets on offer, picking up something from one stall or another before walking at a stately speed (her pregnancy constraining any faster passage) to the decrepit dock just outside of town. It was a few hundred yards downstream from where the Mexican girls once again did their washing and afterwards bathed in varying states of dishabille, albeit in fewer numbers than back in April when the río Bravo had protected them from us stalwarts of the Army of Invasion.

From a safe distance, usually along the road leading away from the dock, Jenny liked to watch the steamboats land and disgorge their cargoes of peloothered 90-day volunteers, a company at a time, Most of them were from their first step on dry Mexican soil whooping, hollering, brandishing their newly issued muskets with bayonets fixed, and swearing to anyone who would listen—and many who would not—that they'd skewer any damned dago who dared to show his face. Jenny did not mind the volunteers, for they mostly ignored her as she soaked in the talk from back home. Needless to say, few Mexicans were ever seen up at the dock or its immediate environs unless they were part of a working party under regular army supervision … and protection.

One day, Jenny was watching one of the newly-arrived companies march past her at a shambling stroll that was all they could muster on account of a surfeit of whiskey and an utter lack of drill. The company stopped and idled for a few moments, all of them busy as magpies chattering with one another in wonder at the novel spectacle of occupied Matamoros. One of them espied Jenny and surreptitiously commented to his fellows about her heavily pregnant state. The beast did not stop with a single off-hand comment, but instead yawped increasingly lewd about her, to the amusement of his fellow volunteers. He then sniffed censoriously that no respectable woman would allow herself to be seen outside her home in such a condition, and so she must be nothing more than … He never finished the sentence. Out of seemingly nowhere, a corporal materialized directly in front of him, towering above him by a clean foot or more, it seemed. The corporal said something quietly to the cove, who immediately shut his trap.

The corporal then strode over to Jenny and swept off his cap in an elegant bow over her proffered hand. "Ma'am, my deepest apologies. Private Forrest is away from home for the first time, and he's just had his first whiskey. As I mentioned to him, he is very lucky that his momma didn't hear what he said, or see him taking that sip of whiskey. He understands the gravity of his impoliteness, and he will not be bothering you any further."

"Why, thank you, corporal. I am deeply grateful." Jenny positively simpered at the attention from the huge man with kind brown eyes and a great brown and black beard.

"My apologies, ma'am. My momma would be just as upset with me for forgetting my manners, as Private Forrest's momma would be with him." He bowed again. "Please allow me to name myself."

Jenny curtsied as prettily as her condition would allow

"Edouard Rocheron, ma'am. Of Ascension Parish."

Jenny curtsied once more. "Edouard. Is that what your friends call you ... or the girl you left behind in Ascension Parish?"

"There is no girl back home, ma'am." Rocheron flushed just slightly above his beard. "But my cronies call me Eddie."

"I am pleased to make your acquaintance, Eddie."

Jenny extended her hand. Rocheron bowed over it once more, and brushed her knuckles with his lips and moustache.

She looked Rocheron directly in the eye as he straightened. "I am Jenny Billings, and you needn't call me 'ma'am.' There is no Mr. Billings. Never was."

Rocheron gawped.

"Now if you'll excuse me." Jenny pirouetted and began to walk away, her maid in tow.

"Ma'am ..."

Jenny turned towards him with the smile of a sphinx.

"I am sorry," Rocheron apologized. "Miss Jenny, may I call upon you?"

"I would be honored." She pirouetted once more and was gone, maid in tow, leaving Rocheron once more gaping at her like a pugilist who'd taken a hard chopper to the knowledge box. Jenny smiled to herself as she heard what she took to be some gentle teasing of Rocheron that hushed the instant he turned back to face his squad.

As the sun set that evening, a couple of hours before the punters had begun to descend upon the cavaulting house, Rocheron showed up at the front door, cap in hand, and uniform and brogans neatly brushed. He took tea with Jenny in the still-empty front parlor, and they talked quietly for an hour, hardly taking their eyes from one another. Sarah joined them afterwards, and within a minute of ascertaining that Rocheron's duties with his company were far from onerous, offered him the position of general factotum and bouncer. Rocheron had shown up as the sun set every night since. He had, by Sarah's account, actually spent more time holding Jenny's hand than dealing with unruly punters. That suited Sarah just fine, because it meant that an increasingly bed-bound Jenny was being well-entertained. It also meant that there had hardly been a disturbance by an unruly punter worthy of mention. That is, Sarah noted, until the night that the peloothered and penurious captain had showed up.

"Oh Eddie, don't look so shocked," Jenny had laughed after a particularly expressive flurry of moans had emanated from the next room. "The captain is getting his money's worth." Jenny patted the bed by her side. "Come sit next to me and keep me company."

Eddie sat next to her and took her hand in his. "Jenny, you shouldn't be talking like that. About to be a mother and all."

Jenny never replied. A loud thump and an unearthly scream issued from the room next door, followed by what sounded like paroxysms of terror. Rocheron muttered an apology to a now wide-eyed Jenny, bolted from her side, and smashed through the locked door of the bedroom next door with hardly a "by your leave." He discovered the young señorita spread-eagled and naked on the bed, her hands bound to the bedposts and her nose and mouth smashed and bleeding. The captain was standing naked—and rampant—over the poor girl, his clenched fist raised above his head.

"Sir …"

"Get out." The captain did not deign to turn around at the interruption. He continued staring at the terrified girl. Blood bubbled from her smashed nose and mouth. "Didn't you hear me, corporal? Get out. This is none of your concern."

"Captain …"

"Corporal, so help me … Get out now, or I will inform Major Rouquette of your impertinence, and then you'll be in the calaboose."

"Captain, no …" Rocheron grabbed the captain's fist. The captain spun around and took a wide, lazy swing at Rocheron with his free hand. Rocheron counter-punched him hard to the bread-basket. As the captain doubled over, Eddie finished him with a tremendous chopper, smashing his beak. The captain collapsed in a heap, bleeding from his nose nearly as badly as the poor girl he'd just disfigured. Rocheron loosened the girl's hands from the restraints and covered her nakedness with a blanket.

"What happened?" Sarah stood at the door, hands on her hips.

"He hit her." Rocheron gestured at the unconscious captain lying naked and bleeding on the floor. "The son of a bitch hit Adabelita. Poor thing."

"Dear God, she's a mess," Sarah sighed. Her face hardened. "Put the bastard in the alley. But not too close to the house. Oh, and leave him naked. Burn his clothes as well. He can go back to his camp in his birthday suit. What he did wasn't decent, so I will not have him treated decently."

"Yes, ma'am." Rocheron bundled the stricken captain into a blanket and unceremoniously threw him over his shoulder.

Jenny touched Rocheron's arm as he brushed past her.

Rocheron paused and looked down at her affectionately. "You should be back in bed, Miss Jenny."

Jenny clutched her shawl more tightly around her shoulders. "Eddie, who was the captain talking about?"

Rocheron looked at her questioningly.

"He mentioned a name."

"Oh, don't mind the captain. He won't tell Major Rouquette nothing."

"Rouquette?" Jenny asked. "They call him 'Carambole'? Right?"

"Yes, ma'am. Gambler. Real popular, though, with the men. Got himself elected regimental major on account of his Indian-fighting prowess—or at least what he claimed was his Indian-fighting prowess. I've heard tell of a different story." Rocheron chuckled as he shifted his load slightly. "Anyway, he and this one." Rocheron nudged the unconscious captain, and continued, "They're a regular pair of old china plates. I'd normally be taking this one's threat to heart, because Rouquette would do 'most anything for him. But the captain's been such a rumhead tonight that he probably won't remember what happened. And even if he did, he'll be too embarrassed to say anything ... particularly after he has to walk back into camp buck naked."

Rocheron thought for a second or two, and then said, "You know, I think that something's up with Rouquette. We've not hardly seen hide nor hair of him since we got to Matamoros, and he's the sort of beast you normally see far too much of. Nobody knows quite why he's not been around at his old tricks, setting up some scam or another. And I've heard tell that when he has been around, he's been keeping company with this regular army sergeant from the Fourth. If you ask me, that sergeant's a real shitpot. Begging your pardon, ma'am." Rocheron bowed slightly, and Jenny curtsied, her eye meeting his in a steady gaze.

Rocheron continued, "He gives me the willies, that sergeant does. Anyway, you'd think that Rouquette was far too much the big bug to give a regular army sergeant the time of day." Rocheron laughed as he walked away. "Anyway, they do seem to be up to something. They probably think they're on the trail of some Mexican *el dorado*. What a joke that is. There aren't two plugged nickels to be found in the same place down here in this Godforsaken land of mackerel-snatchers. I've never seen anywhere so poor."

With that, Eddie Rocheron re-balanced the blanket-wrapped captain's body on his shoulder and rumbled down the stairs to the kitchen and out into the alley.

⌒

Sarah fell silent at this point of the story, so Jenny chimed in, telling me that Sarah went back down to the parlor to resume passing the time of day with the general of volunteers before he visited his pair of clovens, their chicken blood, and their cane switches. The general laid his head back upon her bosom as she drily whispered that one of his captains had been positively beastly.

A regular army captain apparently in his cups had been sitting in a handsome leather and wood chair quietly through all of the hubbub, waiting for his doxy. After Sarah sat down and the general resumed his perch atop Sarah's bosom, the captain snapped from his reverie and said carelessly, "I fear, Mrs. Langwell, that he'll be at it again tomorrow."

"Not here, he won't," Sarah said.

"Then somewhere else."

The general sat up and looked formal, all hint of lasciviousness vanished from his eye. "My boys may be a bit wild, Mrs. Langwell. But I will not countenance such beastliness. The captain will make amends to you and to the girl tomorrow morning. Then my adjutant will see to it that he is on the first boat back to New Orleans—and my adjutant will also see to it that a letter—with my signature—to the governor is in the post leaving on that very same boat." There was a certain hardness to the cast of his face. "I'll make sure that the dastard never walks into a drawing room in the city again. The beast."

"I am much obliged, General." Somewhat mollified, Sarah heaved her bosom for the general's benefit. "Another sherry?"

"Much obliged, ma'am." The general once more laid his head on Sarah's bosom and closed his eyes.

But the regular army captain wasn't ready to change the subject, for he took a lazy pull from his cheroot, gave a slantendicular look at the general that was entirely bereft of any hint of besottedness. "I've always figured, General, that it is a highly commendable act for the great state of Louisiana to have been stripped bare of the flower of her youth so as to rescue our estimable General Taylor from his 'gravely perilous situation,' as that damned picayune New Orleans newspaper put it."

The general continued to nestle on Sarah's bosom, affecting not to hear the captain, who set his small sherry on a delicate table next to his leather and wood chair and warmed further to his task. "In fact, sir, there are so many of them, it seems, that I heard tell from my cousin that there ain't enough honest white men left in some parts of Louisiana to police all the Negroes. It is fantastical that every one of these boys is all riled up and ready to murder any dago where he stands. It surely is a good quality to have in a soldier.

"But that said, sir, I must say that even a slow coach such as our esteemed 'Old Rough and Ready,' … our friends in the penny press call him that now, don't you know. Have you heard the paeans of praise they sing to 'Old Rough and Ready'? The frontiersman who conquers the little brown-skinned papists? Complete balderdash. The old duffer couldn't maneuver a battalion on his own to save his or anyone else's life. And yet, here 'Old Rough and Ready' did what nobody thought he could do: Thrash the dagoes. 'Course, he did miss his opportunity to blow those damned dagoes sky high and on to their Maker 'afore they could skedaddle south. If our esteemed general'd had his wits about him and not been such a slow coach, we could have crossed the Rio Grande while Arista dithered, and then hunted him and all of his men as they fled. We'd've slaughtered them like so many Mexican 'slow deer' waiting in the pen for the butcher."

Sarah petted the brigadier, consoling him as he luxuriated in her bosom.

The captain remained oblivious to his audience. "But I digress, sir. We do not need the volunteers. We need more regulars. Another three or four regiments of doughboys and another couple of regiments of bowlegs, and the dago army would be no more. With respect, sir, we would have had no need for the volunteers, for … and I do mean this with the utmost of respect … they cannot stand in the line with the regulars."

The brigadier groaned faintly into Sarah's milkshop.

"They hardly drill, and they don't know the lash, which we apply to our regulars. It's a tonic, don't you know." The captain sneaked a quick look at the recumbent general. "That and they hardly have an officer worth his salt unless he's from the 'Point. Damme sir, but a volunteer officer can hardly give an order to a private to dig a latrine or to shine his belt buckle, without having to give a stump speech about why the order's a good idea, and why a vote for him in the next election is the best idea since the Declaration of Independence. God help our volunteers if they tried to form a square like the Fourth did against the Mexican lancers. And if we marched 'em south hard, like we did our bluebellies back in the spring, they'd all die of tender bellies or sore feet. My bluebellies of the Third, sir. They can march to the gates of Hell and back and still lick an entire brigade of Mexican cavalry single-handedly. The volunteers cannot. They all look as if they've been buttermilk- or corn-fed since birth."

The general abruptly rumbled to his feet and murmured something about the water closet.

The captain was not to be deterred by the general's departure. "And what's worse is the discipline, sir. They elect their own officers, for the love of God. If my bluebellies were to elect their officers, I would fear for my rank … and my life. They are the scum of the earth, the Third is. All thieving Fenians and Dutchies. Mackerel-snatchers, every damned one of them. They must be led by trained officers, sir. But I would not trade them for an entire army of volunteers. No, sir, I would not."

As the captain settled back into his chair, the general returned to the room, gave the captain a considered look and then turned to Sarah, who had been staring fixedly at a point on the wall over the captain's head. "I believe, ma'am, that I am ready for those two blueskin kinchin morts you promised me."

Hermann and I and a detail of half-a-dozen C Company stalwarts were on a frolic a couple of miles from camp, fetching firewood and water and trying not to sweat too much under the broiling, mid-day sun. There was not a Johnny Raw among our detail, for they had not yet earned the right.

I was relying on Hermann for fresh gossip and news from our business venture, as he had been able to absquatulate from camp on the odd evening. The previous evening, when he had returned late from his sojourn over at the cavaulting house, he and I had quietly split our share of the previous week's proceeds. My share was secreted in a money belt fastened securely about my belly, underneath my blouse. It chafed a little, on account of my belt riding almost directly over it. But that was a small price to pay to know that my $97 in a double eagle and assorted eagles, half-eagles, and small silver coins was as safe as could be, short of resting in the vault at the Bowery Bank.

"Jenny tells me that her new beau is the genuine article." Hermann lifted his cap and wiped his brow.

"What did you think of him?"

"She could not ask for more. I only hope that he can find a way to take her back to New Orleans before the baby comes."

I looked at Hermann agog. "Are you countenancing desertion?"

Hermann replied in a slightly irritated tone. "Of course not. But such matters are somewhat more informal with the Louisianans. They have signed up only for 90 days, and their 90 days will be done soon, particularly as 40 or 60 of those days were gone before they left New Orleans."

I shrugged noncommittally.

"I am worried about Hoggs sniffing around Jenny again," Hermann said quietly.

"In her condition? Anyway, how's he going to get inside the house? Sarah has Luis's Mexican bully backs guarding the entrances, and you told me that Jenny's beau is the size of a small mountain."

271

"Hoggs is an animal, and he wants to exact vengeance upon you." Hermann paused until he had my eye. Then he said off-handedly. "Oh, and Rouquette is back."

I didn't immediately reply. But I realized that he was right, given the Western's story about the louche captain of Louisiana volunteers.

Hermann explained, "Hoggs has been feeling emboldened these past couple of weeks. That is why he dressed you down in front of the company yesterday. Even two weeks ago, he would never have done that. Something has changed, and it must be that Rouquette is back to work his evil."

I burned at the memory. Hoggs had objected to the state of my brogans, which had been better blackened and brushed than his own. Hoggs had from the start bridled at my promotion to corporal (he seemed indifferent to Hermann's promotion to sergeant), and he found a veritable cornucopia of tasks for me to perform, each more humiliating than the next, either supervising the latest miscreant to fall afoul of him or even actually requiring me to perform the task myself. Anything to do with latrines was Hoggs's particular favorite. I assumed that the latter was aimed at undercutting any authority that I might have as the company's most junior non-commissioned officer. Even when I had not been burdened by Hoggs's petty tasks, I rarely left camp. Hermann, God bless his protecting soul, had deemed it too dangerous for me to leave the safety of camp without him at my side. Despite my camp fever, I had not caviled at Hermann's strictures. I had, however, bridled at Hoggs's unwarranted hounding. Unbeknownst even to Hermann, Hoggs had confronted me when we were both out of eye and earshot of anyone else, and I had dared him to try to punish me physically. Hoggs had laughed and not taken the bait. He merely turned his back on me and walked away. I had shaken with unquenched rage and fear.

I put such thoughts aside to focus on what Hermann had said about Rouquette, asking skeptically, "Evil?"

"Yes. Evil. Countenancing what Hoggs did with poor Jenny back in Corpus Christi … That was evil. But that is not all. For I do believe, in my bones, that Rouquette and Hoggs are up to something, and they are in it together."

I scoffed. "They're too late to establish themselves in some gambling ken cum knocking shop like Rouquette had back in Corpus Christi. We and half a dozen others have beaten him to the punch this time."

"No. Worse than that. Robbery ..."

"What? Are they looking for Arista's payroll?" I wasn't being in the least bit serious. Hermann didn't answer. "Hermann, I don't care what the grapevine says about a lost Mexican army payroll. I was there in Arista's tent, remember? There wasn't any treasure chest full of coins to pay the army. If there had been, those two Mexican coves I captured wouldn't have been so busy burning papers. They would've been absquatulating to points unknown long before I hove onto the scene. I sure would've if I'd been in their boots."

"Maybe they had already buried it."

"Where?" I was tired of the rumors. It seemed to be the only thing anyone was talking about these days: Seven cartloads of silver buried at Palo Alto (or somewhere in the Resaca de la Palma, depending upon who was doing the palavering). "If that's all Rouquette and Hoggs are after, then that's harmless enough. Let them dig up on the *resaca* to their hearts' content. Just like the twenty or thirty other expeditions that have been up there in the last couple of weeks. They won't find anything, and they'll be out of our hair ... and away from Jenny. And just maybe that rascal... what's his name? Ramón Falcón. That's right. He ain't dead, no matter what the grapevine said back when Thornton got himself captured. Well, maybe ol' Falcón might happen along and exfluncticate the pair of them. Do the world a powerful lot of good, I should think."

"Perhaps you are right."

We trudged through the underbrush back towards camp for another twenty minutes with our six stalwart doughboys behind us, hauling the firewood cart. We were no more than half a mile from the picket line when a gaudy volunteer, beribboned feathers in his broad brimmed hat and his uniform fairly dripping with all manner of other fantastical accoutrements, stepped out from behind a mesquite and blocked our way. He must have been freshly off the boat, for such finery rarely lasted more than a few days.

"You there," the volunteer said in a stentorian voice.

Hermann and I looked at each other and then back at the volunteer, who had been joined by a dozen or so other volunteers crowding behind him, bayonets fixed to their muskets, laughing like schoolboys about to commit a prank.

I said, "Let me speak to the fellow."

Hermann nodded.

I strode over to him. "Mornin', bud. Welcome to *México*." I pronounced it the Mexican way.

"Nice lot of firewood you have there." The grandiloquent private of volunteers spat tobacco juice suspiciously close to my brogans.

"Yep. Plenty more out yonder for you to gather." I carelessly waved with my left hand.

The volunteer grinned at me. "I heard tell that you doughboys are under orders to collect firewood for us volunteers. I was told that we could pick some up from a fatigue party coming back to camp. And here you are. Mighty obliging of you."

"What? Do I look like your servant, Private?"

"You're a regular. We citizens pay your wages in peacetime. You lazy Paddylander. So I reckon you are indeed my servant."

We were now standing very close to each other.

"You're a private. I'm a corporal, and," I gestured over my shoulder, "he's a sergeant. And you ain't got no shoulder strap huckleberry above the proverbial persimmon in tow. So I suggest that you beat feet. Pronto-like."

"Ain't you the ring-tailed snorter ... corporal ... a fine little fice whoppet, more like." The volunteer looked pleased with himself.

"Let me handle this." I felt Hermann sidle up to me and in a single fluid motion push away my arm, reach to my waistband with one hand, pull my Paterson from where I had stashed it and shove it viciously under the private's chin. With the other hand, he simultaneously grabbed the man's hair and pulled the man's head even tighter onto the muzzle of my repeating pistol. The volunteer's pretty feathered hat fell to the ground. I carelessly trod on it, and then kicked it aside, grinning at the now-cowed son of a bitch.

Hermann breathed heavily on the volunteer. "I do not think you understand what the corporal was telling you, Private."

The private gurgled, his face puce as Hermann once more shoved the pistol's barrel deep under the man's chin.

"Do not move, Private." Hermann did not look at me as he said, "Billy, have the lads take their muskets."

The private twitched under Hermann's grasp.

Hermann tightened his grip and once more ground the muzzle of the pistol into the man's throat. The skin reddened and bled under the assault. "I will kill you as you stand here if you move again," Hermann hissed.

Keeping a slantendicular eye on the private and his cullies, I motioned to our doughboys, and they silently walked over to the other six volunteers, who were now standing like statues behind their leader. The volunteers surrendered their firearms with nary a comment, and our doughboys unceremoniously stacked them on top of our firewood-laden cart.

Hermann once more ground the pistol into the private's chin. "Now I suggest you go and look for your own firewood, Private, and not bother us doughboys any more." With that, Hermann pushed him away, and the private and his minions melted away into the underbrush.

Hermann had us charge our muskets, and we all walked the rest of the way back to our encampment suddenly far more worried about our fellow American soldiers than we were any rogue Mexicans. We left the volunteers' muskets (after stripping them of flints and anything else that might be useful to us) in the underbrush just before we encountered the pickets at the edge of the vast parade ground that we had cleared when we made camp in late May. We did not see those particular volunteers again. So I never learned whether they found their muskets.

"Hey, Gogan." It was Hoggs.

"Yes, Sergeant." As always, I was instantly on guard, even though this time I was in no immediate danger, because we were not alone. I was supervising a couple of privates digging a new latrine, and half the regiment was within earshot, cleaning, policing the parade ground, and doing all the rest of those never-ending tasks that bluebellies have done ever since there were proper armies.

"The pumpkin rind wants to see you." Hoggs' eyes glistened with anticipation. "He's in a right swivet, he is. Never heard him swear before. But he is now." Hoggs chuckled. "What've you done to upset him so, me bucko? Maybe he'll see the light of day and relieve you of those chevrons of yours."

I didn't have the energy to reply. I told the two privates to finish the task and report back to Hermann, who had sent us on the detail.

"Oh, by the way, Gogan."

I turned and gave Hoggs a look of utter boredom.

Hoggs gave me a sickening grin in return. "You know that knocked-up little doxie you and that big-titted bitch are hiding in that whorehouse of yours?" His smile broadened lasciviously." She's mine, and so's her pudding. Always will be … 'til death do us part." Then his grin fell away and his face turned to stone. "And that coot she's doing the gutstick with? I'm going to fix his flint. He chose the wrong bit of quim to tumble in."

Hoggs sniggered quietly as I glanced quickly at the two privates, who were busy digging the latrine and studiously paying us no attention. I couldn't be openly insubordinate to Hoggs in front of them, so I contented myself with a curt nod of acknowledgment to Hoggs, careful to meet his eye for just an instant. Then I retreated wordlessly and made my way over to Grant's tent, stopping only to straighten my uniform and brush the worst of the parade ground dust from my brogans. Grant was sitting on a campstool outside his tent, bareheaded and chewing pensively on an unlit cheroot.

Without looking up at me, he said, "I've been relieved of command of C Company."

"Sir?"

"C Company no longer exists."

I waited Grant out, standing at attention in front of him, my eyes fixed on an imaginary point two feet above the still-sitting Grant's head. But he changed the subject.

"Too bad I'm not headed back to St. Louis for a little recruiting duty. It seems just about every other lieutenant or captain with seniority is headed north to do just that. Captain McCall is leaving for New Orleans tomorrow." Grant looked up at me with a lopsided smile. "Apparently, I am too valuable a commodity to be sent north to my young lady just yet. Surely, Gogan, you know that we pumpkin rinds are mere commodities. No different than you bluebellies, at the end of the day. We're all interchangeable, just like the parts Mr. Whitney designed for his cotton gins. One West Point man is the same as the next, and the lucky ones are going home to recruit soldiers for the new regiments of regulars that Congress just authorized."

"I don't understand, sir ... about C Company."

"It's very simple. What with the men we lost at Palo Alto and Resaca de la Palma and this week's sicklist, not to mention the fact that last week alone five men were mustered out at the end of their enlistments, C Company—even with the Johnny Raws who've trickled in over the past few weeks—is down to twenty-seven Other Ranks in addition to its two sergeants and one corporal ... the latter being yourself, of course. D Company is similarly situated, and each company is supposed to have sixty-four pairs of brogans each. So rather than send us more recruits to bolster our numbers, the big bugs merely condense our companies and drown us in 90-day volunteers in regiments that have never drilled together even once. I imagine that they'll stand up a new C Company at Governors Island. Some lucky soul will get to spend three months recruiting and training them. Then in due course, that new C Company will show up with a couple of fresh shavetails in tow. But the company won't be mine again."

Grant looked positively glum. I remained at attention.

Grant smiled crookedly. "Oh don't worry, Gogan, you're not going to lose your chevrons, and Wurster's going to keep his."

"Sir." I did my best to sound affronted at the notion of my being in the least bit self-interested.

"Sergeant Wurster's going to stay with the company. D Company. Right along with Sergeant Hoggs. For some unknown reason, D Company apparently doesn't have any sergeants left. Sickness ... death ... drunkenness." Grant rattled off the panoply of career-limiting acts for non-commissioned officers. Stupidity and evil were not frowned upon nearly as much. Grant was talking again. "So both Wurster and Hoggs are needed to man D Company. You, my young man, are a different matter. You're coming with me."

"Sir?"

"I have been appointed as the regimental quartermaster. And you, young man, are to be my clerk. Somebody has to keep the books, and I am electing you. You may wonder why I was given such an honor. Apparently you and Wurster are to blame."

Grant looked at me out of the corner of his eye. I remained at attention, fixed upon that imaginary spot just above Grant's head. If he was disappointed by my lack of reaction, he did not show it.

"The pair of you were working too hard one day last fall clearing a boat landing area, and General Taylor attributed our remarkable progress to my leadership and not to your hard work." Grant worked the unlit cheroot for a moment. "Don't think for a minute that this will be some sort of cakewalk. You and I will have our work cut out for us, because the army is going to march to Monterrey and find General Arista and what's left of his army, and defeat them once and for all.

"There are two ways to get there," Grant continued. "By way of Linares, which is the way that Arista went. Half his army dropped dead of thirst, on account of there being no water along the road. We're not going that way. The other route is by way of Camargo and up into the mountains ... they call it the ..." Grant furrowed his brow a minute. "The *Sierra Madre*. That's it. The *Sierra Madre*. We go through a little town called Cerralvo and then down to Monterrey. There's water along the way, and it isn't as hot as the desert route on account of the elevation. But there's a rub." He gleamed at me.

"Sir?"

"There isn't any road from Camargo to Cerralvo, or from Cerralvo to Monterrey. At least not any road you can send Conestoga wagon trains over, or so I hear tell that's what Captain McCulloch and his Texas Rangers've been reporting to the Old Man and Colonel Whiting."

Whiting had replaced the poor, murdered Colonel Cross as the army's quartermaster-general, and he had the unenviable task of straightening out the nightmarish mess that the army's logistics had become since hostilities had begun.

"Pack mules, then, sir?"

Grant nodded. "Yep. The army's going to need thousands of them, and the Fourth by itself will need hundreds. My guess is that we'll have to look far and wide here in northern Mexico to find that many mules."

"Then we'll need to find Juan Pablo to help us, won't we, sir."

"That would be a very good place to start. He and every other *arriero* should be crowding into town right about now. The word has gone out that Perfect Bliss has authorized $25 per month per muleteer."

I whistled involuntarily.

"And no, Gogan, you do not get to change your line of work."

The big bugs were proposing to pay each *arriero* three times a corporal's pay. Sweet Jesus. Mule-skinning for the army didn't pay as well as running a cavaulting house, but still.

"That's not all, Gogan. We have other fish to fry in the meantime."

"Yes sir."

"First things first, you are going to go up to Point Isabel with a letter of introduction from Colonel Garland to Major Thomas—he's the depot quartermaster at Point Isabel. We need him and his minions to know who we are. The regiment is desperately short of every sort of supply. Uniforms, flints for the muskets, you name it, and we need it. We're going to set up this line of communication, and you are going to help me keep it open. That means you'll be traveling to Point Isabel every so often—starting tomorrow, with Colonel Garland's letter to Major Thomas."

"Yes sir."

"You'll be relieved of all your regular duties, and you'll report to me directly. The rest of your time will be your own." Grant fixed his cheroot and glared at me.

"Thank you, sir."

"Don't thank me. I'm trusting you." His expression brightened. "And if you make a blue fist of it, I'll have your guts for garters."

"Again, thank you, sir."

"That's all." Grant waved his hand and turned back to his knife and his whittling. "Oh, Gogan? When you are in Point Isabel, you should stop in and see Sergeant Finnegan. I am given to understand that he is still up there. You can take Sergeant Wurster with you on this trip. I've cleared it with Captain McCall. If you find that Mexican fellow, what's his name? Juan Pablo? If you find him before you go, take him along. Might be helpful in your getting to know the lay of the land."

Oh callooh, callay, oh frabjous day, as that odd fellow, Dodgson, was to chortle a few years later. No more Hoggs.

⌒

# CHAPTER 16

# The Murderous Son . . .

"YOU'RE CLEAN BROKE, AIN'T YOU, BUDDY?" The dealer looked across the plank table at the sucker expectantly, his hole cards sitting contentedly in his hand. The dealer wasn't very good. I had gotten a pretty good idea about his tells merely from having watched the last dozen hands from a safe vantage point behind some other lookers-on. But he was fortunate. Nobody else at the table seemed to know the first thing about the game of bluff. But that was the beauty of running a table in the tent city that was freshly burgeoning cheek-by-jowl with the army's main supply depot at Point Isabel. This base, at such risk in the days before hostilities began, was the transshipment point for the army's supplies and for the volunteers arriving from New Orleans and beyond. Every day, boatloads of greenhorns were deposited on the beach, fresh for the fleecing by even the most minimally competent artist.

The sucker flushed. "I got this here toothpick." He reached behind his head and pulled an enormous knife from a scabbard concealed between his shoulder blades underneath his greasy red woolen shirt. It was of the type favored—and seemingly brandished at every opportunity—by Texas Rangers and just about every other scoundrel between here in Point Isabel and Matamoros. It was nicked and discolored from long use, but he held it up lovingly to the dust-tinged sunlight swirling through the open sides of the tent and mused, "Colonel Bowie's favorite. Sharp enough for shaving ... heavy enough for a hatchet ... long as a sword. Colonel Bowie always swore he could use his as a paddle for his canoe."

The sucker looked like a Texas Ranger, if only because of his enormous slouch hat and the Paterson Colt revolving pistol tucked casually into his belt. His dress was otherwise an indifferent mufti, without a lick of buckskin. Were it not for his armaments, slouch hat, and fantastical beard and moustache, he could have been a mere farmhand. He was so large a man that the enormous bowie knife was virtually dwarfed as he lovingly hefted it in his brobdingnagian hand. I had no idea of his height, but he was as broad a man as I'd ever seen, without the slightest hint of fat.

The dealer pointed to the knife. "What do I want with some scratched-up pen knife from Tennessee? It ain't even a proper Arkansas toothpick made by that feller who made 'em for Colonel Bowie. It ain't got no engraving or nothing, and it's as dull as you are, my friend. It is the saddest excuse for a dirk that I have ever seen," the dealer mocked. "Two bits is all I'll give you for it."

The enormous sucker stirred ominously. The dealer feigned not to notice, although he did push back the tail to his dusty black frock-coat. I wondered what sort of weapon he had concealed there.

Then a voice erupted. "I'll give you a half-eagle for it."

All eyes were on me, and I realized that I'd better make good on my offer. I had been so lost in studying the cards that my desire for the bowie knife had gotten away from me. I dug for the coin, and flipped it to the Texas Ranger, who looked gratefully at me as he handed his enormous knife and scabbard to me. There were a couple of murmurs in the crowd. Like as not, they were wondering what a bluebelly corporal was doing with a gold half-eagle. They were also wondering why I had paid the Texas Ranger double what he'd likely paid for the knife, for it truly was as plain and unadorned a weapon as I had ever seen.

I winked at the Ranger and said loudly, "Don't let the dude horn-swoggle you. Call his bluff. You've got the better hand."

With a sense of immense satisfaction and a broad grin of delight on my face, I skedaddled from the tent to the sound of the Ranger guffawing loudly and the dealer shouting, "That bastard."

Hermann had been asking where the hospital was. He now fell in step beside me. "What have you done now?"

I showed him my knife. "A little more insurance in case I meet Hoggs or Carambole in a dark alley."

"Hmmph." He shook his head and pushed me down a narrow gap between a couple of tents. "We need to go this way."

Hermann had steadfastly eschewed arming himself. He also took a dim view of my continuing to hang onto my Colt Paterson. Hermann nagged me almost daily to leave the damnable gun permanently with Sarah, if only to avoid it being found on my person by a snooping shoulder strap. The weapon was not regulation, and I would almost certainly be accused of theft if some Fenian-hating nativist shoulder strap caught me with it. That would cost me my chevrons and earn me thirty lashes to boot.

So until I left C Company and Hoggs' nearly constant harassment, I had taken Hermann's advice. Now that I was at only Grant's beck and call, I had much more freedom. I also had a horror of wandering about unarmed with the possibility of running into either Hoggs or Carambole, or God forbid, both of them together. The bowie knife made me even happier. My only issue was going to be finding the time and opportunity to learn how to properly use both it and my repeating pistol.

Juan Pablo, Hermann, and I were safe enough here in Point Isabel. We had hopped aboard an empty Conestoga wagon for the day-long ride under armed escort from the Fort Brown landing to Point Isabel. Just before we'd departed, I'd found Juan Pablo wandering around the mule pens and offered him his old job back of working with Grant. He'd readily accepted, and treated me to some good *aguardiente* on the strength of it. Now with the letter safely delivered, Hermann and I were free to visit Rónán Finnegan at the hospital established in the wake of the two battles. Juan Pablo was hoisting an *aguardiente* or two with a buddy of his who was working for the quartermaster at Point Isabel.

Rónán's wan look shocked both Hermann and me. I tried to avert my eyes from the bloody and none-too-clean bandage covering a furrow dug across his ribs by a spent Mexican musket ball. But I found myself drawn to it whenever Rónán coughed and grunted with considerable pain. More than once, I met Hermann's eye, and we each registered our concern to the other.

Rónán laughed—which hurt him every bit as much as his coughing—when Hermann recounted Sarah's and my ongoing argument over whether the dells should use French letters. He looked concerned when I told him of Carambole's apparent return as a major of Louisiana volunteers. He agreed that Carambole and Hoggs would indeed be well employed chasing rumors of Arista's buried payroll, particularly if it took them to the Resaca de la Palma and Palo Alto, rather than mucking about down in Matamoros. He chuckled carefully (thus avoiding a follow-on wince) when he told us about the expeditions from Point Isabel of newly-arrived volunteers who had yet to make their way to Matamoros. Officers and enlisted alike, they headed down to Resaca de la Palma at dawn on what seemed an almost daily basis, only to return hours later, empty-handed, sunburned, and filthy with loamy sand from all the digging.

I related the grapevine's latest twist to Hermann and Rónán: Just before they abandoned Matamoros, the Mexican army supposedly had lowered the payroll treasure to the bottom of a well in one of the wealthier homes to hide it from *los gringos*. According to this story, those cullies who were busy digging up the battlefields were on a fool's errand. Those in the know, on the other hand, were supposedly cracking kens and casas in the better part of town every night and searching wells for the hidden treasure. Juan Pablo had been the first to tell me the story over our drink of *aguardiente*. I heard it again that very evening from Jenny, just before we left for Point Isabel, as I took my ease in the back of the kitchen (which I did almost every night now that I had been freed from duties with C Company). She repeated the tale to me virtually word-for-word, joking that it would be wonderful if the treasure were secreted in the well in the middle of the courtyard of our cavaulting house, because we could all go back north as rhino-fat as Croesus himself. I laughed and told her that, if every wealthy Mexican really put his worldly possessions at the bottom of his well, then every *gringo* ken-cracker, holdup man, and gentleman of the pad ever to darken the streets of Matamoros would've been slipping down every well in town looking for such treasures. But we hadn't had even a single incident at the house, even though thievery of every sort—and worse—occurred nightly. The Texas and Louisiana volunteers and their camp followers were mostly to blame. Locals maintained that the Texians were more vicious, but that the Louisianans were more avaricious. That made sense. The Texians and Mexicans hated each other. The Louisianans were merely taking advantage of the defenseless town to loot it to their hearts' content.

I had dismissed the story then, and I airily dismissed it now. Rónán and Hermann both agreed. Arista's payroll treasure was apocryphal. Even if it had once existed some high-ranking Mexican army officer had long since spiced it and deposited it at the bottom of the well at his hacienda up in the mountains. Or if he were smart, the miscreant would have deposited the treasure safe and sound in the vault of some bank up in New York.

After a while, the conversation died down, and we stared at each other. I wanted to know when we would see Rónán leave this charnel house, where he lay among men dying from diarrhea, dysentery, and seemingly every other plague to have visited man since time immemorial. The doctors weren't going to pay any attention to either Hermann or me. We were mere Other Ranks. Anyway, doctors seemed to be very few and far between at the hospital, and all of them seemed to have fingernails blackened with the blood of every patient he'd seen that day. It brought to mind childhood memories of my father railing about the wickedness and ineffectiveness of the doctors under whose care (presumably complete with blackened fingernails) my mother had died after giving birth to me. Hermann kept glaring at me, as if to tell me to shut pan and not bother any of the doctors, so that they would not make trouble for us.

Rónán congratulated us both—Hermann on being promoted to sergeant, and me on now being able to avoid most of the unpleasant duties of an Other Ranks with my having been seconded to Grant. Rónán, I concluded, had as few illusions about my suitability to be a bluebelly as Hermann and I did, and there was no question that he saw my new situation as one where I would have a better chance of surviving. Hermann and I finally departed to the echo of Rónán's laughing suggestion that I take care not to get into any trouble now that I had so much freedom to come and go. As I followed Hermann out of the tent, I glanced back quickly and saw Rónán's shocked look as he opened the package that Hermann and I had left him. It contained a purse with five gold double eagles.

Several days later, after we had returned from Point Isabel, I wandered through the central square just at sunset, on my way to the dossing house. I glanced over at the immense flagpole that had been erected in front of the mayor's palace. The color guard, complete with the officer of the day and fifes and drums, were forming for Retreat. I swore quickly under my breath, because I was not going to get out of the square before the fifes and drums sounded. I was going to have to stand at attention, saluting, throughout the flag-lowering ceremony.

I had better things to do. I had a business to run. (Or at least I had a job to do in advising Sarah in the running of it, a role Sarah tolerated far better than she might otherwise have.) More importantly, I was just fit to burst over the need to boast a bit to Jenny and Eddie about my new-found expertise with my knife and repeating pistol. The day after we got back from Point Isabel, which had been a hot and lazy Sunday, Hermann and I had hiked out into the brush and practiced with my Colt Paterson until we could both load it and more often than not hit a target at twenty-five paces. Hermann had long since decided that both he and I had better learn how to use it if I wasn't going to sell it or otherwise get rid of it.

I hadn't yet told Hermann that I also knew how to use my knife. On the way back from Point Isabel, Hermann had ended up riding in a different wagon than Juan Pablo and I. As we sat on the sacks of flour, bumping along for hours on end, I showed Juan Pablo my prize. He told me that everyone in Mexico knew how to use a knife. Firearms were scarce, and those that were in the hands of *arrieros* such as himself were often ancient *escopetas* that rarely worked when you wanted them to.

Over the next several days, Juan Pablo had spent more than a few hours teaching me how to use it, as well as how to wear it carefully concealed in a scabbard between my shoulder blades, just like some South Texas desperado—and just like the sucker I'd bought it from. Juan Pablo also incessantly teased me on my still-broken Spanish. Within a couple of days, I thought I was a regular "Cap'n Hackum," although voicing that bit of St. Giles's Greek dredged up the highly unpleasant memory of Lúcás Dineen holding Blackie and me helpless on the porch of Magee's boardinghouse as the boardinghouse burned, murdering poor Mary and Charlie Backwell. When I told Juan Pablo what I thought of my newly-acquired skills, he smiled tiredly and reminded me of that well-known aphorism: Always bring a gun to a knife fight. Otherwise you might get cut. I did not share that aphorism with Hermann.

I wasn't planning to share my new-found expertise with Sarah, either. She fancied Hermann's sentiment regarding my foolish insistence on being armed. Anyway, I'd picked enough fights (if you could call them that) with her over the running of the brothel that I wanted to leave well enough alone. Eddie, though, agreed with me that I should be well armed, for he had a horror of Carambole—and of the captain whom he and Sarah had tossed from the dossing house a couple of weeks back. Carambole's reputation preceded him, and Eddie had clearly insulted the drunken and impecunious captain for his treatment of Adabelita. Eddie didn't know Hoggs, but he took Hoggs's viciousness as an article of faith, if only because he and Rouquette were seemingly as thick as thieves.

The color guard was at attention, and the fifes squealed. As I stopped and saluted, I realized that I was standing next to an old man, swarthy and sunburned and hunched with age, staring at the ceremony with an air of bemusement.

When the fifes sounded the last note of "Retreat," and the color guard marched off, I turned to the old man and said, "¡*Buenas tardes,* señor!"

He started with surprise when he realized that a *norteamericano*— and a *yanqui* doughboy to boot—had greeted him in Spanish. He recovered and told me I spoke Spanish well. I thanked him.

He nodded and replied in Spanish, "I am struck, señor, by the fact that this is the fourth time I have been in a city where I have watched you *yanquis* raise your flag every morning, and then lower it in the evening. In every city I have seen the ceremonies, I have counted the number of stars on your flag, and each time I have counted just a few more, which meant that you *norteamericanos* were just a little bigger and stronger than before."

"When was the first time?"

"I was just a young lad when I came from Spain and landed in New Orleans. We Spanish were settling there in droves in those days. Then the French took it from us and promptly sold it to you *yanquis* for fifteen million of your dollars. There were just fifteen stars on your flag in those days. Five rows of three."

I snapped to attention and give a salute as the color guard marched past us, a file of fifes and drums in tow. The squealing fifes were fighting with the drums over some tune that I did not recognize.

I stood easy after the color guard passed and my companion continued his story. "I left New Orleans and went to Florida. To St. Augustine. One day, several years later, your army marched in and raised its flag. This time, there were twenty stars, and they were arranged in the shape of a larger star. Then I went to Texas. San Antonio de Béxar, where I opened a store. *Los norteamericanos* came once more. This time, though, a different flag was raised after Santa Anna was defeated. It had just one star. But I thought that you *norteamericanos* with all your new stars on your flag could not be far behind, so I left and came here to Matamoros. And what do you know? The *yanqui* flag is here now. With twenty-eight stars. How can we poor Mexicans survive this?"

I said nothing.

Just before he turned and disappeared into the gloom of the encroaching dusk, he said to me, "If I were a younger man, I would go to *la Ciudad de México*. But I am afraid that you *gringos* would follow me, and then *la patria* would be lost forever."

⌒

That night, Sarah told me that Jenny and Eddie were going to have to leave Matamoros.

"But what about Eddie's duties with his regiment?"

"He hasn't been there since the day after you left."

"You mean that he's a deserter?"

Sarah grimaced a little. "Nobody cares about that. Anyway, their 90 days are about up. So General Taylor is sending those useless bastards home. Anyway, Eddie's in hiding here at the casa, because Carambole has apparently put the word out that he will kill him over that business with his sidekick." I said nothing, and she continued, "you know, the kinky one. He ain't gone home yet—and now he's a major, to boot. The brigadier is beside himself over the man's political pull."

"Kinky?" I'd never heard the term before.

Sarah looked at me impatiently. "You know, what he was doing with that poor girl, Adabelita."

"Aaah. How is she doing?"

"Fine. Poor girl's an abigail now. I can't have her with the coves. They'll either be horrified—the decent ones, that is—or they'll want to be with her just to look at her. That bastard ruined her nose and smashed in all her front teeth. She'll never be the same. Her family has disowned her. God knows what will happen to her when we *gringos* leave."

"We make sure she has enough rhino when we leave—more than if she'd continued to wag her tail with the coves."

Sarah rolled her eyes. "Of course, Billy, my love."

"So, what about Hoggs and Carambole … and Eddie?"

Sarah shook her head. "Eddie was lucky. He and Jenny were taking the morning air, and Carambole quite literally bumped into Eddie, right in the middle of the town square. Hoggs was with him, damn his rotten soul. Eddie saluted Carambole, him being a shoulder strap and all. Carambole was a regular Soapy Sam, what with bowing and scraping before Jenny and congratulating her on her expected gift. Hoggs didn't say blessed word." Sarah snorted in disgust. "And then they went on their way. Eddie told me that he would be a dead man if Hoggs's looks could kill."

"I'll bet. And so?"

"It wasn't 'til the next day that some croaksman took a shot at Eddie. Missed him, praise the Lord. Beef-headed moke used a musket. Even though Eddie was okay, Jenny was looking seven ways for Sunday when she heard about it. Absolutely beside herself, cryin' and all. I was afraid she was going to lose the baby. But Eddie just took her upstairs, and she was asleep in ten minutes. I can't imagine a better man for her than Eddie. He wants to marry her and accept that child as his own." Sarah looked positively misty-eyed.

"We all know that Eddie's completely mad about her," I replied, ignoring her news. "But what the Sam Hill is this about him being shot at?"

"That's all I know. We don't know for sure who did it. Jenny's convinced that it was Hoggs."

"Bloody hell."

"Why didn't Eddie go see someone? He could've gone to see Grant." I instantly hated myself, for it was a foolish thing to say.

Sarah gave me a withering look for my pains, and snapped, "Don't be stupid. How could Eddie rap to Grant on Rouquette and Hoggs? Rouquette and Grant don't even know each other. And as you should know, nocky boy, they're not even in the same chain of command.

Anyways, who else would Eddie go to?" She shook her head. "Rouquette's the second-in-command of his regiment. He knows the governor. And the brigadier general of volunteers. Nobody's going to believe Eddie over something like this." She wasn't done, for she once more bore into me. "What's more, we don't really know for certain that it was Hoggs and Rouquette. These days, there's half a dozen shootings and stabbings every night in town. Why just last night, there was a house breaking just down the street. A young man drove away some Louisiana raffle-coffins who were nosing about his sister after they broke in. They came back a little while later, killed the boy and had their way with the girl, anyway. Slit her throat and left her to die in the doorway, naked from the waist down. Disgusting bastards. She tossed her head and forestalled my next question. "So I can't be going to the Old Man with such a matter."

"So, now what?"

"We get them out of here."

"How? Eddie'll be jerked to Jesus for desertion."

"No he won't. He ain't a regular."

I looked at her blankly.

"Old Zach ain't going to be hanging any volunteers. The brigadier himself told me that Old Zach figures that the volunteers ain't subject to the same rules that you bluebelly regulars are. So, them volunteers are just being sent home to face trial ... even when they've croaked some poor greaser. It's worse with the civilians. Perfect Bliss has told the Old Man that he can't do anything to them, for he has no authority over them at all. 'T'ain't constitutional, Perfect told him."

I started to contradict Sarah.

"Let me finish. You are such a know-it-all sometimes. The general also told me that, in most regiments, half the volunteers don't even show up to muster. He hardly knows how to stop them from tearing the town apart, the poor man." Sarah looked positively downcast at the dilemma faced by the brigadier general of volunteers. "His officers are afraid to discipline their men, because they're afraid that their troops will vote for the other guy as justice of the peace or, worse, will torch his barn when they all get home … which they'll start doing almost any day now." Sarah looked triumphant at the prospect. "All these Louisiana and Texas 90-day boys are going home over the next few weeks." Sarah's face fell once more. "To tell you the truth, Billy, I don't think the poor man's heart is in it. He just wants to go home. The governor has appointed some cove named Persifor Smith to be the brigadier-general of Louisiana volunteers over him, and now my poor general just wants to hide over the shame of it all."

"A little pillow talk?" It suddenly seemed so obvious.

Sarah looked daggers at me. "Yes, if you must know. I am a single woman, and he is a fine-looking man."

"Ancient."

"You're just a kid. What do you know?"

I shifted back to the more practical consideration of what we were going to do about Eddie. "So, where's Eddie now?"

"Upstairs. With Jenny."

"What if we're attacked by some ken-crackers bent on croaking us? Or worse, Hoggs and Carambole come back?"

"They wouldn't dare. The house is under the general's personal protection. He's here half the day now that Smith has taken over …"

"And all night, no doubt," I interjected. "But that isn't going to stop Mexican desperadoes. If I were Rouquette, I'd hire a couple dozen of them to rumble us out of the casa. I could hire the lot of them for a gold half-eagle, particularly if I promised them that they could have their way with the place, and loot it to their hearts' content."

Sarah paled. "Rouquette's not going to know that …"

"Rouquette may be a murderous bastard, but that doesn't mean he's dumb. He can figure it out just as easily as I can."

"So what do we do? We can't trust the Louisianans to protect us. And Luis's men won't stand up to a real fight."

"We'll find some more Mexicans of our own. I'll talk to Juan Pablo."

A bell tinkled.

Sarah leaned over and pecked me on the cheek. "You're brilliant."

"What?"

"You've solved everything. Now I can tell the general that he doesn't have to try to protect Eddie." With that she swept from the room with an excited gleam in her eye. Over her shoulder, she said, "I'll tell him now. He'll be so pleased ... and happy with me."

It was too bad that I was never able to follow through on my promise—or, for that matter, to congratulate Jenny and Eddie on their coming nuptials.

CHAPTER 17

# Croake the . . . Greaser

ᢒ───

THE SUN HAD NOT YET RISEN when Colonel Kinney slipped down the pathway between the perfectly aligned and snow-white tents of the Fourth Infantry's officers' row, which overlooked the pickets standing guard beyond the parade ground of the Army of Invasion's digs west of town. The look in his eye kept me silent as I stood more or less at attention out of Grant's way. Grant was standing at the entrance to his tent, his back turned to the world, vigorously brushing out his uniform blouse and otherwise making himself presentable enough for an audience with a field-grade officer—no less a personage than Colonel Jack Hays, himself, commanding officer, First Regiment, Texas Mounted Rifleman—a regiment of volunteers who were as fine a cavalry outfit as any in either army, or so the grapevine maintained. Otherwise known in Uncle Sam as the Texas Rangers, and *los diablos rinches* to *los méxicanos*.

Grant hadn't let me brush out his uniform for him. He had instead given me a speech. "You ain't my dog robber, Gogan. That's what my brethren and I hired Hannibal for."

I didn't ask where Hannibal was. Hopefully brewing some java for the good lieutenant, who would almost certainly share a cup with me. Grant was good that way.

Hannibal had appeared as if by magic a few weeks ago, skin the color of molasses, looking for work. Grant and another shoulder strap had hired him on account of their previous servant, Old Ben, having taken a powder one night for points unknown. Hannibal had confessed to me (over a couple of whiskeys I'd poured for him) that he'd stowed away on a ship from New Orleans after having slipped away from his master on a visit there from some plantation upriver, where he'd been a slave up at the big house—although he used a rather different phrase. On account of his loyalty, discretion, and pleasant mien, he had told me—in those precise words, no less. Hannibal said that he'd heard from other Negroes on the riverboat south to New Orleans that they didn't have slaves down Mexico-way, and he thought that was a "mighty fine state of affairs," particularly as he'd been told that there were plenty of jobs for the asking in Matamoros for a half-eagle or even an eagle a month. I told Hannibal that his secret was safe with me, which, along with an occasional whiskey and good stogie or two, subsequently earned me on more than one occasion some good gouge on Grant's whims and moods.

Grant was talking again. "I don't hold truck with my quartermaster's sergeant brushing out my uniform. It's menial work, and we can't have the ranking quartermaster's sergeant doing anything beneath him …" Grant smiled at my shock. "That's right, Gogan. You're out of uniform again. I have to have a quartermaster's sergeant, particularly for what you're going to be doing for the next few weeks, and I didn't want that Dutchy illiterate whom Major Harrison wanted to assign me." Grant looked at me again. "No, no … I don't mean Wurster. For the love of God, I could outfit the entire army lickety-clip if I had Wurster to guide you about. And he ain't illiterate. But I don't have Wurster. So you're promoted. Not that you deserve it, mind you. And," he gave me a hard, if slantendicular, glare, "you'll lose it the minute you go back to a line company. So when my time's up as regimental quartermaster, so too will your time as a quartermaster's sergeant."

"Yes sir."

So there I was standing when Kinney hove onto the scene, more or less at attention, and at once wondering how quickly I could get my new stripe sown on my blouse and reveling at the thought of no longer having to worry about Hoggs on account of my now being a sergeant just like him (Albeit without the lozenge. But it was nonetheless a big step in the right direction.)

Grant almost jumped out of his skin when Kinney boomed, "Sam, you ain't going to need to be real particular about your uniform. Jack Hays ain't never pissed no West Point water, as you regulars like to say. You and the young 'un'd be better off in mufti." Henry Kinney nodded to me with an amused twinkle in his eye. "Fit in a whole lot better with them Rangers. More comfortable, too." Kinney cocked his eye at Grant's erect bearing, driven in no small part by the tightness of the collar of his blouse.

Grant recovered sufficiently to reply equably. "Henry, I'm going to see a colonel. A colonel leading a crew of rapacious scavengers and scalawags, perhaps. But a colonel, nonetheless."

"True enough. He is the newly elected Colonel of the First Regiment, Texas Mounted Riflemen. But, Sam, that ain't the point. I'm a 'colonel,' if only by courtesy, custom, usage, and the Old Man's patronage. Yet, you call me 'Henry.' It's the same with Jack Hays. He ain't no regular army shoulder strap any more than I am. Why, he was a private no more 'n' a week ago or so. He and Mike Chevallie both enlisted together as privates up Béxar way, although there was no question but that they were going to lead the regiment. An' he didn't get elected colonel of the regiment 'til they assembled at Point Isabel. So, to be clear, Ol' Jack Hays ain't no regular. Never was. Never will be. He's simply the best cavalryman Uncle Sam has. Bar none."

"You mean that my new sergeant over there could have told him what to do before last week?" Grant looked the very picture of innocence as he imperceptibly straightened the red sash beneath his sword belt. "I should've promoted him sooner."

Kinney flashed me a grin and shook my hand. "Congratulations, son. Well done." Then he looked back at Grant and drawled. "Young Billy could've told Devil Jack Hays what to do … while Jack was still a private. But I wouldn't vouch for whatever might've happened afterwards. Not that Jack Hays would've said a word, of course. He's a gentleman, and he would have done Billy's bidding, just simply because that's the way of it, Billy bein' a sergeant an' Devil Jack bein' a private an' all. But Mike Chevallie might've said a word or two, although not to Billy boy's face, on account o' his not liking to give offense unless he's fixing to croake a man." Kinney's face darkened for a moment. "But someone else … Mustang Gray, maybe. Yep, Ol' Mustang Gray would've permanently rectified the slight just as sure as shooting. Right then and there, too."

I shivered involuntarily.

"And thus added to the Texians' share of the murdering down here in Matamoros," Grant observed drily.

Kinney ignored Grant, except to observe, "Sam, do yourself a favor, as we're headed over to see the biggest assemblage of Texians since San Jacinto. Don't call a Texian a Texican. Texicans are Mexicans who sided with us Texians. Of course, that's unless it means a white man who is a Texian. Depends on whom you're talking to, I suppose." He gave me a serious look and elaborated on the subject at hand, "I reckon, Billy m'boy, that you aren't so chuckleheaded as to tell Jack Hays what to do." He thought for a second. "No … I am mistaken. You might be that foolhardy, but you certainly are not that disrespectful."

⌒

I helped Juan Pablo lead the horses over to Kinney and Grant, who were waiting at Grant's tent. As we did, I told him that we were going to see Colonel Jack Hays of the First Texas Mounted Riflemen. I also told him that we would also be seeing a fellow named Mustang Mabry Gray, but that I did not know much about him.

Juan Pablo considered the news for a moment, and then conspiratorially whispered to me in Spanish, "They call Hays, '*el Diablo Yack.*' The most feared *rinche* in all of *Tejas*. Every *méxicano* fears him, even General Canales. But he is not hated."

"Why not? If you give credence to half the stories you hear about him, every *tejano* and Comanche north of the río Bravo ought to hate every *rinche* there ever was, including Devil Jack."

"That is true of most *rinches*. Any *tejano* or *méxicano* worth his salt would kill a *rinche* on sight—that is if the other *rinches* did not

immediately avenge his death. But Devil Jack is different. He has
killed many a Comanche. But they all deserved to die." Juan Pablo
spat on the ground and continued. "As to *méxicanos*, *el Diablo Yack*
has never killed anyone who wasn't trying to kill him first. That is the
sign of a decent man. You know what else? *El Diablo Yack* rode with
General Canales back in '40, when Canales was trying to establish
his independent republic. My cousin rode with Canales as well until
the *federalistas* got ahold of him and hanged him. But that's beside the
point. Thing is, *el Diablo Yack* helped General Canales win a couple of
tough battles, sending the *federalistas* back south where they belong.
But *el Diablo Yack* quit on General Canales and went back north to
Béxar, because he thought that General Canales didn't know what he
was doing. General Canales was very insulted, and he's sworn to take
*el Diablo Yack*'s ears off and tie them to his saddle, like a Comanche
counting coup. But as I said, that's because *el Diablo Yack* insulted his
honor, not because *el Diablo Yack* is a murderer."

Juan Pablo ruminated for a moment, and said, again *sotto voce*,
"But all *méxicanos* do hate *este cabrón* Mustang Gray and others like
him. *Este hijo de puta* Gray is nothing more than a common murderer
… and a cattle thief. Why, he and his 'cowboys'—at least that's what
they called themselves—murdered don Silvestre de León and half
a dozen of his *vaqueros* on the de León hacienda a couple of years
ago, when don Silvestre caught him and his gang red-handed stealing
cattle with the de León brand. Gray and his cowboys had an iron in
the fire ready to brand right over the de León brand on a heifer that
was bleating like a stuck pig. Don Silvestre tried to intervene peaceably, although he was quite firm in pointing out that *el hijo de puta*
was on de León land and the cattle in question were legally branded
as belonging to the de León family. But Gray was having none of it,
and he and his fellow border ruffians shot don Silvestre dead, along
with three of his *vaqueros*. His sainted mother, doña Patricia de la
Garza, sent word to Matamoros of her son's assassination, but nothing came of it and *el hijo de puta* has continued to murder *tejanos* and
rape their women."

The Rangers' camp was set in a field of dried mud on the north bank of the río Bravo, directly across the river from Matamoros. It was cheek-by-jowl with the great earthen ramparts of Fort Texas that Hermann and I and the rest of the Army of Invasion had toiled over during those anxious weeks in April—which now seemed so very long ago. As we rode up from the ferry landing, I noted idly that slender tendrils of weeds were just beginning to poke through the mud walls of the fort, which were just beginning to dry after a drenching monsoonal rain a couple of days before.

It crossed my mind that the weeds were a hopeful sign that the fort might be gradually returning to nature—a notion reinforced by the drying dirt beginning to crumble all along the face of the ramparts, a decay that might just presage the return of some modicum of peace to this pretty valley. I dismissed the thought, though. Uncle Sam was here for the long haul. Anyway, our departure would not end the three-way collision between the Texians and their other *norteamericano* brethren, *los tejanos* and their *norteño* comrades, and the Comanche and Lipan Apache and every other flavor of their red brothers within a thousand miles.

"Henry, you old rascal." A smooth-faced, almost diminutive young man looked up at us. He was the only man we'd seen since we'd arrived at the Ranger camp who was not sporting some form of luxuriant beard or moustache, separated from the two men with whom he'd been talking and approached us. "Welcome to Camp Maggot."

"Why, thank you, Jack. Glad to be here." Kinney laughed as we dismounted and looked about at the camp of the First Texas Mounted Riflemen. "This is a mighty splendiferous shitpot you've got here."

The wind freshened almost on cue, and I gagged from the smell of rotting flesh. The army's slaughtering pens for our food were hardly more than 200 yards downriver—and often upwind—of the camp. Offal from the pens had spread to the river's edge and beyond, lending a grayish tinge to a great semicircle of water misshapen by the slow current. The smell was a perfect match for the utterly motley nature of the camp itself.

The tents were hardly worthy of the name. Makeshift shelters had been set haphazardly in a circle around a small central area that was far too small to serve as a drill field, with no two shelters being remotely uniform with a third. Campfires irregularly dotted the landscape in between the shelters. The general appearance of Camp Maggot could not have been more different from the Fourth Infantry's digs.

The Rangers were as motley as their camp. Not a man was in uniform, although each one looked like the next in his mufti of red flannel shirt, scrofulous vest, suspenders, and filthy trousers tucked into boots of a type I had never seen before—pointed toes and prominent heels to which spurs were attached that jingled merrily every time a man moved even a step. An eastern tenderfoot might have thought that they would be wearing buckskins of the sort described by Fenimore Cooper. Yet not a man was. It was just too bloody hot to wear them. Their slouch hats of dun-colored felt, which were adapted from the Mexican sombrero to shade them from the brutal South Texas sun, could have been a uniform item, yet each man had fashioned his hat to his own particular fancy, thereby adding to the sartorial din.

The members of the First Texas Mounted Riflemen were uniform in one respect, though. Every damned one of them was armed to the teeth. They all bristled with at least two or three knives ranging in size from giant Arkansas toothpicks to folding pocket knives that disappeared into easily accessible nooks and crannies about their persons. Virtually every man had at least one Colt five-shooter. Some even had two, and those who did not generally carried one or two additional pistols of every type imaginable. One man had acquired a giant Model 1842 dragoon's percussion cap pistol and another man was brandishing a tiny pistol not dissimilar to the piece of junk that Lúcas Dineen had sported in Blackie's and my faces on the porch of Magee's boardinghouse. I winced involuntarily at the memory.

Kinney said to Hays, "Jack, I'd like to introduce Lieutenant Sam Grant. He's the regimental quartermaster for the Fourth Infantry. Picked by the Old Man himself for the job. Colonel Whiting, the army's quartermaster-general, has tasked him with gathering mules— on account of his knowledge of horseflesh, which I can tell you from personal experience, is quite extraordinary for a man in a blue uniform. That young stripling over yonder is his sergeant. Billy Gogan's his name. Smart young kid. Helps keep the good lieutenant's skirts clean, I might add. He's the boy with the account books of who owes what to which hombre. He'll be carrying the chink to pay for the mules, an' he speaks the dago lingo as well as any dago born south of the Rio Grande."

We all shook hands, and I tried to hide my embarrassment. My Spanish, although much improved, was hardly that of a native. Between us, Juan Pablo and I could translate well from English to Spanish and back again, But separately? Not on my life. I resolved to work once more with Juan Pablo to further improve my skills, for surely no American would trust a mere Mexican to translate.

"Glad to meet you boys. We're mighty pleased to have you riding with us." Hays said this without a hint of irony, looking first at Grant and then at me. "You don't have much of a retinue, Lieutenant."

Grant crisply saluted Hays, who waved it off nonchalantly. "Well, sir, I'm just a pumpkin rind, myself, so I don't rate any sort of retinue, and I reckon that in the company of your Mounted Volunteers, we're probably in the safest spot in Mexico with all the chink ... gold ... we'll have along to pay for the mules."

Hays nodded appreciatively. "Please allow me to name my companions. My second-in-command, Colonel Sam Walker."

Grant and I crisply saluted Walker, who waved us off with a token tug of his hat and murmured, "Mornin', boys."

Walker was just as slight of build and youthful-looking and unassuming as Jack Hays. For the first time in my life, I was conscious of towering over another man. Yet both he and Hays burned with an intensity of purpose that I had never before experienced. As ludicrous as it sounds, I would have in that instant followed the both of them to the very gates of Hell, blazing away with a Colt's five-shooter in each hand and sending Mexican soldiers to their Maker by the gross. I caught Grant admeasuring them, and thought he would have followed them as well. It was then that I placed Walker's name. He must have been the same Texian gambler who had visited the saloon Brannagh's father had owned in Paradise Square ... a time that seemed infinitely long ago. There couldn't be two Texians named Walker sporting Colt's repeating pistol. The only rub was that Brannagh's character-ization of Walker certainly jarred with the intense and slight man standing next to me.

Hays broke my reverie. "Sergeant, I believe that you've met my other companion. I just heard tell from him that you saved his bacon up in Point Isabel."

I don't know why I hadn't seen the man until now. He was sim-ply gargantuan, towering over everyone there and seemingly as wide as he was tall, and so very much bigger than I remembered him as he gambled away his last bit of chink in that fetid tent up in Point Isabel—and I had thought him huge then.

Hays seemed to relish the moment. "May I present," he intoned with some portent. "Mr. Sidney Moncrief, late of the Carolinas. But we call him Big Foot. Mr. Moncrief is a Carolina planter's son come to Texas in '36 to avenge the untimely death at Goliad of his kinfolk at the hands of that scurrilous dago filibuster, Santa Anna. He has since done me the great honor of serving alongside me in a whole passel of scrapes in these past years. He even saw fit to come back and find me after escaping that damned dago prison down Perote-way."

Big Foot grabbed me in a bear hug and said something endearing to me about having rescued him from that damned square-decker. As he grabbed me, I was conscious of Grant smiling tolerantly.

The languid tone of a man bred and born on some Carolina planta-tion broke the spell. "You know, Colonel Hays, James Fenimore Cooper should capture this scene in his next installment of the *Leatherstocking Tales*. Truly endearing how the young dude saved, as you put it, the

303

heroic Ranger's bacon from that contumelious riverboat sharp. I shall write of it in my next dispatch." I looked at the man sharply, who seemed to have appeared out of nowhere. He was of medium height and a face gone bright red, most likely due to the capacious black frock coat he was wearing despite the heat and humidity, both of which were frightful even at this early hour of the morning. He was the very picture of a man who had passed much of his life indoors.

"Henry, Lieutenant Grant, Sergeant Gogan ..." There was just the slightest hint of forbearance in Hays's voice. "This is Mr. J. T. Pickens, owner, publisher, and roving reporter for *The Picayune*. Late Captain of Louisiana Volunteers with Gaines's Rangers. His partner, George Kendall, apparently has been busy making our good friend and ally, Ben McCulloch, a national hero. Ben told me that, a few weeks ago, Mr. Kendall hired himself on as a "high private" with Ben and his San Antonio Rangers—known to you bluebellies as Company A of our First Texas Mounted Riflemen. I suppose being a "high private" means that Mr. Kendall doesn't have to carry his load of chores and sentry duty. Anyway, Mr. Kendall wrote all manner of dispatches about Ben and his boys." Hays stopped when he saw questioning looks on Grant's and my faces. "Ben and his boys are riding herd over Reynosa-way at the Old Man's behest, scouting out the road to Monterrey through Cerralvo. Old Ben's also been chasing that rascal Canales and his rancheros all over hell's half acre. Except, they aren't peacable rancheros, that bunch. Murdering *banditti*, more like."

As Hays talked, I thought how curious it was that our shoulder straps—regulars and volunteers alike—almost always referred to Mexican *guerrilleros* as *banditti*, an Italian term for bandits. They didn't even call them what the Mexicans called them: *Bandidos* or *bandoleros*, the latter term referring to *bandidos* who belonged to a really large gang.

Hays continued. "Yep, ol' Ben wants to put a powerful hurt on them *banditti* for past sins rendered against us Texians." Hays stopped and looked around at his audience. "So do I, and so does every other manjack in this regiment." His tone softened again. "I also hear tell that Ol' Ben's been chasing them damned Comanche hither and thither —all the while with Mr. Kendall in tow as 'high private.' Now his partner, our companion, Mr. Pickens—'J. T.' to his friends—has kindly offered to join our little expedition in a similar capacity. I reckon he's planning on making Sam and Big Foot national heroes along with Old Ben." Hays allowed himself a tight smile.

Pickens—I never did learn his Christian name—was irrepressible. "I do so kindly thank you, Colonel Hays, for allowing me to tag along. And you are so very right that Colonel Walker shall become a national hero. He is the very apotheosis of Cooper's leading man." Pickens looked to Kinney, Grant, and finally to me for approbation. I tried to keep my expression as noncommittal as theirs. Pickens continued, undaunted, "A hero of the Southwestern Army of Operations sent south by President Houston in '42 to punish the Mexican for his ceaseless raids and depredations on honest Texians and their farms and womenfolk. It was highly infelicitous of President Houston not to see fit to properly equip that gallant little army of unpaid volunteers—not of course that the Texian fisc had a plugged nickel in it on account of the banks not bein' willing to lend the proud Republic of Texas even a bent bungtown copper. And equally of course, President Houston also appointed a man to lead the army who, I am told by the most impeccable of sources, skedaddled back home at his earliest convenience with more than a few men, all of whom were a little yellow about the gills, before the battle royal could commence, thereby leaving Colonel Walker and a few others to carry on the fight—each of whom, I was further informed, was as independent of proper command as a hog on ice. It was a crime how Colonel Walker and ..." Pickens nodded acknowledgement to Big Foot. "Sergeant Moncrief and so many others were captured at Mier after they were surrounded by a Mexican army a hundred times bigger than their paltry force. Dragged south to Santa Anna's lair, they were. From whence they and a few lucky others escaped. Heroes, they are. And their return to arms in the service of Manifest Destiny as the eyes and ears of the conquering Army of Invasion will allow them to exact their revenge against the evil *gachupine*."

Walker looked pointedly at the horizon, his high cheeks coloring slightly. Hays merely looked irritated. Grant's face remained inscrutable, and Kinney's eyes crinkled with amusement at Walker's discomfiture.

Pickens looked at Hays and added quickly, "But we shall do you full justice, too, Colonel Hays. Please have no doubt on that important point." Hays looked even more irritated, but Pickens blithely ignored him and said to no one in particular, "Why, the citizens of my fair city, New Orleans, sent that beautiful bay gelding over yonder to Colonel Walker." We involuntarily looked at a magnificent horse with glistening reddish chestnut coat and black tail and ears tethered some yards away. It must have cost the good citizens of New Orleans a right hefty bundle. "On account of the loss of his horse at Palo Alto, as he gallantly fought off a desperate charge by the Mexican lancers. And that's after he slipped through the entire Mexican army and into Fort Texas at the Old Man's behest, just before the battle was joined, to bring those heroic Cottonbalers the good news that Old Zach was coming to deliver them succor by way of putting a mighty hurt on the dastardly Mexicans." Pickens's face positively shone with enthusiasm.

Walker shook his head, and spoke with a quiet intensity which, like that of Hays, lay ill-concealed beneath his light and chaffing tone of voice. "You do blather on so, J. T. And do you know what the worst of all your humbug is? You have made it downright impossible for me to spend a peaceable week up there in New Orleans—or in New York, for that matter." Pickens eyed Walker with an air of amused tolerance. Walker smiled tightly. "Cap'n Jack is right, J. T. Pay more attention to Big Foot. It'd serve him right for coming along with me to Mier, instead of going home with Jack and Ben McCulloch, as we all should've done."

But Pickens wasn't done with Walker just yet. He pulled a hip flask from within his capacious black frock coat, ceremoniously opened it, wiped its mouth with an enormous violet silk kerchief, and offered it to the assemblage. Everyone demurred. Pickens shrugged and took a mighty swig. The flask disappeared back into the folds

of his frock coat, and he once again speechified to no one in particular, "I think it's brilliant of the Washington City big bugs to offer
Colonel Walker a regular army captain's commission and command of
C Company of that new regiment of Mounted Riflemen—an entirely
new regiment of regulars. He has forgotten more of the equestrian arts
than your best cavalryman in the Second Dragoons has ever learned,
including that born fool, Thornton. No Texas Ranger would have gotten himself captured like that, ignominiously trapped in some thorn
bushes. No sirree. If a Texas Ranger is going to get hisself captured,
he'll be out-numbered a hundred to one, ammunition and water gone,
his horses all broken down, and no hope of escape or victory—just
like at Mier."

Walker had resumed his study of the horizon, and Hays's look
of disapproval intensified before he said, "Mr. Pickens, you will forgive us if we excuse ourselves. Colonel Walker and I must confer with
Colonel Kinney and Lieutenant Grant ..." He paused for a moment,
his eyes flickering briefly at me. "And the good sergeant here. I have
been given to understand that he is fluent in the Mexican language."

⁓

"Gentlemen." Hays nodded to the group standing around a small map
table set up under the shade of a mesquite tree: Kinney, Sam Walker,
and Major Mike Chevallie, a long-standing right-hand man to both
Walker and Hays in exploits too numerous to count, according to Big
Foot, who stood next to Grant and me. Hays had introduced the two
final members of the group as Major Mabry Gray, a man in his late
twenties with vacant blue eyes, a scruffy beard, and the languid air of a
Carolinas planter, and his first lieutenant, a yellow-eyed fellow named
Damien Alston. "Our mission is two-fold," Hays said briskly. "First is
to make our way to Monterrey by way of San Fernando de Presas and
Linares. And if we can along the way, we'll see what we can do to
find those miscreants, Canales and Seguin, and their *banditti*, and give
them a taste of the medicine they've been bringing to South Texas all
these years. We have word that Ben has made matters a trifle hot for

307

them out west, near Mier and Camargo. So we may hope that Canales and the others come east to regroup and recruit new followers to their misguided cause."

There were murmurs of enthusiasm over the prospect of administering a little Texas-style punishment after so many years of Canales eluding capture. I thought about don Guillermo, and how he would have felt being characterized as a mere bandit.

Hays continued. "I take it that all of you boys have heard about what happened back in the springtime, up at Arroyo Colorado to the Rogers party, with those women and children."

We had indeed all heard the shocking news. An expedition led by a Texian merchant named Patterson Rogers, had departed Corpus Christi in late April, bound for Point Isabel. I'd heard tell that he and his party were taking a wagon train of supplies to Point Isabel for the army. Fair enough in view of the rates that merchants were charging the army just then. Only God knew why Rogers was so hellbent on taking Mrs. Rogers, their daughter of marriageable age, and a young child. The army was still ensconced on the north bank of the río Bravo, Thornton had just been captured, Colonel Cross murdered, Lieutenant Porter killed in the search for Cross, and the outcome of any tussle with the Mexicans in grave doubt. But south they came. They camped at the north bank of the very ford across the Arroyo Colorado, where the army had crossed five weeks earlier in the face of the threats of destruction at the hands of the mythical Mexican army supposedly waiting for them on the south bank.

So the story went, they set no guards and awoke at dawn to find themselves surrounded by a couple of dozen desperados. Who was leading that band of murderers, God only knows, although the grapevine had suggested everyone from Ramón Falcón to Seguin and even Canales himself. The desperadoes called out in broken English to the party that they were surrounded with no hope of escape, but no one would be harmed if Rogers and his group surrendered peaceably. After some discussion and further guarantees on the soul of the dearly departed mother of the desperadoes' leader, Rogers surrendered to protect his wife, daughter, and youngest child, and the other women accompanying the supply train. Unfortunately, the leader was not good to his word. The men were instantly bound, their throats cut, and their bodies thrown into the arroyo. The desperadoes took the women along for their entertainment for more than a month, only to leave them with a ranchero along the north bank of the Rio Grande, bruised, violated, and dispirited. The ranchero promptly took the poor women to Matamoros and the protection of the American army, where their horrific story made the rounds quicker than greased lightning.

"Needless to say," Hays smiled grimly. "It'd be mighty gratifying if we were to happen into these particular *banditti*." The group once more murmured its general support. "But we've got a second mission, which I can tell you is far more important to the Old Man's actually getting the army to Monterrey than chasing Canales and Seguin. We are going to have to find as many mules as we can and bring them back to Matamoros and the army, which is why not only are our regular army brothers-in-arms joining us on our little flutter, but also why Major Gray and his boys of the Matamoros Company of Texas Mounted Volunteers are accompanying us south in a supernumerary capacity." I could have sworn that Hays's nose wrinkled in distaste. "Sergeant Moncrief has kindly consented to being detailed to accompany you, Sergeant Gogan, while you are with Major Gray." Gray did not look thrilled with the prospect of Hays's spy being in his midst. Big Foot winked at me as Hays continued, "So I have no doubt that you will be in the safest of hands. Colonel Kinney, would you care to elaborate?"

"Of course, Jack, of course. As you are all aware, Colonel Whiting cannot obtain enough Conestoga-style wagons and oxen for the army's baggage train. What's more, as some of you know from your travels down here south of the Rio Grande, much of the road from Camargo to Monterrey is too rocky for easy transit by wagon. So 'most everything is going to have to be packed in by mule. Colonel Whiting has estimated that we'll need a thousand or more mules, either to haul carts and what wagons we can, or as pack mules. The colonel's got only 200 or so as of last night, mostly left over from the trip south from Corpus Christi, and there isn't another mule to be found between here and Béxar. So we've got to go south a ways to get them from the Mexicans, which is where Major Gray and our regular army guests come in.

"You'll scout out likely sources of mules as you head south with Colonel Hays. Major Gray and his company will head back north when you reach San Fernando. You'll gather up every mule between San Fernando and here as you go. Major Gray's men will play mule-skinner." Gray did not look overly pleased at the prospect. "You'll pay good hard coin—gold and silver—$10 or $15 a head if necessary ... to every *ranchero*, *hacendado*, village *alcalde*, or mule-skinner with healthy mules to sell. We don't want to requisition them, or we'll have a revolt on our hands, which would be Christmas in July for that no-good bastard Canales. Nobody'd be safe on the road unless he was with a company of regulars ... or of Texas Rangers. So pay gold and good silver, we will." Kinney looked at Grant, who nodded. He then looked at Gray, who stared back hard with those vacant blue eyes of his before finally nodding. Gray then looked expressionlessly, first at Grant and then at me, where he lingered with what I took to be a considering, if slightly contemptuous, gaze.

A lieutenant whom I vaguely recognized as being one of Whiting's minions materialized at Kinney's elbow with a pair of privates in tow, each of them in as crisp a uniform as I'd seen in a while. One of the privates proffered a heavily laden saddlebag to me. It was so heavy that I almost dropped it.

"Sergeant," Kinney said to me with a smile. "There's enough chink in that saddlebag to finance Canales for six months. But I'm sure that it'll be as safe as a baby in its cradle by its mother's side with you watching over it. And even better, you will be the most protected man in the army, what with Big Foot as your personal escort ... and in the company of Major Gray and his Matamoros Company ... until you hand the saddlebag back to the good lieutenant." Whiting's lieutenant glared daggers at me, as if I were fundamentally unfit to care for the saddlebag and its precious cargo.

Kinney was done, for he nodded to Hays, who said, "My *tejano* spies tell me that we can find mules down in Refugio and then further south nearer San Fernando. Lieutenant," Hays turned to Grant. "I understand that you and your sergeant have a Mexican fellow who's been a *caporal* for you since Corpus, and that the fellow knows of a few haciendas and ranchos where we might find some mules?"

"Yes sir."

"Can we trust him?"

Grant didn't look at me, although he perhaps should have. Bringing along Juan Pablo had been my idea. "I believe so. But if he doesn't measure up, then simply shoot him," Grant said equably to general approbation.

I fetched Juan Pablo, and we spent the next thirty minutes crowded around a copy of the map I'd found in Arista's tent, discussing the most likely places to find good quantities of mules. Juan Pablo pointed out a dozen locations within easy striking distance of the road to San Fernando, including a couple near Refugio, where he said that he'd bought mules many times over the years. When Juan Pablo finished talking, Hays looked at the group. Nobody said a word.

"So, that's it." Hays flashed a grin. "Hunting for these mules'll give us plenty of cover, because Major Gray's company will take the mules back to Matamoros. The dagoes won't suspect a thing when the rest of us slip off in the other direction."

As the officers' call—for that was what it was as surely as if the Rangers had been a regular army regiment of the line—broke up, Grant and Kinney were hovering in front of me, with Big Foot filling the horizon behind them.

"This is where I take my leave from you, Sergeant." Grant seemed to relish calling me that.

"Sir?"

"You didn't think you'd been promoted to sergeant merely to be my lackey, did you, Gogan? You're going to be on your own on this trip. I have every faith that you will acquit yourself well, although I did have to embellish your equestrian skills just a tad. Colonel Kinney was kind enough to provide some additional bona fides on your behalf." Kinney nodded with a grin on his face. "As Colonel Hays said, Mr. Moncrieff …" Grant looked up at the giant's grinning visage. "Big Foot … will be your bodyguard from now until you return with the mules." As I stared uncomprehendingly at him, Grant said, "What? You really didn't think that I would be going, did you? I've got to work to do, and a quartermaster general to whom I must dance attendance."

Kinney chimed in as he shook my hand. "You'll be fine, Sergeant. Absolutely fine. And I will pass your regards on to that young lady of yours up north. I'm sure she's dying to hear from you."

I will admit that I felt just a soupçon of terror at the prospect of my new assignment. But, then again, I thought, I would be well shot of that bastard Hoggs and his oily sidekick, Rouquette. It wasn't until later that I remembered that joining this little circus would be to leave Sarah and Hermann and Jenny and her new beau in the soup, without so much as a by-your-leave from me.

⌒

Every manjack in the regiment spent the rest of the day preparing for the patrol: Cleaning rifles, muskets, and Paterson repeating pistols, molding bullets, loading spare cylinders, preparing spare flintlocks, sharpening knives, packing beef jerky, reshoeing their horses, and repairing saddles.

Big Foot had sauntered over to me as I was struggling to load my spare cylinder.

"Here, let me show you." His thick fingers were surprisingly nimble as he swiftly loaded the cylinder. "Can you shoot it?"

I nodded.

"Hit anything?"

"At about fifteen, twenty yards or so, I suppose. Tough past that."

"Good enough. These five-shooters ain't much good past thirty yards, even for a crack shot with a steady nerve, and even then you're prob'ly wasting your time. Hell, even Cap'n Jack himself don't use his Colt 'til he can practically touch what he's killing. That way, every

312

shot counts. Why, one time up on Enchanted Rock, he killed a whole passel of Comanche with his Colt five-shooters when they got close. If'n he hadn't had his nerve, they'd've had his scalp, I reckon. He was lucky, though, that they ran off so that he could reload his spare cylinders. It took us boys about three more hours to get ourselves up to him."

"Why'd Cap'n Jack ..." I used the sobriquet self-consciously "... agree to take me along? Lieutenant Grant being ready to let me go by myself, I understand. I seemed to have earned his regard."

Big Foot laughed. "You're the one riding with Cap'n Jack, not your good lieutenant, so with all respect, your lieutenant's view don't signify. Henry Kinney vouchsafed for you. Anyway, Cap'n Jack's got a good eye for horseflesh and a better eye for men. He knows the good ones from the bad, and that's why the boys follow him, regardless of whether he's a colonel of the First Texas Mounted Riflemen ..." Big Foot pronounced the Rangers' official name with a certain ceremonious solicitude. "... Captain of his company of twenty or forty men, or a mere private. Why, when we mustered the Béxar company up in San Antonio last month, Cap'n Jack enlisted as a private. Ever'body knew he was going to be the regimental colonel, but he had to muster in somewhere, and the election waren't going to be held 'til we all got down here. Lemme tell you, though, during the march down here, Captain Acklin was mighty deferential to Cap'n Jack's likes and dislikes. But Jack was even more deferential to Captain Acklin on account of Jack still officially being a private an' all. When we got down to Point Isabel and met up with all the other companies of Rangers, Jack was elected colonel, Sam Walker was picked as lieutenant colonel, and Mike Chevallie became the regimental major—jes' like ever'body intended from the word go." Big Foot looked at me with a devilish grin. "But I wouldn't read too much into your coming along. 'T'ain't nothin' to do with you, at the end of the day. It's that saddlebag with all the chink in it that makes you important. For now, that is."

Later, after we'd finished our preparations, and just as the sun was going down, Big Foot asked me if I'd learned how to use my knife. I demurred, not wanting to appear the greenhorn, notwithstanding what I had learned from Juan Pablo. Big Foot insisted on spending the next two hours showing me the basics of killing a man with knife—Texas Rangers-style. I was very sore afterwards and quite worn out from wrestling with and dancing about a man who outweighed me by a hundred pounds and who was wielding a knife even bigger than the one he'd sold to me.

We departed at dawn the next morning. The regiment fell in silently, double file, company by company. Not a single bugle sounded. Not a single flag or pennant flew. Hardly even a whisper was uttered. I fell in with Big Foot near the head of the column, just behind Colonel Hays, Sam Walker, and Mike Chevallie. Juan Pablo rode by my side, quizzing me quietly on the finer points of Spanish as spoken by the *arriero méxicano*. Right behind us was Mustang Mabry Gray and his company. I could almost feel Gray's malevolence and resentment at being called upon to escort mules instead being invited along to hunt Canales and his miscreants. That sense did not leave me for the rest of the day as I tried to surreptitiously study the man and square him with Juan Pablo's horrific story.

As we headed down to the river, we passed by one of the Negro boys I'd seen working about the camp. He was seated backwards on a donkey, his legs crossed over its rump, playing a doleful tune on a battered fiddle. The donkey was loosely tethered to a small bush and grazing on blades of grass poking up here and there from the hard sand, oblivious to the youth and the fiddle's scratchings. The youth looked up just before Hays and Walker and Chevallie rode past him, abandoned his tune, tugged his forelock, and struck up a lively version of "Yankee Doodle." I mouthed the words "called it macaroni" at the appropriate time, they being the only words of the song I could recall—probably because I had been told by a drunken *Sassenagh* in those halcyon days before I fled the Big Onion that the *Sassenagh* lobsterbacks had originally sung the song to insult the then American colonists by suggesting that the colonists aspired to be suspiciously effete Englishmen of uncertain sexual proclivities. Of course a slumming member of Gotham's upper tendom had interrupted us, sneering that the Jonathans had serenaded their *Sassenagh* foes with the song at some decisive battle in the American Revolution, because all the *Sassenagh* were macaroni-wearing sodomites. I had broken up the fight before it started, and Blackie had thrown both of them into the street to sort out their differences.

I was amused when a couple of Texians behind me sang a couple of snatches of completely different lyrics honoring Uncle Sam's annexation of Texas:

> *Walk in, my long-haired Indian gal*
> *Your hand, my star-eyed Texas*
> *You're welcome to our White House hall*
> ...
> *If Mexy back'd by secret foes,*
> *Still talks of taking you, gal,*
> *Why we can lick 'em all, you know,*
> *An' annex 'em, too, gal;*
> *For Freedom's great millennium*
> *Is working airth's salvation,*
> *Her sassy Kingdom soon will come*
> *Annexin' all creation.*
> ...
> *Singing Yankee Doodle ...*

But the sentiment was quickly smothered as we entered the water, taking care to keep our weapons and powder dry.

We rode hard, straight south, for the next two days, along the very road that Arista and his retreating army had taken just a few weeks before, as they fled from Matamoros and the victorious Army of Invasion. My back screamed, my thighs chafed, and my lips chapped as we rode at what was really quite a breakneck speed, considering the distances we covered. Hays mercifully broke the relentless ride south every few hours, not out of regard for his troops, but to rest the horses and give them a bit of water. Only once we'd tended to our mounts could we all seek shade from the blazing sun for a few blessed moments, save for an unfortunate cove or two seemingly picked at random by Walker or Chevallie in the curtest of tones to ride picket.

Signs of the Mexican retreat were all around us as we rode south: Abandoned artillery and broken-down ox-carts littered the verge, and flags were draped over maguey cactus and mesquite bushes. The flags were already fading from the bleaching effect of intense rain alternating with equally intense summer sun. Worse was the more than occasional stench from rotting carcasses of horses, mules, oxen, and the occasional dead soldier crumpled by the side of the road. We talked quietly among ourselves about whether the Mexicans had survived as any sort of functioning army. The detritus of their march bespoke a monumental breakdown of discipline and morale. I remembered how we had suffered on our march south from Corpus Christi, and we had been superbly conditioned for our march by the seemingly never-ending drilling over the winter. So I could only begin to imagine the slow breakdown of a defeated army not used to marching as it passed over this waterless and burning track without adequate supplies and, by all appearances, no wagons to carry the prostrate, who thus died by the side of the road, only to be found by Hays's Rangers all these weeks later.

We saw no water on our second day, and the further south we went that day, the more frequently we saw the human and equine toll exacted by the Mexican retreat. It was a dispiriting sight, made all the more so by the desolate countryside. We saw no human habitation until we got to Colonia del Refugio, where there presumably was sufficient water somewhere to support a few ranchos and a tiny village. Hays's outriders injuned right up on the ranchos, quickly surveyed them, and slipped away long before anyone spotted them. The rest of us skirted well round the village. As Big Foot said to me at one point, we didn't want the locals seeing us pass through, for only the good Lord knew where Canales or Seguin or one of their confederates might be, and the last thing we wanted was to give Canales the opportunity either to skedaddle before we could find him, or worse, to lie in wait for Mustang Gray's company as it returned north with a thousand mules in tow.

As we rode relentlessly south, listening to stories, first from Pickens and then from Big Foot (both of them were raconteurs of the first order), helped keep my mind off my burning thirst, my chafing thighs, and my aching back. Pickens's loquacity put even Big Foot to shame, although it was Pickens's capacity for needling that really set him apart. Pickens wasn't vicious per se, just seemingly artless in how he brought a topic up and then before he dropped it and moved along to something else, leaving his point lingering for his audience to consider. Eventually, though, as the sun climbed to zenith, even Pickens lapsed into blessed silence.

We roused ourselves only when Hays leaned over to Walker and Chevallie, and the three of them galloped off. I looked questioningly at Big Foot, who said, "Going to talk to Henry, over yonder, who's been riding point for us." I looked at a low ridge ahead of us, where a rider was framed against the sky, waiting for them. "'T'ain't nothing, I shouldn't think."

Pickens roused himself and said to no one in particular, "The regulars sure will be better off with Colonel Walker taking his captain's commission."

Big Foot and I didn't respond.

"But you know what really fascinates me?" Again, Big Foot and I stayed silent. Big Foot was studying the horizon, where Hays, Walker, and Chevallie had conferred for just a moment with Henry, before Henry touched the brim of his hat and disappeared on the far side of the low ridge and they galloped back.

Pickens warmed to his task. "The regulars are all up in arms over it. I hear tell they're jealous that they're stuck in the infantry or quartermastering, or some such, while Sam Walker gets to be a hero, gallivanting about with the mounted infantry—instantly at a rank that it's taking some of those bluebellies a decade or more to achieve."

"True enough," I replied. "But he's a lieutenant-colonel of volunteers now. Surely a step down to be a mere captain."

"Of the regulars? A regular commission? Surely, my dear Sergeant, you'd agree that a captaincy in the regular army must be worth more than a lieutenant-colonelcy in the six-month militia. Why, the First Regiment of Texas Mounted Riflemen will be no more than a mere footnote in history by the new year."

"Well, Grant sure saluted Hays and Walker lickety-split back at Camp Maggot, and he's regular army."

"Yes, but he'll still be a lieutenant six months from now, Walker'll be a captain, and they'll both be regulars. Who knows where Jack Hays will be? Not, mind you, that Jack himself need be concerned. If Old Rough and Ready …" I raised an eyebrow at Pickens using the scribblers' new name for the Old Man. It somehow just didn't seem natural. He smirked at me, before continuing his disquisition. "If the Old Man doesn't want him, then Texas Governor Henderson'll find a way to keep him around—now that the Old Man has got the governor down here as a major general. But I digress. So I put it to you, Billy, m'boy, taking the captaincy with the regulars is a step to permanent seniority for Walker, wouldn't you say?"

I shrugged.

Pickens grinned through cracked lips. "That's precisely why there's a lot of very wrathy regulars on account of Walker's appointment, 'cuz they ain't gettin' it, and this war'll be long over before they get a shot at promotion over Walker's head." Pickens preened at his logic.

Big Foot guffawed behind me. "I reckon he's got you whipped there, *mi amigo*."

"I reckon."

Pickens wasn't quite done grinding his point home. "Anyway, Sam Walker's a damn sight better cavalryman than either Mays or Thornton."

I split a lip as I laughed. "Can't disagree with you there."

Sometime later, I don't know how long after, I had fallen into a bit of a trance under the sun, undulating along with my horse as we suffered through the stifling humidity and heat. Pickens broke my reverie when he started in on how the Louisiana volunteers had been ill-used by Taylor. Big Foot and I were on either side of him. Big Foot guffawed as Pickens prattled on, for it was the second or third time that Pickens had gnawed at the topic. I took the bait just about as fast as I did the last time, anxious to prove the worth of the regulars to this newspaper correspondent. "They're 90-day men. Untrained. I don't want those boys, no matter how tough they are individually, in a regiment of their own in the line next to me, facing Arista's army when we get to Monterrey. They have to be trained to stand in the square and take on a thousand screaming cavalry riding at you full swing, and meaning to use their lances in a business-like fashion."

Pickens sniffed. "There aren't enough of you bluebellies to get the job done. How many of you are there? Three thousand, with every sutler and quartermaster's man and drummer boy thrown in?"

"But 90-day men aren't what we need," I retorted. "We need regiments for the duration. Trained and ready and able to march south. The Louisiana general of volunteers, Lord love him as a customer over at Sarah's place, has only got a mob with him. He'll tell you that himself. And now these Louisiana 90-day yahoos're already going home without having fired a shot—at an organized army that can shoot back, that is. They've been down here just long enough to tear up Matamoros every night for two months and drink up all the whiskey that's been shipped down from New Orleans. Some of them deserve to be hanged or at least flogged for what they've done."

"You can't flog an American. 'T'ain't right."

"It is if he's a soldier."

"No American would submit to being flogged."

"They do." I thought of that poor devil, O'Dea, flogged and branded back on Governors Island, all because he could not take Hoggs's abuse.

"You're all foreigners, Irish, Dutchy, and all somesuch."

"Hardly even half of us are. The rest are buckwheats come from hardscrabble backgrounds." I thought about the native Americans, such as Gaff, who had been part of our training draft all those months ago on Governors Island. Hermann had muttered to me at the time that some of them made the lowliest German beggar in the street look like a prince of the realm. "Anyway, I'm an American citizen."

"Not native-born."

"True. But I can vote as well as the next man can."

Pickens considered my point, as Big Foot said, "I think that we've got some Dutchies from Port Levaca ridin' with us, and there's more of them in the East Texas regiment. An' I'm sure there are Irishmen to be found among us. Hell, J. T., ever' one of us here in the Rangers came from somewhere else. There ain't hardly one of us born west of the Mississippi, let alone west of the Sabine."

Pickens retorted, "A couple more regiments of you Texians, and we'd sweep clear to Mexico City in a month's time."

"You know, J. T.," Big Foot replied slowly. "I'd like to think that we Rangers are the toughest crowd around. Ever' one of us is able to lick 10 Mexicans all by hisself, like you was sayin', J. T., when you was devilin' Sam Walker. But that ain't the half of it. I remember Mier, back in '42. Every fucking minute of it. Damn near the death of me, that was. Down in Perote all those months after we surrendered. It's going to take a hell of a lot of us, all working together, to lick these damned dagoes. I thank God that they're being led by the likes of Santa Anna and not by the Old Man." I smiled inwardly at Big Foot's use of the bluebelly's name for Taylor, instead of the "Old Rough and Ready" of newspaper fame. He might appear to be a lummox, but he had a good ear for things.

"What was it like?" I asked. "At Mier? And afterwards."

Even Pickens tuned his ear to what Big Foot had to say.

Big Foot rode for a while, lost in thought. Then he smiled rue-fully. "Pickens's right in a lot of ways, as much as it pains me to say about a tinhorn scribbler."

Pickens waved away the insult airily. I was beginning to suspect that he was not totally unaware of his persona.

Big Foot ruminated a moment before he began his story. "Somervell's expedition was a star-crossed venture from the day we all gathered in San Antonio to avenge the Mexicans under that froggie general of theirs, Woll, coming up and occupying the town for a week. Nobody thought Somervell was worth a hill of beans. But as it turns out, that's prob'ly why ol' Sam Houston picked him in the first place. 'Cuz it sure was apparent to every manjack in Texas that Houston didn't want a war with those brown bastards, no matter how they provoked us by taking San Antonio. He knew there weren't no money to fight a war. But the rest of us wanted war, money or no money. By God, we were going to learn that varmint Woll that he and his dagoes weren't going to occupy San Antonio anytime they liked. So war is what we got. An' we weren't no gentlemen about it, neither, no matter what Jack Hays or any other respectable Ranger had to say about it. Why, when we got to Laredo, General Somervell issued an order that no one was to go into town. But there were a lot of boys who didn't listen, and they went into town against orders and jes' tore the place apart. Stole everything they could get their hands on. I'll give Somervell some credit. He ordered Jack Hays and Sam Walker and the rest of the steady fellows to force those filibusters to return every bit of what they stole."

Pickens said, "Not that we'll print stories about any of that if such foolishness occurs in this war."

"Not with Jack Hays, it won't. Any man who loots like them critters did down Laredo-way will get hisself shot by Jack Hays. And that's if Mike Chevallie or Sam Walker don't get to 'em first."

"What about Mustang Gray?" I was glad Pickens asked the question.

"He's another kettle of fish, entirely," Big Foot said. "But don't you mind him, none, J. T. Or you either, Billy Gogan. Ol' Mustang wants nothing more than to be part of Hays's Rangers. So he'll be on his best behavior. Don't you doubt that for a second."

Big Foot fell silent after that, and we rode for a bit. I was just about to ask Big Foot to continue his story when he just started talking again. "I reckon that ol' Somervell was just plain embarrassed by what our little army had done in Laredo, and he wanted to do something that would make our expedition worthwhile. But the Mexican army had disappeared back south of the Rio Grande, and there waren't no one to fight. An' we waren't in no shape to fix the dagoes' flint, nei-ther. We didn't have enough horses to chase after 'em. Worse, we were running out of food, and we didn't have much ammunition. So Somervell marched us around a bit, before decidin' to quit. That was when a right dolt by the name o' Thomas Jefferson Green an' about half the men mutinied, on account of their feeling that we hadn't punished the dagoes nearly enough. Green got hisself elected general of the mutineers on the strength of his maintainin' that we should go across the Rio Grande to chase the dagoes—which the mutineers did, along with a whole mess o' the rest of us, marching straight into Mier. Somervell went home tail between his legs with 'most ever'one else. Jack Hays and Ben McCulloch an' a few boys stayed around for a few days, north of the river, keepin' watch over us, and then they went home, too."

Big Foot smiled ruefully. "Me and Sam Walker, we waren't as long-headed as Jack Hays an' ol' Ben. We went across the river to Mier with Green. What a complete bad iron that was. We got to town, requisi-tioned some food, an' rested our horses. Before we knew it, Canales, Ampudia, and every other dago with an *escopeta* was there, shoot-ing at us." Big Foot shook his head. "We was right heroic, though. Burrowing through walls, sneakin' around behind them brown bas-tards. Sam Walker made sure we prospected every pick and shovel in town. An' so we popped a lot of 'em. But they kept coming. They waren't yellow. Not at all. We'd invaded their country. They wanted us dead, and they waren't going to quit 'til they'd quashed us. An' they got to a point where they was going to do just that ... croake the whole lot of us, that is. There waren't nothin' we could do about it—and yet none of us was going to admit that we was in the difficulties.

We ran out of food, first. Then we ran out of water, and finally we ran out of powder and shot. Only then did we even start to acknowledge the corn. Most of us, anyway.

"We was mindful, I shall tell you, of Goliad and the Alamo, an' what ol' Santa Anny did to those poor bastards after they surrendered. So we palavered long and hard amongst ourselves as to whether to surrender at all." Big Foot chuckled mirthlessly. "There was a few who was ready to fight to the death. Another Alamo. And then there war those who allowed that we had indeed been utterly defeated. But not by the enemy. As somebody once told me, we had instead defeated ourselves with our hubris, and we paid for it with the next two years of our lives—those of us who lived, that is." Big Foot gave us a crooked grin. "Anyways, Ampudia promised that we'd be treated honorably. As prisoners of war. So we gave 'em the white flag."

Pickens stayed quiet for once, captivated by Big Foot's story. I shut pan as well, and Big Foot eventually continued of his own volition. "Them dagoes was good to their word. They didn't kill us right off. Santa Anna told ol' Ampudia to march us south, lickety-split, and so we hoofed it south. Imagine marching in boots like these." Big Foot gestured to his boots with the big wooden heels, high arches and pointed toes. They were like nothing I'd ever seen until I found myself around Texians. Perfect for riding and controlling a horse. But I could not think of a worse shoe for a man to walk a thousand miles in. Big Foot continued. "They didn't feed us, neither. An' they beat us. Oh Lord, but some o' the boys got themselves lumped but good in those first couple of weeks.

"So naturally we was all looking for a way to bolt—even though we must've been three hundred miles south of the Rio Grande by then. Maybe that was a good time to bolt, 'cuz the dagoes waren't on their guard no longer." He grinned thinly, "Or maybe it was bad, 'cuz I later heard that if we'd bided our time, we might've been freed much earlier, an' a whole lot more of our boys would've gotten home to their mommas. I don't know whether it's true. But one thing's fer sure. We didn't know that at the time, and every day we war heading further south and away from Texas. So we looked for our chance, and it came by 'n' by one cold morning, at some godforsaken place called Rancho Salado, when 'most all of our escort had stacked their muskets just 'afore breakfast an' left only a couple o' coves to watch us. Captain Cameron led the way. Brave man, he was, disarming the first guard 'afore the dumb plug could cry out the alarm. There were quite a few busted noggins and scragged dagoes 'afore it was all over, though. We marched north, 160 of us. But we never had a chance. Word got out ahead of us, and every Mexican *soldado* and *bandido* came out looking for us. They found most of us pretty quickly, although some escaped capture to begin with. They kept heading north, only to be captured one by one. Others were killed or they jes' died for no reason 't'all. A couple of *hombres* even froze to death in the mountains. A couple more jes' plain disappeared, and no one ever heard from them again. I heard that only two fellas actually made it back to San Antonio.

"The worst of it was the dead Mexican guards—even if they was croaked in a square fight that left half a dozen Texians cold as a wagon tire as well. Ol' Santa Anna, when he heard about it? Well, he wanted us all popped right then and there. Cooler heads prevailed, I guess, because he later ordered that we be punished by *diezmo*." Big Foot explained, "A Mexican army punishment. Means one man in ten was to be killed, and that's what they did. They shot one man in ten."

Pickens couldn't restrain himself this time. "The Black Bean Incident, so my fellow scribblers named it. 'The most inhuman piece of butchery perpetrated by a supposedly civilized country in this century,' my competitors at the *Bee* said. Should 'a' thought of that bit of prosody all by myself." Pickens didn't look despondent, but instead searched for a comment from Big Foot, who remained silent. Pickens continued, "Those dagoes called it *diezmo*. Some damned and fevered fantasy of decimation the bastards inherited from the Spaniards, who inherited it from the Romans before them. The Texians were all made to each take a bean from a big jar. A white bean meant you lived, and a black bean meant you were to be executed by firing squad. I heard you were first, Big Foot, and you figured out that the white beans were the bigger ones, and thus at the bottom of the jar. So you stuck that big paw of yours in and cried out, 'Dig deep, boys'."

Big Foot grunted, "I was lucky. I got a white bean. Seventeen of my cronies and comrades picked black beans. They war all taken outside, lined up against a wall and popped like so many worthless curs. But the Mexicans war such bad shots that a lot of 'em poor devils waren't killed outright. We had to listen to the whole damned affair. Some of 'em just kept screaming." Again, Big Foot chuckled mirthlessly. "Ol' Henry Whaling, well he didn't scream. He jes' kept cussin' them after each volley. They reloaded and shot him ten times 'afore someone took mercy on him and blew his brains out point blank." We rode for a while longer in silence before Big Foot said, "The rest of us got sent to Perote Castle, where we rotted for two more years. Sam Walker escaped, though, and walked hisself all the way to Veracruz and caught a French ship back to N'Awlins. A couple of others escaped as well, including that high-sniffing mud, Thomas Jefferson Green. Me, I never got the chance to escape. And so I finally got released, along with the rest of what remained of our party. I heard tell that the English and the Americans helped get us out.

"You know what the worst of it was?" Big Foot shook his head. "We finally got back to Texas, and it was as if ever'one had forgotten what had happened. I remember how ever'body was screaming for dago blood 'afore we went south with Somervell. When I finally got back to Austin, plumb near three years later, it was as if the whole damned nightmare hadn't happened at all. Except it had. An' we remembered. Sam Walker, me, and ever' damned one of us who got took at Mier and lived to tell about it. You may mark my words. We will fix some flints in this little war of ours on account of it all, and I will croake any son of a bitch I see from those days."

We fell silent for a while. Pickens had a faraway look in his eye, and Big Foot had fixed upon the horizon with an unblinking stare. I brooded upon the nature of the hatred between the Texian and the *méxicano*, and where that left the *tejano*, 'twixt two countries and not entirely of either. I sincerely hoped that don Guillermo had given up his quixotic hope of Mexican rule returning to any of the lands north of the río Bravo, let alone those lying north of the Nueces. Then my mind drifted inevitably to Calandria and that hot afternoon in the barn. I regretted not for the first time my forbearance with her. Not because I had come to a decision about whether to return north to the house of the flowing swallows, but because those fleeting memories left far too much to my imagination, and I was vaguely dissatisfied with myself for harboring such a sentiment, particularly when I could not requite it in other ways.

To break away from such concupiscent thoughts, I asked Pickens, "You've lived a long time in New Orleans?"

"Yeah," he said lazily. "But I wasn't born there. Born in North Carolina. Spent some time in Washington City, too. Came to N'Awlins ..." he dragged out the name as if his mouth was full of cornpone, "... and met up with George Kendall," he explained to my quizzical look. "He'd come down from the Big Onion—your neck of the woods, ain't it?"

I nodded.

"He'd seen the *Sun* and all those other penny dreadfuls up there. He knows Horace Greeley and every other big bug in town. So George and I took leaves from their books. George prevailed upon one or another of Greeley's benefactors to lend us sufficient wherewithal to fund our little enterprise—for a princely fee, of course—which we have long since repaid in spades, thank you very much. Bit touch and go, at first, what with the yellow jack that hit us in '36—and then that damned financial panic—all in the space of a few weeks. What was that born fool Jackson thinking, not renewing the Second Bank of the United States? Destroyed the country for years. Damned buz-wig." Doesn't he know that a great nation such as Uncle Sam can't have twenty-eight different currencies, some backed by gold and some backed by air? We need a national bank, damn it."

"So how'd you and Kendall survive?" I gently guided Pickens back to his story. I really couldn't have cared less about such esoteric matters of banking, just as long as my chink was safe in the Bowery

Savings Bank. A cold shudder ran through me at the prospect of losing what wealth I did have, simply to the malfeasance—or even misfeasance (did it matter which?)—of some fool who allowed his bank to go bust.

"By hook and by crook." Pickens smiled proudly. "I watched the till, and Kendall did the writing. Most of it, anyways. We figured out how to get news of doings up and down the Big Muddy, from Galena to the Gulf 'afore anyone else." He chuckled. "We'd put Kendall or some other correspondent on a northbound boat to Natchez with typeset and a hand printing press. By the time it'd dock in Natchez, we'd have a broadsheet for sale quayside—all before the other papers had even had a chance to talk to anyone. Hell, we'd beat them to press by half a day or more. Then he'd catch the next boat south with all the news coming from the north."

I murmured my admiration.

"Of course, we had our own pony express service as well."

"They also have them up in New York."

"Not like ours, I reckon." Pickens continued blithely on with his story. "'Our Horse' is what we called it. We could get news from New York or Washington a clean day ahead of Uncle Sam. Governments can be so damned incompetent at times. Better off without them— 'til you need them, that is; like for our little war down here. Trains have speeded things up nowadays—leastways, if they're going to the right place."

I nodded.

"I reckon all of it's going to change, though."

"Morse's telegraph?"

"You are a wise aleck, aren't you?"

"You mean 'smart Alex', don't you?" I said. The phrase, "smart alex" (or "smart aleck"), had been popular in New York just before I skedaddled. Some snudge named Alex Hoag and his blowen, a pox-ridden cab moll named Melinda, had started to give brothels a bad name by fitting panels into the sides of the rooms. The idea was to slide the panel open and pilfer the honey from some poor cull's skin as he labored in cunny court, leaving him unable to tip the cow her fees after he'd finished. Hoag became known as "Smart Alex" for his ingenuity, and the panel crib was born, to the everlasting misery of gullible greenhorns everywhere.

"Conceited bastard," Pickens responded amiably.

I grinned and we lapsed into silence for a few moments under the relentless sun. An impulse seized me, and I asked him, "Did you ever run across a cove named Antoine Rouquette? Likes to call himself 'Carambole'."

Pickens appraised me speculatively. "Where'd you run across him?"

"I crossed paths with him last fall, up in Corpus Christi. He was running a faro table in the tent city." I decided to be economical with the context of our meeting. "I heard through the grapevine that he'd signed on and come down to Matamoros. Haven't seen him, though."

Pickens responded, "Nobody has, leastways not since his regiment went home. He did come down, though. Was elected a major, on account of his 'Indian-fighting prowess.' Pure hogwash. That shark knows less about drill than the greenest recruit in a company of blue-bellies. Yet he seems to be at a higher rank every time the Louisiana militia musters. Unaccountable."

Pickens didn't offer more, so I said, "So you've run across him as well." A statement of fact, not a question.

"You could say that. He's a cove, as you would put it, of whom you should stand well clear. That is, if you have any hankering for life. He and his brother are utter locos."

"Brother? There are two of them?"

"Oh yeah. There's Antoine, and then there's Abélard. He's the younger brother. He's worse, by far. Wanted for murder down in Bayou Gauche, in St. Charles Parish. If he ever shows his face there again, they'd hang him the very day they caught him as surely as you'll ask me another question." Pickens smirked. "Son of a bitch seduced the sher-iff's daughter, so the story goes, and put her in the family way. Denied doing it, though, and he refused to marry the poor girl. Her father took his badge off when he heard that Abélard wasn't going to marry the girl, and he went looking for him with his horsewhip. I guess he reckoned to change Abélard's mind and make a respectable girl out of his daughter, even if Abélard liked hitting women more 'n' he liked goosing 'em. The father barely made it from the jail, where he'd hung up his pistol and grabbed his horsewhip, and onto main street before he ran right into Abélard. There were words between them, and Abélard stabbed the father to death with a butcher's knife—just to avoid a well-deserved horsewhipping by a rightfully aggrieved father. Rouquette père had been a butcher, as had every man in his family for a hundred years. He'd died just as those two had gotten old enough to get into all kinds of trouble, but were still too young to stay out of it. Or maybe it simply was something sick inside those two boys that led them to do the things they did. By all accounts, their father was a decent man."

"No mother?"

"Dead, I suppose. Nobody ever talked about her." We both fell silent for a moment, then Pickens continued. "Well, anyway, this Abélard stabbed the sheriff to death right in front of the jail and in front of twenty witnesses. The blood on his hands hadn't even dried by the time he was locked up. But even before he was haled in front of the county judge, somebody broke him out of jail, and he disappeared without a trace. Some said he went north. Others said he joined the army. Who knows?"

"Did Rouquette? I mean, Carambole ... Did he break Abélard out of the old boarding-house?"

"You'd reckon that, wouldn't you? So'd everybody else. Except Carambole—Antoine, as he was known then—had a witness who swore on the Bible that he was twenty miles away. It being Louisiana and not Texas, nobody was inclined to string him up then and there on a mere suspicion without a judge saying so."

"Who was the witness?"

Pickens smiled lasciviously. "He'd been taking his turn up some hoor's frills in some N'Awlins hog ranch or another. A clean twenty miles from Bayou Gauche." He paused for a moment and negotiated his horse around some broken ground. "Well, Antoine pretty much disappeared from Bayou Gauche after that. Folks may not have strung him up out of pure spite, but they were mighty unfriendly. I guess they must'a had their fill of the Rouquette boys by then. So Antoine began working the riverboats. As slick a sharper as there was on the river, with that story and a dozen others trailing after him like a rotten stench. Like how he came by the sobriquet 'Carambole'." Pickens seemed to relish pronouncing "sobriquet." It was as if he'd picked the word up somewhere along the way and was still looking for a news story in which he could use it with a flourish. It was curious that Pickens didn't explain the story of how Rouquette became 'Carambole,' as it was so ripe for the telling. Instead, he asked, "So how'd you run across Carambole?"

"As I said, up in Corpus one Sunday afternoon. He was running a faro game."

"I heard some Dutchy and a young kid broke up Rouquette's game in Corpus last winter. Pretty rare for someone to get the drop on ol' Carambole like that. An' I also heard that Rouquette's looking to square accounts with those two." Pickens looked at me suspiciously. "You know anything about that story?"

I shrugged evasively.

"I also heard that Rouquette stayed down here after his regiment left to settle them boys, and to work some scam or another." Pickens fell silent for a moment, and then he leaned over in his saddle and said to me, "I think Damian Alston got to know Rouquette up in Corpus last winter, when he was running cattle from up Matamoros way. Lord knows what brands he was driving, but you bluebellies didn't care, 'cuz you were eating up a storm and didn't give a hill o' beans where it came from. Anyway, I heard Damian chuckling with Gray about the story a couple of days ago. So, if you cared to ask … maybe he could shed a light."

Two days later, we were just three leagues outside San Fernando de Presas, which appeared from the outskirts to be a quite pretty little town of some 3,000 inhabitants, located in some hill country 80 or

90 miles south of Matamoros. Hays had halted the regiment when our scouts hove into view, escorting three riders from San Fernando flying a white flag. I was called upon to translate a letter that one of the riders thrust into Hays's hands with much expostulation. It was short and to the point by Mexican standards: The local *alcalde* was bending over backwards to avoid a battle in his town, and he was thus taking the liberty of informing us that a company of Mexican lancers were in town, and that they—and the townsfolk—had no wish to mill with a full regiment of *los rinches*. The alcalde concluded his letter by begging our forgiveness as he asked if we would be so kind as to remain outside of town to give the lancers the opportunity to decamp without risk to their dignity.

Hays told me, "Ask the gentleman if Seguin or Canales are here." Walker, Chevallie, and Mabry Gray, all of whom were clustered about us on mounts restless with the tension of the moment, leaned in closer to listen. I heard Big Foot in the background, rumbling about his prayers being met if that scoundrel (I didn't know whether he was referring to Canales or Seguin) was sojourning in town, convenient-like for the taking.

I ignored their stirrings and in the best Spanish I knew greeted the rider in the center, who wore a fanciful—if worn—coat that seemed to denote him as the leader. "Señor, *mi jefe*, Colonel Hays, asks you whether the lancers your alcalde's letter speaks of are men of the army of General Canales, or perhaps Colonel Seguin. I pray that you tell me the truth, for you are speaking to *el Diablo Yack*, himself." I gestured to Colonel Hays, who nodded, as if he understood what I was saying. I noted out the corner of my eye that Juan Pablo seemed pleased with my effort.

"Excellency," the coated rider ignored my sergeant's stripes—which were similar to those used by the Mexican army. "Pray tell his excellency, señor *el Diablo Yack*, that it is only a poor company of lancers visiting our town, and they are unknown to us. They do not wish a fight, and our *alcalde*, don Bartolome Saenz, implores you to grant them a day's leave to allow them to depart. Don Bartolome humbly begs you to respect our town and its women and children. Our men, who are poor shopkeepers and *peóns*, are not men of arms, and they do not seek to oppose your excellencies' entrance to our poor town. The fight of the soldiers is not our fight. They are *federalistas*. They are not of our town. We wish only to live our lives here without interference …" The coated rider's soliloquy faded, and I cocked an eye at him. He rapidly continued. "I give you my word of honor, and the word of my master, don Bartolome, that General Canales and Colonel Seguin are many hundreds of leagues from here."

I translated for Hays, who replied to me, "Tell him that we will camp a mile from town, to the west. There's water over there. We'll not molest the road south for two hours. Then I will put scouts out, and it'll be 'Katy, bar the door.' Tell him."

I did as Hays ordered.

Then Hays said, "Also tell him that I will ride to town under a flag of truce in an hour. I will parley with this don Bartolome and tell him that we mean no harm to the people of his town. He should mark my words, though. We will hunt down any *soldados* or *banditti* who linger, and then we'll hang 'em if they ain't dead yet."

⌒

True to Devil Jack's word, he, Chevallie, and I rode into town, accompanied by Big Foot and a couple of other stalwarts bristling with rifles, muskets, Colt repeating pistols, and Arkansas toothpicks. Pickens tagged along, uninvited, proclaiming that this little expedition promised to be a grand adventure. Juan Pablo had been left in camp to fend for himself, along with the rest of the regiment, as he had decided to remain anonymous to the townsfolk in case he ever ventured this way again. Most of the regiment was busy setting up a bivouac for the couple of days we intended to sojourn outside town, resting the horses, and preparing for the next phase of our reconnaissance. Mustang Gray's company was told off by squad to picket duty a mile or so down each of the roads leading into town, except the one leading south, which Hays had agreed we would not patrol for another hour. The rest of the Mustang's company was broken into two or three additional patrols roving between the pickets.

I momentarily forgot all of that as we made our way over an old stone bridge. A refreshing breeze of cool air flowed about us from under the bridge, generated by the narrow, fast-flowing stream at the bottom of the ravine.

As we rode down the narrow road of alternating dirt and cobblestone leading from the bridge to the town square, our lead rider carried a white handkerchief tied to the end of the barrel of his rifle to signal our good intentions. Every manjack of us, even Pickens—who was tagging along at the rear, taking notes as he went—was ready to use his arms in an instant. Moreover, at the first sound of a shot, Sam Walker was prepared to immediately ride half the regiment into town. But no such shot rang out. Every door was shut tight, and we could have been forgiven if we'd thought that we'd ridden into a town inhabited by ghosts.

That changed as we rode cautiously into the town square. A good measure of the town's populace were braced up against a church as decrepit and unfinished as the cathedral gracing the main square in Matamoros. There was a single, grand house opposite the church. On the two remaining cater-corner sides, there was a series of nondescript one-story adobe buildings. The doors of each one was closed and presumably barred against the feared depredations of the hated *rinches*. The scrum of townspeople seemed to quiver with apprehension as we approached them, and as we rode ever closer it parted soundlessly to reveal a small delegation standing at the entrance to the church. The man at its center wore what appeared to be an embroidered badge of office over his shoulder. I assumed him to be the *alcalde*, for he was flanked by the coated rider to whom I'd had spoken earlier. On his other flank was a magnificently attired and haughty aristocrat, replete with a fine felt hat and gold-embroidered royal blue serape. I assumed that he must be a local *hacendado*, there being little else in the way of commerce to support such an apparently wealthy man. Behind the *hacendado*, partly obscured, stood perhaps the most stunningly beautiful woman I had laid eyes on since … well, I wasn't sure when. She was Calandria's age, and very much in the first flowering of youth, hardly more than a couple of years past her *quince años*. But she was a woman nonetheless, already well-armored in the regal hauteur of the high-born and surcoated in a dress and mantilla of the finest gray silk and lace. She was no doubt the sort of *mujer decente* who, lest some *caballero* were to lay covetous eyes upon her, would never sally forth from her home unless she were on her way to church at dawn, escorted by the very battle ax of a *dueña* who was standing at her shoulder, oozing her contempt of us *gringos* gawping at her precious charge. All of this I captured in an instant. It was only upon a second and far more surreptitious glance that I thought—hoped—that the fine armor of her mien had been betrayed by the merest hint in her eye. Of what, I couldn't tell, although I was seized by a terrible aching to know. Who would have thought we would have been so blessed as to see such beauty in a tiny, one-horse town a hundred miles south of the río Bravo? And what the devil was she doing, standing here in the full view of the *yanqui* barbarians?

Hays and I dismounted and bowed deeply to the *alcalde*, who responded in kind. The coated rider and the *hacendado* also bowed, and the beautiful woman curtsied as delicately as you like. Every man-jack in our little party stirred as if galvanized by an electrical shock. I felt Pickens preening behind me like the cock of the walk, and it wouldn't have surprised me if Big Foot were blushing furiously. For according to the half-a-dozen Rangers who had mercilessly teased Big Foot several times within my earshot since we left Matamoros, Big Foot was as tongue-tied in the presence of a beautiful woman as he was fearsome in battle against the Comanche and the dago.

I sneaked one more slantendicular look at the beautiful woman, and caught her luminous dark eye before we both quickly looked away. I caught Hays eyeing me, so I drew a breath and introduced him to don Bartolome as "Colonel '*el Diablo Yack*' Hays, Commanding Officer of the First Texas Mounted Riflemen, chief scout to, cavalry commander for, and bearer of a proclamation of, our *gran caudillo*,

General Zachary Taylor, Old Rough and Ready, himself." My poetic
license seemed to be proper for the occasion—at least based on what
Juan Pablo had told me of how *los hombres de bien* conduct themselves
in such matters. I nodded to Hays, who stepped forward and unfurled
a rolled folio with great ceremony. He read aloud a short proclamation, which I translated sentence by sentence with only a minimum
of editorial comment. Hays reiterated what he had already told the
coated rider back on the road leading into town: The Texians had no
quarrel with the people of San Fernando, only with the soldiers of the
Mexican army and the wicked *bandolero jefes* Canales and Seguin—
and Colonel Hays would pay much gold and silver for their capture.
Hays concluded by saying that the Texians would also be mighty
obliged if they could purchase fresh comestibles for the regiment from
local merchants. *Los norteamericanos* would pay good coin—gold double eagles, if they pleased—for everything they bought.

Don Bartolome bowed again and introduced the *hacendado*, a
fellow named don Ramón de la Gerza Flores, the largest landowner
in these parts and brother-in-law to the current foreign minister of
*los Estados Unidos Méxicanos*, one don Teodoro Fernandes de la Cruz,
a very great and powerful *hombre de bien*. He also introduced his
niece and daughter of the foreign minister, señorita Isabella Maria-
Magdalena Fernando de la Cruz. Don Bartolome explained to no one
in particular that señorita de la Cruz was to be leaving for *el Ciudad de
México* very shortly, to return to her father's side, and that her uncle,
don Ramón, was to accompany her for safekeeping in these deeply
troubled times. Señorita de la Cruz curtsied once more at the mention
of her name, her eyes focused somewhere beyond the crowd of men
standing before her, and every manjack of us fell in love all over again.
Her *dueña* scowled at us.

Don Bartolome went on to express his gratitude about the Texians
agreeing to respect the sanctity of the town of San Fernando, and he
further expressed with great sorrow that no one in San Fernando had
any information about *el jefe de los bandoleros* for whom Colonel Hays
was looking. Perhaps nothing had been heard, because they were far

to the west, near Camargo, seeking to bring war to that region so as to frustrate the advance of the great *ejército norteamericano*. Don Bartolome smiled broadly when he said that the town's merchants were gathered to greet the famous Colonel Hays, *el gran jefe de los diablos rinches* (I translated this bit as the "great chief of the Texas Mounted Riflemen" in view of the otherwise friendly atmosphere). They would open their stores forthwith and be very pleased to sell all their wares to the visiting Americans. No doubt, Pickens whispered to me *sotto voce*, at the most outrageous prices possible.

"Señor." It was don Ramón, at once beckoning to me and yet as regally distant as befit his station in life. He spoke with a refined Spanish accent of a type I had never heard before. "I would be most gratified if you could extend an invitation to *su excelencia, el coronel* Hays, and his officers to stay at my humble abode." He gestured vaguely towards the grand house on the opposite side of the square. "And, of course, yourself, *sargento* Gogan." He gave me a strangely knowing look.

I bowed to Don Ramón and translated the invitation to Hays and the others (including my own invitation in a suitably off-handed manner). A shadow passed over Hays's brow, but Walker whispered something in Hays's ear, and Hays instructed me to express his gratitude to don Ramón on behalf of himself and his officers for this very kind invitation, "But ..." Hays positively shrugged as he finished, and I translated back that he and his officers would be unable to accept don Ramón's kind offer on account of their pressing military duties, particularly when we were concerned about enemy forces being potentially so close, and the beautiful town of San Fernando thus in danger of unintentionally becoming a battlefield. Hays interrupted me, saying that of course Mr. Pickens, who had sidled up next to Hays and was positively vibrating with anticipation over the invitation, and Sergeant Gogan would be mighty gratified to accept. I smiled broadly at Colonel Hays and finished translating to don Ramón.

"Shall we expect you and Mr. Pickens at your convenience, then, Sergeant Gogan? And, if you would be so kind, Sergeant, please persuade *el coronel* and his staff to dine with my niece and me this evening."

By the time we returned to camp, tents and fires were set, meals were being prepared, and equipment repaired. Walker wasted no time before parading the entire regiment for inspection of horses and arms, reading them the riot act concerning drinking in town. Small parties were to be given passes to enjoy themselves in town that evening, and every man was to conduct himself as a gentleman guest at the house of an honored host. He then conducted officers' call. Pickens and I hung around the fringes and heard Walker instruct his company commanders to leave in camp anyone who was not completely reliable. Meanwhile, four full companies—of the nine present—were to be kept at the ready, with horses saddled throughout the night in case of surprise attack. Hays had quietly slipped beside Walker and cleared his throat when one of the officers, I couldn't see who, asked why such preparations overnight when everyone knew that the damned *gachupine* were too yellow to attack at night. Walker gave way with a courteous nod, and Hays explained that we were as deep into Mexico as any Texians had ever gone—voluntarily, that is, and he reckoned that we were in as much danger of attack tonight as ol' Santa Anna had been that afternoon up on the San Jacinto when he was busy taking a siesta. Anyway, Hays continued, letting small groups go to town tonight to drink a little pulque, lose some chink playing monte, and chatting with the local señoritas might just draw whoever might be lurking out there in the hills into trying to raid the "unwary" *rinches*. That way, we could have a good old-fashioned fandango of our own, Texian-style. Walker and Chevallie nodded their "yea verily" with tight smiles.

I and every other manjack in the regiment, Pickens included, took Hays's admonition to heart, and we spent the next several hours cleaning our Colt Patersons, loading (or reloading, as the case may be) our spare cylinders, making sure of our flints, and sharpening our knives. I also cleaned my musket and repaired the makeshift sling I had fashioned to carry it as I rode, and sharpened my sergeant's sword to a fare-thee-well, all to Big Foot's laughing suggestion that I confine my efforts to my knife and Colt Paterson, as my musket and sergeant's sword were useful only for the parade ground back in Matamoros.

Pickens, Big Foot, and I had just filled our pipes for a quick smoke before we headed back into town with Hays and Chevallie—Big Foot having assured me that Juan Pablo would be safe in his care while I was taking my leisure in the lap of luxury, when we heard a pair of rifles or muskets firing, followed by the lighter bark of several Colt repeating pistols. We looked up to see three horsemen wearing lancers' uniforms riding full chisel, lances deployed, right at Hays, Chevallie, and Walker, who were talking quietly, hardly ten yards from us. The two sentries at the entrance to our camp stood their ground in front of the attacking cavalrymen, aimed their rifles carefully, and brought down two of the riders. The sentries then jumped out of the way of the remaining rider and the two riderless horses that still accompanied him, and drew their Colt repeating pistols. They did not fire, for Hays was already drawing a bead on the remaining horseman with his pistol. There was a single bark and the lone horseman fell to the ground just yards away. His lance slithered to a halt when Chevallie stepped on it. Hays stuffed his pistol back into his belt and shared a look with Chevallie and Walker.

The dust had hardly cleared when Mustang Gray, a dozen of his men in tow, swerved to a halt, showering Hays in dust and gravel. Hays looked up at Gray and said in a clipped tone, "Mabry, let's keep the eyes peeled. I want any bastard approaching this camp who ain't a Ranger dead in his tracks right then and there."

Gray flushed unhappily, saluted, and rode off without a word. His Matamoros Rangers followed, each looking as chagrined as the next.

Hays turned to Chevallie, and then past them to Pickens and me, acknowledging each of us in turn, "Mike, Sergeant, J. T., let me treat you to a glass of pulque to cut some of this trail dust. We can then look in on don Ramón and pay him our respects while J. T. and Sergeant Gogan get themselves set up in the proper clover for a couple of nights."

Three hours later, I was sitting at dinner in the lush courtyard of don Ramón's house in town, my saddlebag of gold and silver specie sitting at my feet, to the general amusement of all. Don Ramón's hacienda proper was three leagues away to the west, nestled in a little valley cooled by a spring, so he told us. But he and his niece, señorita de la Cruz, had ridden to town to see the feared *rinches* for themselves. Hays had smiled thinly at the story as I translated it with a cocked eyebrow that Pickens and Chevallie found amusing (although they turned their smiles away from Hays's glower). I noticed out of the corner of my eye that señorita de la Cruz was looking quite disported by my efforts at translation—and those of trying to keep the conversation going, which pleased me to no end. I wondered how much English she knew, but figured that you didn't need to know any to appreciate Hays's discomfiture, because don Ramón said to me in his wonderfully mellifluous tone:

"You should tell Colonel Hays that if he is *el Diablo Tejano*, then I am caught between his gentle grasp and the deep blue sea." He added quickly, as if to explain how a *hacendado* could have known an old Scottish proverb, "A saying I learned from señora Fannie Calderon de la Barca, the wife of the former Spanish ambassador. She's a *yanqui*, you know. Born in Scotland, but raised in your fine port town of Baltimore. I have found it to be a very useful saying, I might add."

Hays and Chevallie were studying first don Ramón and then me. Pickens stared openly at señorita de la Cruz, who although she affected not to be paying attention was nonetheless all ears. I explained to Hays, Chevallie, and Pickens, "Apparently, the Rangers are not the only enemy facing don Ramón and his little town."

"The Comanche get this far east?" Chevallie sounded almost shocked at the thought, although I was not going to doubt don Ramón—if that's what he meant, based on the chilling stories of Comanche depredation that I'd heard from Texian, Texican, *tejano*, and *méxicano* alike over the last year or so.

I didn't translate, but instead asked don Ramón, "What is the deep blue sea you are facing?"

"Why, my son, our government in *México*."

This I translated to Hays and Chevallie, who leaned back in their chairs to absorb what I had just told them. I didn't bother to translate don Ramón's explanation to me that *México* referred both to the country and the city, depending upon context. Such usage reflected the views of some in the city that the city was the country, and the country without the city was a mere nullity.

"How so, sir?" I didn't wait for Hays to ask the question about the Mexican government, for as I had finished translating, he had shrugged his desire that I forge ahead myself.

Don Ramón smiled and said, "Señor Gogan, that is a very long and complicated story." He pushed his chair back, rose, and continued, "Gentlemen, perhaps we should retire to the patio. We can enjoy some fine brandy de Jerez from when my sainted wife's brother señor de la Cruz was minister to Spain and France, a good cigar, and a little music while I tell you this story." He turned to señorita de la Cruz and said, "*Mi querida*, we needn't detain you with our dark talk of war and rebellion and man's iniquities."

She gave don Ramón a dazzling smile, and said in perfectly idiomatic English, "Of course, Uncle. As you wish. I have no interest in such talk of war, for as you say, I am a woman, and I thus should have no interest in the matters of men. But I do so greatly wish *la patria* be shot of this foolish war and that the *yanqui* invaders, no matter how gracious they are, be the very best of guests, and go home forthwith to *Tejas*." Señorita de la Cruz curtsied in her chair to each of us. Although it lasted hardly a split second, her curtsy seemed a deeply personal acknowledgment to me alone. I glanced about. Every other manjack in that room must have felt the same way. Señorita de la Cruz wasn't quite done, for she gave another volley, "For as much as my uncle is honored to have you fine gentlemen as guests in his humble abode, you are still trespassers in *la patria* and thus must be cast out." She looked us each in the eye, again for no more than the merest second.

I thought Chevallie was ready to drop to his knee and propose at once. Pickens merely leered. Hays smirked ever so slightly, and don Ramón visibly sighed. I thought I could feel the señorita's *dueña* coiled somewhere behind me, a cobra ready to strike the first man who so much as looked slantendicular at her precious charge.

Señorita de la Cruz was undeterred. "But I am always fascinated to hear of the iniquity of men from the mouths of men themselves. It seems only fair that a woman such as I should be forearmed in this world of men. Particularly in the tragic fall from grace of the United States at the hands of the expansionists ... what do they call what those empire-builders want to do? Ah, yes. 'Manifest Destiny,' no? A return to the ways of the *gachupine* and the rest of the wicked Europeans is what it is. How quickly you *norteamericanos* forget your rebellion of 1776." She almost sneered as she switched effortlessly to flawless Latin. "'*Sic transit civitatem in monte*'." She explained herself in her flawless English. "That city on a hill that your Puritan forefathers saw as your God-given right is gone, and you Americans are no better than your English forebears."

With that, she swept as regally as the Queen of Spain from the room, leaving us mere mortal males wrecked in her wake. Don Ramón bowed in surrender to his niece, and we repaired wordlessly to the patio, where we found leather and wicker chairs set in an arc in front of a harpist and violinist, who were waiting for us. Don Ramón sat in the grandest chair and bade us sit as well. Colonel Hays sat to don Ramón's right, and Chevallie on the left. Pickens and I took the end chairs, which were easily close enough for me to provide a translation of sorts if it proved necessary. A servant hovered briefly, delivering the Spanish brandy in the most elegant snifters I had ever seen. Cigars, cutters, and slow matches also materialized at our elbows, and for a few wonderful moments, we five men concentrated on our smoke in a quiet broken only by the soft patter of water from a fountain hidden somewhere in the foliage surrounding the patio. I noticed presently that señorita de la Cruz had returned, and was sitting to the side in the shadows observing us, her expression inscrutable.

Don Ramón finally stirred and said lazily in Spanish, which I translated as best I could, "We *méxicanos* have learned nothing from you *norteamericanos*. We have been independent of the hated *gachupine* for twenty-five years, and yet we have succeeded in frittering away every minute of those twenty-five years. Instead of our government arising from the same excellent principles as yours did—principles that were established while you were still in colonial subjugation to the English—we inherited a way of government from the *gachupine* that has benefited only those who are in power. It all started with *ese de pacotilla emperador*, Iturbide, and continuing to the present day *ese mierdecillo con una sola pierna*, Santa Anna, whom we overthrow, and who keeps coming back like the proverbial bad penny every time he has been deposed and banished for life. They all think that they are Napoleon incarnate, each a cock of the walk strutting about in his fancy uniform.

"When those *caudillos* are each in turn overthrown, those who overthrew them simply step into their predecessors' shoes and feed themselves from the same trough. Each time, more power and wealth has gone south to *la Ciudad de México*, while we here in the north have been starved of all means of preserving ourselves, whether against the creeping manifest destiny of you *yanquis* as you have slowly taken *Tejas* from us or against the depredations of the godless *Comanche*, who raid our villages, kill our men and old women, and take our *señoritas y niños*.

"When *los cabrónes federalistas* do come north, as did that *despreciable creido* Santa Anna in '36, they say it is to 'protect the honor' and 'preserve the integrity' *de los Estados Unidos de México*. Meanwhile, the poor Indian *soldados* are barefoot and hungry, led by cowards who, the minute they win the smallest victory, massacre the survivors, just as they did at Refugio and Fannin. Then they are caught napping as that *idiota*, Santa Anna, was on the banks of that river … what was it called?"

Pickens murmured, "The San Jacinto," as my translation stopped.

Don Ramón ignored him. "The cretin loses the battle and the war, and a mighty limb *de la madre partia* is lopped off, just like the French lopped off the cretin's leg a few years later. Well deserved, I might add—his losing of that leg of his.

"And now as *la patria* twists in agony once more, another limb set to be shorn away, *los tontos en México* are fighting each other harder than they fight *los norteamericanos*. Did you know that there are three brigades of our best *soldados* down south? Think what they could do to stop your General Taylor at Monterrey, and send him packing back north of the Nueces, where he belongs. But those brigades are not coming. Instead, *el presidente* Paredes has sent them to Guadalajara to quell a rebellion. He should have sent them north months ago to help stop you at *el río del norte*. But he did not, because if he did, his enemies would forthwith remove him from power. Well, as you have undoubtedly heard, señor Paredes is no longer in power, despite his dithering and keeping the best of the army close to him. And Santa Anna is back to plague us once more, peg leg and all."

I stopped translating and looked at my compatriots, for whom Santa Anna was truly a bête noire, to see what they thought of Santa Anna's apparent return from exile. They were to a man captivated, so I resumed my task, rapidly trying to catch up to don Ramón.

"Imagine that! *La patria* is lying prostrate before *el otro lado*, and we fight among ourselves like little children, and the best of our army is busy killing their fellow countrymen. It is madness." Don Ramón shook his head sadly. "Utter madness. It is also why I do not spend my life there, in *la Ciudad de México*. I cannot stand to pass my days immersed in that venal and incompetent morass known as our capital, alternately giving the black kiss to that one-legged charlatan, Santa Anna, and then giving the same black kiss to whatever venal *tonto* preceded him or ambitious *pronunciado* who subsequently overthrows him after one terrible debacle or another. But my brother-in-law, señor de la Cruz, has spent his life there in that cesspool. I praise Our Lady of Guadalupé that he has kept his daughter, *mi querida* Isabella Maria-Magdalena, away from there, first in school in France, and now with me. But she must now return there, to that Gomorrah."

I heard a rustle in the shadows, somewhere behind me. It must have been Isabella listening in the darkness to her uncle. Don Ramón continued, oblivious to us all. "I have been so very lonely here, since my sainted wife passed away. Isabella Maria-Magdalena has been a blessing to me these past months. I have not told you," don Ramón's voice became positively conspiratorial, "how special she is." The pride in his voice became evident. "Her father—my brother-in-law—sent her to the finest schools in Spain and France as he served as our ambassador to those countries in years past, and she has been blessed with the finest tutors. Isabella Maria-Magdalena is, how do you *yanquis* say? 'One in a million,' I think. She is better educated than any *hombre de bien* educated in that den of iniquity down south. A proud *méxicana* who not only can spell, but also converse in Latin and Greek with any scholar—and speak as well in English as any of you—as she has shown you. She reads to me in the evening when my eyes are failing me. I think that I have been as happy these past months as I have been at any time since my sainted wife passed away. I wish that I did not have to send her away, back to her father, so that he may be comforted in his old age as he has given me the privilege in these past months of being so comforted."

Don Ramón paused once more, and then he explained. "We received word hardly a few days ago that my brother-in-law, Isabella's father, is seriously ill. Probably from the shame that *la patria* is now prostrate before *el otro lado*. My brother-in-law must be inconsolable—just as I was. I know that Isabella Maria-Magdalena wept for a day. In these parlous times, I shall have to accompany her with every *escopeta* that I can muster. I cannot entrust her safety to anyone but myself.

"We were to leave on the morrow, but we shall remain to host you fine gentlemen until you depart. Then we can make our preparations to head south. We shall be gone from Monterrey long before your *gran cacique* Taylor approaches, and then we shall be safe ... at least until you *norteamericanos* make it as far south as *la Ciudad de México*. God forbid."

Eventually, don Ramón's soliloquy faded away, and the harpist began to play. A violinist and a guitarist eventually stepped out of the shadows and joined her. I was entranced, for I had never heard such music as this, evoking what I took to be both the Spanish and Mexican souls. Pickens was equally captivated, although I didn't know whether by the music or the harpist, for she was very comely. Hays was bored, restless to get back to camp in the hope that something would happen tonight. I could see it in his eyes. He wanted Canales or Seguin or whoever had been in town when the regiment hove into view to do something stupid, such as attack the camp. Chevallie was following his colonel's lead. His infatuation with the beautiful señorita was over, as if the besotted look he had given her an hour earlier had never happened.

When the music stopped for a moment, Hays and Chevallie hastily made their good-byes, chaffing Pickens and me for our prospects of soft featherbeds and baths before we slept. Don Ramón smiled indulgently as we spoke in English among ourselves. Isabella was nowhere in sight, so I assumed that she had retired for the evening.

Colonel Hays and Major Chevallie grasped don Ramón's hand in warm handshakes and bowed as best they could. Don Ramón said and I translated verbatim, "Gentlemen, Isabella Maria-Magdalena and I have been deeply honored by your presence this evening. I do hope that we are able to renew our acquaintances under more peaceful circumstances." Don Ramón then grinned devilishly. "Finally, gentlemen, I will ask your indulgence, and I am sure that you will understand my asking you, if you could be so kind, to please leave at least a little bit of *la patria* behind for us *méxicanos* as you expand yourselves to the Pacific Ocean and wherever else it is you seek to extend the glory of your flag."

After Hays and Chevallie departed, don Ramón bade Pickens and me to sit once more, as the harpist had, in don Ramón's words, one or two more very delectable songs to play for us, which she did. As the harp died away for the last time (the guitarist and violinist having long since departed), I became conscious of a faint and intoxicating aroma of jasmine, a scent I had not smelled in the many months since I had last seen Calandria. I realized with a start that it must be Isabella. I felt myself stir in an unwarranted fashion as she murmured in English, "You are a very pretty boy." My state of intoxication increased as I felt her lean closer to me. "And you speak Spanish so well, even if you do sound like an *arriero*. We shall have to fix your tongue, so that you can speak like a proper *hombre de bien*."

I opened my mouth to reply, but I shut pan when I heard don Ramón's sleepy voice through the gloom. "You must forgive me, señor Gogan, but my niece is most headstrong and prone to talking out of turn to men who are not of our family. You would never know her to have been properly raised as a *mujer decente*. I fear that it is the fault of her father and those schools in Europe, which have filled her mind so with such unladylike thoughts."

I hadn't a clue whether Pickens heard this exchange, and if he did, what he thought of it.

⌒

The clean sheets that night, the close shave administered the next morning by don Ramón's valet, and the beautiful music of don Ramón's magnificent in-town casa were a distant memory by the middle of the morning the regiment departed, and I was once again marveling at how humidity and dust could coexist as well together as they did on the southern side of the Rio Grande Valley. But complement each other they did that late summer of 1846, to the enduring misery of every manjack in the Army of Invasion.

Dawn had barely been a thought when the regiment broke camp and followed Hays north, up the Matamoros road, looking for all the world like the mule-gathering foray we'd advertised in San Fernando for two-and-a-half days. Hays halted our column of five hundred brilliantly disciplined and trained scalawags and desperados after an hour or so of hard riding. A pair of pickets from the rear guard raced forward within the minute and reported that no one had followed us from town. Other pickets on our flanks and from up the road each reported in turn that not so much as a señorita bound for the San Fernando River with her morning wash had ventured out yet. Walker and Chevallie grinned broadly at this successful bit of deception.

Hays merely said, "Pass the word for Major Gray."

The call echoed down the column, and Gray rode up lickety-split, wearing an ill-concealed grimace of discontent on his face, an expression which had hardly departed his visage since the three Mexican lancers had slipped right past him and his pickets. I had heard through the grapevine that Gray had actually volunteered his men for that all-important picket duty when we had most feared attack from the company or regiment of Mexican lancers that had so recently hotfooted it out of town as we arrived. (The actual size of the Mexican cavalry detachment had been a matter of considerable debate among the San Fernando townspeople while we were there, so we had not been entirely sure whether half the Mexican army's cavalry were about to descend upon us.) Gray apparently had hoped that a good show against such an attack might cause Hays to relent and assign another company to mule-gathering duty, thereby sparing Gray and his boys from the ignominy of it all.

By all accounts, Gray's embarrassment had descended first into sullen despondency and then into deep discontent expressed only in muttered tones to his lieutenants while we lingered in San Fernando. But by the morning we left, his discontent had spread to his company's rank and file, which was now little short of openly mutinous. They were a scabrous lot, even by comparison to Hays's boys. Gray had ventured south by himself to Point Isabel in May 1846, looking to join Hays and the First Texas in a capacity he thought would befit his lofty status as the premier gentleman of the road, high pickaroon, and cowboy extraordinaire south of the Nueces. It was not to be. The word was that one or two of Hays's company commanders would have been happy enough to take Gray on as a private, but no more. Hays, Walker, and Chevallie had wanted no part of even that. So Gray raised his own independent company of scouts and mounted rifles for a twelve-month enlistment from his pick of the many-splendored filibusters, sneak thieves, smugglers, and the myriad other *norteamericano* sweepings to be found littering the streets of Matamoros in that June of 1846. He had been lusting ever since for the honor of being included in the First Texas, and thus universally adjudged to be a proper part of the Texas Rangers.

"Major," Hays said drily. "This is where we part company. As we've discussed, you'll head north with Mr. Pickens and Sergeant Gogan and the gold and silver, picking up every mule—and anything that even resembles a mule—between here and Matamoros. You'll deliver them safe and sound to Colonel Whiting, and then you'll report to Major Bliss for further duties. Understood? Any questions?"

Gray shook his head and saluted as crisply as any Texas Ranger I ever met, pivoted his horse and galloped back to his company. I followed him, and within five minutes, we were headed north full chisel, and the First Texas had disappeared in a cloud of dust, heading due west at a similar speed to God knows where.

Five days later, we hove to in front of a small tumbledown rancho just south of Colonia del Refugio. It must have been the thirtieth place we'd visited, gathering ten mules here, two-score there, and half-a-dozen at yet another little rancho. Judging by the size of the corral just outside a thorn fence encircling the rancho's *jacal*, I was hoping to add two score or more mules to the herd of five hundred we already had in tow. A growing number of Gray's cowboys were now tending the herd. Every one of them, when his turn came to drive, coax, and threaten the mules in something approaching the right direction, loudly acted the wet dog at the prospect of doing such "dago swelter."

I heard to my left a nasally voice express that sentiment for what seemed to me to have been the fiftieth time that morning. The voice added, "I thought that I'd signed up to croake these god-damned greasers 'stead o' grafting like one." He sounded to me like he was fresh from the Big Onion on account of his hard accent.

Gray turned in a sudden fury towards the voice. "Who was that?"

"S'me, Cap." A foxy-faced man rode forward towards Gray as if he were being impelled against his will.

"Come 'ere," Gray snarled.

The man sidled his horse up alongside Gray, the two mounts nervously pawing the dust. Without a further word, Gray grabbed the bridle of the man's horse and leaned over and floored the poor slubber with a vicious chopper to his knowledge box. Claret sprayed from foxy-faced man's shattered nose, splattering Gray, who immediately released the bridle of the man's horse so as to settle his own startled mount. Alston confirmed my general impression of misanthropism by swatting ineffectually at the bleeding man, who was sagging in his saddle, and his horse as they crashed into him and his mount. I felt a couple of drops hit my face, and I was sitting on my mount a clean ten feet away.

Gray spurred his horse, crying, "Let's get a move on, god damn it."

Gray, Alston, Big Foot, and I spurred our mounts in unspoken concert. We rode through a narrow opening in the rancho's thorn fence into a small dirt courtyard bounded by two slovenly *jacales* on one side and a slightly larger and slightly less slovenly *jacal* on the other side. The latter looked to be housing the ranchero's family, if only on account of the short, fat Indian woman standing in the entrance, suckling her child. Behind the woman and suckling infant, I could see through an open window two or three much prettier girls sitting on the only bed in the *jacal* as they sewed and jibber-jabbered with each other while casting covert glances at the goings-on outside. To one side in the courtyard, an old woman was spinning yarn on a makeshift spinning wheel. Another old woman was kneeling not far from her, busy grinding corn on a *metate*, a flat mortar of grayish stone. A much younger woman, probably her daughter, caught my attention as she bent over at the waist, stiff-legged, helping her mother form the ground corn into tortillas. The smell was indescribably delicious, and I wondered for a moment whether we might be able to tarry long enough to consume two or six tortillas filled with some of the *queso fresco* sitting in bowls next to the *metate*.

Pickens had followed us into the courtyard, for I heard him murmur, whether to himself or someone else, "If these peasants had Uncle

Sam's machinery, they would soon be as rich as any Yankee industrialist in New England."

Alston must have heard him, for he laughed. "Not that any dago *hombre* would be caught dead doing women's work. Lazy bastards, they are. Cowards, too."

He was right—about their being idle, that was. There were three men in the courtyard in addition to the ranchero. All of them were squatting in the dirt in the inadequate shade of the thorn fence, well away from the industry of the women on the courtyard's far side. All of them seemed able-bodied, but they had hardly stirred when we rode in. We hadn't interrupted their morning's work, for there was nary a tool in sight. Nor did it seem that they were openly lingering in the courtyard so as to try to protect their ranchero if things went wrong, for they were bereft by all appearances of even a knife, let alone an ill-concealed *escopeta* or cutlass. Nonetheless, Alston had signaled a couple of his cowboys to keep an eye on the idlers, which they did on mounts snorting restlessly, their hands resting on their Colt repeaters in their holsters.

The rest of the company—aside from those who were disconsolately tending the mules we'd already gathered as they continued their way north—swirled some 90-odd strong around the fenced perimeter on mounts stirred to snorting excitement despite the heat and our many hours of travel that morning. Three or four of them dismounted and bounded another low thorn fence, which demarked the perimeter of a large corral erected cheek-by-jowl with the rancho's tall exterior thorn fence. The mules, cows, and pigs ensconced within scurried hither and yon, screaming, braying, and mooing in protest at the hullabaloo of our arrival at the rancho.

I didn't wait for any pleasantries from the ranchero, who was giving us a broad, gap-toothed grin of supplication. "Five *gringo* dollars for each mule. And we'll take two cows as well, for tonight's dinner. Ten dollars apiece for those."

The ranchero opened his mouth to bargain and then shut pan as he caught sight of the thunder on Gray's face and Alston's malicious grin.

"How many mules do you have yonder?" I drew my purse from under my serape, and the ranchero approached me, impelled involuntarily by his avarice. My mount bridled briefly, and I clutched the purse reflexively.

"Fifty, *su excelencia.*"

I translated.

"Great, jumping catawampus! Success!" Gray exclaimed. "That is outstanding, Gogan. Maybe you and your little brown mule-skinner were worth bringing along. And, perhaps, just perhaps, we can finally be done with this damned foolishness and get back to smoking these brown dastards 'afore Hays gets done with them. All right, Gogan, pay the fucker, and let's be quit of this shithole."

I counted $270 in eagles, double eagles, and half-eagles. I leaned over to pour more chink into the ranchero's hand than he was likely to see in ten lifetimes. The ranchero said, "Please leave me my bull and one cow, and at least a few chickens. Let me feed my family." He gestured to the fat Indian woman and suckling infant.

"Count yourself lucky that you've got your chink." I didn't translate chink, but he knew what I meant. "Good day, sir."

With that, we stormed out of the enclosure to see cows and mules being led away from the breached corral under heavy protest, and pigs and chickens running amuck in every conceivable direction, chased by hooting and hollering men with crazed looks on their faces. Pickens was staring at the spectacle in a slightly stupefied fashion as I cantered past him.

⌒

Several hours later, I was riding just behind Gray and Alston, when one of Gray's minions, a fellow named Jedediah Paige galloped up. A sergeant, I assumed, for although he had no insignia he carried himself as only a potentate with sway over a very small empire would. He tugged his slouch hat to two officers. "Dwyer just told me that he ain't seen his brother, Timmy, since we left that rancho back there. Figgered he's back there doing the dog's rig with one o' them brown cockatrices."

Gray swore. "Damien, you stay here. I'm riding back to find Dwyer the younger. He shall rue the day his bitch mother whelped him."

"And make his greaser bitch rue the day she sold him her honey pot." Alston answered, grinning lasciviously.

Gray did not deign to answer Alston. Instead, he asked Pickens. "Want to ride along? Better than eating dust with these damned shavetails."

Pickens shook his head and said to no one in particular, "My posterior pains me. No more hard riding for me today."

Just before dusk, Pickens, Alston, Big Foot, and I rode up on an old man encouraging a donkey straining against the traces of a two-wheeled *carreta* improbably overloaded with melons of half a dozen different varieties.

I greeted the old man. "¡Hola, señor! Where are you going with such a heavy load?"

The old *carretero* was so tired that he hardly reacted to my greeting him and speaking to him in Spanish. He merely gestured vaguely north.

"To Matamoros?"

The *carretero* nodded.

I looked at Alston, who read my mind and grinned his agreement. The old man read my mind as well, for he was already nodding when I asked, "Will you sell me your entire load of melons? It'll save you a long trip. Twenty dollars?" I had more than $200 left, and it was unlikely that we'd find any more mules between here and Matamoros, just fifteen miles up the road. We had all the mules expected of us and many more besides, which pleased me mightily. Better, I'd come in well below budget, and as the remaining chink wasn't mine I wasn't above spending some on the melons.

Juan Pablo, who had been out surveying the mules and making sure that none of them were pulling up lame, wordlessly materialized at my elbow. For an hour, he, Big Foot, Pickens, and I ferried melons from the *carreta* to nearby riders. Other riders appeared as if by magic, grabbed one or three melons and disappeared, often without so much as a muttered thanks. When we reckoned that everyone had had his fill, Juan Pablo and Big Foot fashioned a series of impromptu saddlebags out of the ponchos and blankets donated by every manjack within hailing distance to carry the rest of the melons, and they distributed them among the remaining outriders.

When the *carreta* was empty, Juan Pablo sent the *carretero* packing, and he soon vanished south. We gave him no more thought other than to smile at the memory of gorging ourselves on several melons each, rendering ourselves filthy with the sticky juices, which seemed to snare every grain of blowing sand.

We ambled along all that afternoon, sweating in the breathless air, and watching bluish-gray storm clouds forming over the río Bravo to our north. Pickens and I had been riding side-by-side for an hour or so without having said so much as a word to each other. Alston was riding alone fifty yards in front of us.

Big Foot and Juan Pablo were riding from string to string of mules out of a sense of duty that I had long since given up. All I could think about was drinking several gallons of cool water when we reached a rancho that Juan Pablo had told us was on the southern outskirts of Matamoros, its prime feature being an inexhaustible well of sweet water that the ranchero was perfectly happy to share—for a price.

Pickens looked up at the lowering sky and muttered, "In for a blow, ain't we."

"Yep." I wanted to return to my solitary contemplation of my misery. I was in no mood for Pickens's pleasantries.

Unfortunately, my reply, even as sour as it was, seemed to energize Pickens. "You know, Billy m'boy, I been thinking about what you said last night about the state of the Mexican peon, and what a sad fellow he is, all in hock to the *hacendado*."

"Almost as bad as being a bluebelly." I couldn't bring myself to be completely rude to Pickens.

"'Leastways, you've got an end to your enlistment. Those poor beasts. They're condemned to eternal peonage. Even that ... what was it you called him? The *carretero*. He's got twenty dollars from you, and most of it will find its way into his master's pocket. Worse than a darkie's lot, really."

I looked at him slantendicular-like.

"One day, anyway, you'll be free. Not them peons. Say, you ought to come work for me when you're done ... maybe after the Old Man's done with Monterrey? There won't be any more shenanigans after we thrash the dagoes one more time. They don't have that much fight in 'em." There was just a hint of a grin underneath Pickens's mutton-chops and ten-days' growth of beard.

I grunted.

"They really will be done after this. Just you see. Why, we'll have Matamoros as our port on the Rio Grande. The peons as far south as Monterrey and the mountains will all be freed, and God-fearing American folks'll be farming in the Rio Grande valley lickety-split."

"America's manifest destiny, no doubt. With or without slaves?" I muttered under my breath as I eyed the looming storm slowly drawing closer. A gust of wind cooled the sweat soaking my forage cap and the back of my neck, and I shivered slightly. I threw back my serape and opened my blouse to allow the breeze to dry my shirt.

Pickens affected not to hear me. "You're too smart to stay a blue-belly, m'boy. Hell, you're the only bluebelly I've ever known who could read and write even a little, an' you can do a whole lot more 'n' that if you put your knowledge box to it. And you can jabber away to them brown monkeys like you were born to it."

I didn't have the energy to tell Pickens that Hermann could probably read and write as well as Pickens, who had told me that he'd only had one year of schooling, but had picked up his Shakespeare as a thespian in Washington City when he was "a mere stripling just like" me.

"Why, m'boy, you told me yourself that you can declaim Cicero, whoever the hell he is. You're wasted as a bluebelly, Gogan. You ought to come up New Orleans way, and we'll put you on salary at the *Picayune*, cleaning up my 'peerless prose' and Kendall's as well. His is worse." Pickens snorted with delight. "Hey ... I like that ... 'peerless prose.' I'll have to get someone to say that when they're talking about the *Picayune*."

I sought to deflect him. "J. T., where the devil does the name '*Picayune*' come from?"

Pickens took the bait. "Why, Billy m'boy, it's quite simple. When Kendall and I started selling the *Picayune* back in the '30s, we sold it for a *picayon*, a Spanish coin then in general circulation." He said this last bit quite loftily. "Worth just half a bit. Everybody else was charging a short bit. So we have made a right hit of it, charging half the price. 'Course, we charge a short bit nowadays as well, because we're the best newspaper in the city. And that price increase is all pure profit."

"You and Kendall have gathered quite the pocket full of rocks from running your paper, haven't you?"

"We sure have." Pickens seemed to savor his success for a moment. "But, even so, we ain't the only rag in town—even if we are the biggest toad in the puddle. You've got that rag, the *Commercial Times*, with that third-rate joke writer, Thorpe. You know that he has the unmitigated gall to be writing a book about Resaca de la Palma? Wasn't even there. He was sojourning up at Point Isabel."

"I don't recall any newspapermen there that day, J. T.," I observed.

"Well, I'm not going to dispute that point. 'Course, I was hard at it up in New Orleans, raising my company of volunteers, don't you know."

"Comfortably away from Mexican musketry."

"Well, I ain't writing a book about a battle I wasn't at, like Thorpe, am I? In any case, I'm down here now, acquiring a righteous set of saddle sores helping these *rinches*, as the dagoes call 'em, chase those damned *banditti* to hell and gone." He shifted himself in his saddle uncomfortably. "Well the *Commercial Times* ain't the only doubtful rag we've got in New Orleans. Our fair city also harbors that treasonous fish wrapper, *la Patria*. S'posed to report all the news right from Mexico. They can speak the lingo—unlike the rest of us. Those bastards at *la Patria* think that we Yankees are imperialists—just like the British—for wanting Texas to be part of Uncle Sam. They went into conniption fits over the prospect of these United States stretching clear to California. They don't understand. It's America's God-given right. A matter of manifest destiny." He paused and gave me a slantendicular glance. "As you put it just now."

And then he veered right back to his previous topic. "Seriously, Billy. You've got a head on your shoulders. Your lieutenant ... Say, what's his name?"

"Grant?"

"Yep. That's him. He might miss you keeping his books and pattering with the browns in their lingo about mules and such better'n they can. With you, we could beat those boys over at *la Patria* at their own game. Except we'd have real analysis, instead of that dago propaganda they keep spewing out. No one would look askance ..." Pickens looked proud at having used the word. "... at you skedaddling to make some chink. Hell, man, half your Irish brethren have taken French leave when they've had the chance, and they ain't got a prospect among 'em."

I glared at Pickens.

"I know ... I know ... Don't get sore. I heard from your pal Wurster when I was dipping the wick over at the Great Western's place that you two have a pact not to skedaddle 'afore we've licked old Santa Anna." Pickens, as manic as I'd seen him in a while, changed the subject once more. "Man, you talk about having a pocket full of rocks. You and Wurster and the Western must be absolutely loaded from that little dossing crib of yours. That is simply a license to mint double eagles."

"We've done fairly well. All the Western's doing, though, mind you," I allowed.

"She told me that the French letters were your touch. Very classy." Pickens furrowed his brow for a moment. "Say, you told me that your lieutenant," Pickens thought for a second, "Grant. That's right. He's got a girl back up in St. Louis that he's sweet on, right?"

I shrugged noncommittally.

"He writes letters to her, don't he?"

"I suppose. I certainly don't read them."

"He seems competent enough, and he sure can talk like a book."

"But only when he wants to," I said.

"Well, that's exactly what I like about him. He ain't gimbal-jawed at all. But when he do talk, he makes a lot of sense. I want to publish his letters in the paper. He'd be our occasional correspondent from the Fourth Infantry. He could even use a pseudonym."

"You're kidding."

"No. I'm as serious as a Quaker. All the smart shoulder straps are doing it. Why, that fellow Henry ..." Pickens explained, "Captain over in the Third. West Point man, don't you know. He's been sending letters to the *Spirit of the Times* up in New York regular-like since he got to Corpus Christi last year."

"I suspect that Grant'd have me bucked and gagged, if I were to suggest it to him. I'll pass on that, thank you very much. I am quite certain that Grant looks upon you fellows as little better than a blight on the army."

"I'll bet you're dead wrong. You just ask him."

We rode for a moment or two in companionable (on his part) and blessed (on my part) silence.

"You've been sore at me ever since I told you about my office slave, haven't you?"

"You bought him on account of his pleasant mien, no doubt," I observed sourly.

"Yeah, I know. The Western told me about that little dusky wench you was doing the four-legged frolic with up in the Big Onion. How you were sweet on her an' all, and how her mother sent her away. A touching story, I'm sure. But you're right, though. That's exactly why I bought Sandy. When I interviewed him, he was as personable a darkie as you could ask for, I could understand what he said, he could read and write and he kept himself clean. Ain't much use having an office slave if he can't help around the office, and I sure don't want no damn Negro…," the latter not being the word he used, "if he's odiferous. Paid a pretty penny for Sandy, I did."

"Might be better if you paid him his wages, like Grant does with Hannibal."

Pickens prattled on as if he hadn't heard me. He hardly seemed aware of my presence now. It was as if there was another, more appreciative audience for his stories.

"I don't have anything against Negroes." Manifestly not the word Pickens used. "Why, Sandy's the best colored man alive—true and faithful as steel. He'll be living on easy street as long as he lives. I wouldn't have it any other way."

I continued to look at the lowering sky as we ambled on. My thoughts turned to Brannagh and that stormy afternoon we had spent in the coolness of her mother's parlor sheltering ourselves from the thunderstorms. In retrospect, they seemed genteel in comparison to what would likely be on us in an hour or two. I passed from such pleasantness to the memory of holding dear Mary's dead body in my arms, a memory that seared more hotly than it had since my earliest days in Corpus Christi. I picked in a desultory fashion at why that was so, and came up with no good answer, and then I descended down that well-worn path to the guilt of having somehow been the proximate cause of her death (through the agency of that malign bastard, MacGowan) and thence to the more certain knowledge that I had betrayed Mary even further, by not being there to protect and raise Fíona—the money I sent to Mrs. Shipley (more than enough to keep Fíona, Mrs. Shipley, and all of Mrs. Shipley's childer in the clover) did little to assuage my guilt.

Yet in the balance it wasn't Mary, but instead Calandria, and the memory of her interleaved with surprisingly lustful thoughts about the impossibly remote señorita Isabella Maria-Magdalena Fernandes de la Cruz, whom I'd never see again, and who left me curiously saddened and feeling more alone than I had felt recently. I resented Calandria's intrusion into my memories, and thought briefly of circling back to memories of Ireland, my father, Cousin Seamus, and Evelyn—and poor, murdered Father O'Muirhily, whose only sin was to protect me from MacGowan while he saw me to the *Maryann* and the safety of the New World. What a good man he was. I could only hope that he—and my father both—would have looked upon what I had done since I landed at Bulgers Slip those many months ago. I couldn't hope that they would find all that I had done to be admirable. But I did hope it was enough. My father had cruelly died at the hands of the *Sassenagh*, true enough, and his death had burdened me for a very long time. Father O'Muirhily was different. He had died because of me. I had helplessly watched the Irishman murder him as casually as can be, in front of ten score oblivious souls as *Maryann* was edged away from Lavitt's Quay on her way to anchorage in Lough Mohan. I had done nothing. My ineffectuality and my inaction galled me to no end, even now nearly two years later.

As a deflection, I wondered idly whether Pickens or Chevallie or even Big Foot had similar sorts of thoughts about señorita de la Cruz. I was quite certain that any memory Hays might have had of her probably had long-since vanished, so single-minded was he. Indeed, I wondered if he thought about dimber morts at all. He wasn't a sodomite. I was certain of that. Such longings simply were not part of his nature. As unassuming and unprepossessing as he was in nature and appearance, the man was a warrior, and that was simply all there was to it. I wished that life were as simple and focused for me as it seemed to be for the likes of Hays and Walker. But it was not. And with that, I had come full circle back to Calandria.

I wondered whether I really should take French leave and pass the remainder of my days on that south Texas hacienda where the swallows flitted about. It was a place where I could plant myself and tell the world (and myself) that I belonged, even if part of the reason I would be there was merely a meretricious ploy by Calandria to preserve her family's hacienda. Serafina, I thought, had purer motives in that regard than her sister. Thus it seemed better if Hermann were to absquatulate north to Serafina's waiting arms while the going was good (i.e., he was still alive and near enough the Rio Grande to find a horse and ride hell for leather north to where he'd never be found). That would preserve the hacienda without there being an air of the meretricious. Then again, perhaps the both of us could go.

I gradually left such feelings where they belonged, and I eventually returned to the lowering sky, the smell of more than a thousand mules, my weariness, and Pickens's prattling to his imaginary audience. "You know," he said. "I've been doing a powerful lot of thinking since I've been down here. This is mighty fine country. Like I said, I think good, honest white men'll be settling that Rio Grande valley lickety-split—on both banks, north and south. It'll do those poor brown peons a powerful lot of good when that happens. They'll be able to get jobs from the Jonathans, and that will allow them to break their bonds of servitude to those *gachupine hacendados*." As I decided that Pickens did not know the difference between a *gachupine* and a *criollo*, I caught him looking at me out of the corner of his eye, as if to see the effect of his words on me. Notwithstanding his glance, he continued without missing so much as a beat. "And we need the Jonathans settling the valley. Not slave-owning chivs."

"Chivs?"

"Old-style cotton and tobacco planters in white-columned manses with crowds of darkies to do their hard work for them, while they duel and flirt their lives away."

"As in an overweening sense of chivalry?"

"You're a bit dull this afternoon, aren't you, Gogan. Must be all that melon you ate. As I was saying, if the chivs settle the valley, there'll be more slavery there, and everywhere else we're taking from the dagos, than you know what to do with. Already enough of it in Texas, as it is. I do hail from a southern neck of the woods, and I do own my own office slave. But I must tell you that I've long held that too much of a good thing is still too much." Pickens ruminated. "Hell, if those Mississippi planters did start planting cotton down here, they might just try to enslave these poor brown peons, just like they've done with the coloreds. Be cheaper than paying those black-birders who bring the Negroes in from the Bight of Benin, say what? Wouldn't that just beat the band if we started having brown slaves as well as black?"

I shook my head in general disbelief.

"'Course, all of this hypothecatin' do tend to beg the question of how far south we *yanquis* go." Pickens pronounced "*yanquis*" as close to the Mexican as he could, which resulted in a rather loose approximation. "We go too far south, and we're going to have to assimilate a whole lot of folks of the brown-skinned persuasion. I can tell you from personal experience that there are a whole passel of white folk back home who won't take too kindly to that. Hell, they think we've already got too many of the blacker persuasion as it is, let alone all the Irish and other Papists who are flooding in from the Old World."

Pickens stopped to see if I was listening. I affected to ignore him.

"I do have to say, though, Billy boy, that most of these peons might just be better off under that Mississippi planter than in debt servitude to the local *hacendado*."

I looked over at Pickens in shock.

"So you are listening."

I gargled something about a peon being able to buy his way out, at least.

"Oh hogwash, Billy m'boy. That's just gammon and spinach pitched by fat-arsed dons and padres stinking of incense. These poor bastards are born into the debt of their fathers, and every year thereafter until they join the angels, they dig themselves in deeper with the *hacendado* for everything from the meat he eats to the clothing he wears. Even worse is the church, taking its two bits for every birthday that rolls around, not to mention what they charge for a marriage. You go ask that fellow Juan Pablo what it's all about."

I had, and Pickens was right. Even Kinney had told Hermann and me about how feudal life was on the hacienda. But then I thought about don Guillermo—tamping down thoughts of Calandria—and the utter loyalty of Pedro and Maria to doña Alandra. That was not a relationship borne of debt, but something else entirely … almost family. Stronger than some families (to wit, my cousin Seamus, damn his rotten, deceased soul).

"'Course," Pickens waxed pedagogical over my ruminations. "Neither of 'em are free. But then again, they ain't white, neither. So there ain't a whit of difference between 'em on that count. But you know, I reckon that an enterprising colored man can earn a pretty penny for himself, particularly if he's smart. Why, Sandy has proba-bly earned enough to manumit himself—that is, if I were willing to sell him to himself." Pickens chuckled. "No way a lazy peon down here can do that. There's not any opportunity. Look at this place … Remember the women working hard at that one rancho, and Alston pointing out all those dagoes just lazing about?"

I glanced around the barren plain, and once more contemplated the coming storm. Then I thought of Matamoros. The only com-merce visible in the town was what we *yanquis*—more like *gringos*—had brought with us. In fact, if you ignored the dust and palm trees, Matamoros two months after we *gringos* had descended upon it wasn't so different from what you found in New York—brothels, taverns, gambling hells, newspapers, and a burgeoning trade in luxury goods. We really were an Army of Invasion, maybe even of annexation. And the average *méxicano*, if he had a bit of wit about him, was cottoning on to our American ways—I thought of Juan Pablo making a year's wages in less than a month—and chasing the almighty chink just as hard as any *gringo* did.

Pickens bored into my thoughts once more. "And I'll bet you dollars to doughnuts that the average colored man lives one bodacious huckleberry above the peon's persimmon. You've seen those *jacales*?"

I nodded.

"They live worse than Mississippi field hands, for pity's sake."

"Maybe so. I've never been to a Mississippi plantation, so I can't say how slaves live. But I have been to the Gates of Hell, and the Old Brewery, too, back in New York. You've been there, haven't you, J. T.?" I hadn't a clue as to whether Pickens's travels during his days of living in Washington City had led him that far north. "The denizens of those ghettoes were once slaves, or their parents were. Compared to the way they live, I reckon I'd rather live in a *jacal* up on Padre Island, thank you very much, eating fish and melon and chasing pretty girls."

"But you are misapprehending the point, my dear fellow."

For a self-taught man with no schooling, as he was fond of telling me, Pickens did have a certain turn of phrase.

"Peons ain't living on Padre Island, Gogan. And they certainly ain't living free and easy. They're sweating in the humidity and dust down here, south of the Rio Grande, on some hacienda, where a *jacal* ain't so nice, seein' as it's not by the ocean. Anyway, my Louisiana brethren tell me that they, as slave-holders, are obligated—by law and as a matter of economic sense—to house their slaves and feed them three squares a day. It'd hurt their investment otherwise. Anyway, since they outlawed blackbirding all those years ago, all the more reason not to work your darkies to death. A good buck Negro," once again a word that Pickens manifestly did not use, "or a breeding wench is worth a king's ransom these days. So no man with an ounce of common sense is going to starve his slaves. The same goes for doctoring. I send Sandy to my own doctor, and I pay all the expenses. You go ask your *compadre* Juan Pablo if his *hacendado* ever did that. 'Course, I've yet to see a decent Mexican croaker. So maybe that ain't the best point of comparison. And I reckon that no one down here ought to be getting sick. Anyways, I heard that these *hacendados*'ll throw a peon out on his posterior the minute he can't work anymore. You can't do that with your slaves up in Louisiana. It's against the law. A master is legally bound to care for his slaves from the minute they're born until the day they die."

I was at a loss for words, although I had a hard time envisioning most masters solicitously caring for their slaves in their dotage or on their deathbeds.

"You know what else, buddy? From what I've seen, the average field hand gets better treated by his master than the average bluebelly does by his officers—although you have quite the sweet deal with that shoulder strap of yours, what's his name?"

Amazing. An hour ago, Pickens was ready to hire Grant as an occasional correspondent, and now he couldn't even remember the man's name. Sweet Jesus. I laughed. "Grant. U. S. Grant."

"Hell of a name."

"Yep. But he answers to Sam."

"That's a good thing."

The rain was just moments away now. I could smell it on the wind, which was beginning to really pick up. We were in for a hell of a blow.

The storm was almost upon us when Alston finally signaled to Big Foot and Juan Pablo to call in all the strings of mules and batten down for the blow. He'd been talking about doing so for the last hour. Quite properly, he was balancing stopping before the storm hit so that we didn't lose any mules against the desire to close the gap between us and Matamoros, so that we could make our final push past the routine patrols of the Second Dragoons. For only then would we be safe at last from any possibility of a cutting-out expedition by Canales's or Seguin's *guerrilleros*.

As we began gathering the mules, the squalls began to spit enough rain to temper the choking dust clouds raised by the wind and the ceaseless galloping back and forth of the 40 or so Rangers busy securing the mules at Juan Pablo's direction. We were about half done, and the rain was beginning to pelt more seriously, when a messenger on a well-lathered horse raced directly towards us, shouting, "Canales. Canales is abroad—so says the Mustang," even before he'd swerved to halt next to Alston.

"Where?" Alston asked, his voice tight with anticipation.

"We heard tell of riders as we headed back looking for Dwyer. Then one of our pickets was told that Canales is abroad, looking for Devil Jack. So the Mustang wants to find Canales and fix his flint for good."

"Son of a bitch," Alston rasped.

"Mustang says come quick. Every manjack you've got. Ammunition, too. All of it." The messenger met Alston's hard gaze as he said, "The Mustang told me to tell you to 'fuck the damn mules'." The messenger glanced at me after he said it.

Alston looked at Paige. "Gather 'em up, Jedediah. The mules. Tether 'em together. We leave in ten minutes. Bring the two pack mules with the spare ammunition. You ..." Alston pointed at me. "You stay here with your brown pal. Everyone else goes." Alston saw that Paige was still hovering, with a questioning look that met first Big Foot's eye and then mine. Big Foot paid him no mind. There was a lust in his eye that I'd not quite seen before. Alston said to the both of them, "Go! God damn it. Ten minutes."

Paige shrugged almost imperceptibly, and was gone hell for leather hallooing orders to all within earshot. Before you could shake a stick, Alston was leading forty Rangers south, full chisel, Big Foot in the van, raking his mount bloody with his spurs. Pickens went with them, his sore buttocks forgotten. "Wouldn't miss this for the world, my boy," he said to me as he spurred his mount and galloped away.

⌒

Within ten minutes, Juan Pablo and I finished tethering the two score and a half of the leads from the mule strings in as tight a circle as we could such that the mule strings radiated outwards as crookedly and irregularly as suited the mules' whims. The rain had already begun sheeting down on us, as if driven by the very hand of God himself, the thunder banging overhead like Hephaestus working his forge. Nary a lick of lightning could be seen in the deepening gloom. Juan Pablo yelled at me over the roar of the storm, "Keep your powder dry, *mi compañero*. I have a very bad feeling."

I had already secreted my cartridge box and a spare flint for my musket under my serape next to my Colt revolving pistol and extra cylinders. Juan Pablo had also handed me what little powder he had, although it was already starting to cake, and was likely useless until it had been thoroughly dried in the sun and once more pulverized. Even though I was curled over, shielding the powder from the worst of the rain, I didn't expect it to remain dry for very long. Juan Pablo took up position next to me, to the windward. I could barely see beyond the mesquite bush next to me, which added to my own mounting sense of foreboding. I tried to leaven my dread by figuring that any miscreants bent on doing us harm were quite unlikely to be abroad, let alone with mischief on their minds. I also told myself that even if they were, their powder was just as likely to be as wet and useless as ours threatened to be.

Juan Pablo and I remained huddled like this, for how long I couldn't tell. The storm gradually began to wane and the sky to lighten. Without speaking, we both got to our feet to survey the mules. Juan Pablo went one way, and I went the other. The mules, which were still strung together and tethered to bushes in a broad circle, had huddled even tighter during the worst of the storm, thus decreasing the exterior circumference of the now thoroughly snarled herd. I became lost in the task of disentangling the worst of the knots of mules, which were by now very cranky from the wet and the suddenly chill wind that cut through their wet coats as easily as it did my sodden blouse.

I stopped cold when I realized that the mules weren't stirring merely because I was jostling and cajoling them. Something else was out there. Perhaps a wolf or cougar drawn by the lure of an easy meal now that the storm was over? Big Foot had told me one night that cougars liked the mountains, whereas wolves didn't really care much one way or the other, a fact which I thought in a very detached way was quite unfortunate, because wolves like to hunt in packs. Bloody hell.

I gently pulled my Colt from my belt, checked the percussion caps on the cylinder as best I could without disassembling the pistol, and prayed that I didn't have more than one or two misfires. I also felt for my knife. My musket was fifty yards away, leaning up against the mesquite bush where Juan Pablo and I had sheltered. My cartridge box was hanging next to it. Both of them were sheltered underneath my nearly sodden serape, which I'd spread over the bush. Juan Pablo's and my horses were tethered to the very next bush, and I prayed once more, this time that the wolves were more in the mood for mule than horseflesh.

The gloom brought on by the storm was already deepening into twilight, which put me at an even further disadvantage. So I resolved to set about spooking the wolves. I didn't cry out, for I also feared spooking the mules into trampling me ignominiously into the muddy sand. I slowly crept out from the depths of the maul of mules towards the perimeter, which pressed towards me as the mules sought to pack themselves ever more tightly to protect themselves from whatever it was that was threatening them. I swore under my breath, struggling to keep to my feet, as the panicking mules evermore roughly buffeted me about. The pack finally spit me out, stumbling but upright. I was very thankful that my Colt was still in my hand. I drew my knife as I caught sight of one of the intruders.

They weren't wolves at all. They were a far more deadly species of predator, *los guerrilleros*. The only redeeming virtue of the situation was that their *escopetas* and antique flintlock and wheel lock pistols were likely useful only as clubs, for the *guerrillero* with his back to me was wetter than I was. They'd probably spent the entire storm injuning up on us. I hoped that they hadn't seen Alston and his forty Rangers thundering south at full chisel, lusting to get into the action of capturing Canales before it was all over. Otherwise they'd know that they had plenty of time to find Juan Pablo and me.

I briefly considered murdering the *guerrillero* with a knife to his throat, as Big Foot had shown me back at Camp Maggot. But I dismissed the thought. I didn't trust myself to kill in cold blood, and the last thing I wanted to do was to get into a noisy scrap with an angry *guerrillero*. That would surely bring the rest of them running. I crept out into the brush beyond the mules, praying that Juan Pablo had noticed the mules being spooked and had been lucky enough to escape detection.

A moment later, I heard an *escopeta* discharge, a man scream in mortal pain, and another man chortle triumphantly. I reckoned that they must have been able to shelter their powder, after all.

I burrowed under a bush fifty yards from the mules and watched the *guerrilleros* as the afternoon faded from gloomy twilight into real dusk. There weren't many of them, five or six at most. But even that few were too many for Juan Pablo and me to face alone—that is, if Juan Pablo were still alive. So I contented myself with hoping that Juan Pablo had found a hidey-hole and was watching *los guerrilleros* work patiently to little avail trying to disentangle the mules, either to steal them or scatter them to the four winds. I wondered where they had come from. Then I realized with a start: They'd been wandering about and had likely run into the *carretero* whom I'd so recently enriched. I wondered if they'd stolen the *carretero*'s earnings. I couldn't conceive of it being otherwise. The poor man probably wasn't even alive. Bastards!

"Look, *mis amigos*, a little chicky away from its nest." *Los guerrilleros* had found me.

I whirled about and fired my Colt in the direction of the voice, which had begun to snarl. The flash blinded me, and the report deafened me. The voice choked and stopped. I heard men rushing blindly through the underbrush towards me. One man stumbled over my feet. I shot him. Another came lunging towards me, and I heard someone screaming, "Croake the greasers. Croake the fucking greasers!"

# CHAPTER 18

# A Baile for Jenny

"To be clear, Sergeant. You and your Mexican mule-skinner were alone, guarding the mules when the *banditti* attacked?"

Perfect Bliss glared at me without a great deal of empathy as he paced back and forth. I was standing at attention, eyes front, at the apex of a semicircle of very unwilling participants in this audience with Bliss. To my left was my entire regimental chain of command, starting with Grant, who was next to me, and ending with Colonel Garland at the far end. I could feel all of their eyes (save Grant's) boring into me as Bliss conducted his inquiry into what had happened during the trip back to Matamoros after Major Gray's company separated from Hays and the First Texas. To my immediate right stood the Mustang, flanked by Damien Alston and Big Foot, each of whom, if not as perfectly ramrod straight as the regulars, was at least making an effort to remain at attention.

Truth be told, the audience really wasn't with Bliss. It was with the Old Man, for this semicircle of unwilling attendees stood just twenty paces away from the front of his tent, which was set in the pleasantly cool and moist shade of a great live oak at the edge of the Army of Invasion's parade ground. The Old Man, his countenance inscrutable, was sitting on his campstool just by the tent's entrance, seemingly unaware of this little morality play unfolding in front of him.

Bliss was all boiled up. Whether with me, someone else, or merely the situation in general, I couldn't tell. It really didn't matter, though, because I was going to be the one to catch it. I was the only bluebelly

there. Even Big Foot had a leg up on me. Although he was a mere sergeant, just like me, he was also a Texas Ranger, and the Rangers were
the Old Man's eyes and ears searching out the enemy. Perhaps even
more importantly, Big Foot was a volunteer.

So I considered my answer carefully, once more revisiting all that
had happened on the trip. The two days it took to gather up the scattered mules and then to return to the army's digs on the west side
of Matamoros had been like holding a match for light in a powder
magazine. Gray and Alston and their men, a surly lot at the best of
times, were rumbling with rage at having chased over hell and gone
all for naught only to return to find that the *banditti* had bamfoozled
them and raided the mules while they were gallivanting about. What
I should say—and to whom—had only begun to preoccupy me once
Big Foot and I had shooed our shavetails to the entrance to the quartermaster's holding pens. Grant had found me just minutes after Gray
and Alston and their company of Matamoros street-sweepings had
cleared out for Camp Maggot (save for a few sullen ruffians detailed to
remain with Big Foot and me until we had turned our mules over to
the quartermaster's mule-skinners).

Whiting's lieutenant had been hard on Grant's tail, looking for
his saddlebag and what remained of the gold and silver coins that it
had contained. He also wanted an accounting from me, which I gave
him settled to the half-penny. (The $20 we'd squandered on the mel-
ons was safely tucked away in the much larger, but not as large as it
could have been, category of "mules lost due to enemy action." I was
mighty gratified that in the end very few mules had been lost—less
than fifty, which paled before the thousand or more we brought in.)
My efficiency earned me a wintry smile and a look of relief that I,
a fast-talking—and painfully young—sergeant entirely unknown to
him other than by the bona fides presumably offered by Kinney and
Grant, hadn't skedaddled off into the far back of beyond with enough
gold and silver to last the average bluebelly a couple of lifetimes. I
didn't think it would have been wise to tell him that I didn't give a
tinker's dam about the money. Why would I? I had as much—and far

more besides—sitting on account at a reputable bank in New Orleans, not to mention what was left in the Bowery Savings Bank.

(Hermann, the Western, and Jenny had similar accounts with similar amounts of chink. The general of volunteers had prevailed upon one of his minions to arrange the bank accounts, an emolument for us borne of the general's affection for the Big Western and his gratitude for the services she had rendered. Every last penny in our accounts had been earned by the sweat of the score of Mexican dells who were all more or less happily—or, so I assumed—earning a year's wages or more every week at our riding academy, servicing shoulder straps, volunteer and regular alike, all the while subject to the Great Western's eagle eye.)

From the moment I gave Grant a tired salute, it seemed as if he already knew that something was up. Once the mules had been turned over to the quartermaster's mule-skinners, Grant hustled me away without my giving Big Foot so much as a by-your-leave, although he did manage to give me a weary smile and wave as I looked back. Grant quickly marched me to his tent in the very heart of the Fourth Infantry's officers' country, sat me on his campstool, borrowed another, sat down, offered me a whiskey, and asked me if I was all right. I damn near blubbered at the asking. But I recovered, drank a bit of the whiskey, felt its fire explore my innards, and finally told Grant bits and pieces of what had happened. I didn't tell him everything, for I wanted some maneuvering room—for what I didn't then quite know, but I wanted it nonetheless. I must have said enough, though. For when I'd finished, he murmured, "It's true, then." He ordered me not to move from the stool and disappeared. I sat there, wishing myself into invisibility as the Fourth Infantry's brass sauntered by on one errand or another without any of them even once acknowledging my existence.

Grant returned eventually and escorted me to Colonel Whiting's lair on the river, just upwind of the mule holding pens and cater-ways from the newly-built landing. A paddle-wheeler chugged patiently quayside as a flood of colored and Mexican laborers swarmed over it like locusts, feverishly extracting every box and container to be found and placing them into waiting Conestoga wagons. There Grant left me for two days with the strictest of orders not to speak to anyone, not even to Hermann—about anything. Somebody must have also warned Hermann off, for I saw neither hide nor hair of him, nor of the Great Western or Jenny—or Eddie Rocheron, for that matter. I was entirely behind the purdah.

Before reveille on the morning of the second day, Grant sent Hannibal to warn me to be standing by, square-rigged, and squared away before the wind for an audience with the big bugs. An hour later, Grant marched me to the Old Man's tent as smartly as you like, with curious eyes cast our way as we went. My entire chain of command and Major Gray, Damien Alston, and Big Foot were already assembled in that small semi-circle in front of the tent. Bliss was pacing its diameter. The Old Man sat behind him on his campstool, affecting not to notice the passion play unfolding in front of him. Colonel Whiting and Colonel Kinney stood a little to the right of the semi-circle, at once detached, yet very much involved. At the apex of the semi-circle, there was a gap of a few feet between Major Harrison, now the Fourth's second-in-command, and Mustang Gray. Grant and I gave the group the crispest salutes in our inventory as he deposited me in the gap. He remained beside me.

Bliss began without preamble. "Stand easy, Sergeant, and tell us your story of what happened the day you were attacked."

I paused when I reached the point in my story at which I'd been attacked as the storm ended and night fell. Bliss asked me bleakly whether Juan Pablo and I had been alone with the mules when the *banditti* attacked. I answered him truthfully. We had been alone. Lieutenant Alston had taken all of his men, Big Foot included, south to join Gray in the hunt for Canales. Bliss looked at me hard, and asked me what happened next.

"Pretty simple, sir. Mr. Pickens and Sergeant Moncrief found me. I don't know where they came from, but they saved my skin. And within a couple of minutes, there were more of Lieutenant Alston's men milling about, looking for *guerrilleros*."

"Did they find any?"

"Sir?"

Bliss was glaring at me again. "Did they find any more—what did you call them? guerrillas? ... Bandits ... Did he find any of those brown devils alive?"

"No sir. Not a trace other than the bodies. The rest of them, if there were any, had disappeared by the time the lieutenant's platoon got there, just as the sun was coming up."

"Whose bodies?"

"My *arriero*, Juan Pablo. He must have been killed by the shots I'd heard. But I didn't see his body until later."

"Who else?"

"Two of the three who came after me ... Well, sir, I'd never seen them before ... and they were dead. But the third." I glanced at Kinney, who had hardly acknowledged me since I'd arrived. I swallowed hard. "The third ..."

"Speak up, man."

I gulped and thought about what had happened after I'd emptied my repeating pistol at the *guerrilleros* who had discovered me cowering under that blasted mesquite bush. I'd stayed put just a few feet from the two dead bodies for what seemed like hours, praying that there was no one else around. My Paterson's cylinder was empty, and I couldn't find my spare. My musket and my loose ammunition were where I'd left them, too far away to chance making a dash for them. So my knife was all I had to protect myself and my saddlebag laden with gold and silver. The third man stirred occasionally, thrashing an arm about and muttering prayers and imprecations that I could only half hear. Eventually, I found my two o'clock in the morning courage. (You know, the sort of courage that is entirely unprepared, but which is ready for the unexpected occasion—at least that's how Napoleon referred to it, or so I am told.) I crawled over to the wounded man and put my knife to his throat hard enough to draw blood, which glistened black in the newly emerged moonlight. I was ready to press it home, when I realized I knew the man, and I knew too that I could never kill him, even though he had just tried to kill me.

Remembering that sense of shock, I looked Bliss in the eye and then Kinney. "It was don Guillermo Ñíguez Rodríguez, sir." I also caught sight of Alston and Gray in my periphery. Alston's eyes flickered slightly. Gray continued to stare ahead, indifferent and detached. "He was a friend and neighbor of Colonel Kinney's. I came to know don Guillermo and his family last winter, when the army was in camp back in Corpus Christi. But he went south months ago to join Canales and his *guerrilleros*. Leastways, that's what I heard at the time."

As Kinney stared at me intently, I reflected upon my answer and upon the fact that I hadn't told the half of it.

Don Guillermo opened his eyes, and he had seemed to recognize me even though it was still very dark out. I tucked my knife away in its scabbard and looked at his wound. One of my bullets had shredded his shoulder. Blood was everywhere. I unbuttoned my blouse and used it as a filthy bandage.

As I did so, don Guillermo began whispering to me in labored Spanish. I tried to quieten him, to save his strength. He waved me off and continued whispering, and I finally understood what he was telling me, "Go home, my boy. Go home to Calandria and the flying swallows. She needs you. Protect the swallows ... remember ... remember the swallows." He licked his lips and closed his eyes.

I wanted to scream, for there was naught I could do for him. We were miles from camp and a sawbones to tend his shattered shoulder—if such a croaker could even begin to help him. God knows that most of the time they could hardly help themselves, let alone their patients. They had certainly not helped my father, when he died in that fetid, pox-ridden gaol cell in Richmond Prison, nor had they helped my mother when she died giving birth to me. So I just sat there in the mud, helpless, watching don Guillermo slowly bleed to death, soaking my sodden blouse.

The sun had just begun to peek over the horizon, when I heard, "What the Sam Hill are you doing?" I damn near jumped out of my skin. It was Alston. He murmured softly, "Jedediah."

"Yeah, Cap?"

Alston pointed wordlessly. In one swift motion, Paige pushed me aside, drew his Paterson, and fired a single shot. Don Guillermo's face exploded.

Bliss testily brought me back from my thoughts. "We don't have all day, Sergeant. Was this 'don Guillermo' alive?"

Alston's eyes flickered once more. Only the Mustang and I saw it, and he remained detached, as if his life were not swinging in the balance.

I remembered the last thing that Pickens had told me before he skedaddled to a waiting riverboat and passage home to New Orleans. "Don't let the West Pointers get ahold of them," he'd said, referring to Gray, Alston, and Big Foot. "You'll need them. Every damned last one of them. Even if they are murdering scoundrels." I'd looked at him, not understanding him. "The Army, man," he explained impatiently. "The Army. They'll need the Rangers in Monterrey." I'd nodded, and he'd left without saying another word.

Until that instant, standing there in front of Bliss, who was growing more impatient by the second, I had not made my mind up what exactly I should say of the matter. "There was nothing I could do, sir. Don Guillermo was dead. That's when Lieutenant Alston and his men found me."

"Hmmph. They weren't there during the scrap with the *banditti*, you said earlier?"

"Yes sir. That's right. Lieutenant Alston and his men had been called south by Major Gray the night before. Major Gray had sent a rider to find us, and he—the rider—told us that the Major and the rest of the company were hot on Canales's trail, and to come quick. And to bring the ammo packs. All of them." I stopped for a moment, and I once again felt all eyes boring into me. "Sir."

"Yes? Well, go on."

"I want to make it clear that Sergeant Moncrief was ordered to go south by Lieutenant Alston. He …" I paused theatrically. "He wanted to stay with me, just as Colonel Hays had ordered him to. But Lieutenant Alston ordered him to go south with everyone else. 'Every manjack available' were the orders, sir." Out of the corner of my eye, I could see Big Foot's look of relief. Alston was wooden-faced. Gray looked off, as indifferent as ever to the dramaturgy.

Bliss paced along the semicircle's diameter for a moment. Then he changed the subject. "Sergeant, what do you know of events that befell Major Gray and his men as they searched for Canales?" I looked at Bliss quizzically, trying to force his hand, for we both knew where this was going. Irritation flickered across Bliss's eyes, but he yielded nonetheless. "Involving civilians being killed."

"Not much, sir." Not far from the truth, insofar as it went. I'd seen nothing, of course. But I had learned enough from Big Foot, far more than I cared to divulge. "I understood from what Major Gray's men were saying to one another that there had been some sort of altercation at one of the ranchos where we'd bought mules."

"An altercation," Bliss repeated skeptically.

"Yes sir."

"What else?" Bliss asked harshly.

"I was given to understand …"

I paused for a second, drifting in my mind's eye back three days to when Big Foot told me his story in an appalled tone of voice. We had been riding together, alone, with a string of mules and Juan Pablo's horse in tow. When he started talking, I hardly listened. I was too deep in my own funk, ruminating about Juan Pablo's death and, worse, don Guillermo's final moments and the prospect of having to tell Calandria that I'd been the one who had killed her father.

Eventually, though, the enormity of what Big Foot was telling me gradually began to intrude as we rode through the ever-present and ever-miserable heat. "When we heard that the Mustang was hot on Canales's trail, I was ready to wreak the vengeance of the Almighty, himself, on the greasers," Big Foot was saying, seemingly to no one in particular. "Dear God, how I'd looked forward to it since Perote. We rode hard south to find the Mustang. Damien put riders out two, three miles on either side of us, so we wouldn't miss him. The rain held off behind us, so we didn't have to worry about our powder if we ran into Canales before we found the Mustang. Not that we wanted to. There were only forty of us, and if we found Canales and all of his *guerrilleros*, we might 'a' had just a few more of them greasers on our hands than we'd 'a' cared to.

"Anyways, we never did find the Mustang, and we saw nothing of Canales. We rode clear down to that little rancho where Dwyer was s'posed to be havin' a bit o' fun with that damned dago bitch. I was with Damien and Jedediah and a couple of others when we piled into the courtyard. The *ranchero* came out with his woman. She was feeding her whelp, just like the last time. Damien didn't even open his mouth, and the *ranchero's* blabbering on in gibberish about something or other. We couldn't figure what it was other than we reckoned he was telling us that Dwyer was gone, west with the Major, all of 'em lickety liner.

"Damien asked the *ranchero* why the Mustang had gone west. *Irregulares*, the Mexican told us. *Tanta guerrilleros.* Damien turned to leave and then I saw him."

I almost asked, "Who?" But I said nothing.

"That son of a bitch. Grinning like a fucking baboon, he was, standing in the middle of this miserable, little rancho in the middle of hell's half acre. He was grinning the same way he'd grinned when he was holding that damned jar of beans down Salado-way all those years ago." I must have looked at Big Foot quizzically. He reminded me. "The Black Bean Incident at Rancho Salado. The *diezmo*. Looking at that god-damned bastard brought back all those fucking screams as our boys was shot to death. Two or three, or even five or seven, shots to kill each man, and the ones who wasn't dead yet begging those damned dagoes to put them out of their misery, proper-like. What a fucking mess that was.

"Well, I hadn't seen the fucker since then, and now, there he was. I was ready to smoke him as he stood there before me. I really loved the look on that bastard's face when he realized who I was. We just stared at each other for a while. And then he was dead, a fucking great hole in the side of his head. Ol' Jedediah Paige killed him. He'd been there, too, at Salado. Just a kid, he was, then. Not a rustler or a killer. Not yet, anyways. Two years in Perote Castle would twist any man, and it twisted young Jedediah Paige something awful. Anyways, Paige must 'a' seen that bastard an' me lookin' at each other and realized who he was.

"Well, all hell broke loose after that. The *ranchero* was dead. So was his wife. Their whelp was on the ground, screaming, until somebody shot it. My Colt was in my hand, and I'd used it a couple of times. I reckon I killed a fellow coming out o' one of the smaller *jacales*. I didn't get off my horse. Several other fellas did, though." Big Foot chuckled sardonically. "And they carved some topknots off'n the ranchero'n his wife better'n the Comanche could 'a' done it. Then it was over. There waren't a soul left alive in that rancho, 'cept the women in the *jacal*. They was all screamin' like banshees. A couple o' boys—I don't know who, an' even if I did, I ain't sayin' who they was—well, they went in there. Into that *jacal*. When they came out a few minutes later, there waren't no screaming no more.

"Damien didn't say a word to any of us. He just shooed us out o' that little rancho like the missus'll shoo her man out of a saloon. As we left, the storm hit, an' half our powder was wet 'afore you could 'a' counted to ten. So we didn't go looking for the Mustang no more. Damien headed us back north, instead. Nobody said much of anything the whole way back, and absolutely nothing about what happened back at the rancho. I think that everyone was praying that Canales didn't find us. I sure was. By 'n' by, we got back to you an' poor ol' Juan Pablo, and the rest you know."

"Why'd you tell me? You could hang for it. All of you could. Sweet fucking Jesus, man."

"You needed to know that what you did waren't wrong. You just defended yourself when you was attacked. So don Guillermo died proper-like, even if you was the one doin' the killin'," Big Foot murmured bleakly. "What we did down at that rancho was different, an' it war wrong. Them poor greasers down there at that rancho was just plain murdered—all o' them 'ceptin' that grinning fuck from Salado. He deserved to die. But the rest of 'em didn't, even if they was jes' greasers. An' I helped kill them poor devils, though I didn't kill no one 'til after the shooting started. But I was there, and I did some killing."

With that, we stopped talking. Within a few hours we were in Matamoros, and I was disbosoming carefully edited bits of my soul to Grant and Kinney.

Bliss broke into my reverie. "Don't try my patience, Sergeant. Just tell us what you know."

I looked Bliss square in the eye. "All I heard, sir, was that there was an altercation at one of the ranchos at which we'd bought mules, and some Mexican civilians were killed."

"Who told you about it?"

"I don't rightly remember, sir. I just remember generally hearing about it. I don't even know who was fighting and who was killed."

"You didn't think to ask about what had happened and who was involved?"

"No sir." I met Bliss's eye "I was a little preoccupied at the time …" I trailed off, hoping I hadn't been too insolent in alluding to don Guillermo's and Juan Pablo's deaths.

Bliss ignored it. But he wasn't done. "You heard nothing about women being murdered? And …" He turned and almost beseechingly half-looked at Taylor, who didn't react. "And worse than that done to them?"

"No sir."

I could feel Big Foot rustling involuntarily.

"Hmm." Bliss paced some more. "Major Gray? What of this?"

"Whatever happened, Major, it wasn't us." The Mustang stood negligently, with a seemingly amused glint in those dead blue eyes of his. "Me an' my Matamoros cowboys were busy chasing that varmint, Canales. Too bad he gave us the slip."

"No doubt." Bliss gave Gray a brief, icy glare. "In light of my questions, it should come as no surprise to you, Major Gray, that the General has received numerous reports of a massacre at a place called Rancho Guadalupe. They have come from all parts of the Mexican citizenry. Indeed, some of our informants are gentlemen, and they possess the highest credibility. They are also deeply shocked that we North Americans, as they call us, could have committed such a terrible misdeed. As one of them said to me, 'You *norteamericanos*'"—I was impressed with Perfect Bliss's accent—"'are not the godless Comanche, and you are not the heartless *gachupine*, whose yoke we threw off just as you did the yoke of English tyranny. You *yanquis* are the paragons of the New World. At least you should be,' he said to me." Bliss paused for a moment to collect himself. "Major Gray, I cannot tell you the depth of shame I personally felt over what that Mexican gentleman told me. The General is of a similar mind. Such iniquities irreparably stain the escutcheon of this great Army of Invasion. The killing—and worse—of innocent women and children cannot be countenanced." Bliss hardened his glare, meeting Gray's eye. "So, Major, what do you say of it?"

Gray looked at Bliss steadily, all the amusement drained from his face. "It must have been Canales cutting up the didoes on his poor fellow countrymen for the sin of having sold us all them mules."

"Cutting up the didoes … Do tell." Bliss switched his gaze to Alston. "Lieutenant? What do you have to say?"

"Sir?" Alston was staring rigidly a thousand yards behind the Old Man's tent.

"What do you know of this?"

"Not a thing, sir. We did visit one rancho, looking for news of Major Gray after he sent for us. But when we left that rancho, they was all breathing just fine, 'specially the women-folk. An' we didn't know the name o' that rancho 'til you told us … Sir."

Bliss spoke once more, as if he hadn't heard Alston. "What of this Mr. Pickens? The news correspondent." Taylor swore under his breath. "Has anyone seen him? I want to hear from him what he

380

knows. God knows what he and his fellow scribblers might publish about this story."

There was a long silence. I dared a glance. Colonel Garland, Major Harrison, and Grant were all standing to my left, each of them looking off at a different bit of the horizon than his companions, and all of them seeking to distance themselves from this sordid tale. Gray was smirking once more, and Alston had a carefully blank look on his face.

Big Foot broke the silence. "He's gone, sir."

"Gone? Gone where?"

"N'Awlins ... sir." Gray's smirk broadened. "He is quit of this war. On account of the hard riding and all, I reckon."

Taylor swore again, a little less softly than before.

"And what of this story about Rancho Guadalupe? What does he know?" Bliss's gaze bored in on Big Foot. (Actually, Perfect had to stare up almost to the clouds on account of Big Foot being damn near a foot taller.)

"There ain't no story to tell," Gray interjected calmly. "Nothing happened before J. T. left. In fact, he was very disappointed that he didn't have a story for all the hard riding we did. He was taking back only one letter he wrote while we were down in San Fernando. He showed it to me. Speaking about the couple of days he and Sergeant Gogan spent enjoying the hospitality of a rich man in town and his daughter. A beautiful young woman, by all accounts. I'm sorry I missed meeting her. J. T. was a little disappointed on account of us not finding Canales. He wanted to make Damien here ... Lieutenant Alston, beggin' your pardon, sir ... a hero in his newspaper. But there wasn't anything to be done about it, on account of ol' Canales having given us the slip."

Bliss paced before he spoke again. "General Taylor has determined that he cannot convene a board of inquiry over this incident." Bliss turned a wintry smile towards Gray. "He doesn't have the jurisdiction, you see. You're mere volunteers. All of you. And volunteers are civilians in the eyes of Congress, even when they wear the uniform of the

United States Army." Bliss paused to eye the Rangers' mufti. "The Articles of War don't give the General the power to try civilians. So there is nothing that he can do. He cannot even turn you over to the local *alcalde* for trial, because you are not Mexican. But you should not misunderstand me, Major. If you and your men were regulars, you'd be court-martialed and hanged, given what we know of this massacre. Consider yourselves lucky. Dismissed."

Gray's insolence paled just a trifle.

⌒

Hermann and the Great Western heard my tale out wordlessly, as we sat at the big table in the kitchen, untouched cups of mescal before us. I left nothing out. When I was done, I drained my cup in a single swallow. Hermann and the Great Western exchanged glances, but they did not ask me any questions, for which I was thankful. I hadn't the energy to explain more.

Instead, Hermann said, "I received this." He was holding an opened letter.

"To me?" I felt a spasm of irritation that either of them would read my mail. Not that I'd gotten any. Ever.

"No." Hermann said gently. "To me. From Serafina."

"She wrote you? Is all well back there? How's Calandria?" Maybe I could find a way to tell her of her father's death without her hating me for all eternity. "How's Serafina, and doña Alandra?" I looked at Hermann like an expectant puppy.

"They … they are all fine." The ponderousness of tone I had known when I first met Hermann, and which had almost vanished in the last few months, had come roaring back hand-in-hand with his Teutonic accent. Hermann and the Great Western exchanged another glance.

She took up where Hermann had faltered. "Billy, honey. It's about Calandria."

I stared at them, not quite comprehending.

"She's gotten herself married, and she's with child."

382

⌒

Hermann did not show me the letter, but he told me what he knew. Some cowboy hove into Corpus Christi about the time that the army marched south. The *gringo* adventurer had attended church beneath the live oak where I had met Calandria and where Hermann had met Serafina. Within the month, the bastard had put her in the family way, and they had been hastily married. Serafina and her mother were naturally horrified at the fall from grace of such a beautiful *mujer decente*. Serafina also wrote of plans seemingly afoot to displace her and her mother from the house of the flowing swallows and send them back to their digs in Béxar. To allow room for the growing family, don't you know. I growled that we should both take French leave, borrow a couple of horses from Big Foot and his compatriots, and have a discussion with this *gringo* interloper about dispossessing Serafina and her mother.

I spent the next few hours swimming in the bottle of mescal that had been sitting on the table when I had listened to Hermann and the Great Western floor me with the news. The next twelve hours after that—which was until I showed up again to run errands for Grant—I spent laboring mightily between Adabelita's legs, a welcome development that came about purely by chance. I had escaped the kitchen and the empty mescal bottle just after the sun had risen, intending to sleep off the booze in bed in my little room, alone save for my miseries. I nominally had a tent in camp (by myself, on account of my lofty status as a sergeant and the fact that I was not attached to one of the companies of the line, but instead was the ranking regimental quartermaster's man). I rarely used the tent, because my purely military duties were few. Indeed, I rarely attended drill, and that was only if the entire regiment was at it (which had been but once or twice since we'd left Corpus Christi), and even then, I generally mucked about with the horses, mules, and whatnot, and did not march in the ranks. A beautiful existence for a man who just a year earlier had been a raw recruit stuck under the thumb of a sadist. But I was not appreciating such amenities as I slouched none too sober to my little room and the straw mattress where I hoped to escape the memories of what I'd seen and done in the last few weeks—and to escape the unpleasantly graphic thoughts engendered by the news of Calandria's betrayal.

The hall was pitch black other than for the flickering light cast by the single tallow candle I was carrying. I started involuntarily when Adabelita appeared silently at my elbow and looked mutely and impassively up at me, her eyes dark and luminous above her smashed nose and misshapen cheek. She had hardly spoken since that bastard had caved in her face. Her silence was to be expected, for she had a terrible, nasally lisp that made it difficult to understand her when she spoke. We looked directly at each other for some seconds, her face shadowed by her dark hair in the dim candle-light. I smiled at her to let the moment pass, and went into my room and sat heavily on the straw mattress. As the mattress sagged under me, I could feel the frame of the bed cutting into the bottom of my thighs. I focused on the sensation for a moment, wondering how long it would take to induce a raging case of pins and needles.

Adabelita followed me in, wordless and uninvited, gently closed the door behind her and sat next to me, her legs curled up under her white cotton Mexican frock. I did not look at her, and instead held my head in my hands, focusing on the bite of the bedframe into the bottom of my thighs. I could feel her warmth and smell next to me, although we were not touching. It comforted me. We remained that way for quite some time until I leaned back and looked at her. She was staring at me as impassively as before. I leaned over and gently kissed her smashed nose and cheek. She opened her mouth, and I felt the awful scars left by her vanished teeth. But her scent stirred me now, and it was not very much later when I expiated myself between her thighs, mewling like a baby into her long black hair coiled in the crook of her shoulder. She came to my room every night for the next week save two, when my obligations to Grant called me away one night and when Sarah found one task or another for me. I don't know that Adabelita spoke twenty words to me during that entire week. But it was enough for me to know that her world had shrunk to working for Sarah and seeking solace for herself with me. I whispered ten thousand words to her and, I suspect, communicated little.

◦—

Notwithstanding the fleeting solace I found with Adabelita, I cannot say I took particular pleasure in the week leading up to Jenny's nuptials. I should have at least been more gracious about it all, for I wished Jenny and Eddie and their forthcoming child—Eddie viewed the coming birth as if it had originated from his own loins—all the happiness and more that this world and their future back in the Louisiana swamps could offer them. (Apparently, the district of Eddie's birth was lousy with swamps. A more unpleasant-sounding place, I could not imagine.) Moreover, I had never before been intimately involved in a wedding. Cousin Seamus had been married years before I was born. My father had never remarried after my mother died, and there had been no one else in my family. When my father attended the occasional wedding of a friend or colleague, I was not invited, for in those days children did not attend such adult gatherings, even if they were immediate family members. So the novelty alone of Jenny's and Eddie's looming nuptials should have piqued my curiosity. But it did not. I'm not sure what I was thinking that week, but I am certain that I had had no mind for the living and their futures.

Perhaps I was grieving over the deaths of don Guillermo and Juan Pablo, or perhaps even the shocking story of the dead *ranchero* and his murdered family, which even on the telling of it by Big Foot remained surreal and remote. But I didn't think so. What I felt was instead far more narcissistic, self-pitying, even. I was grumpy and discontented. I even got as ugly as a tarantula with the newly promoted (to replace Juan Pablo) *caporal* of our *corrida*. The promotion did not work out well. The dastard became increasingly indolent and insolent with each passing day. So I cuffed him in front of his men, pulled my knife, and threatened to exfluncticate him if I so much as glimpsed his filthy dago idleness again. In the wake of this hitherto unknown (to myself, at least) capacity for mindless outbursts of rage, I retained a sufficient sense of self-preservation to want to avoid crossing Grant in a passing moment of indiscretion borne of my current state of mind. So I hid from him as best I could, and kept as formal a barrier between us as possible when I couldn't avoid him. I also did my best to stay well out of Sarah's way, which was easy enough as she was up to her neck in wedding preparations. It was harder for me to avoid talking to Hermann. He knew merely by looking at me that something was wrong—something that I could not bring myself to explain to him. All I knew was, now that I'd given him and Sarah at least the contours of the story, I did not want to talk further with anyone about what had happened down south—or about anything else, for that matter. So I avoided him and Gaff and the few other remaining castaways from C Company who were now amalgamated into D Company, an outfit I knew little of and cared for less.

But I couldn't completely avoid Sarah. Not for very long, anyway.

⁓

At first, I thought I was safe enough. Sarah had joyfully asserted herself as mother *in loco parentis* of the bride, moving heaven and earth—no expense spared—to transform our now-closed brothel into a beautiful venue for dear Jenny's wedding. But early on the Monday before the wedding, Sarah unceremoniously kicked open the door to my little room and shooed poor Adabelita from my bed, who ran, clasping my coverlet about herself. I was left naked as a robin.

Sarah affected not to notice. "You have to find us a brother of the surplice," she intoned. "Got to have one to marry the bride and groom."

"What?" I scratched my head and tried unobtrusively to cover my nakedness, but there was nothing at hand.

"Here." Sarah threw me my pantaloons.

Decent once more, I said, "I understand that we need a preacher. But why ask me to find one? You know better than anyone that I don't hold any truck with autum bawlers and black boys, regardless of whether they're Holy Rollers or mere dog collars. They simply do not signify in my life. For the love of Christ, Sarah, I don't go to church."

She started to remonstrate, so I hastily added, "Much, anyway. And that's beside the point. There's got to be some holy joe attached to one of the volunteer regiments who'd be happy to take a double-eagle for half-an-hour's work and the promise of pleasure with one of our dells."

"You would think so, wouldn't you," Sarah said primly. "But you'd be dead wrong, Billy boy. Eddie's a mackerel-snapper, jes' like you and Hermann. They all are up there in Louisiana. Turns out Jenny is, too. Who'd have known? Every damned one of the preachers attached to the volunteer regiments is a Protestant, and not a one of them will do a mackerel-snapper wedding, even if I held a nice big barking iron to his godforsaken head." Sarah answered my unasked question. "So we've got to find a Romish priest, just like the one you found back in Corpus, over at the Colonel's house."

"But ..."

"Hell's bells, Billy, every brown dago is a mackerel-snapper. You can't get around this country without inhaling a snout full of incense, and Matamoros is lousy with churches. You're a smart boy, you've a pocket full of chink, and you can speak their lingo. There's got to be one of them dago incense-burners willing to do it, even with Jenny's belly the way it is. Just offer them enough rhino. Anyway, it'll do you good to stir out of this damned room for a few hours." She turned away from me, dismissively, and surveyed my room. "Adabelita? Oh there you are, honey. Do be a dear and clean this damned place up, lickety-split."

⌒

I was really cut up rough at Sarah having roused me from my funk, and I was of no mind to accomplish anything useful. As a result, I was at quite a loss about how to fulfill Sarah's directive. The obvious solution was to find a Mexican priest, just as Sarah had suggested. But Juan Pablo was dead, and I didn't know anyone else whom I thought could help me find one. I would have swallowed my pride and gone round to see Hermann for some ideas. But D Company was busy marching about smartly, and Sarah had said to me with a ghost of a smile before I'd decamped that Hermann wasn't going to be around later, because he was going to be supervising his corporals, Gaff chief among them, in drilling a handful of hay-foot straw foots fresh from the tender mercies afforded by Governors Island. I was avoiding Grant, which left me fresh out of people whose brains I could pick for ideas. That is, until I remembered Henry Kinney. I eventually moped my way around to Kinney's digs near the mule pens without any real plan in mind, and within a few minutes we were each looking at the other in pained silence.

I opened my mouth first, but Henry cut me off. "Save it, lad. What's done is done. Don Guillermo was a fool to go south last winter. You and I spoke of this when he went, and he was killed, just as I said he would be. The only real bother in it all is that you were the one who had to end up doing the killing."

I stood there, saying nothing. There was nothing for me to say.

Henry looked at me speculatively. "You didn't tell Bliss the whole of it, did you?"

I shook my head.

"How bad was it?"

I found my voice. "As bad as you can imagine."

"Jack Hays? Sam Walker?"

"A hundred miles south."

"Good, then Jack'll have a clean conscience, when he sees Bliss this afternoon. He rode in this morning with three or four of his boys, looking for the Old Man. Word on what we should be expecting down Monterrey-way, I expect."

"Most like."

"So it was Gray, and his cur, Alston?"

"Just Alston. Gray was busy chasing ghosts." And so I gave him the details of both the Rancho Guadalupe massacre and don Guillermo's death as I knew them, finishing with Pickens's admonition about the Old Man needing all of his eyes and ears.

Kinney sighed. "J. T.'s right, although I'd dearly love to see that bastard Gray dancing at the end of a rope. He's a murderer, no doubt, and a blight on South Texas. He's given me and *mis amigos tejanos* no end of trouble over the years. It sounds as if Alston and Paige are just as bad. Murdering don Guillermo in cold blood as he lay dying was bad enough. But all those people at that rancho. For the love of God. That wasn't war. It was savagery, pure and simple." Kinney shook his head tiredly. "Doña Alandra can never know how her husband died. It would break her heart even more. And she can never know of your involvement."

"Grant knows about what I told Major Bliss. You're the only one who knows the whole story, other than Hermann." I didn't have the energy to explain about Sarah. "I had to tell him."

"On account of that pretty little thing, Serafina, no doubt. Your friend should pay attention to her. She is very special, and she cares very much for him."

I nodded.

"I'm sorry about Calandria, my boy."

I shrugged. There was nothing to say.

"You didn't come just for this, did you? Although I do commend you for finding me."

I shook my head and told him about needing to find a Catholic priest, and my not wanting to use a Mexican priest, if I could help it. I'd decided that Juan Pablo's death was not why I was avoiding that alternative. But I could not articulate why I felt that way.

Henry thought for a moment. "You know, Perfect Bliss told me about a couple of American Catholic priests who've been here in Matamoros for the past few weeks. The big bugs sent 'em down from Washington City to help the Old Man with all of the Catholics in the ranks. Pretty smart move, if you ask me. I've met one of them, Father Rey, and he seems to be a square sort of fellow. I think that you and I should pay him a call and see what he can do."

⌒

Father Anthony Rey sat across from me in the shadow of his tent, which sheltered the two of us from the heavy afternoon sun. Henry Kinney and Grant sat cater-ways to us, across from each other. Kinney had insisted on Grant accompanying us, as he was the officer to whom

I reported. "It's only proper," Kinney had said, adding something about the importance of bluebellies observing the proper chain of command. I acquiesced, which required me to seek out Grant, notwithstanding my prior intent to avoid him until I'd put myself into a better frame of mind.

I found Grant up at the quartermaster-general's operation. His back was to me, and before I'd even made my presence known to him, he turned around and said, "Good. I was just thinking about you, Gogan. You've been making yourself mighty scarce since our audience with Major Bliss." Grant considered me for a moment. "Well, no never mind. You're entitled to a day or two after what happened down there. But that's over now, and you're going to be a very busy quartermaster's sergeant until the army marches to Monterrey. We're receiving a shipment of new uniforms and brogans in the morning. I'll need you to inventory them." I saluted him and said I'd be there at dawn in the morning. He nodded.

"Sir, there is one other matter."

"Yes?"

"Are you available to accompany me to see Father Rey this afternoon? Colonel Kinney will be coming along, and he suggested that you come as well." Grant arched his brow higher than I thought possible. "It's concerning a marriage." Grant's eyebrow arched even higher. "Not mine, sir." A look of considerable relief. "It's Mrs. Langwell's ward, Jenny Billings. You remember her, sir. She was one of C Company's washerwomen back in Corpus. Some bastard ..." Grant winced at my oath, and I kicked myself for forgetting that Grant was likely unique in the army for his dislike of the profane. "Someone, we never found out who, kidnapped her, and Mrs. Langwell rescued her." No need to complicate matters by bringing up Hoggs's misdeeds at this late date. "She's pregnant, sir. And a Louisiana volunteer named Eddie Rocheron—he's been working for Mrs. Langwell over at her house in town—well, he wants to marry her and raise the child as his own back in Louisiana—even though he's not the father."

Grant's equanimity was impressive. "You mentioned that Colonel Kinney is involved?"

"Yes sir."

"Hmm. Anyone else?"

"Not other than Mrs. Langwell, sir. And Hermann … I mean, Sergeant Wurster, sir."

"I figured that your sidekick was not going to be too far away from this tale. Where is he this afternoon?"

"Drilling D Company recruits, sir. Mrs. Langwell's tasked me to find a preacher to marry Eddie and Jenny this coming Saturday. They're due to take the steamboat up to Point Isabel on Sunday."

"I see." Grant's browed wrinkled. "I take it that the banns of marriage haven't been read yet?"

"No sir."

"Might be important, particularly seeing as this Louisiana volunteer's planning on marrying a woman pregnant with another man's child. Or am I missing something?"

"No sir." Grant forbore further comment, so I continued. "They are very much in love, sir, Jenny and Corporal Rocheron. I went to Colonel Kinney for some advice on where to find a preacher, and he told me about the two Catholic priests. He knows one of them, a Father Rey."

"I take it that they are the two priests whom Secretary Marcy sent to the General last month?"

"The same, sir."

"Useful service they're providing."

"Yes, sir."

"You don't have much truck with that sort of thing, do you, Gogan?"

"No sir. But …"

"A lot of your countrymen—excuse me, I mean to say those who come from the country where you were born, you now being a citizen of these United States—set a great store by it."

"Understandably, sir." Then I took a chance. "I think that a Catholic priest or two down here will do a lot for those bluebellies who can't readily go to a proper Army chaplain."

Grant looked at me closely. "Why's that?"

"If you'll excuse the blunt language, sir, but there's more than one Protestant chaplain with the regulars who's convinced that we Catholics are secretly plotting to bring the Inquisition from Spain to Uncle Sam. Not to mention the chaplains attached to the volunteer regiments." Grant said nothing, so I plunged ahead. "And some of your fellow officers, both regulars and volunteers, order their companies and battalions to Sunday services conducted by such bigots, where they are forced to listen to scurrilous anti-Catholic sentiments. It doesn't signify well for morale, sir." I started to say something about it being a cause of desertion, but decided that was a step too far.

To my surprise, Grant voiced what I had been thinking. "And here I was thinking that it was illiberal officers and sergeants too free with the buck and gag who caused the wave of desertion this past April."

"Sir."

"Come along, Gogan, before you get yourself into real trouble. Let's see if we can honey fuggle your Catholic preacher into marrying these two." Grant took off like greased lightning, and I fell in behind, conscious that our appointment with Father Rey was not for another few hours.

Thus it came to pass that the four of us were sitting comfortably (everyone except for me, that is) after introductions had been made and tea enjoyed (at Father Rey's insistence). Father Rey puffed contentedly on his pipe for a moment before looking at me and saying, "Colonel Kinney tells me you are fluent in Spanish, my son. Can you converse in Latin as well?"

"I learned my Spanish from a Mexican *arriero*. So I speak it like a peasant, and not like the proverbial huckleberry above the persimmon, Father. My Latin is that of a schoolboy raised in Ireland."

Rey waved away my reticence and smoothly switched to Latin with an apologetic wave to Kinney and Grant (both of whom smirked to themselves), and I hung on for the ride. "My son, what is being asked of me is difficult, and in view of the needs of the Army in this time of war, I must proceed with great caution. I note that the Church commands her pastors to publish banns of marriage for three successive Sundays, so as to avoid the knowledge of impediments to marriage not becoming known. But I understand that there are some uniquely extenuating circumstances. Please tell me."

I apologized once more for my poor Latin, and then told the story of Jenny Billings and Eddie Rocheron to Father Rey, Jenny a poor washerwoman who found herself with child out of wedlock and Eddie a Louisiana volunteer who wanted to marry her and raise the child as his own, and the need for them to marry before they departed for New Orleans at dawn on this coming Sunday.

"As a good son of the Irish Catholic Church, Sergeant Gogan, you must know that the command to publish banns may be suspended only for very just and grievous reasons. So to that end, I must ask you bluntly, who is the father of the child?" He observed me for a moment. "For example, my son, and please forgive me for asking, but you are not the father, are you?"

"Good Lord, no, Father," I blurted in English. Grant and Kinney both hid smiles.

"Then who is?" Rey asked in Latin.

I replied in Latin. "She was … Jenny was … kidnapped, Father. And raped." I then told him the story of Jenny and her lost beau, Kenny O'Leary, and his descent into madness and despair, before being murdered by Hoggs. Out of the corner of my eye, I could see Grant picking up on the odd word or two—knowing of the story as he did. Kinney seemed to be on another planet, as far as I could tell.

"Do you know who kidnapped young Jenny Billings?"

"Yes, Father. But I cannot say, for I cannot prove it."

"You must tell me, and I shall treat it as a matter of confession, for we are speaking in Latin." Father Rey gestured ever so slightly towards

Grant. I nodded and told him all that I knew, careful to use the most obscure language I could muster.

When I was finished, Father Rey looked at me thoughtfully for a moment, and then made his mind up. "This is a very unusual matter. You have made some allegations that you clearly would not care to have known, particularly in view of your not being able to prove them." Rey stopped for a moment, and my heart lurched. "I thank you for having been honest with me about the matter, though, for it makes a great deal of difference." I tried my best to hide my palpable relief as Father Rey continued. "Miss Billings could easily, through no fault of her own, be cast from polite society as a fallen woman. Yet God has seen fit to deliver her through her beau, Mr. Rocheron. Although you may have been reluctant to seek me out for your own private reasons," he smiled and I flushed, "you did so, and I commend you for it. I believe that I can be of some use here, for marrying Miss Billings and Mr. Rocheron under these circumstances would be the right thing to do, once I have satisfied myself with an interview with the prospective couple."

"Thank you, Father," I said in English.

I smiled at Kinney and Grant, and began to take my leave, when Father Rey said to me, still in Latin, "You should visit me again, my son, for I see a great weight upon your soul. Confessing your sins to God is the right and proper thing to do, even for a man who professes himself to be ungodly."

⌒

"A stag party," Hermann intoned. "That's what we are, a stag party. Unleavened by the fairer sex." I didn't think I'd ever heard Hermann grouse about the lack of feminine companionship before.

I groused in solidarity with him, if only to curry favor after having actively avoided him for a week. "Unceremoniously turfed from our abode is what we are."

"Place of business," Hermann corrected me.

"Former place of business," I replied. Hermann grunted his assent, and I continued. "But I do have that little room in the back, so I view it as at least a *pied à terre*."

Gaff chortled. "You speaking Mexican, again, Gogan? You do kill me with them fancy words of yours." I had grown to appreciate Gaff's obdurate refusal to acknowledge in private either my first name or the fact that I was a sergeant. He had referred to me as "Gogan" since the day we had met those many months ago. In public, though, he was flawless in observing military courtesy, which I also appreciated.

Hermann continued as if he had not heard either of us, "And it is the venue for tomorrow's wedding and the *baile*. Sarah has spoken, and that is all that need be said on the subject, my friend."

I looked at him sharply, but his face remained serenely bland. This was another first, Hermann acquiescing to Sarah's whims and demands without visible struggle. I didn't know what to think of it.

Hermann raised his mug and looked at Gaff, Eddie, and the half-score of Eddie's friends seated about a rickety table in a cantina just off the main square, their red faces animated by a hilarity fueled by *pulque*, each batch stronger and in a dirtier jug than its predecessor. Hermann and I had also stood the table to a vast quantity of American whiskey of the lowest kind, imported at great expense from New Orleans for the pleasure of shoulder straps, punters, and adventurers taking advantage of new vistas opened up by the occupation of Matamoros. All of it, whiskey and *pulque* alike, made Con Donoho's Binghamton whiskey back in Gotham seem by comparison to be the very taste of ambrosia.

"We should take the occasion of this ... stag party ... to wish our good friend and loyal comrade, Eddie Rocheron, a bon voyage as he departs on his journey into matrimony." I thought I detected just a hint of melancholy in Hermann's eyes as he said this. Was he sweet on Jenny? I dismissed the thought. He'd had far too many opportunities to have made such feelings known to her long before Eddie had ever hove onto the scene. What else could it be? I was at a loss. Had Serafina given him the boot as Calandria done to me, and he simply had not told me? Hermann waved his glass about and said, "To Eddie and his new bride." Hermann raised his mug for not the first time since we'd arrived. I'd never seen him in his cups as much as this.

We toasted.

Eddie flushed and rumbled to his feet. "And our new baby."

We toasted again. One of Eddie's friends rose, feet planted apart, body swaying, and befuddled for words. His companions laughed and hooted and drank whiskey. Finally, he focused enough to say his piece. Hermann and I looked at each other. We could hardly understand him. He spoke in that curious Acadian accent that I'd heard every so often since the Louisiana volunteers had descended upon Matamoros, which not even a born Frenchman could have ever properly deciphered, let alone an ex-Irish schoolboy who'd slept through as much of his French classes as he had dared. There were more whoops and hollers and laughter as the man tried to gather himself. Gaff and Eddie were roaring at each other about something. I'd never seen Gaff at the center of things like this before. His eyes were as bright and feverish as any of them, and he seemed to understand whatever it was Eddie and his friends were jibber-jabbering about.

Eddie saw me staring at him and his rumbustious friends in incomprehension, and so he explained to me that his friends, all of whom he'd known since birth, were going to keep the circumstances of Jenny's pregnancy a secret from Eddie's mother on account of her being a devout Catholic and all. I cocked an eyebrow and asked how that would be possible, seeing as Eddie had only been in Matamoros since June, hardly nine weeks since, and Jenny was, to put it charitably, a fully paid-up member of the pudding club. Even a devout Catholic woman, I observed, particularly as she'd given birth herself, was going to know that the pudding took nine months to rise. Eddie laughed and told me that he'd been gone from home for nearly two years, on account of a spot of trouble.

"You didn't kill a man, did you?" I blurted out, thinking of Rouquette's murderous brother. I also realized with a lurch in my belly that I hadn't told Hermann of what Pickens had said. There had been so much else to discuss on those rare occasions when I'd been of such a mind.

"Good Lord, no," Eddie spluttered.

His friends laughed convulsively, as if it were the funniest thing they'd ever heard. One of them shouted derisively. "Tell him, *mon ami*."

"Well, there was a girl." Eddie swayed a little, seemingly baffled about what came next.

"Yes?" the chorus chanted.

"Her daddy was a church deacon."

"You have not a child already, have you?" Hermann was aghast.

Another of Eddie's friends cried amid a fresh gale of mirth, "He was too much of a ham to actually have done the trick with her."

"Ham?" Hermann wrinkled his brow.

"An incompetent who passes himself off as otherwise." I chuckled. "So apparently Eddie liked to let on that he knew what he was doing, his failure to 'do the trick' notwithstanding. You can figure out that last bit yourself."

My observation produced a further paroxysm of laughter, replete with red faces spitting their whiskey and *pulque*. One of Eddie's friends asked innocently, "How much of a ham were you, Rocheron?"

Eddie went red with embarrassment.

"Where were you when Daddy found you?" Eddie's friend persisted.

Eddie looked as if he wished he were at the very apex of an infantry square, awaiting the entire Mexican army's charge rather than here, being grilled by his friends.

"Whose porch was it?"

"Oh, Eddie," Hermann groaned in sympathy.

Eddie's friend explained, "It was a bright and sunny Sunday in spring. Daddy was busy at church, listening to the sermon and saying his 'Our Fathers.' So his girl, a pretty little thing named Mary Domithilde ..."

"She was double-arsed, for the love of God, and she had the face of a horse," someone else observed. "The back end."

"That is not very nice," Hermann remonstrated.

"But true," Eddie acknowledged unhappily.

"The only girl in the parish who would talk to him." Another jibe from the peanut gallery. "And that's because she wanted to find herself in the family way."

"Why would a respectable girl do that?" Hermann asked.

Eddie's tormentor crowed with still more laughter. "The only way she was ever going to leave the house. Her Daddy was a tyrannical fellow, and no dowry was going to be big enough to marry her off respectably. Not to a sane man, anyway."

Eddie was busy looking for a hole into which he could crawl.

"So what happened?"

A chorus responded, but Eddie's voice cut through the blather. "Boys, let me tell my own tale of woe. For I was a mighty curious young lad, as you might expect." There was a mixed chorus of boos and cheers that faded away as Eddie raised his hand, a small grin on his face. "I was, to use Gogan's words, a concupiscent young cove, and our dear Mary Domathilde was buzzing with me something awful. So all I saw was what I wanted to see."

"Have we not all," murmured Hermann, thoughtfully.

"I skipped church one Sunday to go fishing, and paid mightily for the sin. I was cutting through Deacon Levesque's vegetable patch on my way to the creek, and I ran into Mary Domithilde. Never did puzzle out why she wasn't in church that morning. Anyway, we started talking. We never even got to fooling around." Eddie looked shamefaced. "All I did was kiss her for a second, and Deacon Levesque was there, beating me about the head and shoulders, threatening to kill me or to have me hanged for despoiling his only daughter. I ran, hardly even stopping at my house to say good-bye to my mother. I left her alone there, and went down to New Orleans and worked … and sent my money to my mother."

"That is very true," cried one of Eddie's friends. "She lives better now than when you were at home."

"So you cannot go home?" Hermann asked.

"Well …" Eddie paused.

"He can go home now," came a cry from the crowd. "The feared Deacon Levesque has gone to meet his Maker. And good riddance to that old hard shell. Better than that, 'afore he croaked, he married off Mary Domithilde to some bonehead who had all the land, slaves, and means adequate to maintaining her. Of course, why the dummy married her is beyond any of us. Mary Domithilde's dowry couldn't have meant that much to him. But marry her he did, and now he's one gone coon. He's got a child as well, and now Mary Domithilde has a triple arse, and he ain't said a word about it. So Eddie's safe to come home."

"Does your mother know you are coming?" Hermann asked dubiously. "As you are to be a father, and she to be a grandmother, so soon?"

Eddie nodded happily, and everyone went back to drinking. I drifted to the edge of the group to be alone with my thoughts.

"You have been very distant, my friend." Hermann was at my elbow, appraising me tolerantly. "Do you want to talk about it all some more? About don Guillermo? Or Calandria?"

"No." I couldn't understand what held me back from unburdening myself after my initial telling of the story, and I couldn't articulate the why of it to Hermann—or to myself, for that matter. I softened my tone at the look in Hermann's drunken eyes. "I'm sorry. I can't."

Hermann nodded and changed the subject. "Hoggs is now a deserter."

I looked at Hermann sharply. "Why?"

"No one knows. But his stripes are gone, and they will flog and brand him if he is caught. Perhaps even hang him." Hermann smiled humorlessly.

Hoggs jerked to Jesus at the end of a rope? I grinned with a sudden frisson of what Cicero called *malevolentia* and what Hermann had explained to me at some point the Germans call *Schadenfreude*.

It was as if Hermann had read my mind, for he said, "I, too, want to see him hang. But we have other matters to concern us. Hoggs is still dangerous, for this is a lawless city, and easy to hide in."

"You think he's with Carambole?"

"That is what the grapevine says," Hermann replied. "I do not know, nor is it very important. I will not be happy until Hoggs can no longer get at our little Jenny."

"What's to worry? Big Foot's got the watch on her tonight with a couple of his scallywags. Tomorrow night she and Eddie will be married, and by dawn they'll be onboard *Neva*, making their way safe and sound to Point Isabel and thence to New Orleans."

"What if he is in Point Isabel?" Hermann asked. "Eddie and Jenny will have to pass through there when they leave *Neva* and board their ship to New Orleans."

I pointed to Eddie's friends, who surrounded Eddie and Gaff. They were singing a song in that tongue of theirs that I could not understand. It must have been bawdy, for they were all making suggestive gestures, and I thought I heard one or two French words I'd learned in school that described a lady's unmentionables.

"Carambole hasn't been heard from, either," I said with more hope than knowledge. "I'll bet *guerrilleros* croaked them while they were looking for that treasure up at the battlefields. You've heard the stories about entire groups having gone missing while they've been up there."

"They are too smart for that to happen ... and too mean. They are around somewhere. I can feel it here." Hermann touched his chest.

"Did you know that Rouquette has a brother?"

Hermann stared at me, astounded, as I finally recounted the story that Pickens had told me.

⌒

The slowly setting sun momentarily framed Father Rey in a halo as he faced the altar and lifted his arms, palms open to God, celebrating mass before tying the knot between Jenny and Eddie. In that glorious, sun-filled moment, I could have believed in the Almighty, himself, had I been of a mind to do so. In the next moment, the sun descended, and the halo was gone, and so too was the joyously bright glint reflecting from the gold and silver cross that Father Rey had brought with

him to crown the temporary altar set up along one side of the courtyard of our casa, an altar every bit as beautiful as the one gracing the
courtyard in front of Henry Kinney's house back up in Corpus Christi
all those months ago.

Notwithstanding my momentary epiphany having been extin-
guished by the setting sun, I was very glad that we had shut down our
brothel earlier in the week, and scrubbed the casa clean of anything
that could have even begun to hint at venery. Sarah, Hermann, and
I would have sooner faced our Makers at the end of a rope than to
have subjected Father Rey to any such indignity. So thorough had
we been that, although there were a score of Sarah's erstwhile—and
newly wealthy—mabs scattered throughout the crowd witnessing the
nuptials, they were as respectable-looking as any gaggle of *mujeres
decentes* from the finest families to be found in Matamoros, decked out
as they were in their brand-new gowns and colorful rebozos, which
Sarah had given them.

The sun retreated inexorably, and Father Rey was now shrouded
deep in shadow as he intoned in Latin:

> *You both appear here before me as the servants of
> the Christian church, and before these witnesses, to
> promise matrimonial love and fidelity to one another,
> and to have your union hallowed by the blessing of the
> church.*
>
> ...
>
> *In entering the condition of matrimony ye enter upon
> an inner union, and a partnership which embraces
> every condition of your lives, and indeed a contract
> which should be incapable of dissolution throughout
> the whole duration of your lives.*

Jenny (and likely everyone else standing in the courtyard behind her,
other than me) couldn't comprehend a word Father Rey said, but as

a woman about to be wed, she understood the import of his grave and portentous utterings. Such knowledge, and the comfort that these words gave her, rendered her as she knelt before him as radiant in her gravid state as any virginal bride from the best of families, dressed simply in a gown of dark blue silk that camouflaged her condition admirably.

Hermann had walked down the aisle with Jenny, resplendent in his new first sergeant's uniform (his promotion coming in the wake of Hoggs having seemingly taken French leave—which had left Grant and others scratching their heads), and he was as pleased to be giving Jenny away to Eddie as any father could have been to give his own daughter away. Kneeling beside Jenny, with as wide a smile on his face as was humanly possible, Eddie was every bit as resplendent as Hermann, his uniform of his lately disbanded regiment of Louisiana volunteers cleaner than it had ever been before. Only the good Lord and Sarah Langwell knew how it had come to be so clean, for Eddie had been wearing it as we stumbled to our beds at 5:00 o'clock that morning, considerably worse for the wear.

Father Rey finished his Latin droning:

> All this ye now promise before God, and this promise
> is an irrevocable one, which should bind you till death
> do you part.

And now it was to be done, for Father Rey asked in English, "Wherefore I ask you in the name of the Lord: Do ye appear here of your own free will, and unconstrained, to repeat before me, in the presence of these witnesses, the declaration of your matrimonial contract, and to obtain the blessing of the church for the same?"

Two voices rang out as one, "I do."

The rings were blessed before the altar, and Father Rey turned back to face the couple and the congregation, intoning in English, "And now I ask thee, Edouard Modeste Rocheron ..." I wished in that instant to wisecrack about Eddie's modesty. "Dost thou take Jenny

402

Anne Billings here present to be thy Christian wedded wife, before the Lord God and his holy church?"

"I do."

Father Rey turned to Jenny. "In the same way I ask thee, Jenny Anne Billings, dost thou take Edouard Modeste Rocheron here present to be thy Christian wedded husband, before the Lord God and his holy church?"

"I do."

The service meandered on for a bit after that, and I could hear the crowd just beginning to become restive. Not a word was uttered. But there was a rustling of wool and cotton and silk as many began to fidget just a little, whether they were Sarah's mabs, D Company's blue-bellies (at least, all those who could be liberated wholesale from their evening duties at camp), or Devil Jack Hays, Big Foot, and a half-dozen other stalwarts from the First Texas Mounted Riflemen. (The latter were all as pleased as Punch to have received our invitation, for it allowed them to flee Camp Maggot and its olfactory offenses. A few of the Rangers were sojourning at Camp Maggot, while Devil Jack consulted with the Old Man and Perfect Bliss about the coming assault on Monterrey.)

There was but one regular army shoulder strap in attendance at the nuptials, and that was Grant, who stood with Henry Kinney. Whether Grant's presence was driven by a sense of duty to protect Father Rey from what might befall him in this former knocking shop, or simply out of polite curiosity, I could not say. But after Father Rey announced in English,

> As the servant of God, I ratify the marriage concluded
> between you, and bless you in the name of the Father,
> the Son and the Holy Ghost ...,

intoned just a bit more prayer, bid the newly-married couple to turn to face the crowd, and proclaimed, "May I present to you Corporal and Mrs. Edouard Rocheron," Grant clapped as loudly as anyone, and perhaps had a moist eye in addition to the broad grin only partially hidden by his huge, reddish-brown beard.

⌒

Sarah threw an A-1, copper-bottomed shindig to honor Jenny's and Eddie's wedding. It was most manifestly not a fandango, Sarah had sniffed a few days ago, when I questioned her about some arrangement or another and used the term. Fandangos were common, she snapped. Any old cove off the street could come—if he had two bits to his name. This reception was a *baile*. A *baile* for Jenny. Invitation only. No riffraff, and certainly no scum. And limits on the booze for those yahoos I'd insisted on inviting—Big Foot, Colonel Hays, and their boys (thank God, Mustang Gray and his Matamoros street-sweepings were elsewhere, or I would have been hard-pressed not to invite at least a few of them, if only for appearances' sake)—and the D Company bluebellies whom First Sergeant Wurster had insisted on inviting.

Thus, in keeping with Sarah's lofty ambitions for the event, there was nary a drop of *pulque* to be found, merely a well-diluted brandy punch that one of Sarah's erstwhile mabs, a bleak and fetching lass reputedly from a good family fallen on hard times, had told her was proper for the occasion. I don't think Sarah's plan for limiting the booze like that had worked very well, for by the time that we'd cleared away the altar and the musicians had set up near where the altar had once been, there was more than one D Company bluebelly with a red face and softly maddened hilarity that was suppressed only by First Sergeant Wurster's stern warning of the prospect of a bucking and gagging for any D Company bluebelly who even so much as thought of getting out of line during either the nuptials or the *baile*. The Company moreover had strict instructions to return to camp very early, under the command of a sergeant whose name I did not know (and steadfastly refused to learn, for D Company was not my company, and C Company as I knew it was gone). Corporal Gaff was to remain behind, afterwards, to help Hermann and Eddie's friends escort Jenny and Eddie to *Neva* for their trip home to a new life.

Notwithstanding the relative shortage of Mr. Grog, the tables inside veritably groaned with food for all concerned, and while the musicians set up for the dancing, the guests tucked themselves in for a fine feed. I was busy running hither and yon on any of two-score or more tasks that Sarah, who was conducting the proceedings as if she were a female field-marshal as formidable as that Anglo-Irish Duke of Wellington at Waterloo, had assigned me, when Big Foot accosted me with Devil Jack Hays in tow.

Hays said to me in a low tone, "I want to thank you for that unpleasant favor you did Gray and that straw boss of his, Damien Alston. In a better world, they deserve to hang, as does Jedediah Paige, for what they did down at Rancho Guadalupe. But you saw, as do I, that we are at war with the dago, and we will need the likes of Mustang Gray and his Matamoros Company, if we are to take Monterrey. There will come a time for a reckoning with the Mustang over this and his other misdeeds. But now is not that time. So I thank you for it, as painful as it has been for you."

With that, Hays was gone, and Big Foot looked unhappily at me. "I doubt we'll see each other 'afore we get to Monterrey. We ride in an hour."

"That why no drinking?" I asked.

"Jack ain't got no use for the hotheaded. Anyways, I ain't too crazy about headin' south with a case of the jimjams. That bastard Canales is in the neighborhood, harrying us and generally runnin' around like a chicken with its head cut off. He ain't goin' to take our whole regiment on. But he'd be tickled to death if he were to catch Devil Jack riding with just a small group."

"Be safe."

"You, too. We'll hoist a proper whiskey together in Monterrey. You name the tavern or *pulqueria*."

We shook hands and hugged, and Big Foot disappeared in pursuit of his boss.

Father Rey and Lieutenant Grant must have been hovering, for no sooner had Big Foot departed, than first Rey and then Grant were grasping my hand, Grant with an ironic twinkle in his eye and word-less, and Rey with a look that met me straight in the eye.

Rey said, "Find me on the march south, my son. There will be plenty of occasions for us to talk then, for Major Bliss has asked me to come along." He looked at me gravely. "I am very serious, my son. Find me. I fear that we have much to talk about, before you can unburden your soul."

I flashed a glance at Grant, and his look was entirely more sober than before.

I involuntarily promised Father Rey, "I shall, Father. I shall."

When the music started, I put the lot of them from my mind, along with any thoughts of war yet to come. A man with a battered trumpet was leading the band. Rumor had it that her had recently made it to Matamoros from Tampico, having absquatulated on account of some mix-up or another for which he was to have been jerked to Jesus. He was quite the novelty to the *méxicanos*, for brass musical instruments of any kind had hitherto been unknown in the Rio Grande Valley, and he was thus a welcome addition to the little band's flageolets, violins, and guitars. The trumpet-player was no match for the colored fellow up at Magee's saloon, or any other colored trumpet player I'd ever heard in the Big Onion (it being a simple fact of life that no white man in town, whether native, Irish or otherwise, had even a soupçon of the *teas* of even the most mediocre Negro). But he worked hard to infuse a bit of Mexican *teas* into the proceedings, and there was soon a lively succession of reels, quadrilles, and waltzes to which everyone was dancing.

During one of the more temperate waltzes, Hermann and Sarah danced gracefully by, each with eyes that self-consciously did not stray from the other's. I thought nothing of it, for Adabelita had found me, and I was unwillingly joined to the crowd, Adabelita in hand and arm, milling and swirling about the well in the center of our courtyard. When we were done, Adabelita leaned comfortably on my arm as I drank off a brandy punch. One of Sarah's erstwhile mabs traipsed up and whispered into Adabelita's ear. They both giggled, and the girl thrust something into Adabelita's hand with a fresh gale of laughter and retreated posthaste. Adabelita looked at the objects and smiled. I asked her what they were, and she told me that they *cascerrones*, which were perforated, paper eggshells filled with gilt and glitter and confetti, and then sealed with a bit of wax. She said that it was customary for a man who was sweet on a girl to break a *casceron* over her head to show his intentions. I made to snatch one of the *cascerrones* from her, but she held them out of my way, giggling. Then she lisped into my ear that, at a carnival—and Jenny's *baile* was such a carnival—a señorita could break a *casceron* over her beau's head, and he was bound to break one over her head. She stuffed one of the eggs into my hand and then reached up on the tips of her toes and broke the second egg on my forehead, just above my nose. Bits of colored paper flitted down my face. Adabelita proffered her face to me, and I gently broke my egg over her mantilla—I had bought it for her to wear to the wedding—and she laughed more than I'd ever seen her laugh before.

And then the *baile* was over, and it was time for Eddie and Jenny to go, for *Neva* sailed for Point Isabel in less than an hour. Sarah and Jenny embraced, their eyes suddenly wet with tears. I looked away, and stuffed my repeating pistol into my belt, and I made to follow Hermann and Gaff. They were joining Eddie's friends, who were the couple's escort to New Orleans and a new life, to see the group safely to *Neva*. Jenny and Eddie were safe here, and they would be safe aboard *Neva* once her gangplank were raised. It was during the short journey to the quay when we all expected Hoggs to make his move—if, indeed, he actually did.

Hermann said, "Stay here with Adabelita and Sarah. We won't be long. Somebody should stay behind to mind Luis and his men. They should be enough to hold the fort." With that, Hermann shrugged. I looked at Sarah, and she nodded.

Jenny embraced me. I felt the crush of her belly and breasts against me and forgot my moment of disquiet. "Godspeed, Billy Gogan, for you are a fine man." I kissed Jenny's forehead to hide my own tears, which quickened of their own volition. I shook Eddie's hand, and we embraced, and then the group was gone through the main door, which I bolted behind me.

"Where's Luis?" I asked Sarah and Jenny, as we settled in the kitchen to wait. They both shrugged, and Sarah said, "He's out posting our guards at the front gate, and he'll be back, by and by."

Adabelita poured me a freshly-brewed cup of joe, and I squeezed her hand in thanks. We then sat to wait for Hermann and Gaff to return.

For an hour, Sarah and I sat at the kitchen table, our coffee long drunk and our mescal untouched, while we stared at each other wordlessly. I felt for all the world like a cat on hot bricks, waiting for Hermann and Gaff to return with news that Jenny and Eddie and their Louisiana escort were safely tucked in on *Neva*, and she was chugging her way downriver to Point Isabel. Sarah must have felt the same, for she finally snapped and liverishly told me to "do something useful," at which point I slipped out the back door, and left her sitting in the kitchen with my Colt Paterson's repeating pistol in her lap and Adabelita sitting next to her, staring at me with those large, dark eyes of hers as I left.

I instantly regretted being outside with only my Arkansas tooth-pick to defend myself. It was as black as the Earl of Hell's weskit, the moon having long since yielded to a suffocating blanket of clouds hanging low in the sky, which foretold a hot and steamy start to the morrow without much promise of any rain to break humidity's hold. There was not a soul about, and Sarah and Adabelita, safe behind their barred doors, felt as far away as if I'd been miraculously transported to the Antipodes. The vagaries of the alleys and street were such that I had to wend my way around an adjacent casa before I could make my way to the front gate, which was barred and guarded by a Mexican man hired by Luis some weeks before. I did not call out and ask for admittance, because I was curious about the other side of the block.

Ten minutes later, I was once more at the back door. I knocked, but there was no response. That was odd, I thought, for both Sarah and Adabelita had said they would remain in the kitchen by the door until I returned. I swore silently and once more made my way around through the alleys to the front door's entrance to the courtyard. My heart stopped when I rounded the corner. The damn door was swung open, and a figure was peering inside the courtyard. It was not the Mexican man. The figure had something in his hand, but I could not tell what. Beyond him in the courtyard were several more figures, their faces unrecognizable in the flicker of a couple lanterns they were holding over the well at the courtyard's center as they pushed together, straining to look down inside.

A voice called out in English from further down the street, "He ain't here."

The figure at the door swore.

I pressed myself against the wall. Moonlight had once more worked through the clouds and dissolved the inky blackness into pale shadows. I stood there, debating whether to cut and run to the quay. Surely Hermann and Gaff must be making their way back from *Neva* by now. I hoped they were, anyway. Looking for Big Foot was out of the question. The Rangers' camp was on the far bank of the river. Then I remembered that the officer of the day and the guard were hardly two or three streets away at the Halls of Justice on the Plaza de Hidalgo, across the way from the unfinished cathedral and next to the city calaboose. Five minutes to get there. How long to get back with the officer of the day and the guard? Worse, would the guard even respond at the word of a mere bluebelly?

The voice from down the street called out again, "Still ain't found him."

A voice from inside the compound called out, "We know you're out there, Gogan. We'll find you. Show yourself, and save us the trouble of finding you hiding in a gutter and killing you there. We have the cows, Gogan. We'll kill them both, if you don't show yourself."

I should have known the voice, but I couldn't quite place it.

Another voice laughed mockingly, "I got the Western and I got your Colt's repeater, Gogan." It was Hoggs, cackling. "I'm gonna blow her brains out with it. You worthless turd."

What the hell was he doing here? Then I realized that the other voice was Rouquette. So they were together. But why were they here? Jenny was gone. What does Hoggs care about us now, other than mere, opportunistic murder? This invasion was anything but opportunistic. There were perhaps six or eight bully backs with them, maybe more. But why?

"I'll kill the brown bitch, Gogan. Right after I knock the rest of her filthy teeth out." Carambole was not cackling. He was deadly serious. I heard Adabelita squeal in pain and terror. It ended abruptly, and I prayed that she had not just been killed.

I jerked my knife from its scabbard between my shoulder blades and crept closer to the figure peering through the door. I had progressed only a few steps before I felt someone rushing past me. I slammed myself against the coarse stucco of the wall, and I felt the wind of the man from down the street who had called out earlier, as he rushed by. I'd completely forgotten about him. He pushed roughly past the man at the door, saying, "Keep your eyes peeled, *panocha*, and quit yer gawping at the proceedings." He gestured towards the open gate. "It ain't gonna make the treasure appear any quicker."

Treasure? What treasure?

"That little prick, Gogan, is around somewhere. Don't let him sneak up on you."

I did just that, for the man at the door continued to crane his neck around, transfixed by the goings-on inside the compound. In two steps, I was on him, my hand over his mouth and my toothpick under his ribs, twisting deep inside him. He sagged into my arms. I grabbed what had been in his hand before it fell to the ground. A barking iron, a great big dragoon's flintlock. I was in business. It hardly occurred to me just then that I had killed a man in cold blood.

"Go ... gan." Hoggs elongated my name mockingly.

"The guard's on its way, Hoggs," I shouted back. "You're trapped. There's no money for you here. We put it all in a bank in New Orleans. So you are on a fool's errand, Hoggs, and you'll jerk to Jesus for naught."

"Then the cows are dead." Carambole's voice was curiously devoid of emotion.

Sarah cried out. "Don't come in. They'll kill …" She finished with a suppressed scream suffused with pain.

I called out. "Hoggs, you've missed her. She's safe and on her way home. You'll never find her now."

There was silence.

"You'll never get Jenny, Hoggs."

"I don't give a fuck about her or the whelp in her belly. Zuckes like her are nothing but dog's meat. I'll be getting me a whole passel of fresh cherries with the chink coming our way."

Carambole hissed. "Shut pan, Abélard."

Abélard … Rouquette's brother. The one who murdered the sheriff. Hoggs! I should have known that's why they kept finding each other like a pair of bad pennies. I was almost laughing as I called out, "Hey Hoggs. Your name really Abélard? That's a mighty pretty name for a sodomite."

Adabelita screamed and I rushed in without thought, my great dragoon's pistol pointing at where I thought the voices were. As I rounded through the entrance, I stopped in my tracks and stared helplessly. Carambole was holding a huge Arkansas toothpick of his own to Adabelita's throat, blood welling from the flesh where the point pressed. Carambole had roughly plastered his hand over Adabelita's mouth, and she was having difficulty breathing through her damaged nose. Her chest was heaving with the effort, and her eyes were bulging with terror.

"Thought that might get you in here." Carambole chuckled mirthlessly.

I looked around. There were two men busy hauling something from the well. Behind them, near the entrance to the house, stood

Hoggs, his hand and arm wrapped around Sarah's neck and mouth. He held what I thought to be my Colt's repeating pistol in his hand, pointing it vaguely in my direction. I wondered for an instant why he didn't simply shoot me. Too noisy, I realized, and they didn't want to raise an alarm when they didn't yet have whatever it was they were looking for. To the side stood Luis, our major-domo, and I remembered that he hadn't been around much until earlier in the day, when he had made much of setting a guard for Jenny's *baile*. I swore to myself over my foolishness at not realizing that matters were afoot, and felt slightly ill at the realization that I had just gutted Luis's man guarding the gate. Luis had always made nice with Sarah, bowing, scraping, and acceding to her every wish and whim. She had paid him well for his pains, and this was what he was serving back. The betraying bastard. Next to the major-domo stood Damien Alston and Jedediah Paige. Now there was a surprise—until I remembered Pickens saying something about Alston having met Carambole in Corpus Christi last winter. I wondered idly where Gray and the rest of his Matamoros Company were.

"How do, Gogan?" Alston grinned wolfishly. "Thanks for the other day, by the way. I appreciate your looking out for my neck. I ain't too keen on getting it stretched." He considered me briefly, his grin still in place. "Although I'd 'a' taken exception to you and the Western not invitin' us to that shindig earlier today—if it weren't for the fact that we … the Mustang and the rest of us … are a hundred miles from here. So I quite understand your oversight."

I was wordless. And I felt vaguely foolish, standing in the court-yard, my bloodied knife in one hand and dragoon's pistol in the other.

The two men at the well grunted, and a big chest crested over the well's coaming. Carambole moved closer to the well, dragging Adabelita with him. As he did, she tried to bite his hand, which remained tightly across her mouth. He retaliated by viciously twisting her head. The major-domo, Alston, and Paige all inched closer as well, seemingly impelled by a lust for whatever might be inside. Hoggs loosened his grip on Sarah as he stared at the chest. She struggled with him, but she didn't break free. Hoggs tightened his grip on her, hissing into her ear. I stood there, bewildered.

"Open it," Alston said harshly. "Open the fucking thing."

The chest fell heavily to the ground. The two men, whom I now recognized as members of Gray's company of Matamoros street-sweepings, pried the chest open with a crowbar that I recognized as being Eddie's. The hinged clasp bent under the crowbar's assault, and then flew from the chest as if spring-loaded. The chest's lid crashed open, tearing a leather hinge away. One of the men close by swore under his breath.

"What is it?" Alston's face tautened in the curious blend of pale moonlight and the weak and flickering light from Paige's lantern. "What?"

"It's empty. The fucking thing is empty."

The major-domo began to laugh and shake his head sadly. His laugh was cut short as Paige drew his Paterson and shot the man dead.

"You idiot," hissed Carambole. "You'll rouse every manjack between here and the officer of the guard's post."

I taunted Carambole. "They're already on their way."

"Shut pan, or she's croaked." Carambole renewed the pressure from his knife to Adabelita's throat, and her eyes once more bulged with terror. I felt a pang of shame that my bravado had cost her and not me.

Hoggs whispered viciously to Sarah, "Where is it? The chink?"

Sarah said nothing, and shot me a questioning look.

I replied sarcastically, "I told you. We've sent it all to a bank in New Orleans. All of our profits from the bordello. You're too late, Hoggs."

"I'm not interested in your pussy chink, Gogan." Hoggs jammed my Paterson under Sarah's chin and hissed in her ear, "Where's the damned treasure?"

Again, Sarah said nothing. I simply stared in shock that anyone would think that there was a treasure at the bottom of the casa's well.

"You mean you had no idea it was there?" Hoggs's voice betrayed utter disbelief.

"We didn't know, Abélard." I chuckled. "Anyway, it looks like you either had bad gouge from him," I jerked my thumb at Luis, the blood welling from his chest turning the stones black in the moonlight, "Or, worse, someone spiced it from right under your nose. Oh," I added helpfully, "it really is time to go, there, me bucko.

Hoggs glared, first at me and then at Sarah. He twisted her arm in frustration. She groaned softly.

"Gogan's right, Damien. Let's dust it." Paige's tone to Alston. "There ain't no chink, so there ain't nothing for us."

Alston didn't respond. He instead jerked his head towards Carambole. "Let the bitch go. And Gogan. Her, too." He jerked his head towards Sarah. "No more killing tonight."

"They'll peach on us."

"Not him," Alston smiled thinly, referring to me. "If he was going to have us hang, he'd have done it already. So he can't go splificatin' now. Raise too many questions. Anyways, iff'n you scrag 'em, the gunplay'd only raise a real alarm." Alston gestured to Paige and said, "Bad enough he shot the dago. So let them go."

Hoggs interjected. "I don't fucking care. Croake both the bitches. Then we croake Gogan. Wearing them stripes. Insolent fuck."

"You will not kill Gogan." Alston's words were deliberate and spaced. He gestured at Hoggs. "Jedediah, put a gun on the bastard." Paige smiled and raised his repeater.

"Hoggs, let her go." It was Hermann. Where he had come from, only the good Lord knew. It didn't matter, though, for Hermann was pressing a bayonet against the small of Hoggs's back.

Sarah was instantly free when Hoggs instinctively raised his hands and involuntarily dropped my repeater to the ground, whereupon it discharged. Where the bullet went, I hadn't a clue. Sarah picked the pistol up and held it to Hoggs's temple. Hoggs quivered. The yellow cur. As I stared, transfixed at this turn of events, I caught a blur of motion in my periphery. Carambole was dragging Adabelita towards the front door.

"No." Involuntarily impelled past my lips.

"Or what?" Carambole hissed.

"Give me the girl, and you live."

Carambole snorted derisively.

Alston chimed in. "We all leave now, Rouquette. For the love of Christ."

Carambole edged towards the door. I beat him to it. "Let her go and you walk. Even Hoggs."

Carambole rejected the offer with a derisive snort. As he did, I noted that Alston, Paige, and their two men had quietly decamped into the house.

I ignored Carambole's stubbornness, and said to Hoggs in as gentle a voice as I could, "Abélard, come over here."

Hoggs walked away from Sarah and my repeating pistol as if in a trance, his eyes fixated on his brother's. Carambole edged closer to the door, Adabelita still in his grasp.

I stepped away from the door. "Let her loose, and you can both go. You and Abélard. Quickly, before the guard comes. We can settle accounts later. Like gentlemen."

Hoggs reached Carambole's side, and Carambole started to release Adabelita. Then he stiffened his grip at the sudden commotion behind me. I turned instinctively. It was Gaff and the officer of the guard, a lieutenant I didn't know. Boiling through the open door behind them were a dozen bluebellies, bayonets fixed to their muskets. They jerked to a precipitate halt behind their lieutenant and Gaff, who were gawking at the spectacle of Carambole holding Adabelita in front of him, his knife once again pressed to her throat.

"Dear God," the lieutenant murmured.

Adabelita stamped hard on Carambole's foot. He released her involuntarily. She bent over, and a small knife appeared in her hand. Carambole grasped for it with his left hand, keeping his knife hand clear. Adabelita drove her knife through his grasping hand, and Carambole screamed as she pulled the knife free. She backed away from Carambole's clutches only a step or two before Hoggs pushed her roughly back into Carambole's grasp. With an odd and slight smile, Carambole sliced his huge knife across Adabelita's throat. Arterial blood spewed from the gaping wound. I stared for an instant at Carambole raising his knife, which glistened dark and wet in the moonlight, high above his head, as if in triumph. Adabelita fell to the ground like a rag doll, and Carambole and Hoggs both turned to run to the back door, despite Hermann and Sarah blocking their way.

I looked at Adabelita crumpled on the ground, her life's blood staining the stones black in the moonlight. Something snapped inside of me, and I lunged at Carambole, dropping my barking iron as I went. Carambole and I grappled briefly like two wrestlers looking for a fall. I found myself holding the wrist of his knife hand away from me. His left hand hung uselessly at his side as I drove my Arkansas tooth-pick deep into his belly and up into his vital organs. I twisted the knife and rammed it home once more, and only then withdrew it. To my horror, Carambole's bowels followed, hooked on the pommel of the knife. I jumped back to free my knife, but Carambole's bowels kept following me, unraveling until I flicked them clear of the knife's pommel. By that time, Carambole was on the ground, dead, smoth-ering poor Adabelita, and Hoggs was firmly in the grasp of a pair of bluebellies, his hands secured roughly behind him. I stood there, wet with Carambole's blood and bowels, as Sarah and Hermann pulled Carambole's body from Adabelita. Sarah instantly cradled the poor, dead girl to her bosom, mindless of the gore that blackened her gray silk gown. I stared at the spreading stain and the gaping, rictus grin that Rouquette had slashed across Adabelita's throat, and I could not bring myself to stoop to take her from Sarah's arms.

As Hoggs was led away past me, he leaned over and hissed so that only I could hear, "You're a fucking dead man, Gogan. A fucking dead man. That was my brother you murdered."

I looked at Hoggs and heard the words, "I didn't murder the bas-tard. I executed him."

~

# PART THREE

# A Grand Fandango

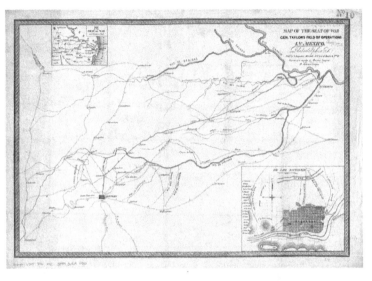

*Map of the Seat of War, General Taylor's Field of Operations.*

# CHAPTER 19

# Go It, My Boys

THE ARMY WASTED NO TIME in bringing Hoggs to trial in a hot stuffy room in the upper floor of the calaboose. All the better for him to be hustled down the back stairs to the scaffold erected in the middle of the yard formed by the former Halls of Justice once the five members of the court-martial, none of whom I knew, had finished deliberating and had sentenced him to be scragged. When the trial first got under-way, I hadn't recognized Hoggs's defense counsel. But I admired the way he fought a valiant rearguard action to save his client, particularly when the prosecutor, who was a bumbling fool, had after two or three tries where objections were lodged as to the form of the questions and other sundry legal niceties elicited testimony from Grant that Hoggs had shot poor Kenny in the back as Kenny dashed for the Rio Grande in a fit of madness on that terrible night in April. On cross examina-tion, Hoggs's defense counsel asked Grant what Old Zach's standing orders had been that night.

"Shoot any deserters the minute they get to the water's edge, sir."

Every member of the court-martial nodded appreciatively. They were, after all, West Point regulars to a man, so Grant later told me. Hoggs expressed his satisfaction with his counsel with an expression of righteous justification. I, on the other hand, cringed inwardly as I waited for the defense counsel to ask Grant about my having hesitated to shoot Kenny. I couldn't imagine Hoggs not having said something to him about it.

But Hoggs's defense counsel didn't ask, and it was only then that I realized who he was: Lieutenant Longstreet, one of Grant's closest friends in the Army of Invasion. Grant was the squarest cove I knew—aside from Hermann, that is. So I asked myself whether Grant asked Longstreet to avoid the subject for my sake, or whether Longstreet hadn't asked about it, simply because it was of absolutely no interest to anyone but me.

The moment passed, and Grant left the stand. He was followed in rapid succession by Hermann, Gaff, and the lieutenant who had led the guard to the house. All of them testified about the attack on our casa, and none of them mentioned Carambole. None of their testimony boded well for Hoggs's neck.

I testified next, confirming what the others said about that night. Again I was spared embarrassment. Neither Longstreet nor the bumbling prosecutor asked me a single question about Carambole. It was as if he hadn't been there that night, or if he had been there, it was as if I hadn't croaked the son of a bitch.

Equally interesting was the absence of Alston and Paige and their henchmen from the testimony. Neither Longstreet nor the prosecutor asked me or any of the other witnesses about them. I figured that they weren't needed to convict Hoggs of desertion, and they certainly weren't going to exculpate him of that crime. It was odd, though, because if you'd not been at our casa that night, and you'd listened only to the testimony at Hoggs's trial, you'd have concluded that Hoggs had mounted the invasion all by his lonesome.

Sarah took the stand next, and the cheeks of every man in the courtroom blanched at her chilling testimony about rescuing Jenny from Hoggs's assault at Carambole's tent brothel. Sarah then testified about the night at the casa. Hoggs had stormed into the kitchen, demanding at knifepoint, "Where's the treasure?" Sarah fluttered her pretty little Mexican fan over her décolletage as she testified that she knew nothing of any treasure—and told Hoggs just that. I wondered if they heard a word she'd said.

The court-martial panel lost their appreciative smiles when Sarah testified that Hoggs had backhand slapped her across the face for "lying" to him, and then hit her several more times, each time demanding that she tell him where the treasure was hidden. Hoggs had then produced the majordomo out of some shadow or another and cuffed him viciously. Luis had quailed under the blows, whining that, if there were a treasure chest, it was likely hidden in the well, because that was where all wealthy Mexicans hid their treasures. Hoggs cuffed him again, demanding to know what was in the chest. The majordomo had grinned in supplication, but said nothing. Hoggs jammed a small knife to Luis's throat, and he promptly gave Hoggs the office. The treasure was supposedly Arista's payroll. The majordomo's master had apparently hidden it when the Mexican army abandoned Matamoros after they lost at Resaca de la Palma. A cool quarter of a million *escudos* in gold and silver. A fucking king's ransom. Sarah played the crowd when she testified that the box was empty, and everybody in the courtroom tittered appreciatively. Neither lawyer asked her the obvious question of where she thought the missing treasure might be.

A man's neck for an empty chest. There was little to be said after that, and Sarah was excused. Hoggs didn't testify in his own defense, because as Grant explained to me, a man cannot be compelled to testify against himself, which was a useful right to have when that testimony would only heighten the odds that he'd be scragged.

During his closing argument, Longstreet put the best face he could on Hoggs's case, pointing to Hoggs's years of loyal service and his participation (if one could call it that) in C Company's magnificent charge at Resaca de la Palma. Longstreet had questioned Grant at some length about the charge, highlighting Grant's leadership and bravery—much to Grant's discomfiture and Longstreet's evident pleasure. The prosecutor had long recovered from his earlier fumble, and he talked to the court of two matters only: Hoggs's desertion, which by itself justified hanging, and his beastly kidnapping and ravishing of Jenny Billings. The court took fifteen minutes to convict and sentence Hoggs to be branded with a "D" for desertion, drummed out of the army, and then jerked to Jesus for desertion—there was not a single mention of his other crimes.

The result cheered me to no end. Hoggs was evil, and he had done evil things. The world would be better off with his soul safely shuffled off this mortal coil—however unwillingly it went. Hermann disapproved of my exuberance, cautioning me that it is no small thing to see a man swing, even a man as evil as Hoggs. I remonstrated with him, pointing out that he, Hermann, had once told me that we would have to destroy Hoggs in order to save ourselves, that he not too long ago had said that Hoggs should swing. But it was to no avail. Hermann demurred.

I had fully expected Hoggs to be frog-marched out the door and down the back stairs, straight to the scaffold, but I learned that when a capital punishment was rendered by a court-martial, the commanding general had to review and affirm the decision. I was shocked to learn the next morning that Old Zach was not in a hanging mood. He had commuted Hoggs's sentence to a mere thirty lashes—and no branding—reputedly after looking at Bliss and asking, "Why hang an experienced man when we have but five or six companies in each regiment of regulars, and each of them is grievously under-strength? Why, damn me, sir, I cannot rely upon the Volunteers to lie in the line against the dago lancers. I must have regulars!" With this, Old Zach commuted Hoggs's sentence, even though enough of Hoggs's dirty laundry had been aired at his court-martial to hang him twice over. Hermann approved, declaring that thirty lashes would set Hoggs straight. I sourly responded to Hermann that he'd better be damned careful or one night he'd find himself stabbed to death as he slept.

⌒

Hoggs received his thirty lashes without a murmur, and the very next day he carried a 70-lb. pack on shoulders possessing hardly a fleck of skin, so thoroughly had he been laid into. What's more, he was a model soldier during every step of the 220 miles of hard marching from Matamoros by way of Camargo, our jumping off point on the río Bravo, and south through the mountains to the army's camp at Walnut Springs, a beautiful wooded park with a river running through it that overlooked the walled city of Monterrey and its burgeoning defenses. I thought Hoggs's fortitude to be supremely out of character. Yet despite my lingering concern that Hoggs was no more than a "Yes sir, kind sir, three bags full, sir" sort of bluebelly whom I didn't trust even one whit, I told Hermann as we made dinner together one night just before we marched into Walnut Springs, that he had been right about Hoggs, and I had been wrong. I also told him that his positive effect on Hoggs was no mere fluke, for I had watched the entire company mature and improve in the weeks following Hermann's formal promotion to company first sergeant. I wasn't the only one to see it, either.

On the march from Camargo, we stopped at Mier just before we got to the mountains. This was the town where five years before Walker and Big Foot had surrendered and one could still see the pockmarks from the Texian invasion. While we were camped there, the regiment was paraded and inspected by Major Harrison. As he inspected D Company, Harrison publicly commended Hermann as "the very epitome of what a first sergeant should be, exercising a perfect influence on the moral and physical efficiency of the company's rank and file." Hermann took the praise from Harrison with characteristic modesty. When I tried to congratulate him later, he later told me to just shut pan and make dinner.

I later remarked to Grant that Hermann truly deserved such praise. Grant agreed. "There's little that I would dispute with what Major Harrison said. A company first sergeant is the most important man in the company—the company captain aside. He is responsible in no small measure for setting the proper command tone for the company. If he does so poorly, or not at all, he can do more damage than even the company captain. There is no question in my mind that Sergeant Wurster has done a better job at it than any sergeant I've ever met." Grant looked thoughtful for a moment. "I think that he'd make a fine officer, if the opportunity presented itself." Grant looked me in the eye as I nodded agreement. "You've got that sort of potential as well. If you don't get hanged for your pains, that is."

"Sir?"

"You heard me, Gogan. You're an entirely different sort of soldier than your friend. You play fast and loose. But you get results with it. And you are smart."

I choked off my initial impulse to retort with wounded pride, and instead shut my pan.

"But your manner is heedless, Gogan. Impulsive. And, I think, you are occasionally inclined to shade the truth."

There was no avoiding what Grant had to say next.

"I can't prove it, and I don't want to, but I think there is more to what happened down south with the Rangers than you let on—either to me or to Major Bliss."

I tried to look shocked.

"Don't worry, Gogan. Nobody else has figured it out—at least, I don't think so. And I'm not going to put you on report over it. But you witnessed something out there in the desert. And you haven't told us quite everything you know about it. Why, I don't know. But you haven't." Grant stopped for a moment, before continuing. "And that gets to the nub of it. You played fast and loose for a reason, and I suspect for a quite good reason. Probably to protect someone. Who and why, I don't know, and ..." he studied me thoughtfully. "I don't think I want to know."

There was no good response to what Grant had said. So I once again shut pan. It was some time later when I asked Grant, "So, how does one become an officer in the regulars?"

"Go to West Point."

"Can bluebellies go?"

"I don't know. I'll have to think upon that a spell." Grant looked at me with a serious expression. "But you should be careful what you wish for. Army life is not for the family man. Or for courting nice young ladies." He smiled a little crookedly. "I do long so for St. Louis and the sight of Miss Dent."

I smiled equally as crookedly, thinking of poor, dead Adabelita, Brannagh's banishment, Calandria's betrayal, and Evelyn's deathly silence. "I don't have a young lady, sir. At least, not anymore."

"Sorry to hear that."

It was some three weeks later that Sarah, Hermann, and I were among a thousand or so spectators crowding the crest of a low hill—which I reckoned was just about every manjack and camp follower who could slip away from his or her duties, several score of the womenfolk having braved the trip south along with their soldiers. The hill was just south of our camp at Walnut Springs, about a mile north of the main defenses of the walled city of Monterrey, which lay before us on the northern bank of the Santa Catarina River. The city's defenses were dominated by a huge structure called the Black Fort, which lay just north of the city proper. The grapevine had reliably informed us that this formidable redoubt was on the site of an abandoned cathedral built with walls of black basalt. It now visibly bristled with all manner of artillery and hundreds of troops.

Most of the spectators, particularly the volunteers, hadn't even bothered to bring their muskets. So the gathering more resembled a Sunday afternoon promenade along the Battery at the bottom of Manhattan than it did the beginning of a battle two hundred miles south of the río Bravo and the nearest succor for our little army. A number of big bugs, including the Old Man and General Worth and General Twiggs and all of their respective minions, stood by themselves on a little promontory slightly in front of the rest of us, with a slightly better view than most. Every one of them had a spyglass glued to his eye as we all watched a regiment of Mexican lancers, resplendent with pennants of red and green and uniforms of bright red, forming in a long line to the west of the Black Fort, perhaps a mile from us. We heard trumpets sound in snatches as the breeze allowed.

Hays's regiment was just a few hundred yards in front of us. The Rangers were dismounted, checking their repeating pistols and rifles, and watching the steady advance of the lancers. Just behind the Rangers and there to watch the show from the front row was Old Zach, seated on Old Whitey. He had ridden forward away from the rest of the big bugs a few minutes earlier. With nary a bugle or other apparent command, the Rangers mounted their horses in almost perfect unison and split into perhaps a hundred groups of five. Each little impromptu squadron began advancing towards the lancers, picking up momentum as it passed through the mesquite and underbrush.

I could feel the anticipation ripple through the several hundred spectators on our ridge. The volunteers from regiments representing half the states in the Union, it seemed like, jibber-jabbered like magpies. We regulars watched the Texians in admiring silence. The Mexican line was also advancing, lances lowered as they went from a canter to a near gallop. Still their line held admirably well. The collision of the two advancing lines seemed inevitable. Then a bugle sounded. The lancers wheeled in formation and ran hell for leather towards the city and flashes rippled along the parapets of the Black Fort and from batteries hidden along the outskirts of the city, followed seconds later by a fusillade of angry barks of the smaller artillery pieces and the more occasional booms of larger pieces. But the Mexicans had opened fire at quite an extreme range. The Rangers had stopped short—again with nary a visible signal from anywhere—when the lancers had retreated, and the instant the first cannon boomed they ran full chisel for safety, and were long gone by the time grape and canister battered the underbrush like a storm's violent gusts of wind and hail. Solid shot from other cannon crashed through the underbrush much closer to the retreating Rangers. One errant shot went very long, crashing into the dirt just twenty feet from the Old Man. He calmly looked at the furrow dug by the shot, and then quietly wheeled Old Whitey and cantered leisurely to safety. His escort, shoulder straps and bluebellies alike, had jumped for dear life when the shot landed, and they gladly retreated pell-mell in the Old Man's wake.

Most of the Rangers paced Old Zach as he retired. But several score remained behind, just out of range of the larger artillery pieces, which occasionally boomed again, their solid shot falling well short. Then the Rangers began a game, which I recognized from Big Foot's description as having been borrowed from the Comanche, showing off and boasting of their prowess to their enemy on the eve of battle. The

Rangers, singly and in groups of two or three, began circling around the northern face of the Black Fort and then running parallel to the hidden batteries defending the town west of the fort to the base of Independence Hill at the western-most edge. Occasionally, a single Ranger or a pair or three of them would wheel and bolt full chisel towards the hidden batteries or the fort and then just stop. As soon as there was a flash from the fort's parapet or from one of the hidden batteries, the Rangers closest to the gun just fired would dart in one direction or another and gallop to safety long before we heard the report and longer still before the solid shot arrived. They resembled nothing so much as the swallows in the rafters at *la Casa de Las Corrientes de Golondrinas*, flitting hither and yon at breakneck speed, with seemingly nary a care in the world.

Within a few minutes, a few of the more daredevil Rangers began to dart much closer, often within just a few score yards of the earthen works surrounding the Black Fort's basalt walls, waving their hats and shouting at the Mexican artillerists on the parapets. The Mexicans promptly switched their ammunition to canister and grape, but they were no more successful. As soon as there was a flash, the Rangers in harm's way darted hither and yon, and the grape and canister scythed futilely at now unoccupied underbrush. I heard someone remark that the Rangers appeared to be little boys testing the first frail ice on an early winter's morning, all to see how far they could go before they fell in.

After an hour, the Rangers tired of their games and rode off. The fort then turned its attention to us spectators on the hills. A gun flashed and then boomed. By unspoken agreement, a group of us scattered. It was only as the solid shot landed in a spray of dirt just yards from where we had been standing, that I heard the rushing sound of its flight. Having found the range, the Mexican guns began to make hot work of it for us. I heard more than one admiring comment about the Mexican gunnery as the crowd swayed to and fro, avoiding the solid shot as it landed just short of where we were and crashed towards us. At one point, Hermann murmured his agreement.

Sarah snapped derisively in reply, "Probably that damned mick, Riley, and his turncoats serving those guns. They were the ones who made it hot for us at Fort Texas. Them dagoes couldn't hit the broad side of a barn."

I shrugged noncommittally. Half the army was standing on the little ridge, and thirty guns in the fort hadn't been able to hit a single one of us. Sarah looked slightly annoyed at my indifference. But I shrugged that off as well. It was dinnertime, and I was hungry.

~

The next afternoon, Old Zach split the army. He sent Worth west with his division of regulars and Hays's Rangers to secure the road to Saltillo and to invest the west side of the town. To cover their move, they marched west behind the ridge we'd been standing on the day before. Of course, the attendant blare of the bugles, flutes, and drums, and the general bobbery of moving two-and-half thousand troops in an organized fashion, brought observers with telescopes to the ramparts of the Black Fort and to the top of Independence Hill at the western extremity of the town, where the Bishop's Palace proudly sat. Twiggs's division, of which the Fourth Infantry was part, had been paraded to our east, safely out of range of the Black Fort's guns, to cover Worth's movement west against any Mexican sortie from that direction.

Grant, the regimental quartermaster, and I, his sergeant, did not parade with the Fourth. We were not part of the line. We were regimental staff. Grant had nonetheless supplicated with Colonel Garland himself to join one of the companies, if only as a supernumerary. But Garland turned Grant down flat, telling him that his place during this battle was not engaging the enemy in combat, but instead was with the horses, mules, tents, latrines, kitchens, and dinner—"for the benefit of the bluebellies, don't you know, and a damned fine job you've been doing, too. So keep at it. That's the spirit." Grant did the next best thing, which was to find himself a grand seat for several hours on the ridge facing the Black Fort watching all of the comings and goings and commotion. I stood atop the ridge with him, having shirked as many of my own duties as I dared (including leaving some Mexican laborers to dig latrines on the threat of exflunctication if they weren't finished in a right soldierly fashion by the time I returned to pay them). We were accompanied by every other idler and fellow-shirker in the army, although there were far less of us rubberneckers than the day before, what with a third of the army marching away with Worth and another third of it parading with Twiggs. Unlike the day before, everyone was carrying a musket or some other weapon or another.

Worth's regulars made slow work of it as they marched west cross-country, first to the Monclova road and then south along the base of a great hill that stretched thousands of feet into the air. Pioneers cut paths for the artillery, which lagged behind even the slow-moving infantry, first through the underbrush and then through fields full of standing corn and the Good Lord knows what else. By the time that the sun had set behind the mountains, we heard cannon fire and musketry. We couldn't tell what was happening, because dusk was rapidly approaching and Worth's Division was about three or four miles away from us. It was not until much later that the grapevine told us that Hays's Rangers had been advancing south along the Saltillo road, when they were ambushed by infantry and dismounted cavalry hidden in the cornfields lining the road. Under a hail of musketry and cannon fire from Independence Hill, the Rangers retreated, set camp and began foraging for food and water. As they did, they were attacked again, this time by about 500 lancers and *irregulares*. The Rangers repulsed them forthwith as darkness fell, killing some 200 or more of them, while losing only one man themselves.

This news and the near-perfect condition of the Fourth's new latrines cheered me to no end. I was actually whistling a bit as I recruited a couple of Mexicans fresh from laboring on the latrines to carry warm food down to the trenches in front of the mortar and howitzer battery. Word had come back to us that the Fourth would not be returning to camp this evening. They had been assigned to dig in below our only battery of anything worthy of the name, siege artillery, to protect the redlegs from surprise attack. Old Zach had apparently adjudged the Fourth, which now comprised just six reduced companies (one of which was on guard duty at Walnut Grove), to be fit only for garrison duty. Not surprisingly, the prospect of guard duty and digging in around the mortar and howitzer battery did not appeal to anyone in the Fourth. Word had come down that they would not be joining the rest of Twiggs's division of regulars for the assault planned for the next morning on a redoubt on the extreme eastern side of the city. Our scouts and Mexican spies had dubbed it *la Teneria* on account of an old and disused tannery that lay somewhere behind the reddish gash of fresh earth where the earthenwork redoubt was apparently still under construction. The tannery and its earthenworks anchored the Mexicans' eastern flank against the little river alongside which the city of Monterrey lay. The redoubt lay cheek-by-jowl with a nest of single-story, whitewashed buildings with flat roofs. The word was that Old Zach was planning the attack to distract the dagoes into defending the eastern approaches to town, thus pulling them away from the hills to the west, where the real assault was to come at first light, courtesy of Worth's division.

The grapevine was abuzz with what was in store for Worth and his men tomorrow. They were to charge up and capture four hills, two on each side of the river. The main prize was the bishop's palace, which crowned Independence Hill at the western edge of the city, just north of the river. From those hills, we were going to turn the Mexicans' own cannon on the town and bombard it before assaulting it from the west. We all thought that to be just desserts for the misery those cannon had caused Worth's division over the past day or so. Few of us thought that assault would be without a heavy cost, though, if the four hills were stoutly defended. I hoped that Big Foot would stay safe, although that was unlikely, as he was always looking to be in the thick of it, and the Rangers were going to lead the assault, along with the Fifth and Seventh Infantry, and Childs's Battalion of redleg infantry.

The food I had managed to bring down to the battery only partly sweetened the sour mood pervading D Company, and I made two more trips before the company had eaten its fill. Grant organized other details to feed the remaining companies, whose denizens had grumbled while they dug and looked longingly at D Company's boys as they ate. I thanked Grant, which he repaid with a short lecture about how a good quartermaster's sergeant would have seen to dinner for every one of the five companies. Grant finished with a wry smile, observing that a competent regimental quartermaster would have instructed his sergeant to make sure that the entire regiment was fed.

I walked down to the battery once more that night. Hermann was standing in the middle of a broad trench that the five companies of the Fourth had fashioned from a natural depression in the plain that gradually descended towards the Black Fort. D Company's bluebellies were working like demons all around him in amidst the flickering torches. Several hours of regiment's hard labor had cleared the trench of all vegetation, erected an earthen parapet, and cleared all standing bushes and similar vegetation as far down the gentle slope of the plain as I could see by a flickering torch planted in the parapet. Hermann wiped the sweat from his forehead with a filthy red handkerchief, his shadow cast eerily against the back side of the trench, above which stood the army's two 24-pounder howitzers and a single, 10-inch siege mortar, affectionately known as the old witch's soup pot. The battery's redlegs were swarming over the three artillery pieces, making ready to commence firing at dawn—just as soon as they could see the Black Fort.

Hermann was in a foul and somber mood, notwithstanding the pleasure of my company and the chow I'd brought down. I wasn't sure what had precipitated his foul mood. Perhaps it was the prospect of spending the night out in the muddy trench that the regiment had just dug, a prospect made all the more unpleasant by a sudden cut of cold wind and several desultory waves of drizzle. But it surely wasn't the prospect of being part of the Greek chorus observing the battle without participating. Hermann was far too smart for that, notwithstanding the general mood of D Company's bluebellies disappointed at being left out of the next morning's attack. It was only after Hermann had finished tending to his men that he and I sat at long last. As we did, he observed sourly, "There will be a butcher's bill to pay tomorrow."

I replied with a mirthless chuckle, "You and Grant. He's all doom and gloom about our prospects tomorrow at both ends of town. Something about the guns and the hills. He wasn't very happy about either of them." I motioned towards the redlegs laboring above our head, busy covering the powder and shot with waxed tarpaulins to keep it dry. "Rather like you, as a matter of fact." I then nodded in the direction of the Black Fort. "You don't think they'll attack tonight, do you?"

"Why would they?" Hermann groused. "They can stay dry tonight, drink their *pulque* and *mescal* to their hearts' content, and keep their powder dry." He glanced up at the sky. "While we get wet, our powder gets damp, and we have only that to prepare our way tomorrow." He motioned towards the mortar and howitzer battery above us.

"You really don't like that old witch's soup pot, do you?" I gestured to the massive 10-inch mortar that was the centerpiece of the tiny battery.

"My friend, I would be a very happy man, indeed, if we had a score of those witch's soup pots, as you call them. The ten-inch mortar is a perfectly fine piece of artillery. Modern. Not like the junk that the Mexicans have left over from what the *gachupine* brought here a hundred years ago. I thank God for that. But they have a lot of pieces tucked in that *gottverdammten* fort, and there are very likely many more on top of that *gottverdammten* hill with the bishop's palace." Odd, I thought, that Hermann should have sworn, much less have sworn in German, which I had not heard him speak in a very long time. Hermann continued, "Only the Lord knows where else they have artillery hidden. How many different places did you see flashes coming from yesterday and today? Thirty? Forty? With that many pieces, even if they are only ancient Spanish bronze and brass, the bastards can do us a lot of damage. One old soup pot and our two 24-pounders, however modern they are, and however well handled, are not going to be enough to reduce the Black Fort. If we could

432

reduce the Black Fort, we wouldn't have to attack uphill over there."
Hermann pointed to the west side of town, beyond which Worth's
division was passing as uncomfortable a night as the Fourth, for they
had not taken their tents with them.

"That's what Grant told me."

"He's right. We need more guns. Proper siege artillery. Big mor-
tars and such."

"Grant told me that the army has them," I said. "Howitzers even
bigger than our 24-pounders. 32-pounders. Big enough to destroy
stone. The Washington big bugs simply did not send them to us."

Hermann replied, "Even with guns as big as that, we would still
need twenty pieces, and even all of Childs's Battalion doesn't have the
men to service them. Fifty pieces, if we could have them. Forty years
ago, Napoleon used artillery by the hundred to wreck the Prussian
army. And here we are with three pieces, not counting that arrogant
bastard Bragg and his 6-pounder flying artillery, and they're utterly
useless here. Even the Bull Battery's 18-pounders we had at Palo Alto
would help. Why the Old Man left them at Camargo, I will never
understand. These three pieces sitting above us will not even be able
to suppress fire from the fort, and that can be the only reason we are
sighting in from here. We should reduce those redoubts over there."
Hermann pointed in the direction of *la Tenería*. "We also could reduce
the works on the other side of the Black Fort as well—where the lancers came from yesterday—if we wanted to attack there. And we could
avoid having to attack those hills and that *gottverdammten* bishop's
palace, which just has to be as full of *bandoleros* and other riff-raff as a
well-fed maggot is of meat. But that fort. Were those greaser bastards
to screw their courage to its sticking place, as you like to say, they
could make hot work for us." It was the first time I'd heard Hermann
refer to our enemy as "greasers," a term that every other manjack in
the army seemed to have adopted since shortly after we arrived in
the Rio Grande valley. "We simply cannot storm the Black Fort," he
groused. "Not without the big guns. They would kill us all ten times
over. And the Black Fort must fall for Monterrey to fall."

"You are a true beacon of joy, my benen cove."

"Do not get me started on how few men we have here."

"Six companies of the Fourth," I responded. "Every company badly reduced in number, and one of them on guard duty with the baggage train. Every other regiment of regulars is nearly as attenuated as the Fourth." I raised my eyebrow. The Fourth was barely at half-strength, even with the fresh drafts we received in June and July. Only the Seventh and Childs's Battalion were at anything approaching full strength among the regulars, and the assault on Independence Hill would rectify that oversight. We did have the volunteers, full regiments from Ohio, Tennessee, and Kentucky, as well as a battalion from Baltimore, some 3,000 volunteers in all. More than half our army, and every manjack among them, from colonel to private, was untested in battle.

"We need Pillow's division," Hermann lamented. "Even if they are just volunteers. We left far too many of them in *das gottverlassen* charnel the Mexicans call Camargo."

I shivered at the memory of the sick and dying in camp at Camargo. The toll had been a hundred times heavier, it seemed, than our losses in battle at Palo Alto and Resaca de la Palma, combined. An unhealthy spot it was, with hundreds dying of the fever when the backdoor trots didn't take them. But Camargo was nonetheless our sole link to Matamoros and the United States. So we had to hold the spot. But I put such thoughts from my mind. They were too horrifying to dwell on. I said, "I can understand why the Old Man left Pillow behind, though. He's a born fool. A real feather-brain." Hermann smiled faintly at me, as I continued. "Disloyal to a fault, so they say. You've heard the story about the redoubt he had built at Camargo, didn't you?"

"No," Hermann replied.

"You'll like this one. I heard it from one of Gray's bully backs a couple weeks ago. After we marched south, Pillow had a redoubt built to defend Camargo in case Canales or some other *jefe de los bandoleros* attacked. Good idea, you might think. But there was a fly in the ointment: Pillow personally designed the redoubt. He put the ditch inside the parapet—on the wrong side, for love of Christ. Rendered the damned redoubt completely useless. Of course, nobody told him that he'd messed up. It gets even better. The fool also built it so small that, even if the ditch were outside the parapet, the redoubt would have kept out only an attack by midgets. Fine for Lilliput, but not to stop Canales. Pillow was so proud of it, though, that he showed it off to some visiting scribblers. So while he's showing these coves around, some shoulder strap on horseback leaped over the entire parapet and ditch, as if he were riding a steeplechase. Everybody started laughing. Apparently Old Pillow was so boiled up at having been so thoroughly bamblustergated, that he put the poor cove on report."

"I am not surprised. I have not heard good things about General Pillow."

"I heard Grant and a couple of others talking one night about him. According to them, Pillow is President Polk's old law partner, and he can't march a platoon in a straight line for all the tea in China. He's down here for one reason, and only one reason—to keep an eye on Old Zach. I guess the Washington City great pots can't have Old Zach getting too popular. Wrong political party, or some such foolishness. Worse is the fear that the old codger would want to become president in '48 on the strength of what he's doing down here. Utter bosh if you ask me. Anyway, so the story goes, Pillow thinks that the Whigs are more the enemy than the dagoes, and Taylor, if you will remember, is a dyed-in-the-wool Whig."

Hermann reproved me. "I truly wonder at your language, Billy. You speak Spanish better than any man in our little army. You respect the Mexicans. You even fell in love with a beautiful *tejana*. So, how can you denigrate them so by using the term 'dagoes'?"

I shrugged, forbearing mention of Hermann's casual use of the other epithet, "greaser," which had so recently come into general use. Both words fit. The Mexicans were the enemy, no matter how lovely their spring ewes. But I didn't explain any of this to Hermann, and instead went back to the topic at hand. "No wonder General Pillow was left behind. But we could have brought his regiments—all four of them. It would have been a fourth division. Could have made all the difference."

Hermann snorted derisively, "And leave the king without a kingdom? With a fast ship to Washington City to bear such ill tidings?"

"A heavy price to pay, my friend, to keep a political spy at arm's length."

We stared at the black wall of the night. Hermann then turned to the few men still laboring behind us. "Get your asses in gear, *sie gottverdammten Faulenzerin.*" He looked back at me and handed me an envelope. "Give this to Sarah for me," he said. "She'll know what to do with it."

I nodded.

"You should write one as well. Perhaps send it to that girl in Ireland. You haven't written to her in weeks."

———

Back in camp, Sarah said the same thing to me about writing a letter to Evelyn when I handed her Hermann's envelope half an hour later. She was making herself busy tidying up around her tent and little wagon—the same one she'd driven south from Corpus Christi. She then looked at the envelope more closely and wrinkled her nose as she read the address written on the front of it.

I ignored her request to write a letter to Evelyn, and instead asked her what the matter was.

"Nothing."

"It's something," I said in as light a tone as I could. Then comprehension dawned. "You've been doing the sentimental with him, haven't you? All this time. Behind my back." I stared at Sarah in amused wonder. "Even while you were entertaining the general. And here it is that I thought you fancied me." I laughed. "Even as wet behind the ears as I am. I still thought you fancied me."

"Billy Gogan." Sarah had her back turned to me as she busied herself with some task or another. "Shut pan. You are not the center of this universe. No matter what you might think."

436

I laughed again. "That's why you insisted on not opening up our knocking shop again after the wedding. Light dawns upon the doltish. You cost us all a load of chink when you closed up. Matamoros is lousy with volunteers fresh off the boat. I always wondered why you followed us, side-saddle on that mule, parasol in your hand, and wagon in tow. You've already got enough chink to retire to New Orleans and live in style for a hundred years, and if you'd stayed in Matamoros, you could've made another fortune by Christmas, and retired to Paris or London or any damn place you pleased."

"Billy Gogan." Sarah sounded defiant. "I will open another dossing house. It will make more chink than the last one, and you will resume receiving your annuity, my avaricious little china plate. Just as soon as Old Zach takes that damned town."

"You're in love with him, aren't you?" I asked as gently as I could.

Sarah turned to me, tears glistening on her cheeks in the dim light of the nearby fire. "Bring him back to me, Billy Gogan."

⁓

I ended up writing a letter to Evelyn. I hadn't intended to. But I felt a little empty deep inside as I sat in my tent, listening to the drizzle pattering overhead, hoping that it did not overwhelm the tent's thin muslin. Why I felt that way, I couldn't fathom. But I had to fill the emptiness, and writing the letter to Evelyn seemed to be the best way. I certainly wasn't going to find succor with Father Rey. My opportunity to disbosom my soul to him had been foreclosed, at least for now. Father Rey accompanied the army on its march from Matamoros to Monterrey as far as Camargo. I had actively avoided the good Father on a couple of occasions on the march, even to the extent of walking in the opposite direction when I caught sight of him—an army of seven thousand or so is not a very big place if you truly wish to avoid someone. Camargo had rapidly become a charnel house of every kind of fever and disease that could plague an army, and so Father Rey remained behind to tend to the sick and dying. Once we'd marched south and he was no longer with the army, I wasn't sure what I felt about having avoided him. And now I was assuaging an emptiness by writing to a girl whom I'd not spoken to nor heard from by letter in nearly two years, and who I was sure had long forgotten my very existence.

I left the letter with Sarah a couple of hours later, and I apologized for tormenting her so. Her tears had long since dried and vanished and her armor was back in place, so I was thoroughly prepared when she told me off for being such an insensitive bastard. As we parted, though, she once more entreated me to bring Hermann back to her safe and sound.

I was up before dawn the next morning, along with every other manjack in the army, every one of whom, regular and volunteer alike, had a bit of a pinched look about him as the First Division's and Volunteer Division's regiments formed in the brush and fields to the east of our idyllic camping ground. It was not the miserable drizzle and chilly air they minded, though, because for the first time in many days I did not hear a single fool ask someone whether he had yet seen the elephant roar—a question that so many, volunteer and Johnny-come-lately regular alike, had taken up asking those of us who had seen the claret drawn at Palo Alto and Resaca de la Palma. Grant found me before I'd found my first cup of joe, and we headed to the ridge to watch the day's proceedings, as he put it. We were not of the line, he informed me, and he had once more been ordered to attend to his duties—which consisted of watching the regiment's baggage and tents—rather than finding a spot with the Fourth as its five small companies occupied the trench below the mortar battery.

A shavetail friend of Grant's, I didn't know who although I recognized him as a bowlegs with the Second Dragoons, cantered up to us on horseback and said to Grant, "Twiggs is indisposed."

"Indisposed?" Grant gave him a shocked look.

"Took a purgative, he did. Told his aide-de-camp that it was far better to have a clear bowel if you were going to be gut-shot. Apparently lessens the likelihood of mortification."

"What an old granny."

"Quite, and now he's completely hors de combat. But it does point out the prospects of an officer who manages to find himself in the right place. It's Garland leading the First Division today. A lieutenant colonel, second-in-command of his regiment when the war starts, and he's commanding a division by the third battle. I wonder if he knows that his attack is a mere diversion to the main affair with Worth. Were I commanding the First, I'd be mightily tempted to take the town myself," the shavetail mused. "I'd like the odds of general rank and the thanks of Congress for such a crowning glory, although think of the claret needed to take that." The shavetail waved his hand in the direction of the raw earthenworks of *la Tenería* and the town to the right of the redoubt, where we could see tiny figures scurrying about on the rooftops.

Grant wasn't following his friend's gaze. Instead, he murmured, "I'd just as soon see such prospects at my more pedestrian rank. Along with the opportunity."

The shavetail gave a short, barking laugh. "You'll not be regimental quartermaster forever, my bene cove." I positively goggled at the shavetail's use of the argot.

Grant reacted as well. "You sound like my young sergeant over there."

"As does any Irishman from New York." The shavetail glanced my way and winked. "Anyway, you'll get your opportunity. There's not a man who's forgotten what you did at the Resaca." Grant flushed as the shavetail continued. "You'll get your brevet. You've just got to remember to get yourself mentioned in the dispatches, that's all. Anyway, grit ain't what it's cracked up to be. Not without something more. Just remember that codfish, May, and that equally daft bastard, Thornton. Both were looking for glory, and they both got some good bowlegs croaked on the strength of it. You on the other hand, you're the talk of the army."

Grant glared at the shavetail in embarrassment.

The shavetail grinned mischievously and winked at me again. "There ain't a regular who's not heard the story of you coaxing your mule trains along with hardly more than a patient word whispered to a mule or one 'o your dago mule-skinners. There ain't another mule-skinner or quartermaster in the army who could induce a mule to throw his heart into the work, 'ceptin' with a powerful volley of Sunday-school words. Anyway, you did a better job of keeping your bluebellies fed on time on our little peregrination south than any of the other regimental quartermasters. So, my friend, you've gotten yourself to be a right popular young cove with our shoulder strap aristocracy."

He was right. Grant was the talk of the army. Sarah had told me that, over in the Fifth, some cove'd joked that Grant had upset the entire creed of the quartermasters' corps, which was built upon the foundational gospel of mistreating mules (who died of the blues as easily as our volunteers) and bluebellies alike (with mistimed supply trains of food, uniforms, ammunition, and everything else that an army on campaign requires in the vastest quantities). And he had done so simply by being good at his job. In the three weeks we marched south, I never heard a sour or sharpish word from Grant, who was everywhere, all the time, full of purposeful energy. I cannot tell you how many times he cleared knots of stalled mule trains where the road petered off into nothingness and the quartermasters stood helplessly with evermore cranky and disputatious mules, waiting for someone else to do something. Somehow, Grant knew to almost magically appear and do what he did that day in the Aransas Bay, when he sorted out Hoggs's hash under the Old Man's eagle eye. Solve the problem, and keep the supply train moving. On the one or two occasions that Canales or some other brigand was whispered to be in the neighborhood, Grant knew to call for a company of bluebellies to be in the right place, such that we hardly cared so much as a tinker's curse whether there were any brigands about. Best of all, Grant made sure that the Fourth was the best feed in the army. Breakfast and water for canteens at dawn, before the regiment marched. Rations for the noon meal as they marched, and a hot dinner as the sun went down for each ravenous and footsore bluebelly. Grant was a wonder. Yet Major Harrison paid him no mind save for the occasional sneer.

It was almost as if the shavetail read my mind, for he turned more serious. "Remember, Sam, be political. Don't get Harrison all wrathy with you, and a first lieutenancy will be yours for the asking, with a brevet captaincy to follow on the morrow."

With that, the shavetail drifted off in the general direction of the Second Dragoons, who were now formed further down the ridge, their horses restless with the excitement of it all. Grant switched his gaze from Garland's division assembling on the plain to the little trench containing the two hundred men of the Fourth guarding the even smaller battery situated just above them, and then back again. He continued restlessly switching his gaze until a wave of excited murmuring and finger-pointing rippled down the line of idlers and spectators. A Mexican cavalry officer was riding the length of the Black Fort from west to east, carrying a small gold-fringed green and red and white pennant. He was escorted by a pair of lancers carrying much larger flags, one of them the national Mexican flag fringed in gold. The three riders formed the apex of a V, each wing of which must have contained an entire squadron of lancers. We could hear exuberant cheers course from the fort's battlements as the procession passed by.

A shoulder strap next to Grant swore a surprised oath, and Grant snatched away the man's telescope—with a muttered apology. "What …? Look at this, Gogan." Grant thrust the telescope into my hand and pointed to the cavalry officer. "It's a woman, by God." And then Grant did something I'd rarely seen—he swore. "That damned dago officer is a woman."

And so she was, long black hair flowing beneath her shako. She must be beautiful, I thought, to have such a regal and erect bearing in the saddle—and strong, to be carrying even that small a pennant.

As the woman officer and her escort disappeared back into the safety of town and the cheers from our enemy slowly died away, I sensed Hannibal hovering with two cups of hot joe. As he gave me my cup (God bless him for it!), I whispered to him. He nodded and vanished into the crowd of idlers. Grant seemed prepared to query me, but his attention, and that of every manjack on that little ridge, was diverted by a solitary bang from our ten-inch mortar. A redleg officer came flying up the hill on horseback towards us. He hurriedly turned to look at the Black Fort through his spyglass. He cursed quietly as the shot exploded harmlessly several score yards short of even the protective earthen breastwork girding the fort. The howitzers followed, with similar results, but the redleg shoulder strap had already departed, hell-for-leather bound back to the battery. He returned for the next several salvoes, steadily and efficiently walking them into and over the breastworks and then over the basalt walls of the Black Fort itself. We all cheered as bits of stone flew furiously as our shells exploded upon its parapet. But the smoke cleared to reveal that no real damage had been done.

Grant was damn near dancing with barely suppressed frustration. "Our guns will not do. They will not do at all. There is nothing left but to go it, my boys. Go it hard. Give 'em the bayonet."

It was as if Garland's division had heard the imprecation, for bugles sounded and to the beat of fife and drum, the division rumbled down the road to the east of the Black Fort, the Third Infantry in the lead, followed by the First, and trailed by the Baltimore Battalion of volunteers. Hardly had they begun to move, and the Black Fort finally began to reply to the pesky barks of our battery. There were half-a-dozen flashes from the fort's parapet, the whine of shells in flight and then the glacis in front of the trench guarding the battery, so recently cleared by the Fourth, exploded in mud and rock. Every doughboy in the trench ducked as a solid shot ricocheted over their heads and buried itself in the mud and wood revetment behind them that supported the battery's parapet. The redlegs were seemingly indifferent, for the little battery roared in defiant reply. And thus it went for some time, as we watched Garland's division take the road towards town.

Grant vibrated next to me. "Flank to the east, man. Flank to the east."

I almost asked why, but there was no need, for in that instant, the east-facing wall of the fort erupted in a dozen flashes. There were no explosions, but men began to crumple as shot bowled through the ranks of the First and Third. The First and Third increased their pace and double-quick timed their way to the relative safety of the buildings on the town side of *la Teneria*, where the Black Fort could not bring its guns to bear. But now they faced the prospect of musketry from Mexican soldiers secreted on every rooftop in the buildings on the edge of town, most of them safe behind makeshift parapets. The Baltimore Battalion was next through the gauntlet, and I could see tiny figures at the head of the battalion gesticulating to their men to hold steady in anticipation of what they were about to receive. But the prospect of being flayed by Mexican guns was all too much, and as the next salvo flashed from the parapets of the Black Fort, the ranks of the volunteers quivered, folded, and then broke under the onslaught. Scared men fled into the chaparral to the east of the road, seeking shelter at any cost. I thought in that instant of Taylor's commuting Hoggs's sentence to hang, and appreciated his sentiments in having done so. There were so few of us veteran regulars to attack this great fortress of the Mexican north.

Then I felt Hannibal at my side, pressing the reins of two horses into my palm. "Godspeed, my friend," he whispered into my ear. I turned to thank him, but he had already absquatulated as quickly as I'd asked, thus denying Grant the opportunity to demand that he take the horses away.

I heard Grant exclaim, "What the Sam Hill ..." and I followed the line of his sight to the trench in front of our little battery. The Fourth was beginning to form to the east of the trench, as a regiment of volunteers, the First Kentucky by the look of them, entered the trench from the west. I admired the steadiness of both regiments as they maneuvered amidst the continuing, if now somewhat more sporadic (now that attention had shifted to Garland's division) fire from the Black Fort. The Fourth issued from the trench in a formation of three companies in preparation to join the battle. Hardly a hundred men, and not nearly enough to rescue Garland's division. I wondered where the other two companies were.

Grant spoke again, pointing at the horses that Hannibal had brought to me. "What the devil, Gogan? Where did these come from?"

I shrugged.

Grant looked back to the Fourth as it was preparing to march to the road that Garland's division had so lately traversed. "I have to …"

"Sir?"

"Join them." Grant gestured to the Fourth. "You stay here. With Hannibal."

"Sir."

"Oh, all right, Gogan."

And with that, we were gone, our moral courage to obey our orders gone with the wind that had driven away the early morning drizzle. Shot and shell followed us in our two-hundred-yard dash to the battery, all of it falling short, although I felt dirt and rock splatter me at one point. Grant rode to the head of the column, which was now formed, bayonets fixed and faces grim, and ready to march into harm's way. Major Harrison nodded at him tightly, and Grant rode alongside him. He and I were the only two on horseback. Every other of 90-odd in our three companies was marching, including Harrison himself, who led the tiny formation in perfect cadence, his sword stiffly held at shoulder arms, down the road to where the rest of Garland's division was fighting for their lives.

I fell in alongside Hermann. He nodded and smiled tightly, before roaring at D Company, "Dress the ranks, there!" Hoggs's legs quivered back into step, his face reddening under Hermann's glare. Not another man of the attenuated D Company noticed.

"REGIMENT." I could hear the hoarse strain in Harrison's voice. "DOUBLE QUICK TIME. MARCH."

The command echoed down our tiny column, and we lurched forward. I cantered my horse to keep pace. I could see ahead of us that the First and Third were taking a terrible punishment from Mexican musketry from the roof of what seemed to be every house in the neighborhood just in front of us. The Baltimore Battalion had recovered their courage, for those who still lived were now racing, higglety, pigglety, and pop, to support their brethren regulars in the desperate fight at the foot of town. Behind us, both regiments of Butler's division of volunteers had formed in a column, and were advancing to support us. The flag of the First Tennessee led the way, accompanied by drums and fife. The First Mississippi and their magnificent Whitney rifles followed, their colonel, a fellow named Jefferson Davis, a martinet of a West Pointer who, according to the always well-informed grapevine, had married the eldest of Old Zach's daughters many years ago over the Old Man's vociferous objections. She and Davis had been star-crossed lovers, for just a few weeks after they were married, she'd died of a malarial fever that had almost killed Davis himself. Relations between the Old Man and Davis had remained frosty ever since. I didn't give a rap about Davis's love life, though. I admired him for the ceaseless drilling of his regiment ever since they'd arrived at Matamoros. I'd seen him slogging his complaining volunteers across the drill field at Camargo, fever and the blues among the ranks be damned, until they could form a square to repel a cavalry attack almost as quickly and efficiently as a regiment of bluebellies. It seemed to be paying off, for his volunteers were holding their columns very prettily indeed, as they began their advance, even in the face of the carnage to come and the shame of the Baltimore Battalion breaking under salvoes from the Mexican cannonade. The First Tennessee, in the lead, were increasing the pace, and they seemed bound and determined to hold their formation equally as well as the Mississippians.

Diversion, Hell. We were going to take this blasted city by main force, one bayonet at a time, shot, shell, and women cavalry officers be damned. And in the moment, I once again appreciated how and why Grant had disobeyed his orders to stay in camp and had joined the fight. I even forgot how damned terrified I was.

⟶

"REGIMENT," snarled Harrison. "RUN!"

I spurred my horse to keep pace with the sweating faces of the Fourth as we began to hurtle towards *la Teneria*. I could hear and see shot and copper shell all around us, but none came near. What the dagoes were shooting at, I could not tell. But it wasn't us. The raw earthenworks were now just a couple of hundred yards away. Faster and faster we went, our column keeping formation as we ran. We presented a mighty narrow target for the still-silent redoubt's defenders to aim at.

We were close enough now, just a stone's throw away, that I could see individual faces as *la Tenería*'s garrison began popping their heads above the parapet and through the embrasures and sally ports. There must have been two or three score of them. I could see cannon being run forward as well. I wondered what they were waiting for. We would be on them in just a few seconds.

Then I wondered no longer, for an eruption of solid shot, grape, exploding shells, and musketry destroyed the world around me. It came from all directions, mowing down entire ranks of our tiny column. Miraculously, Grant and I, the only two horsemen, both stayed in our saddles.

CHAPTER 20

# Revenge

⌒

"GOGAN!" GRANT MATERIALIZED NEXT TO ME as I tried to control my terrified horse. I was still holding onto my shattered musket, more out of shock than sentimentality. It had just saved my life by stopping a piece of shrapnel or a musket ball or God knows what from slicing open my belly. The Mexicans were still firing at us from not two, but three locations: *La Teneria* in front of us, which continued to ply us with musketry and the occasional whiff of grape and ineffectual small solid shot, the Black Fort, whose much larger solid shot had torn great furrows through our ranks, and still more solid shot (once again of seemingly smaller caliber) from somewhere else behind *la Teneria*. I couldn't easily see where at a glance, and I wasn't going to stay still long enough to study the welter of buildings to find the hidden battery.

I looked around in some confusion. Hermann and Gaff and Hoggs and the rest of D Company had vanished, save only for the bodies, a score or more, that littered the field of trampled cornstalks. I silently thanked the Gods that be, when I did not see Hermann and Gaff among them. Some of the bodies were still moving. One was crawling on the ground, his entrails spilling onto the dirt. Another was sitting and staring at a missing arm as the blood pulsed from a torn artery. Grant was the only other sentient being in this abattoir, and he was yelling at me. "Damn it, man. Give me your horse. Hoskins has mine. He's injured."

I looked over at where I had last seen Grant on horseback, a dozen yards away. Lieutenant Hoskins was mounted on Grant's horse, trying despite his injured arm to control the terrified creature while at the same time purposefully gesticulating with his sword. Probably trying to gather survivors. Then Hoskins was gone, and the horse was riderless and running hard, away from the shot and shell and musketry.

I jumped off my horse and offered the reins to Grant.

"Save yourself, Gogan. Retreat into the sugarcane field, yonder. Find the others. Stay low, or you will die. I will find you." Grant mounted the horse, crouching low in the saddle. "I'm going to round up the survivors over there." He pointed to where the riderless horse had been, and then stormed off, crouching even lower in the saddle, his horse a live shield against *la Teneria's* musketry splattering the cornstalks that still stood haphazardly in his wake.

I was not entirely ignored by *la Teneria*, though. Several shots plinked at the few shattered cornstalks still erect in my immediate environs. After one tore away the top of a cornstalk hardly a yard from me, I felt a tug at my cap. I ducked instinctively, and sat involuntarily in the dirt and mud and broken cornstalks. I pulled my cap off and marveled at the two holes in it. The musket ball that had made them must have passed hardly more than an inch from the top of my head. I looked at my blouse, and it was torn in a place or two as well. I sat, oblivious to the storm of shot and shell howling around me, stupefied at my luck, and helpless to console the men dying around me. Their screams and moans eventually, and very gradually, faded away, so that I did not have to hear them anymore amidst the din and fury of the battle.

⌒

An insistent and maddening tattoo of drums and the accompanying screech of flutes and rapidly tramping feet roused me, whether from sleep or mere reverie, I didn't know. How long I'd been sitting there in the dirt, surrounded by my dead and dying comrades, I didn't know either. I scrambled to my feet and looked towards the commotion. It was the First Mississippi, fifty yards away, in a column of black slouch hats and red shirts deploying into a line and advancing directly towards me at double quick time. To their left, the First Tennessee had

448

already formed a line, and they were aiming at the dry moat defending *la Teneria*, straight across the very ground upon which we of the Fourth had been destroyed.

"JACKSON FENCIBLES. HALT. FIRST RANK, KNEEL." The line of sweating Mississippians did as they were bid, oblivious to my presence now hardly more than ten paces from them. A captain paced in front of the line. "Aim for your targets, boys."

I shivered with a frisson of horror. I was directly in the line of their fire. I bolted towards the captain, who had located himself safely to the side of his company, his sword raised. He looked at me distractedly as I scooted to his side. He shook his head and returned to his task at hand. "FIRST RANK. READY. AIM. FIRE."

The volley coincided with renewed fire from *la Teneria*, solid shot flying (thankfully) overhead, and grape and canister scything down still more cornstalks in front of us—I thought madly, how could there be any left standing? The larger cannon of the Black Fort boomed once more, and I saw a couple of gaps open in the line of Mississippians. Not the company in front of me, but a different one. But neither company swayed in the least, and the captain pacing in front of his company seemed entirely unperturbed.

"SECOND RANK. ONE STEP FORWARD. MARCH. KNEEL." The captain raised his sword and once more cautioned his men. "Make your shots count, boys. Aim at a dago ... and a live one at that." He raised his sword and watched the parapet of *la Teneria* until there was movement. "READY ... AIM ..." He held them a moment longer, until he saw heads pop above the parapet to sneak a look at the regiments arrayed before them. His sword flashed down. "FIRE."

A ripple of fire erupted from the company and the heads disappeared below the parapet. The captain then brought the first rank forward again, and they knelt, waiting. The captain peered through the smoke, looking for another target.

"There." I pointed at the very top of a head bobbing along the parapet. "And there." I pointed at a second head, which promptly disappeared.

The captain nodded appreciatively. "FIRST RANK. READY. See the targets, boys. Don't waste your shot and powder."

He got no further, for half a dozen rifles erupted simultaneously, and the remaining head disappeared with a distinctly unnatural jerk. Another head appeared in an embrasure where a Mexican gun was being run out. Several more rifles fired and this head disappeared as well. The gun remained silent as several more shots poured into the embrasure. I thought I could see movement. Presumably the gun crew taking cover. A taste of their own medicine, I chuckled to myself.

"Damn it, boys!" the captain swore in frustration. "Wait for the command."

"Let them fire at will, Captain McManus." It was Davis, the regimental colonel, sitting astride a magnificent charger that stirred nervously with every report of a rifle. Davis leaned over and soothed the horse, calling him "Tartar." Davis then said to McManus, "We don't have our orders, yet. So we cannot advance."

"Aye, sir."

"We cannot attack like the Fourth did …" Davis stopped and stared at me. "Saw what happened, sergeant. Damned shame. Good regiment, the Fourth." He looked at me again. "That's a damned fine knife. Good for killing the dagoes."

I stared at my knife, which I was clenching in my hand. I must have drawn it at some point, although I had no memory of doing so, nor of why I had done so. I also unconsciously touched the butt of my repeating pistol stuffed into my belt, and reassured myself that I hadn't lost it.

The pop of rifles firing continued to ripple up and down the line, as men aimed, shot, reloaded and looked for fresh targets. Davis paced impatiently as he watched *la Teneria*, where all of the guns had fallen silent. We hadn't seen a single head pop above the parapet in a couple of minutes now. We could hear the crackle of musketry coming from deep in the town, from somewhere behind the redoubt. I wondered if Garland's division had progressed that far into town, and whether they were somehow firing into the redoubt.

450

"Great God," Davis muttered to himself. "They're not firing. If I had thirty men with knives like yours, sergeant, I could take that fort now, before they start murdering us as we stand here." He glared at me. "You'll come with us, of course."

It was not a question, but I nodded anyway as Davis vibrated with frustration.

A great cheer arose further down the line, and a man waving a sword began sprinting forward, with a hundred or more men of the First Mississippi in close pursuit.

"Damn it," Davis swore. "McClung's charged. He's bloody charged without me." He waved his sword. "Go, McManus, go. Take the damned fort."

McManus yelled, "JACKSON FENCIBLES. Follow me, boys. CHARGE."

"Go with them, boy," Davis said to me. "Go with them."

And so I did.

⌒

I looked to my right as I ran, repeating pistol in one hand and knife in the other. Every company in the First Mississippi was charging now. I looked to my left and saw that the First Tennessee was charging as well. An unearthly guttural yell was being raised by both regiments, a sound unlike anything I'd heard before, but which I would come to know so well in a later war. I could only hope that it put the fear of God into those *méxicanos* in *la Teneria*, for it caused me to shiver and they were my fellow countrymen. The glacis to *la Teneria*, which was little more than the most gentle of slopes, was now venue for the foot-race to determine which regiment would storm the little redoubt first. I saw the First Tennessee charge up the glacis to the moat and leap over it in almost a single leap. I wondered wildly as we ran whether that fool, Pillow, could have had a hand in designing it.

By the time I looked forward again, the Mississippians and I were at the base of the redoubt. Someone lifted me, and I was among the first to scramble over the parapet, my heart pounding in my ears. When I looked up to gain my bearings, I saw that resistance was already largely broken. Many of the redoubt's denizens were absquatulating across the creek that ran along the open backside of *la Teneria*, and heading full chisel to another redoubt about two hundred yards away, on slightly higher ground above the far side of the creek.

One or two had remained, suicidally determined to make a fight of it. One of them, his shako tilted crazily upon his head, raised his musket to shoot a First Mississippi officer as he stuck his bare head through an embrasure and slithered past a now-abandoned cannon. I drew a bead on the Mexican with my Paterson, but another First Mississippi shoulder strap had materialized right next to the man and calmly shot him at nearly point-blank range with an enormous percussion pistol. The man's shako flew off as his head and shoulders whiplashed violently. He then collapsed and lay still.

I knelt and pulled a couple of coves up and over the parapet as they were being boosted from below. One man gave me a courteous, "Much obliged." I smiled at him. In the next instant, he fell. A musket ball through his throat. I looked aghast at the moat, where Tennesseans were indiscriminately firing up at the parapet, not knowing whether we were friend or foe. I began shouting and waving, imploring the Tennesseans to stop firing into us. Others on the parapet took up the cry, Captain McManus among them, and the firing abruptly ceased. But it was too late for the courteous man. He was already dead.

Tennesseans scrambled from the shallow moat through a gun embrasure, and passed flags through. A great cheer coursed across the redoubt as the First Tennessee's regimental flag and Old Glory were unfurled. A platoon of Mexicans on top of an abandoned building to our east fired one last volley, killing and wounding several Mississippians as they swirled about the interior of the redoubt. After an enraged hail of fire was returned in their direction by Mississippians and Tennesseans alike, the Mexican platoon's commander promptly raised the white flag of surrender.

The redoubt was ours.

"Three cheers for old Tartar. Look how he follows his colonel," someone called from further down the parapet. And so it was. The horse was cantering along the base of the parapet as Davis ran along the top, sword drawn. "Three cheers."

The huzzahs that followed merely added to the pandemonium. The two regiments were now milling about both the exterior of the redoubt, awaiting their turn to scale the parapet or be hauled through an embrasure or sally port, and interior of the redoubt, which was open on the city-side all the way to a creek, which was a hundred yards away, about half the distance to the second redoubt.

I stared at the second redoubt for a moment, wondering why they were not firing their cannon. They could have made *la Teneria* a killing field with grape and canister, but they must have been unable to depress their cannon muzzles sufficiently to do so. Thank God.

But the Mexicans did what they could, and peppered us with musketry. We were too far away for it to be very effective, but every so often, a man fell. So random was their firing that a musket ball struck a Mexican officer who had just surrendered his sword and was being herded with his men at the point of the Tennesseans' bayonets to one corner of *la Teneria*. The man collapsed to jeers and catcalls from the *yanquis*, who were still milling aimlessly about, every damned one of them unsure of what to do next, private and shoulder strap alike. I studied the chaos for a moment and then realized that, in the several minutes since we'd swept into the redoubt, nobody had paid the slightest attention to taking advantage of our having breached the Mexican defenses. The whole eastern part of the town seemed to be at our mercy—if we acted quickly.

But that wasn't my job. I was a sergeant in a regiment that hardly existed anymore. Unsure of whether my friends were alive or dead, equally unsure of what to do next, and without any particular destination in mind, I turned to walk along the parapet towards the open end of the redoubt. As I did, I kicked the rifle so lately held by the courteous man.

"Go ahead. It's yours." I looked back to Davis, who was standing on the parapet and gesturing at the rifle. "Don't forget the cartridge box. Meacham won't be needing it. God bless his soul. It's a Whitney.

Doesn't take a bayonet, but you have that knife of yours ... and that revolving pistol ... where in God's name did you find that? Beautiful. They're as rare as hen's teeth in these parts."

"Thank you, sir." I gently relieved the dead man of his cartridge box, and picked up the fallen rifle, thanking the poor devil under my breath.

"Follow me, and you can use those weapons on the dagoes up there." Davis gestured to the redoubt above us. "They call it *el Diablo*. The devil's corner. It's the key to the eastern side of the city. While we're about it, maybe we'll find what remains of your regiment for you. I'm told that all three of Garland's regiments are tucked in down there, somewhere. House to house. Great God, what a way to fight."

I had been wrong. Somebody was thinking about what to do next.

Ten minutes later, Davis led fifty of us across the narrow creek to the protection of a stone wall. Half-a-dozen marksmen with those glorious Whitney rifles remained on the *la Tenería* side of the creek, kneeling or standing as they surveyed the nearby rooftops, which had been fortified with impromptu parapets of sandbags, for the enemy. The marksmen made a rich practice as scores of Mexicans recklessly exposed themselves so as to take better aim at us as we splashed across the creek. Musket balls plinked off the ground, bushes and everywhere we weren't as we dashed madly for the wall's protection. Miraculously, nobody was hit.

Once we were against the wall, it was a different matter. In short order, one man was killed, shot in the face, and another wounded in the neck, as they tentatively poked their heads above the stone wall.

A lieutenant, somebody said his name was Russell, organized us for a desperate run over open ground up the slight incline of the hill and glacis to the redoubt's wall. "Knives. Check your knives, boys. We'll be needin' 'em. Check your loads and put fresh caps on." There were about forty of us, all told, who were going to make this charge and about ten or so more who were going to lay a covering fire onto the fort and the rooftops while we ran. Half our complement went to one end of the wall, and the rest of us went to the other, where a couple of sharpshooters were already sniping at anything that moved on nearby rooftops and *el Diablo*'s embrasures. Russell reassured us that his sharpshooters would shoot dead any Mexican bastard who popped his head up on the rooftops facing the open ground we were going to have to traverse. Despite his efforts, none of us were looking very pleased.

"There! There!" cried a Mississippian, pointing to a group of a score or more Mexicans on a rooftop about fifty yards or so away. They could shoot behind the wall we were huddled against. One of them, an officer, waved his sword in our general direction. A score of Mexican muskets aimed at us and fired a ragged volley.

Mississippi rifles swung around and took aim at the Mexicans, who were starting to scuttle away.

Russell admonished our sharpshooters. "Draw a bead, boys. Don't waste your shot."

Half a dozen reply shots spat out spasmodically. Four Mexicans dropped. One of them fell from the roof to the ground in front of the white stucco building and twitched for a moment before lying still. The other three simply disappeared.

The officer's head popped up. Rifles fixed upon him.

"Don't shoot." I only realized afterwards that I had spoken.

Several heads turned and looked at me in shock. One man, who had kept his eyes fixed on the officer, exclaimed, "Good God Almighty. It's a woman. What the blazes is she doing there?"

Russell shook his head in disbelief and put his hand on a man's rifle as it was raised. "Don't kill her, lads. 'T'ain't right."

Somebody in our group, I couldn't tell who, cried out, "Dad blame it. Kill the fucking bitch. She's leading them musketeers up there, and they're trying to stifle us."

"No." It was Davis. "You will kill anything else up there that moves. But not her. We do not make war on women and children. Even if they make war upon us."

The woman disappeared, and we saw nobody else pop his head up on that roof. But the image of her face stayed with me. I had an aching to know her, although, curiously, it was almost as if we had already met. It was an unaccountable thought, and it took me a very long way from the stone wall in front of *el Diablo*.

"Dan, form your men. Get ready on my signal. We'll have word in just a moment from General Quitman. I'm going to see him directly."

~

Fifteen minutes later, small plumes of dirt spat up where spent musket balls were dogging Davis as he weaved his way helter-skelter across the creek and open ground for the safety of the stone wall, where he heaved himself, next to Russell, who was busy conferring with one of his sergeants. Once he was safely tucked in, Davis kicked the wall in frustration. A red-shirted man jumped out of harm's way, and damned near got himself shot by the Mexicans for his pains. His companion impudently observed that the man was right to risk enemy fire rather than getting in their colonel's way, "Seein' how hell-fired wrathy the Colonel can get when he's crossed."

Davis was ranting to no one in particular as he caught his breath. "Of all the blasted, ill-considered, god-damned, stupid orders it has ever been my displeasure to obey in the twenty years since I went to the 'Point, this one takes the cake."

"What's that, sir?" Russell turned from his sergeant and saluted Davis, even though they were both crouching tightly against the wall. "We're ready to go at your sign, sir."

"We aren't going, Dan."

"Sir?"

"I've been ordered to pull everyone back across the creek. Christ in Heaven! We've lost good men this morning, and now these ass-backwards, nancy-boy numbskulls want us to withdraw all the way back … and give these blasted dagoes back that fort we just stormed."

"Jesus H. Christ, sir."

456

"I know, Dan. That's why I came out so strong with General Quitman. Hell and damnation, man, I told him that we were born fools for retiring like this. But he told me that the regulars, Garland's division, have been cut up something awful, and Old Zach ain't inclined to put more of us into the grinder 'til he figures out what to do next. So, back to the suburbs we go."

"Yes, sir."

"Deploy skirmishers as we go. You direct them. I'll take the main body back across the creek to the fort. Maybe Old Zach will relent, and let us keep the damned thing as a trophy. We paid enough for it."

Russell slithered over to our waiting group. "You men, form a line. Two yards apart, to the creek. Kill any son of a bitch who shows himself. We're getting out of here."

A couple of men looked relieved. *El Diablo* was not an attractive direction in which to go. Back to *la Teneria* seemed the far more hospitable course.

~

I tagged onto the end of the skirmishing line, and fired my new-found Whitney half a dozen times in the next five or ten minutes. I had never shot a rifle such as this, and I gloried in its accuracy. I think that I actually killed one poor bastard who had been dumb enough to show his entire torso above a sandbag parapet, and I know that I sent stone chips flying into the face of another as I hit the corner of a wall. Other skirmishers were doing even better, and Mexican fire slackened to virtually nothing by the time I splashed across the creek, following at the tail-end of the skirmishing line.

As I reached the bank of the creek, I turned and studied the nearby rooftops before I made my final run to safety. I didn't see anyone. So I turned to follow the rest of the skirmishing line. But they'd vanished, and I was momentarily alone in the middle of the battle, with not another live human being in sight. The sudden loneliness seemed to be saving my life, for a sole target such as myself would make poor practice for a squad of dago musketeers. The feeling none-theless sent a creepy shiver down my spine. A spatter of musketry from *el Diablo* ended that feeling of loneliness, tearing at the weeds and kicking about stones hardly ten yards in front of me. I started to run in the direction of *la Tenería*, but another hail of musket balls kicked up dust and whacked at the weeds directly in front of me. I veered to my left and suddenly found myself in the shelter of a street in the town.

I thought about reversing course to try to make it back to the fort, but thought the better of it as a volley of musketry from near overhead fired in the direction of the *la Tenería*. I sat for a moment, reloading my Whitney rifle and checking the loads in my repeating pistol. As I finished, another volley forestalled any further thought of dashing over the open ground to the fort. I instead crept slowly in the other direc-tion, down a narrow, cobblestoned street that was blessedly shaded from open view. I plastered myself to the walls along one side of the street as I went. They were some seven feet high, and thus afforded me protection as I searched the sky above for lurking musketeers and every so often checked behind and in front of myself to ensure that the street was still empty. So intent was I on this 360 degree surveillance that I almost walked into a musket as it was poked through a loophole per-forated in the wall of a residence. I stopped cold, hoping to dear God, wherever he may have been, that the musketeer had not heard me.

I looked behind myself. I realized, to my horror, that I must have made a turn or two as I was creeping along the walls. I hardly knew the direction I had come from, let alone where I was headed. I stopped and waited. I could hear a voice in Spanish, hoarse with tension, swear, "¡A *la verga*! Where have *los puta gringos* disappeared to?"

It must have been the musketeer, for another voice standing fur-ther away from the other side of the wall, clearly an officer or ser-geant, snapped, "¡*Cállate, pendejo! Los camisetas rojas están de vuelta.*" He wanted the man to shut up. The redshirts were coming back. The Mississippians. Coming from the north. Thank God, I thought. The musketeer asked, "which way is north?"

"*A la izquierda. Pinche idiota.*"

The direction I was traveling, assuming that the two Mexican soldiers were facing the street. I wondered how the devil I'd gotten so disoriented, because I thought the street was running east and west. I looked up to see how the sun's shadows were tending. But I realized that was a fool's game. It had been hours since the battle had begun, and I didn't know whether it was morning, noon, or late in the afternoon. The sergeant or officer spoke again, ordering the musketeer to go up to the rooftop to keep watch. Reinforcements were on the way, he said, and they would guard the wall. The musket scraped clear of the wall and vanished. I crept underneath the loophole and past the locked gate. My shirt and blouse were soaked with my sweat, and I felt exhausted. But I could not stop to rest. I had to find the Mississippians—or somebody American, for God's sake. Otherwise, I was going to be dead—or worse.

I crept along as quietly as I could towards the sounds of fighting, which were intensifying by the moment. It was almost as if the Old Man had sent the army back into the streets of Monterrey. If he had, then I could find them and rejoin them, just as long as I could find a way to safely cross over from the Mexican lines to the American side. I turned a corner to the right, which should have been the east, if I was heading in anything like the proper direction, and suddenly found myself at the edge of a small, eerily silent city square. The silence was quickly broken as a series of ragged volleys were exchanged. I plastered myself against the wall, staring in wonder at a most fantastical sight: a score of dead and injured men lying in the center of the square, all topsy-turvy, Mexican and American alike. A Mexican woman was shuttling from one wounded man to the next, Mexican or American it did not matter a lick to her, giving water to one man, binding the wounds of a second, and comforting a third as he died. I heard commands in English on the American side and in Spanish on the Mexican side, imploring their men to avoid hitting her. I continued staring at the woman, stunned by her selfless courage, as she continued to move among the wounded, seemingly oblivious to the musketry peppering all about her. Her luck came to an end, though. She fell, twitched, and struggled for just a brief moment. Then she died. I heard groans of shame and pity on both sides of the square.

～

I slipped away from the carnage, back down the street I'd just traversed and then down a different street. I eventually found a broken door, thinking that perhaps I could get to a roof to see where I needed to go. I clambered over the splintered wood into a cool courtyard full of lemon and orange trees. I grabbed myself a low-hanging orange safely below the level of the wall surrounding the courtyard. Then I looked over at the house. There was a bluebelly sentry posted at the door, and he was smiling at me silently. Why there had been no one guarding the gate to the street was well beyond my ken.

"Hey there, brother Jonathan."

I looked up towards the voice, and saw another bluebelly, wearing Third Infantry insignia, clinging to a branch at almost the top of the tree, shaking it. He had a bloodied bandage around his head.

"Catch the oranges, and take them inside." I looked at him as if he were a born fool, and he explained. "There's a collection station for wounded in there."

"Okay. Toss them down here."

He tossed the oranges to me, one by one, and I caught them and placed them gently on the ground. We'd gathered perhaps thirty or so, and the tree was starting to look a little bare, when a hail of musket balls ripped through the tree. The bluebelly barely reacted, and continued to methodically pick oranges and toss them to me.

"Get down from there," I called up. "Don't get yourself killed."

"Don't worry, these *méxicanos* can't hit nothing. And the laddies in there need the fruit. Half o' them poor bastards are going to croake before this day is out."

"Bad in there?"

A tight "Yep" was all I got from him.

"Well you watch yourself. Those musketeers may be bad shots—and the good Lord knows they've managed to miss me all day. But even bad shots occasionally hit what they're aiming for."

"True enough."

Another volley ripped through the tree. A little closer this time, and more focused upon the intrepid orange-picker, who called down to me, "We're about done here." He shinnied down the tree as a third fusillade of musket balls battered the branches above him.

He vigorously brushed the palms of his hands against each other, as if to say, "Job well done." He said, instead, "We ought 'a' tell that shoulder strap inside to get a couple of boys up there on the roof. We got some hard bargains who ought 'a' do the trick."

"Hard bargains?" I looked at the orange-picker a little slantendicular like. "You mean hard cases showing a streak of yellow?"

"One and the same, my bene cove."

"You were a lobster back, once upon a time, weren't you? Only you coves say 'hard bargain'." He chuckled as I asked, "Skedaddled from Canada?"

"Yep. An' a wild goose, to boot. You're County Cork, aren't you?"

"Ayut. Bred and born."

"Tipperary, meself. We're practically neighbors."

"We're both a long way from home, buddy."

"What home? Rotten potatoes and god-damned Methody middlemen turfing poor folk from their land?" He looked at me a little closer. "You don't sound like you was whelped in a bog."

"I wasn't. But I still had to skedaddle."

"Murder?" There was an amused twinkle in the orange-picker's eye. "Or'd you make some little chick-a-biddy a member of the pudding club?"

I laughed. "Didn't hush no bloke back in Éirinn. And there's no by-blow to be found. Not on my account, anyway."

"Danny McCormac."

"Billy Gogan."

We shook hands, and I asked him, "Have you seen anything of the Fourth in town, today? I got separated from them a while back."

"Yeah. Just a block or so over, as a matter of fact. Say, wait a minute. You're Gogan, right?"

I nodded.

"Fella. A sergeant like yourself. Older though. A Dutchy. He was asking after a 'Sergeant Gogan'."

"I reckon that'd be me."

"Well, he's alive and well," McCormac said to my relief. "Leastways he was an hour ago, 'afore I got carted over here, dead to the world." McCormac pointed to his bandage. "Then I woke up as fit as a fiddle, and here I am, gathering oranges. Shoulder strap inside won't let me go."

We were just carrying the oranges inside, when a voice said, "Damn it, Corporal. One sentry at post. That's fucking madness."

I couldn't see very well in the cool dimness, but I imagined the corporal flushing as he whined, "There ain't no one else, sir."

There were twenty or thirty wounded men crowded in the room. The shoulder strap looked the worse for the wear as he pushed away a surgeon's mate trying to bandage his mangled and bloodied arm. A blasted marvel, I thought, finding a croaker's man so near harm's way. I silently gave him my thanks for having the iron to venture out here, and I simultaneously prayed that I would not need his services this day.

The shoulder strap looked at the orange-picker. "Ah, good, McCormac, get those oranges distributed." He then looked at me. "From the Fourth, Sergeant?"

"Yes sir. Have you seen them? Got separated from them this morning outside *la Tenería*."

"Heard about that. Damned bad business sending three unsupported companies up like that. But we haven't seen them since we got sent back into town. I reckon that they're a couple of blocks thataway." He pointed vaguely with his good arm in the direction McCormac had indicated. Then turned back to me." I need a good sergeant to organize the less wounded. We're not ready for the dagoes to attack us."

I thought for a moment about whether to openly demur, and then decided not to. I probably stood a better chance of finding Hermann by staying and helping, if for no other reason than I was more likely to stay alive that way. And I was more likely to avoid the hot water if I stayed than if I skedaddled without absolution. Plenty of time to go once the coast was clear. In the meantime, I'd do what I could to help. "Sir, do you have anybody topside? On the roof?"

The shoulder strap shook his head, and winced involuntarily at the effort.

"If I might suggest, sir, perhaps we should get someone up there as a lookout at least. The *méxicanos* are using the roofs to move around the city."

The shoulder strap said nothing.

"How many able-bodied men are there, sir?"

"You. That hard case corporal. The sentry out front. No one else. I was busy collecting strays when I got winged. My company got scattered over tarnation when we got into town." He smiled sardonically. "I'm a shoulder strap, don't you know, and I've got to have men to lead, so I was doing the next best thing when this happened." He gestured at his mangled arm. "Kind of like rounding up cattle in the spring, back home—rounding up stray bluebellies, that is." McCormac had sidled back alongside me, having distributed the oranges. The shoulder strap continued. "And now we have the famous McCormac. He's from my company. He was a goner when he got dumped here. Now look at him ... Back from the dead."

"A good man, sir," I said. McCormac looked appreciative. "If I may, sir. I think that we ought to barricade the street door to the courtyard. I walked in and nobody challenged me. We wouldn't want any unwelcome guests doing the same, sir."

The shoulder strap looked at me. "Good idea, Sergeant. Should've thought of it, myself. Make it so. I reckon we can use a few lightly wounded to guard the door and put the more fit onto the roof. There's a ladder over there."

"Yes, sir. Corporal?" I called into the darkness of the room, not knowing quite where to find the corporal whose head the shoulder strap had bitten off.

"Yeah, Sergeant?" The whining corporal, an indolent-looking cove from the First Ohio—a volunteer, and not a regular—materialized out of the gloom.

"Do you know who's able to move around and hold a musket?"

"I dunno, Sergeant."

"Well, find out, god-damn it."

"Don't get your dander up, bucko. You ain't my company sergeant." He made to slip away into the shadows.

I grabbed him by the shoulder and collar and pulled him back.

As I did, the shoulder strap coldly said to the corporal, "I'll have thirty lashes on your back and your stripes if you talk to a sergeant that way again."

There was dead silence in the room. Even the most badly wounded were looking at the three of us.

"Now," I said to the corporal very evenly. "Get the surgeon's mate and he can tell us who's fit enough, and then let's sort out one detail for the front, and another for the roof. Got it?"

"Yes, Sergeant." The corporal vanished. The shoulder strap and I looked at each other.

"Fucking volunteers," he said equably. "O'Brien's the name. Second lieutenant. First Infantry. I was with Backus until I got winged."

"Gogan, sir. Quartermaster's sergeant with the Fourth."

"Didn't want to count beans, today?"

"Came down with Lieutenant Grant, sir. He's my boss."

"Sam Grant's a good man. A classmate of mine. Is he okay?"

"He was the last time I saw him, but that was a while back."

The corporal came back with the croaker's mate in tow. His hands and arms were slick to his elbows with blood. I tried not to wretch at the sight—and the smell.

O'Brien queried the surgeon's mate, "How many of these fellows can we give muskets to?"

"They're all injured to one degree or another. Even yourself." He paused. Then he said with reproach, "Sir. Every one of you belongs in a hospital."

"That's not answering my question. There's ten thousand dagoes out there who'd love to slit the throats of every man in this wretched house. We have to try to defend ourselves … until help comes." Those who could were getting to their feet and gathering around O'Brien and me. O'Brien spoke to the group at large in a voice that quavered slightly with the effort, "I want to know how many men we can put on the roof with how many muskets, and how many we can put on the front wall, guarding that broken gate. It's asking a lot of you. All of you are injured. Some very gravely. So I am asking for volunteers."

Hands were raised, and a number of men called out.

I said, "Those of you who can climb, muster by that ladder over there. I need six of you. Bring your muskets, and bring your cartridge boxes. And bring extras of both if you can." Men started shuffling towards the ladder. "McCormac, get them all up topside and set a sentry. The most able-bodied go first."

"Yes, Sergeant." McCormac began bawling orders at the motley lot of injured men, some of whom were looking skeptically at the ladder.

"Corporal."

"Yes, Sergeant." I noted with satisfaction that the First Ohio corporal snapped to as well as any regular.

"Get the rest of the men who can walk and hold a musket out there into the courtyard. Make some loopholes," I ordered, thinking of what the two Mexican soldiers I'd seen earlier must have done. "Then, one man per loophole. Two loaders per loophole. At least four muskets per loophole, if we have that many. And cartridge boxes."

The corporal grumbled to himself, but led five fellows out into the bright sunlight of the courtyard. Perhaps two score or more still lay on the floor. Some of them were entirely motionless. Probably dead. Others were thrashing about quietly. The sudden activity seemed to have inhibited the moans of pain. The surgeon's mate wiped his nose with a bloodied rag, stuffed the rag into his pantaloon pocket, sighed and bent over the man closest to him, who was moving feebly and gurgling.

I turned away, unable to watch. I said to O'Brien, "Begging your pardon, Lieutenant, but why don't I go topside? I'm not sure you can make it up there. Perhaps you might look at the front door?"

O'Brien looked as if he wanted to say something about my having decided which of us would go where. But instead he smiled and nodded and went out into the courtyard, tenderly guarding his injured arm as he went.

McCormac was making heavy weather of moving the six injured men to the roof. I helped him shove, cajole, and encourage them up the ladder. There was more than one suppressed moan of pain as we did. One man shrieked in agony as I manhandled him. He bled all over my blouse. He had been gutshot, yet somehow had gotten to his feet and staggered over to the ladder, ready to help. The surgeon's mate rescued him from my tender mercies, clucking his concern as he led the poor man away.

I grabbed my rifle and raced topside. I was relieved that there weren't any Mexicans in sight. Fusillades were still being traded, presumably across the square I'd seen earlier. But I couldn't see any actual movement. McCormac and I situated the five remaining men in pairs, one of them with McCormac. The more mobile man to shoot, and the less mobile to reload. I counted cartridges and musket balls and distributed them as evenly as I could among the three pairs of men. I told McCormac to keep his eyes peeled, and that I'd be back in a jiffy.

Before I left, McCormac pointed again to where he'd last seen Hermann, three houses away. He then pointed to several rough-sawn planks lying on the roof. They looked long enough to span from one roof to another over a narrow street. I looked at other, nearby roofs. Almost every one of them also had two or three rough-sawn planks lying on them.

As I looked at them, McCormac said, "Them dago bastards are smart. That's how they're traveling from roof to roof. We haven't figured it out, yet."

I grunted noncommittally. But I knew how I was going to find Hermann when the time came.

Down below, in the courtyard, O'Brien had worked wonders. Furniture had been dragged out of the house to reinforce the barricade at the front door. Loopholes had been hacked through the wall, with two men stood at each loophole: One to shoot, and one to load. Each had three muskets and enough powder and shot to keep them well-occupied for some time.

But a look at the faces told me that resistance would be measured in minutes. Not one of them had any color, and most of the loaders looked as if they were ready to drop from the loss of blood and the pain of moving about. O'Brien was sitting on the ground next to one of the loopholes, his back against the front wall, his face ashen and lathered with sweat.

"Gogan," he croaked. "If we're attacked, take who you can from the roof and run. There's no holding this for long. There aren't many left inside who are still alive."

I stared at him. His eyes closed, and I thought for a moment that he'd died. But he opened his eyes again and focused on me with effort.

His voice slurred. "Don't …"

Whatever else O'Brien had to say went unsaid, for he was dead.

"Corporal."

"Yes, Sergeant?" The Ohio volunteer looked at me with a sense of dread.

"Take down the barricade."

"Sergeant?"

"Unblock the doorway, god damn it. You heard me."

He began pulling the table and broken benches away. I helped him. Everyone else stared, all of them physically incapable of helping. When it was done, I called the surgeon's mate over and told him to surrender when the time came, and not to waste a single life defending what couldn't be defended. I told him that I'd send help if I could.

I ran back into the house and up the ladder to the roof and found mayhem.

⌒

McCormac was dead. So were the other five men. They'd been slaughtered by a volley fired at near point-blank range by a platoon of Mexicans just as my head broached the roof's combing. McCormac had saved my life before he died, though, for he had put the planks down to the roof of the house opposite the Mexican platoon, which were struggling to reload their muskets. I stood tall for just a moment, found their officer, who was giving halting commands to reload, and shot him down with my Colt Paterson. I stuffed my pistol into my belt, grabbed my Whitney rifle, and ran like the devil over the planks, threw them into the street below and ran across to the other side, threw the planks from that roof over to the third house, clambered over and stopped cold. There were four or five Mexicans lying dead or dying on the roof. Three very alive Mexicans were busy shooting into a group of three bluebellies scrambling for cover on the next roof over. I recognized the bluebellies instantly: Hermann, Hoggs, and Gaff. Every one of them was bearing a charmed life as the Mexican fusillade whined harmlessly past them.

I drew my repeating pistol and shot the three Mexicans dead. They died without knowing that I had even been there.

Hermann stood up, looking at me with a dropped jaw. Hoggs and Gaff were busy reloading their muskets. I looked around. There were no planks for me to bridge the street with.

"Billy." Hermann's summons was hardly more than a throaty whisper. "The building underneath you is empty. Go down and cross the street and into our building. Our boys are in there. They'll be waiting for you. We are getting ready to pull out. We've been ordered to retreat."

I nodded.

Hermann smiled thinly and said, "When you go, run like the devil."

468

I took Hermann's advice, and I moved very quickly indeed. As I dashed across the street, half-a-dozen musket balls whined past me and they caromed off walls on both sides of the cobblestoned street. I spilled through a suddenly open door to the house opposite, landing stomach-first on a hard dirt floor, my Paterson in one hand and my Whitney rifle in the other. I looked up, feeling vaguely foolish. Grant was leaning over me as if he were looking at what the cat had just dragged in. He had a whisper of a smile on his face. "You're missing your shako and your musket, Sergeant. But at least you're not too late to join us. Remind me later to ask you where you've been gallivantin' off to all day."

I jumped to my feet to salute him. I almost knocked myself out with my Paterson when I did so. I hastily stuffed the pistol into my belt and saluted him properly. A couple of bluebellies standing behind him looked sniggered at my discomfiture. It momentarily relieved the pinched look from their faces.

Grant briefed me without further ado. "We've been ordered to withdraw. The dagoes are buzzing around us like flies, and we've got to get two blocks to where the rest of the regiment is holed up. Then we're going to withdraw back to *la Teneria*. Wurster's up topside. He's volunteered to command a rearguard. That'll give us a chance to get out of this house without too many casualties. Gaff and Hoggs are with him. They will cover us while we move along the street to the next house, where we've already got a few boys holding down the fort. Then we'll cover them, while they join us."

Grant seemed to be the only shoulder strap in evidence, although there were one or two corporal's and sergeant's stripes in the crowd of thirty or so filthy bluebellies. So he was not entirely without help in guiding this remnant back to safety.

"I'll join Sergeant Wurster, sir. That is … if you don't mind, sir."

"Thought you might say that. Dangerous."

I shrugged with an equanimity that I did not feel. "I've got this." I touched the butt of my Paterson. "Five shots, when I reload." I lifted my Whitney. "And I have this. It'll give you a little more cover."

Grant nodded, and I clambered up the ladder to the roof.

"*Für die Liebe Gottes*, stay low," Hermann hissed. "There is a whole platoon on that roof across the way. Where you just were."

"Jesus." I shuddered involuntarily.

Hoggs moved uneasily. Gaff chuckled.

"Let me switch my cylinder. I only have one shot left. Rifle's loaded, though."

"We have six loaded muskets up here."

"What're you planning?"

"We put a volley into the platoon over there." Hermann gestured to the house across the street, where I had killed the three soldiers. The Mexicans were settling into two ranks, getting ready to blow the four of us off our roof. "Just as our boys go down the street, we'll disrupt the dago volley, and direct their fire our way. Then you and Gaff and Hoggs go. I'll be right behind you after I give them another couple of rounds. We'll leave all the empty muskets here. Too cumbersome to carry."

"You'll not get off this roof by yourself," I replied. "Send Gaff and Hoggs ahead. I'll stay with you. If I can reload my cylinder before the show starts, we can have something to shoot with as we hoof it."

Hermann shrugged philosophically. "Reload. I'll ask Grant to hold still until you're ready. Can you finish before ... ?" He gestured at the Mexican platoon. Thankfully, the lot of them were still fumbling about trying to reload their muskets.

I already had slipped my pack off, and was switching cylinders, checking my loads in the spare cylinder as I slid it into place. I prayed that I didn't have any misfires. I hadn't had any yet today, so I must have done a good job loading and reloading my cylinders last night. My Colt's repeater was now loaded. My fingers trembled as I reloaded the cylinder I had just removed from my repeating pistol. Finally, I finished, and slipped the spare cylinder in a safe place I could reach. The Mexicans were still mucking about, and they didn't seem to be in any kind of all-fired hurry to kill us. Thank God.

I nodded to Hermann, who whistled down to Grant and the waiting bluebellies. They erupted out of the doorway. Several of them stopped in the street and peppered the Mexican platoon atop the house across the way. Their officer disregarded the danger, stood tall and raised a sword high into the air, where it flashed in the sunlight. The officer's command trilled unlike any military command I had ever heard, for it was given by the voice of a woman. I stared at her, astonished. She was the very same woman with the same long, lustrous hair whom Jeff Davis had forbidden us to kill as we were pressed up against that stone wall beneath *el Diablo*. Probably the same woman who had led the Mexican lancers. There surely couldn't be two of them in the Mexican army.

Hermann seemed to read my mind. "Aim at the musketeers," he said quietly. "Not at the officer. She can't hurt anyone … Ready … Now!"

Three muskets and my Whitney rifle blazed at the same time the Mexican platoon fired at us. I dropped my Whitney and picked up a second musket and glanced at Hermann. Why I did, I could not say, for my job now was to keep up the fire at our enemy as best I could. But look I did, and my heart sank at what I saw. Hermann's shoulder was bloodied, and he was looking at his useless arm in sheer frustration at not being able to pick up his musket. Gaff, who had made his way to the ladder to make good his escape, read my mind, and began dragging Hermann to safety, ignoring his protest that he wanted to stay. Hoggs was moving to help him.

I returned my attention to the roiling mass in front of me. Our little volley had hit a couple of them, and disconcerted the rest quite nicely. I fired my musket into the center of the Mexican soldiers, picked up Hermann's second musket and discharged it without looking to see what effect I was having. I reached for my Paterson. As I did, I heard a clattering behind me, and then a canister shell from Old Zach's 10-inch witch's soup pot seemed to explode inside my head.

⌒

471

It was quite some time later, how much later I don't know, when I tried to swim to the surface. I couldn't quite make it, but I could still smell jasmine and the scent and the sweat of a beautiful woman, and I could feel the softness of her holding me.

She murmured, not quite lovingly, "*Pobrecito*."

THE END OF BOOK TWO

# Acknowledgments

⌒

*Billy Gogan, Gone fer Soldier* was borne of the same quiet moment in May 2009, when my wife, Pat, encouraged me to first put pen to paper and begin to tell Billy Gogan's story from the beginning. At every step of the way, Pat has encouraged me to stay the course and finish Billy's story. She truly is, and always has been, the "indispensable woman."

Larry Habegger has been similarly indispensable these past several years. We found each other in a round-about way, and we worked together for a long time to take a shaggy first draft and slowly produce, first *Billy Gogan, American*, and then the book you see today. I cannot sufficiently express my appreciation to Larry for everything that he has done, both in being a brilliant editor and in taking the lead in getting the book published.

Deanna Spear was invaluable in her editorial comments. I drank deeply from the water to which her comments led me.

I do not speak Spanish, and as wonderful as Google Translate, Spanish-English dictionaries, and the many-varied and wonderful works on Mexican slang, I needed help. Juan Legares provided that help. That said, this truly is a point at which I must say that all the credit for the Spanish in this book is his, and any mistakes are mine, alone.

Eugene O'Driscoll rendered me an invaluable service in helping me get the Irish "right" in *Billy Gogan, American*, a contribution that has paid invaluable dividends in *Billy Gogan, Gone fer Soldier*. Again, all the credit for this work is his, and any mistakes are mine, alone.

To Joe Levine and his wonderful team at CC&G, I can only say thank you for developing such a fantastic website and social media presence. Jen Lipford I must thank for being so very patient with me in filming a piece for the website. They have all taught me so very much about the "brave new world" of book marketing on social media.

To Blake Henderson, and all the others upon whom I inflicted early drafts of the book, many, many thanks for your warm words of encouragement along the way. And so many thanks to Wendy and Mark Battaglia and Christina and George Lemperis for hosting such wonderful book signings.

Finally, I return to Pat, my wife, and my children and their spouses, and their children. Thank you for putting up with me and for enduring the early drafts of the book – even when, for my children, those drafts sounded like me lecturing your thirteen-year-old selves. (My apologies for having been that way.)

## Acknowledgments for Pictures and Song Lyrics

"A New Map of Texas, Oregon, and California," S. Augustus Mitchell, Accompaniment to Mitchell's new map of Texas, Oregon, and California, with the regions adjoining, North Pacific Bank Note Co., 1925), high resolution map courtesy of Paul Norrell, found at (https://www.worldmapsonline.com/ (accessed August 24, 2018).

"Territory Claimed by Texas," Charles Kendall Adams, A History of the United States (Boston, MA: Allyn and Bacon, 1909) 296; high resolution map courtesy of the private collection of Roy Winkelman and Maps ETC, a part of the Educational Technology Clearinghouse, produced by the Florida Center for Instructional Technology © 2009, College of Education, University of South Florida, found at http://etc.usf.edu/maps/pages/800/804/804.htm (accessed August 24, 2018). "Map of the Seat of War Gen Taylor's Field of Operations in Mexico," S. Augustus Mitchell (1846), high resolution map courtesy of Norman B. Leventhal Map & Education Center, https://collections.leventhal-map.org (accessed August 24, 2018).

## Acknowledgments

"*Battle of Monterrey*," Justin Smith, *The War with Mexico*, volume I (New York: MacMillan, 1919) 240, electronic copy courtesy of Wikimedia (accessed September 21, 2018).

Lyrics for Yankee Doodle, Rough and Ready Songster: Embellished with Twenty-five Splendid Engravings, Illustrative of the American Victory in Mexico (New York: Nafis and Cornish, circa 1848).

# About the Author

Roger Higgins and his wife are traveling this great country of ours and meeting all sorts of very interesting people. They remain immensely proud of their four children, their children's spouses, and their grandchildren. As Mrs. Higgins patiently observed to her husband when he ruminates about the trials and tribulations of raising children, it was together that they went four-for-four with their children, hitting safely at every at-bat. Not a bad day in the batter's box.

SNEAK PEEK AT BOOK THREE

# *Billy Gogan,*
# *Sheltered by the Enemy*

⌒

SAN LUIS POTOSÍ, MÉXICO
OCTOBER 1846

*The Battle of Monterrey is over, and the American army was victorious. The Mexican army retreated south to San Luis Potosí with only one prisoner, Sergeant Billy Gogan of the U.S. Army's Fourth Infantry Regiment.*

She came again today, the woman in white did. Shimmering in the light above the surface of a calm sea. I longed to swim that long journey upwards to the woman's promise of a sweet hint of jasmine and her soft touch and her scent. But it was not to be, and I once more sank away from the light and the touch and the smell, unable to break the surly shackles binding me cruelly to the sharp and icy rocks of an inky-black Tartarus, where the familiar horrors patiently waited to visit me once more.

The dreams—if they may be called that—began as they always did, with the familiar, cackling laughter of that bastard, Hoggs. I screamed silently at Hermann, as I had so many times before, to watch out, to protect himself, for I could not help him. But my warning was of no use, just like every other time this horrid apparition visited me. As inevitable as the denouement of a stage play, blood bubbled from Hermann's wound. Gaff is nowhere to be seen, and Grant is screaming that he can wait no longer. Sarah Langwell, her magnificent bosom heaving with grief, glares at me reproachfully, although I'm never quite sure whether it's because I didn't bring Hermann back to her or whether it's on account of the life blood pumping out from the rictus grin slashed across poor, dead Adabelita's throat. I try to explain, but like every time before this, I am helplessly mute. Sarah turns from me in disgust.

Eventually, they all fade back into the inky blackness. In predictable due course, their fading faces are replaced by the waxen slackness of Mary's visage, still so lovely in death as I cradle her in the muck of Mulberry Street, amidst the smoke and stench and roar of Magee's boardinghouse going up in flames. I look up. Fíona's frightened eyes are fixed in aghast fascination upon her poor, dead mother. Then she looks up, her eyes boring into me and she wordlessly asks, "Why?" Yet again, I cannot answer, and she buries her face in Mrs. Shipley's skirts, looking elsewhere for solace. I then hear Magee rumbling above me. I raise my gaze to the hatred glittering in his eyes. Behind him, a shadowy figure dressed in funereal black, whom my former headmaster had called "MacGowan," black-haired and blackened in soul, is controlling Magee's nemesis, Cassidy, like a puppet on a string. That murderous devil, Lúcás Dineen, and his brother, Cian, are also dancing to this devil's tune. They in turn melt away into the icy black water. All that is, save MacGowan, who stares me in the eye as he casually murders Father O'Muirhily at Lavitt's Quay and then points to a motionless figure lying unconscious in a bed. I recognize the figure. Poor Phillip Murray, whose head I'd cracked with an errant cricket ball. Not the same, anymore, Headmaster had said. Poor bastard. But Murray'd had it coming, God damn him.

A spasm of fear shudders through me just then, as I see my beautiful cousin, Evelyn O'Creagh, whom I've loved for as long as I can remember. Her cowardly father, Seamus, who sent me away from all I knew without so much as a "by your leave, sir," stands behind her, warning me off, his hand protectively on her shoulder. Then I remember why the stab of fear. Evelyn whispers, "Write to me, promise." I try to promise, but I can't, and I am left staring, transfixed, as her father's house burns, its occupants screaming helplessly as they died.

The embers from the house slowly fade away, and Evelyn's golden ringlets transmogrify into the dusky and dark-haired Calandria. Ah, beautiful, voluptuous and available Calandria. Beckoning like a succubus. I come closer, but she evanesces into the ether as an unknown man's mocking laugh echoes. She leaves me with the image of her father as he lies dying in my arms from the very wounds that I had inflicted upon him. My hands still covered in blood, I am standing in the middle of the Texas prairie, miles from anywhere. Grant is there on horseback staring down at me with a look of puzzlement. After a while, I espy Father Rey looking at me seriously over Grant's shoulder in the heat and humidity of the Army of Invasion's encampment outside Matamoros. He says to me, "I am very serious, my son. Find me. I fear that we have much to talk about, before you can unburden your soul." I want to tell Father Rey that I will seek him out on the march to Camargo, but I never can, for I know that my intent is a lie.

A stentorian voice from offstage tells me that all those who are close to me have died—or hate me for allowing those deaths—and that they have all died for my unexpiated sins. I try to think of someone I have not hurt. I can think only of the woman in white, whom I don't even know. She cradles my head in her lap and murmurs to me not entirely unsympathetically, "Mi pobrecito."

I am left with only my father's ghost hovering over me, his face etched with unhappiness. And I ask myself, where in the Sam Hill am I? And why have I visited so much pain upon those close to me?